written by

THIERRY SMOLDEREN

art by

ALEXANDRE CLERISSE

DIABOLICAL
SUMMER

Facebook: **facebook.com/idwpublishing**
Twitter: **@idwpublishing**
YouTube: **youtube.com/idwpublishing**
Tumblr: **tumblr.idwpublishing.com**
Instagram: **instagram.com/idwpublishing**

ISBN: 978-1-68405-425-1   22 21 20 19   1 2 3 4

LETTERS BY
FRANK CVETKOVIC

TRANSLATION BY
EDWARD GAUVIN

EDITS BY
JUSTIN EISINGER AND
ALONZO SIMON

DESIGN BY
RON ESTEVEZ

Chris Ryall, President, Publisher, and Chief Creative Officer
John Barber, Editor-In-Chief
Robbie Robbins, EVP/Sr. Art Director
Cara Morrison, Chief Financial Officer
Matt Ruzicka, Chief Accounting Officer
David Hedgecock, Associate Publisher
Jerry Bennington, VP of New Product Development
Lorelei Bunjes, VP of Digital Services
Justin Eisinger, Editorial Director, Graphic Novels & Collections
Eric Moss, Senior Director, Licensing and Business Development

Ted Adams, IDW Founder

Antoine LAFARGE

DIABOLICAL SUMMER

A Novel

Publisher's Note

In light of certain facts that have surfaced since this book was first published, the author has elected to append a second part to the original work.
All the questions that haunted him for almost twenty years have thus been answered at last.

Original Title: DIABOLICAL SUMMER

© CLERVILLE Editions, first edition, 1987

to Michelle G.

How many times, since the summer of '67, have I gone over that day in my head...

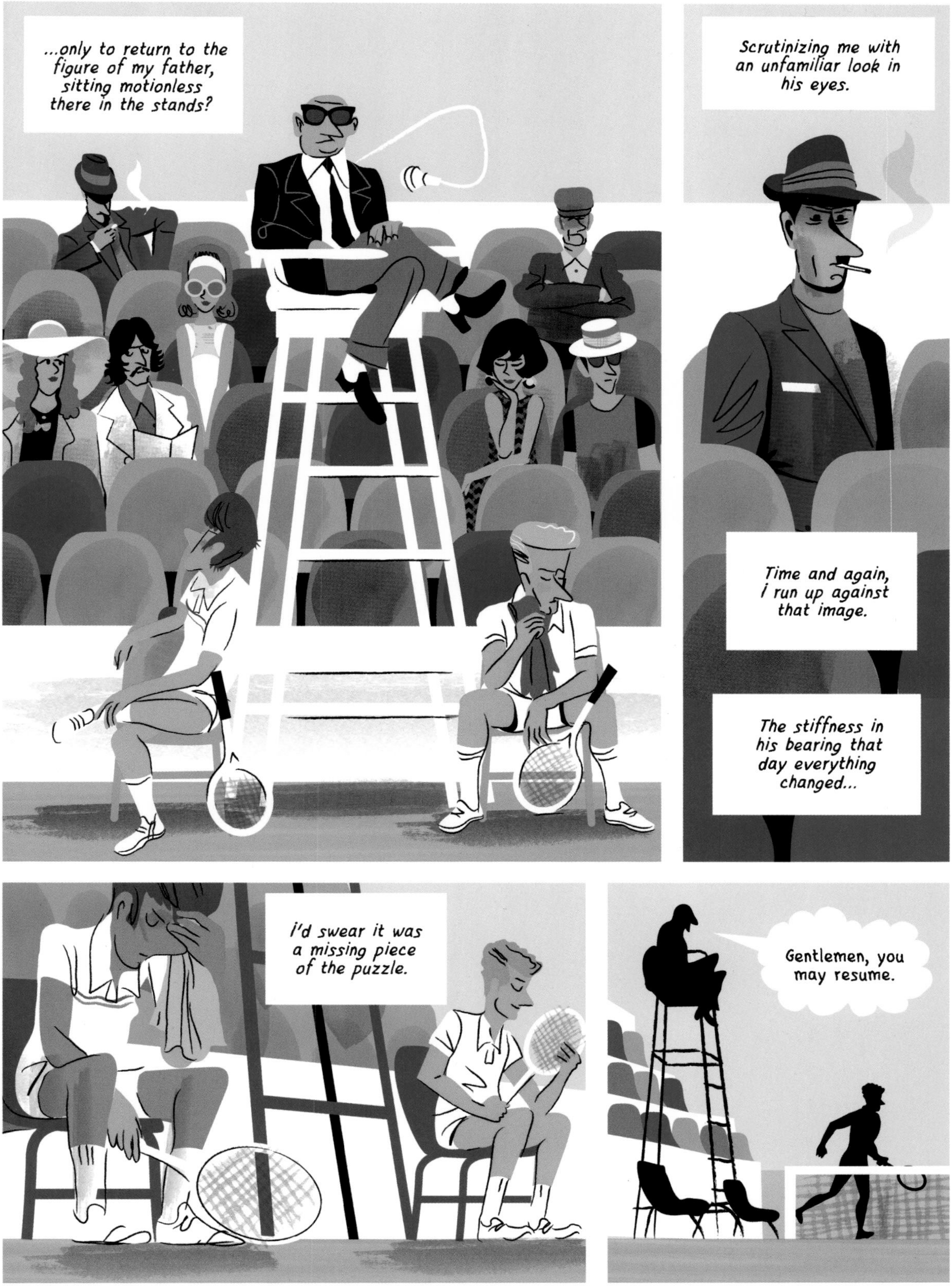
...only to return to the figure of my father, sitting motionless there in the stands?
Scrutinizing me with an unfamiliar look in his eyes.
Time and again, i run up against that image.
The stiffness in his bearing that day everything changed...
i'd swear it was a missing piece of the puzzle.
Gentlemen, you may resume.

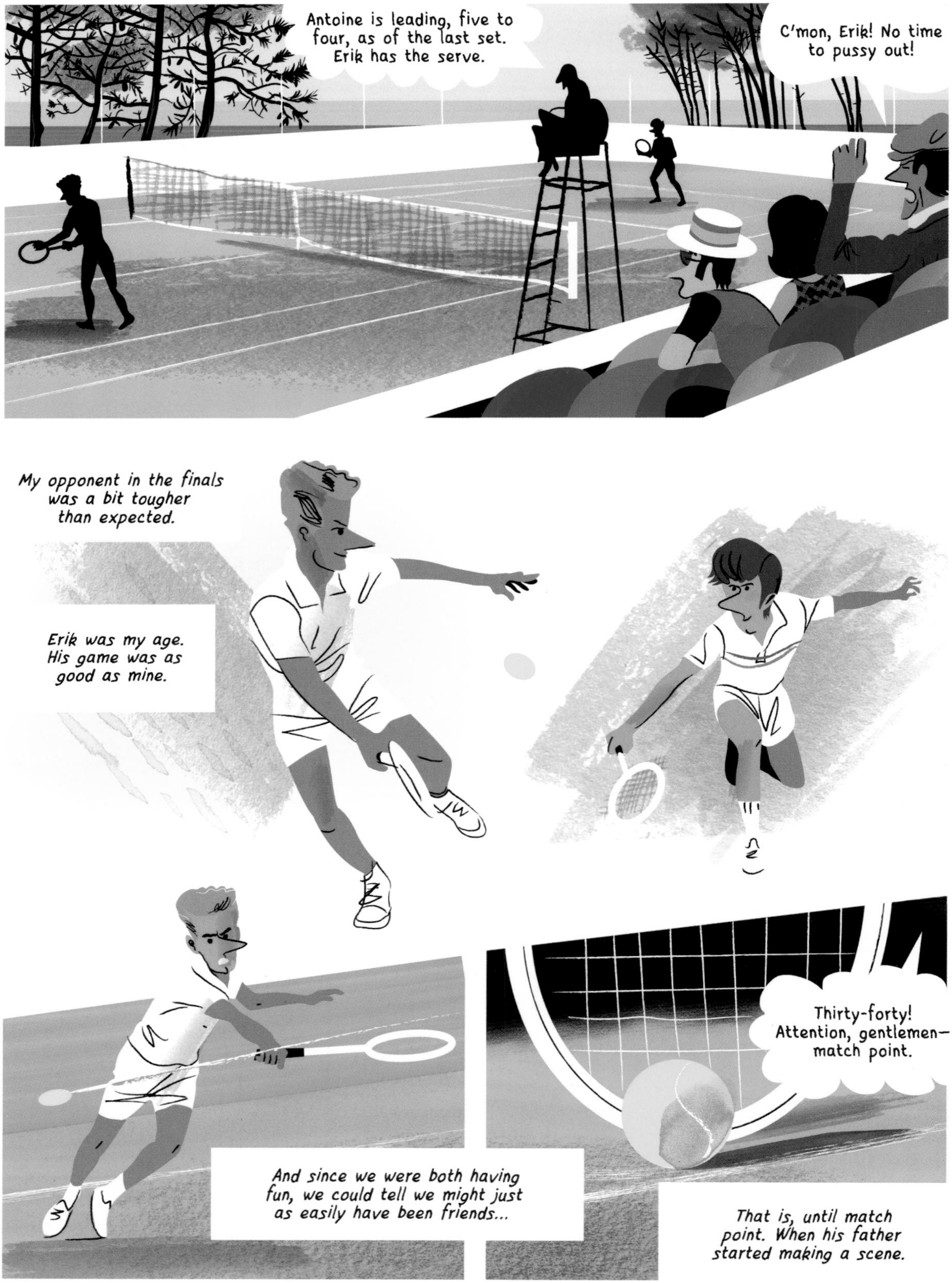

Antoine is leading, five to four, as of the last set. Erik has the serve.
C'mon, Erik! No time to pussy out!
My opponent in the finals was a bit tougher than expected.
Erik was my age. His game was as good as mine.
And since we were both having fun, we could tell we might just as easily have been friends...
Thirty-forty! Attention, gentlemen— match point.
That is, until match point. When his father started making a scene.

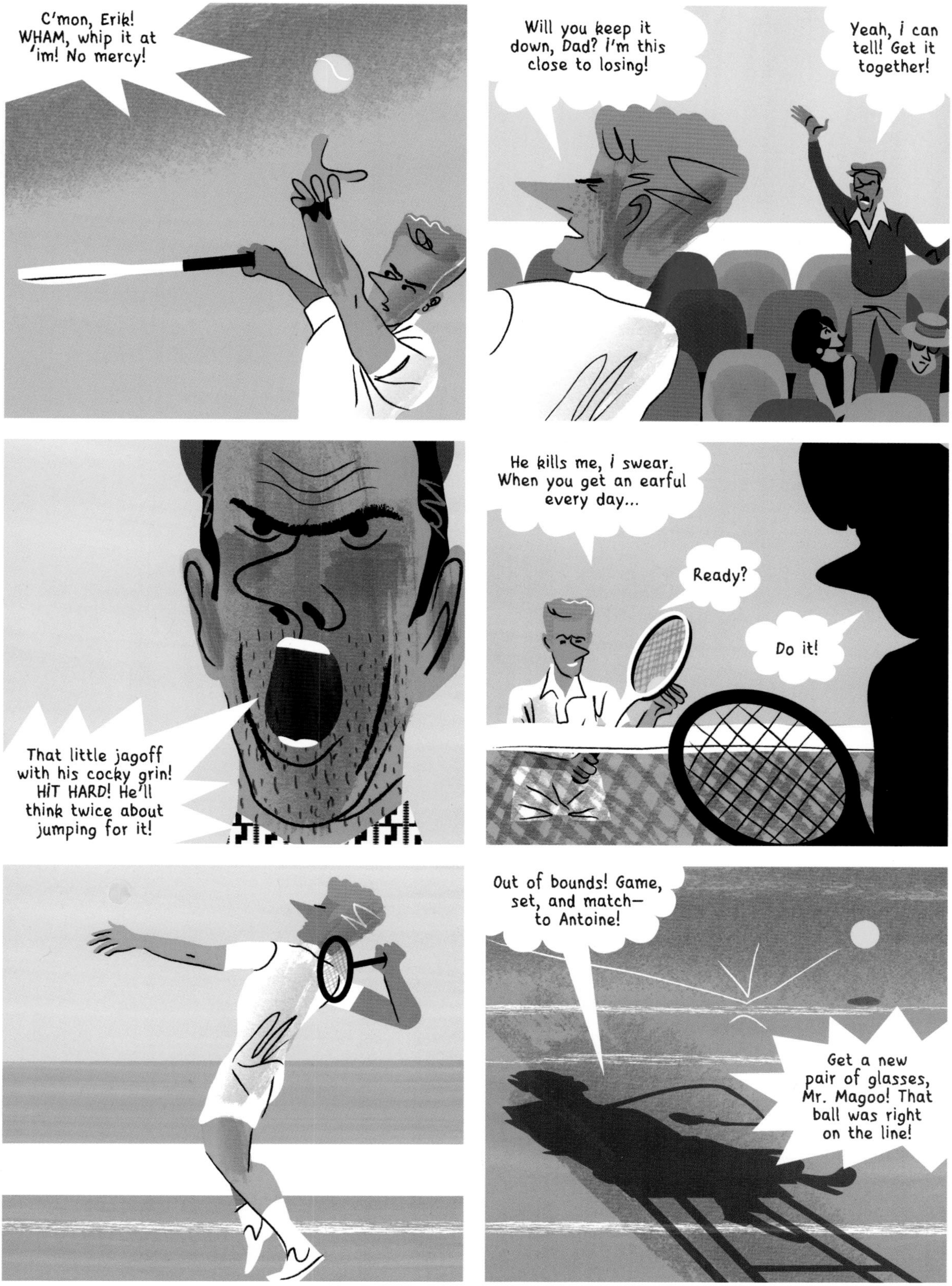
C'mon, Erik! WHAM, whip it at 'im! No mercy!
Will you keep it down, Dad? I'm this close to losing!
Yeah, I can tell! Get it together!
That little jagoff with his cocky grin! HIT HARD! He'll think twice about jumping for it!
He kills me, I swear. When you get an earful every day...
Ready?
Do it!
Out of bounds! Game, set, and match— to Antoine!
Get a new pair of glasses, Mr. Magoo! That ball was right on the line!

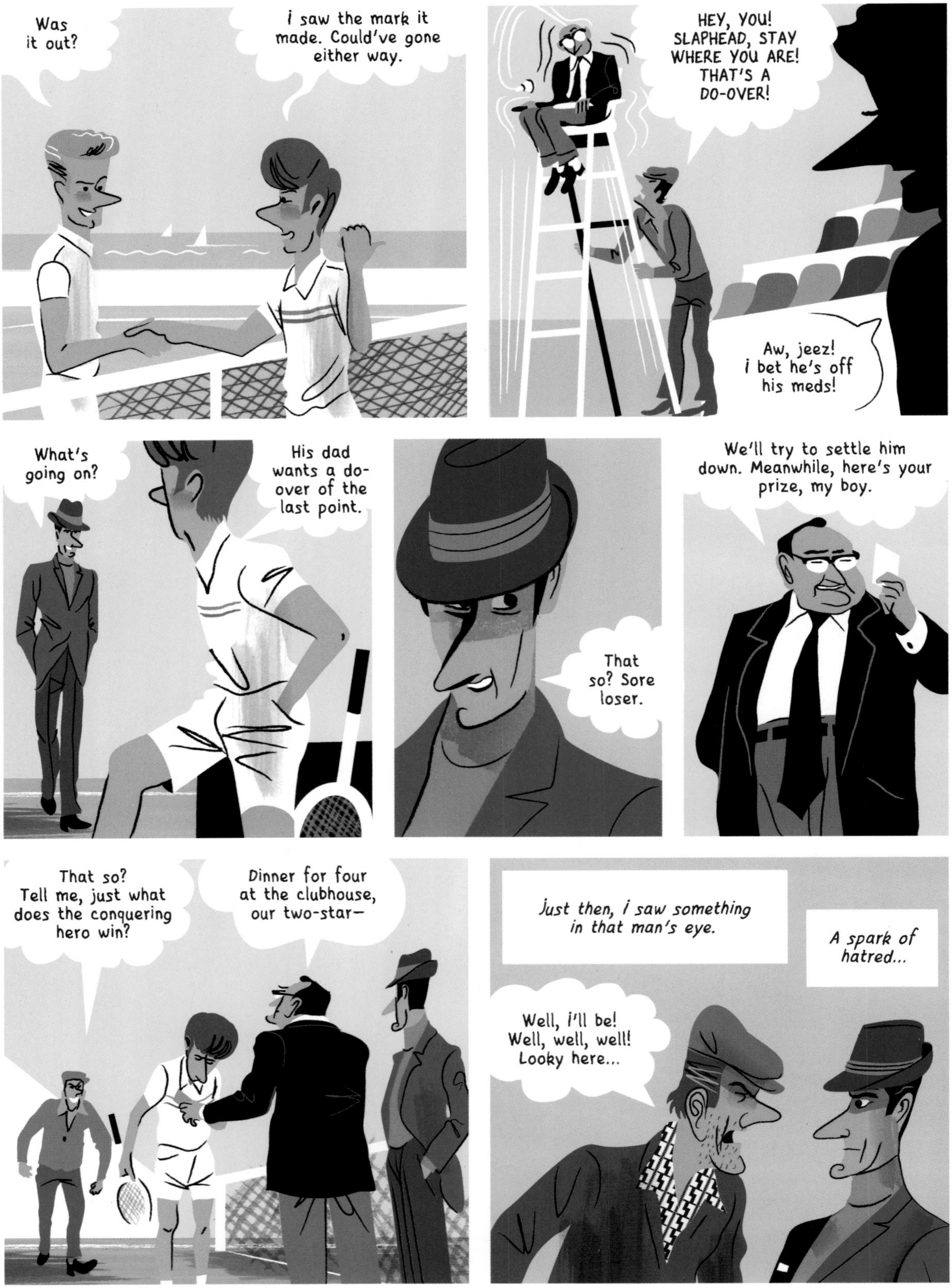

Was it out?
I saw the mark it made. Could've gone either way.
HEY, YOU! SLAPHEAD, STAY WHERE YOU ARE! THAT'S A DO-OVER!
Aw, jeez! I bet he's off his meds!
What's going on?
His dad wants a do-over of the last point.
That so? Sore loser.
We'll try to settle him down. Meanwhile, here's your prize, my boy.
That so? Tell me, just what does the conquering hero win?
Dinner for four at the clubhouse, our two-star—
Just then, I saw something in that man's eye.
A spark of hatred...
Well, I'll be! Well, well, well! Looky here...

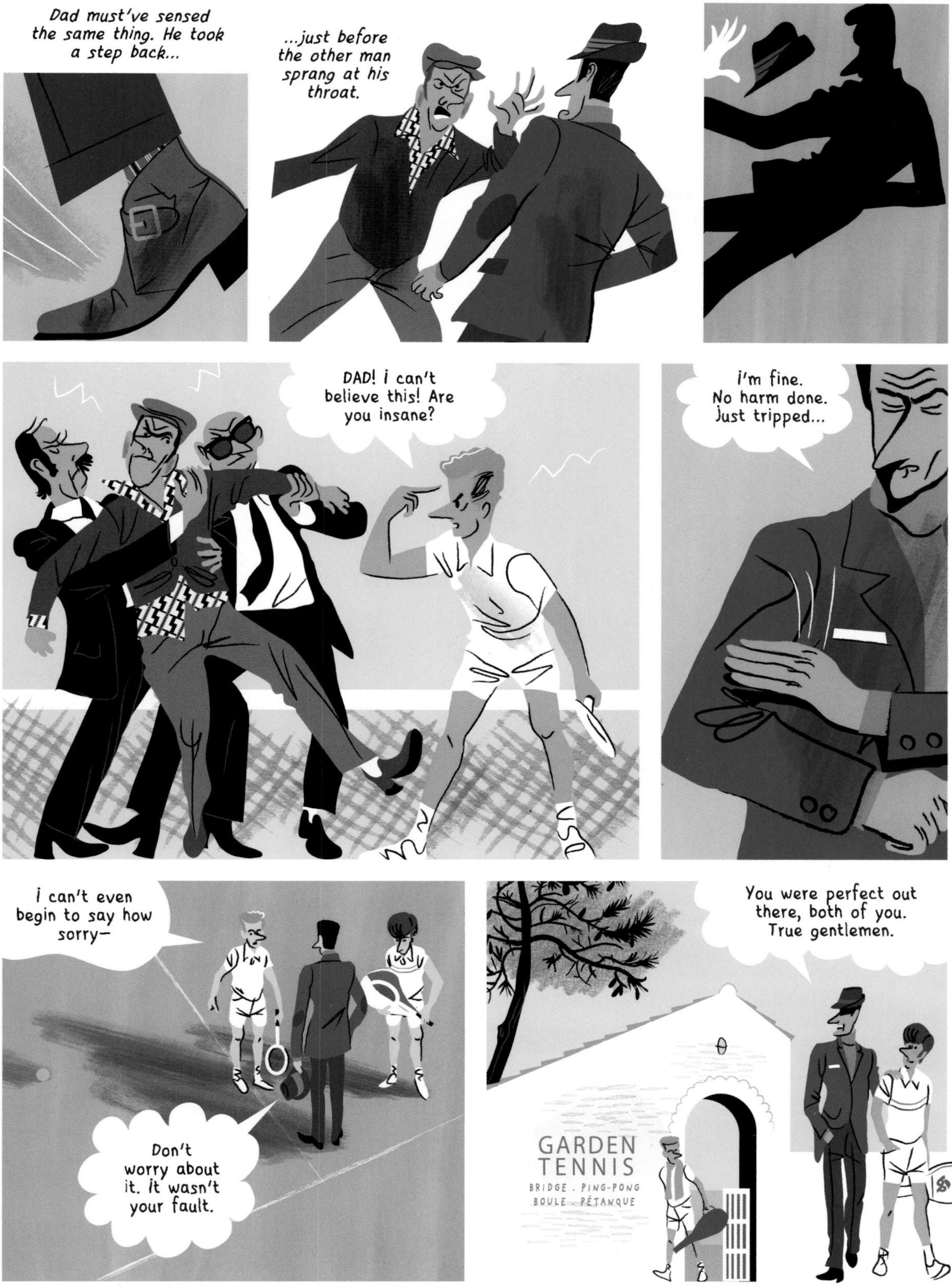
Dad must've sensed the same thing. He took a step back...
...just before the other man sprang at his throat.
DAD! I can't believe this! Are you insane?
I'm fine. No harm done. Just tripped...
I can't even begin to say how sorry—
Don't worry about it. It wasn't your fault.
You were perfect out there, both of you. True gentlemen.
GARDEN TENNIS
BRIDGE . PING-PONG
BOULE . PÉTANQUE

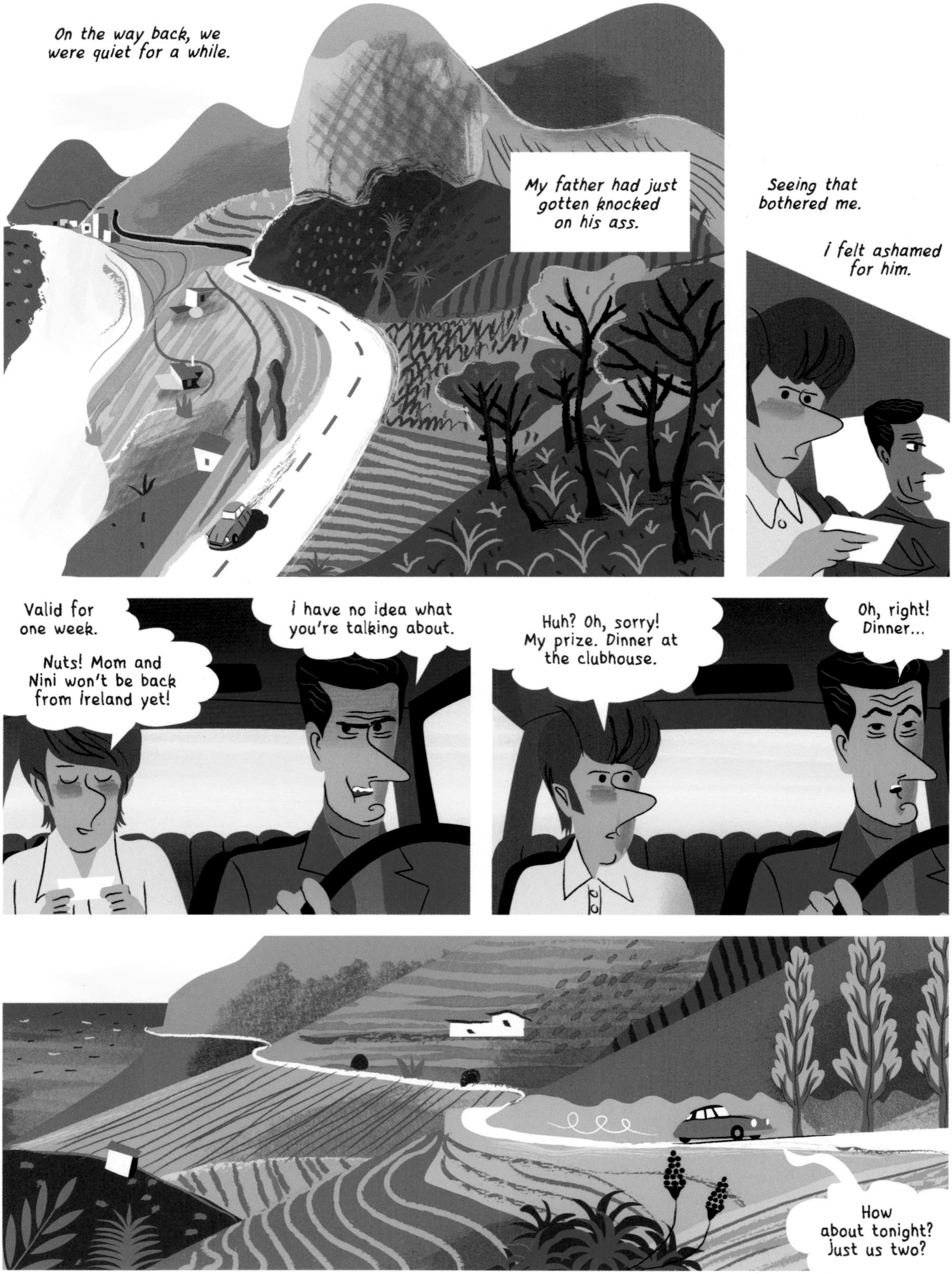
On the way back, we were quiet for a while.
My father had just gotten knocked on his ass.
Seeing that bothered me.
I felt ashamed for him.
Valid for one week.
Nuts! Mom and Nini won't be back from Ireland yet!
I have no idea what you're talking about.
Huh? Oh, sorry! My prize. Dinner at the clubhouse.
Oh, right! Dinner...
How about tonight? Just us two?

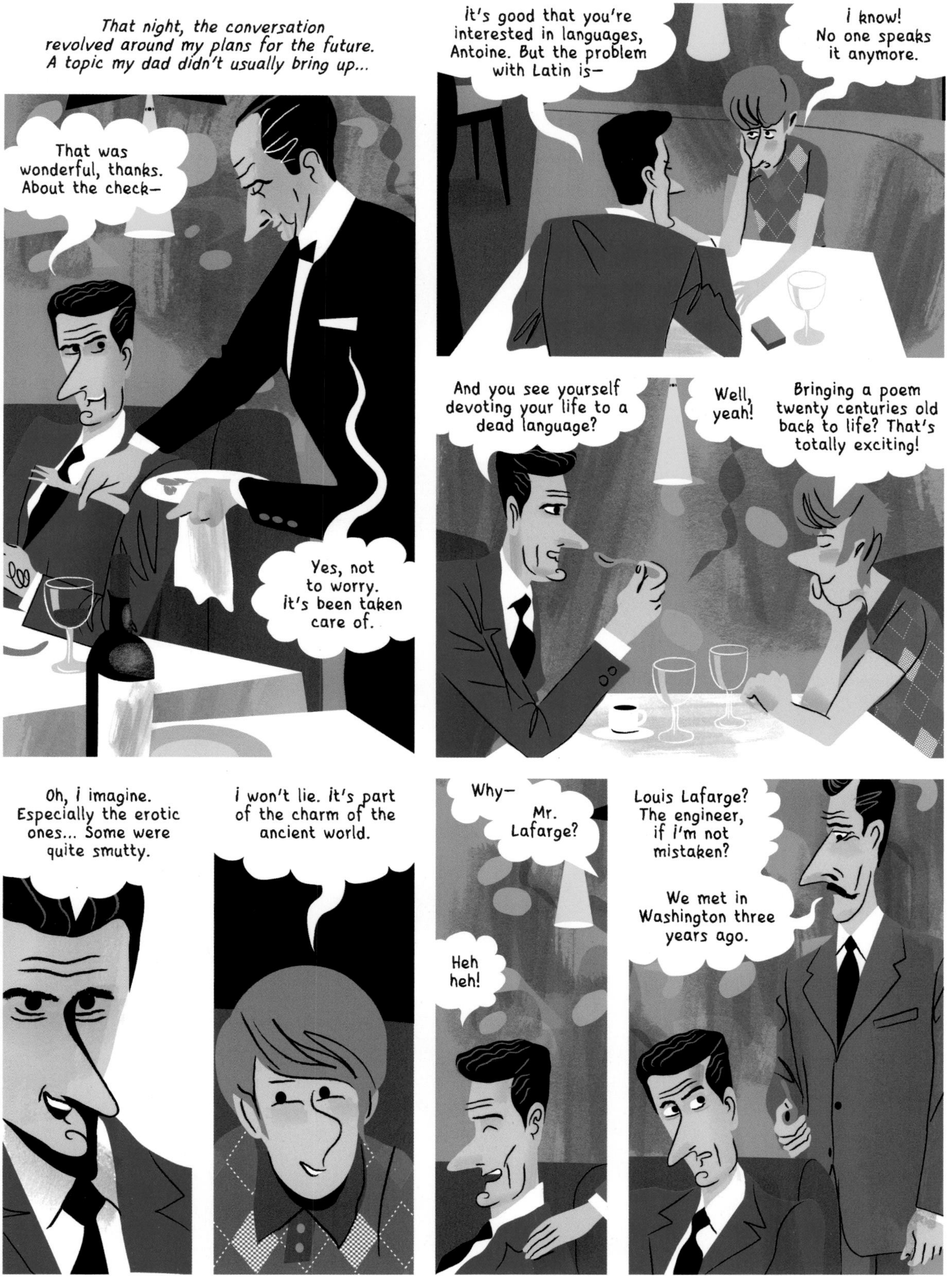
That night, the conversation revolved around my plans for the future. A topic my dad didn't usually bring up...
That was wonderful, thanks. About the check—
Yes, not to worry. It's been taken care of.
It's good that you're interested in languages, Antoine. But the problem with Latin is—
I know! No one speaks it anymore.
And you see yourself devoting your life to a dead language?
Well, yeah!
Bringing a poem twenty centuries old back to life? That's totally exciting!
Oh, I imagine. Especially the erotic ones... Some were quite smutty.
I won't lie. It's part of the charm of the ancient world.
Why—
Mr. Lafarge?
Heh heh!
Louis Lafarge? The engineer, if I'm not mistaken?
We met in Washington three years ago.

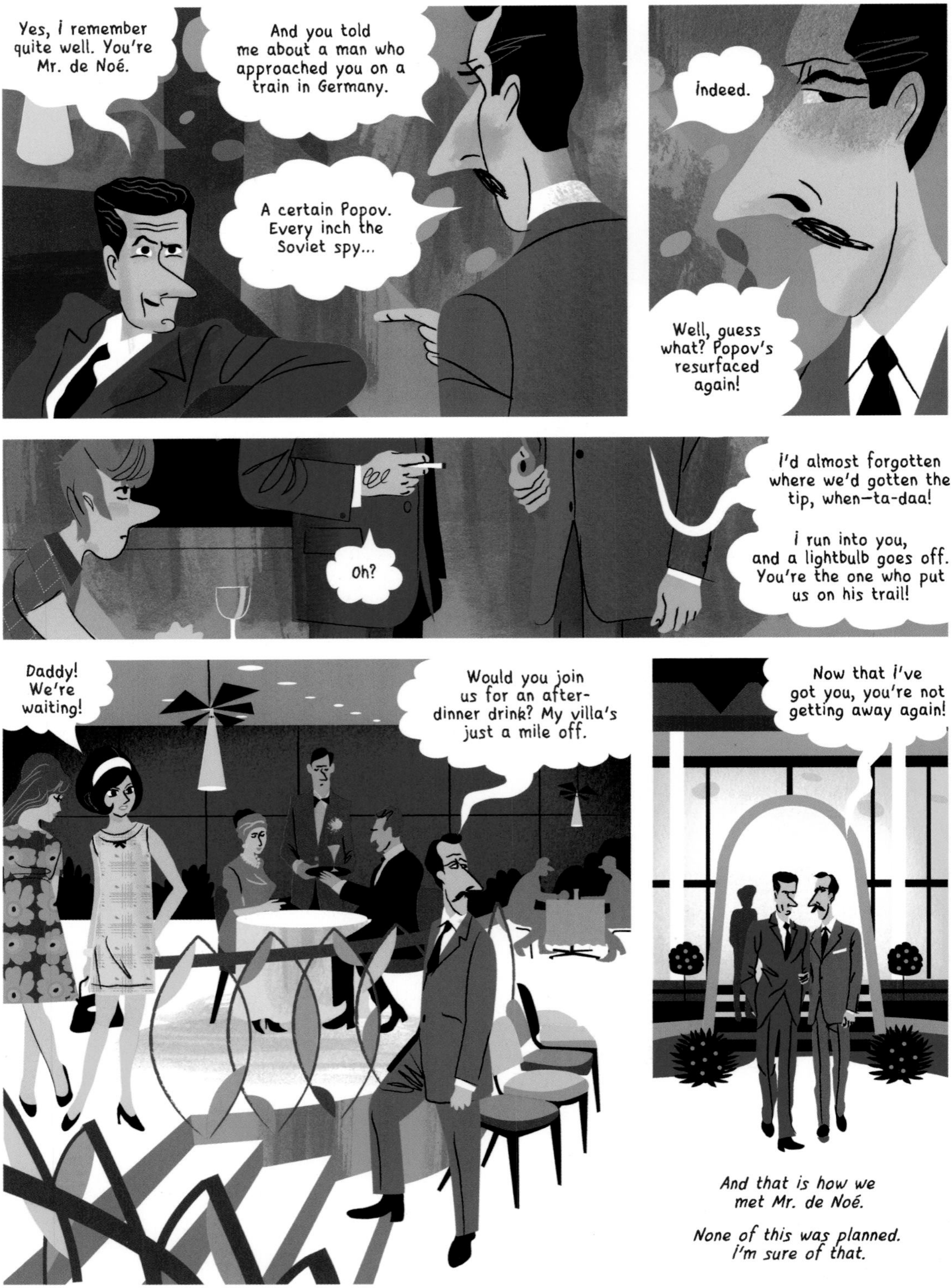
Yes, I remember quite well. You're Mr. de Noé.
And you told me about a man who approached you on a train in Germany.
A certain Popov. Every inch the Soviet spy...
Indeed.
Well, guess what? Popov's resurfaced again!
Oh?
I'd almost forgotten where we'd gotten the tip, when—ta-daa!
I run into you, and a lightbulb goes off. You're the one who put us on his trail!
Daddy! We're waiting!
Would you join us for an after-dinner drink? My villa's just a mile off.
Now that I've got you, you're not getting away again!
And that is how we met Mr. de Noé.
None of this was planned. I'm sure of that.

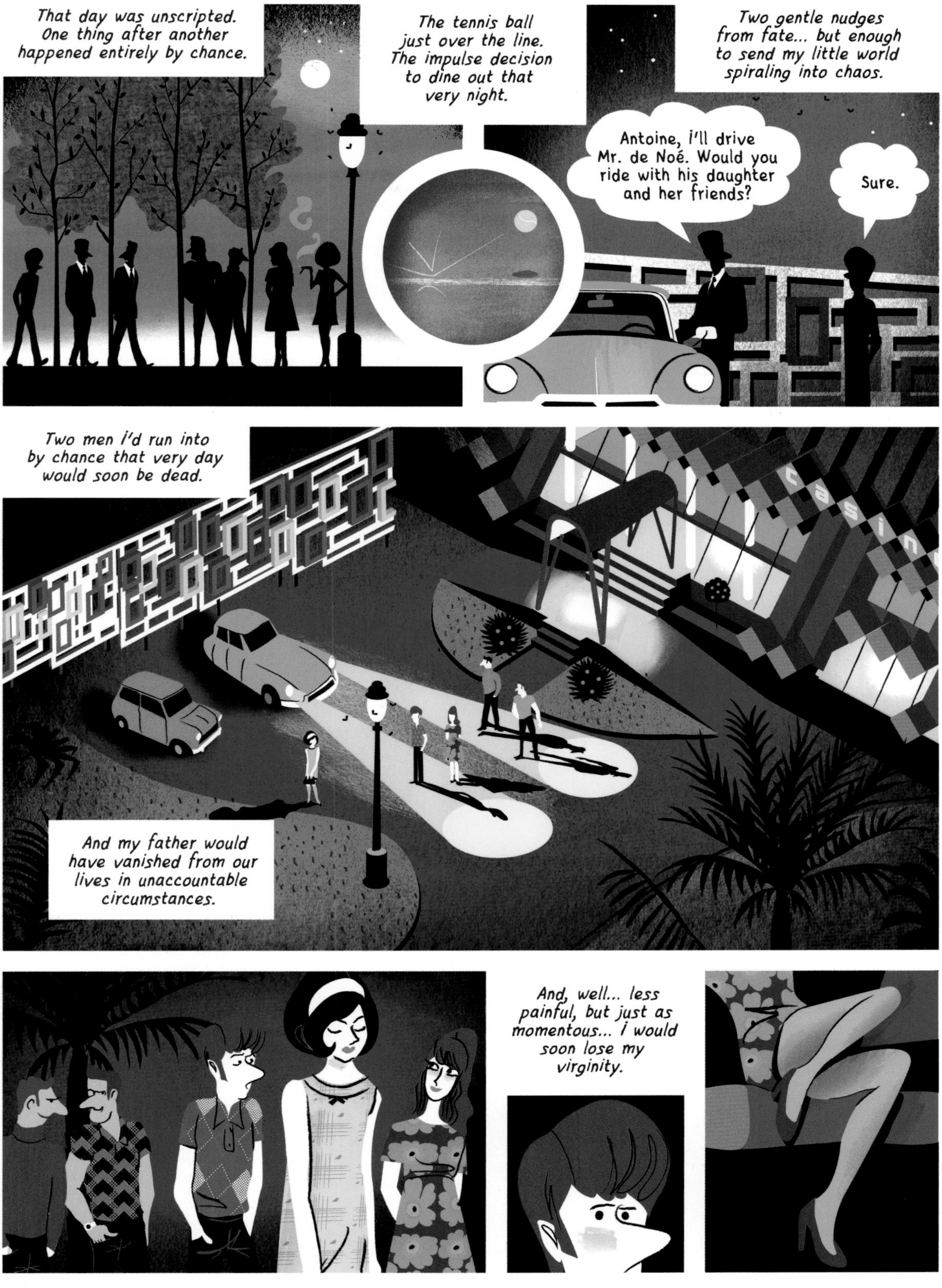
That day was unscripted. One thing after another happened entirely by chance.
The tennis ball just over the line. The impulse decision to dine out that very night.
Two gentle nudges from fate... but enough to send my little world spiraling into chaos.
Antoine, I'll drive Mr. de Noé. Would you ride with his daughter and her friends?
Sure.
Two men I'd run into by chance that very day would soon be dead.
casin
And my father would have vanished from our lives in unaccountable circumstances.
And, well... less painful, but just as momentous... I would soon lose my virginity.

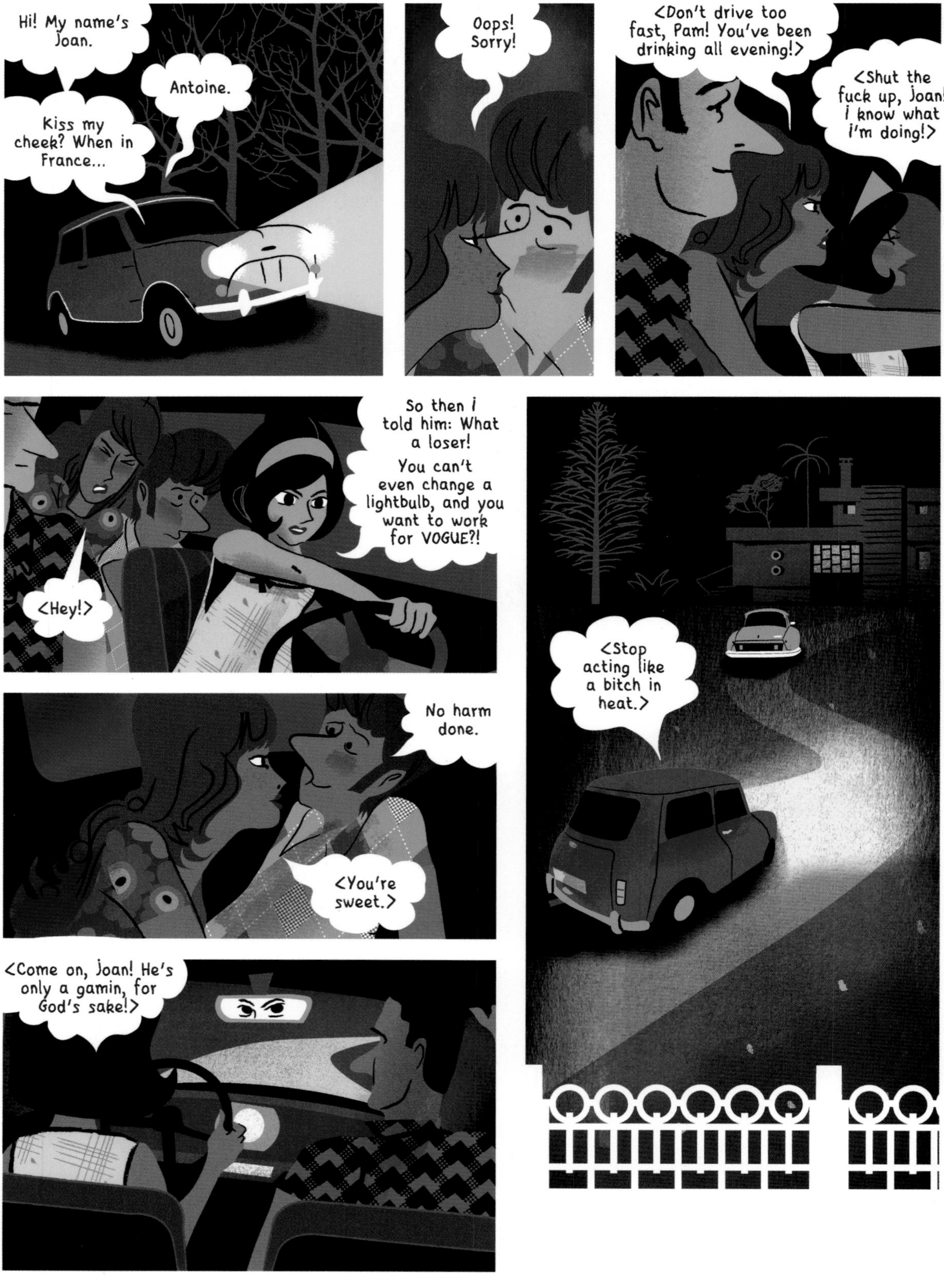
Hi! My name's Joan.
Antoine.
Kiss my cheek? When in France...
Oops! Sorry!
<Don't drive too fast, Pam! You've been drinking all evening!>
<Shut the fuck up, Joan! I know what I'm doing!>
So then I told him: What a loser!
You can't even change a lightbulb, and you want to work for VOGUE?!
<Hey!>
No harm done.
<You're sweet.>
<Come on, Joan! He's only a gamin, for God's sake!>
<Stop acting like a bitch in heat.>

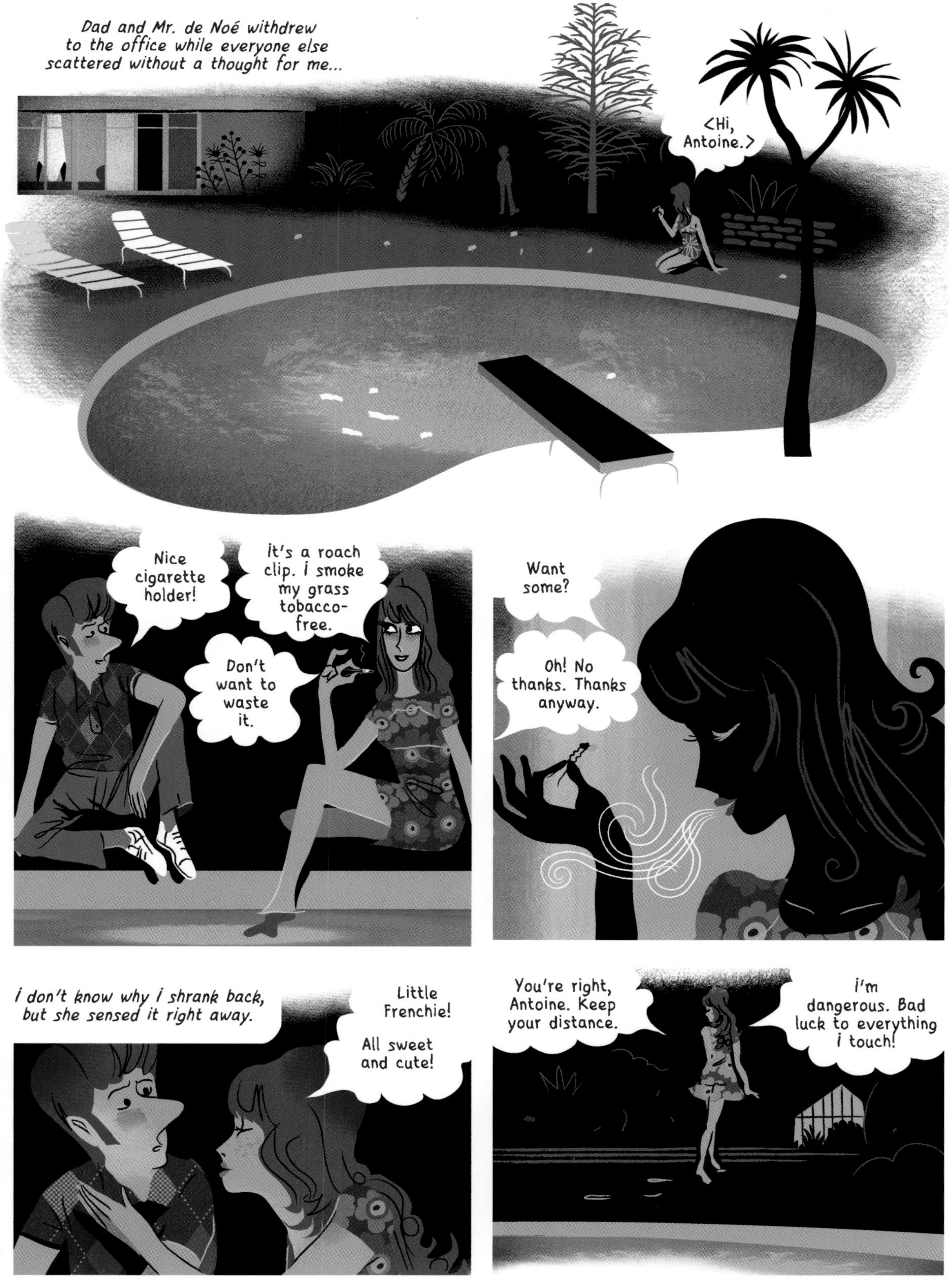
Dad and Mr. de Noé withdrew to the office while everyone else scattered without a thought for me...
<Hi, Antoine.>
Nice cigarette holder!
It's a roach clip. I smoke my grass tobacco-free.
Don't want to waste it.
Want some?
Oh! No thanks. Thanks anyway.
I don't know why I shrank back, but she sensed it right away.
Little Frenchie!
All sweet and cute!
You're right, Antoine. Keep your distance.
I'm dangerous. Bad luck to everything I touch!

Hey! We found him!

Pamela de Noé must've swallowed a radio once.

Your father was wondering where you'd run off to.

No worries. Just admiring the pool...

Every quarter hour on the dot, she'd broadcast an update on her plans, her mental state, her desires and frustrations...

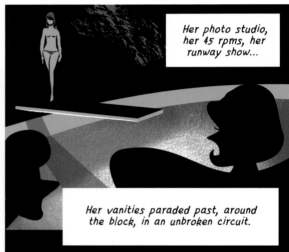

Her photo studio, her 45 rpms, her runway show...

Her vanities paraded past, around the block, in an unbroken circuit.

That night, however, someone was about to steal the spotlight.

Hey!

What's gotten into her, flaunting herself like that? Does she think she's the only one here?

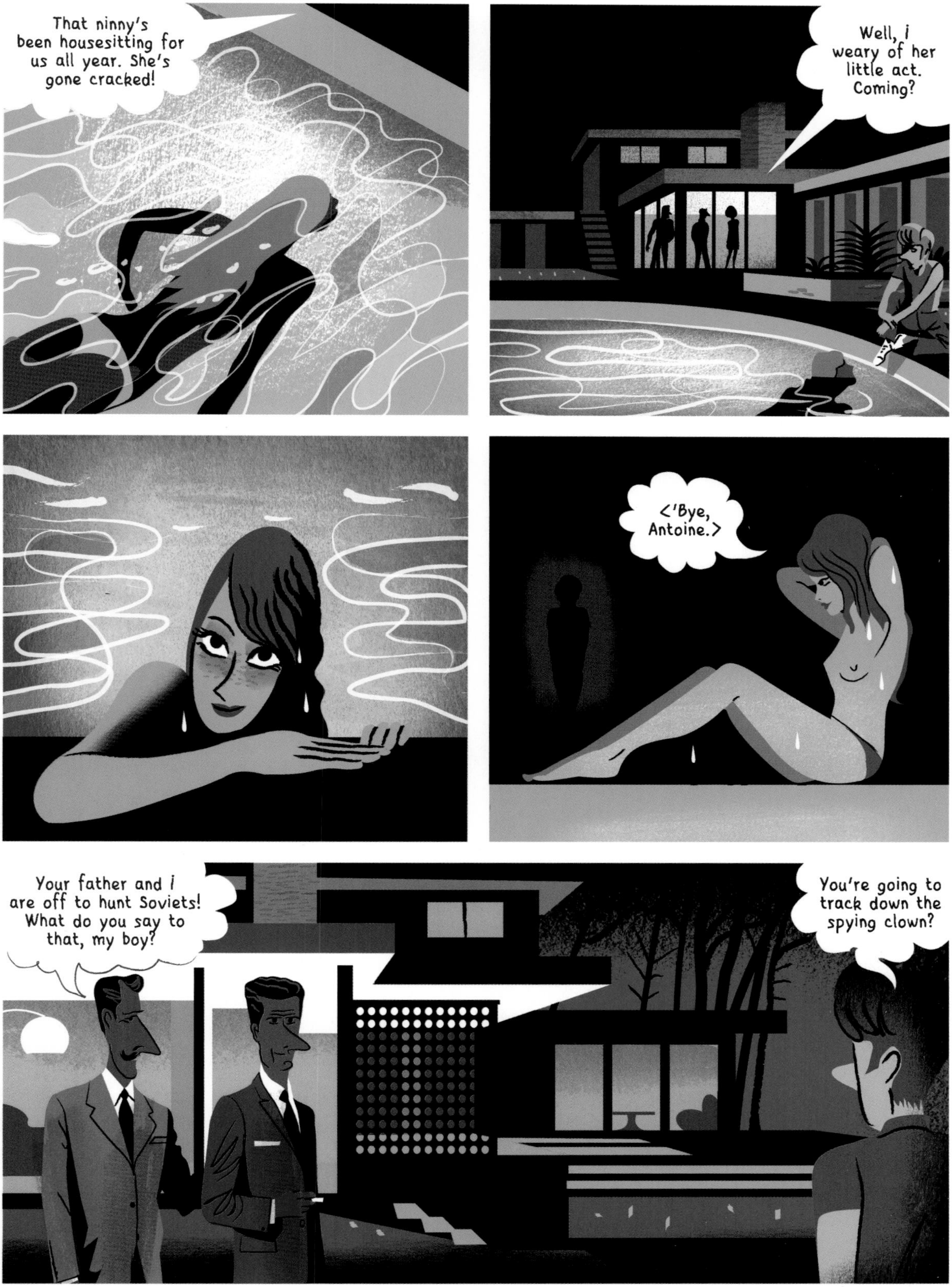
That ninny's been housesitting for us all year. She's gone cracked!
Well, i weary of her little act. Coming?
<'Bye, Antoine.>
Your father and i are off to hunt Soviets! What do you say to that, my boy?
You're going to track down the spying clown?

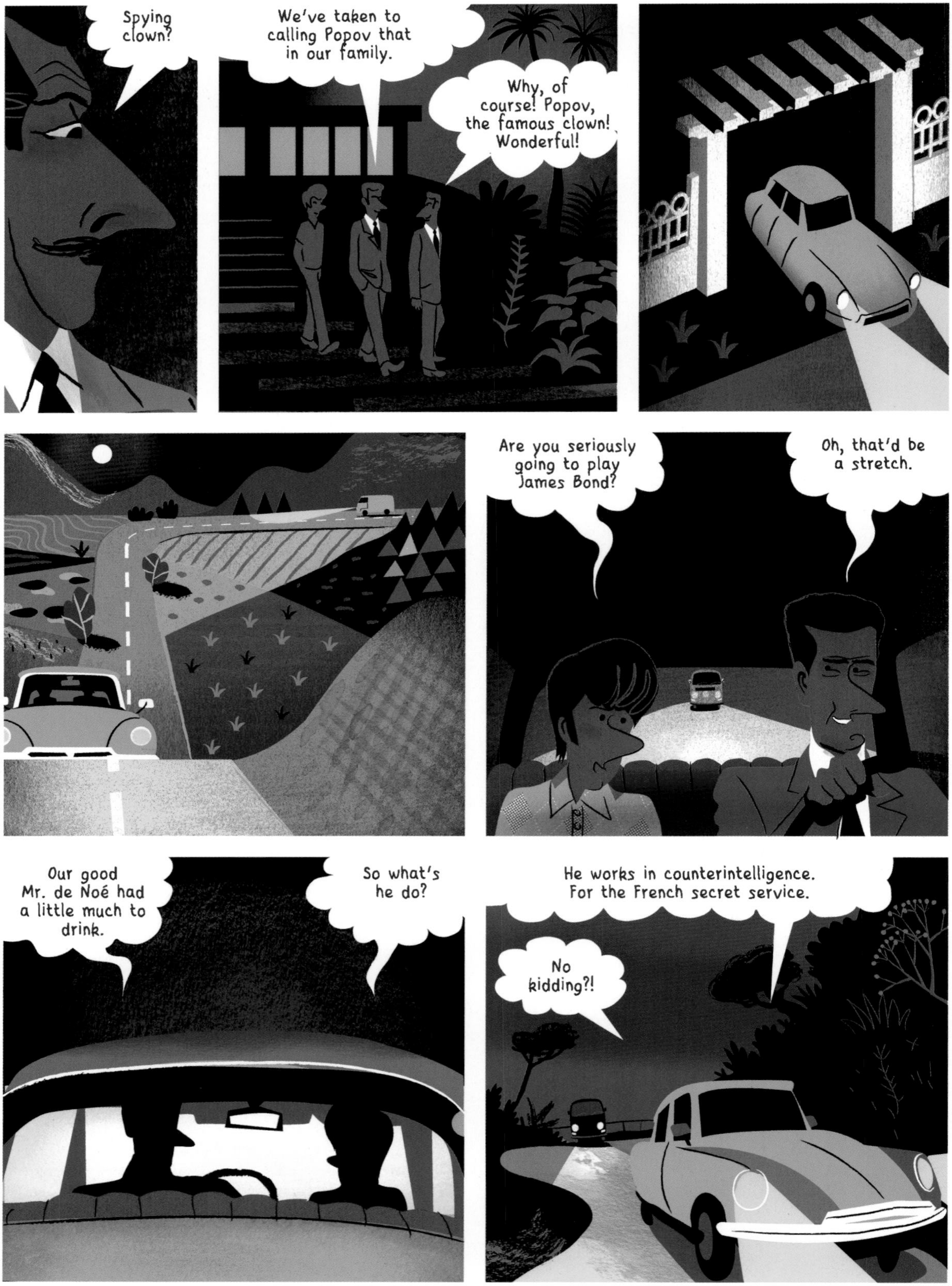
Spying clown?
We've taken to calling Popov that in our family.
Why, of course! Popov, the famous clown! Wonderful!
Are you seriously going to play James Bond?
Oh, that'd be a stretch.
Our good Mr. de Noé had a little much to drink.
So what's he do?
He works in counterintelligence. For the French secret service.
No kidding?!

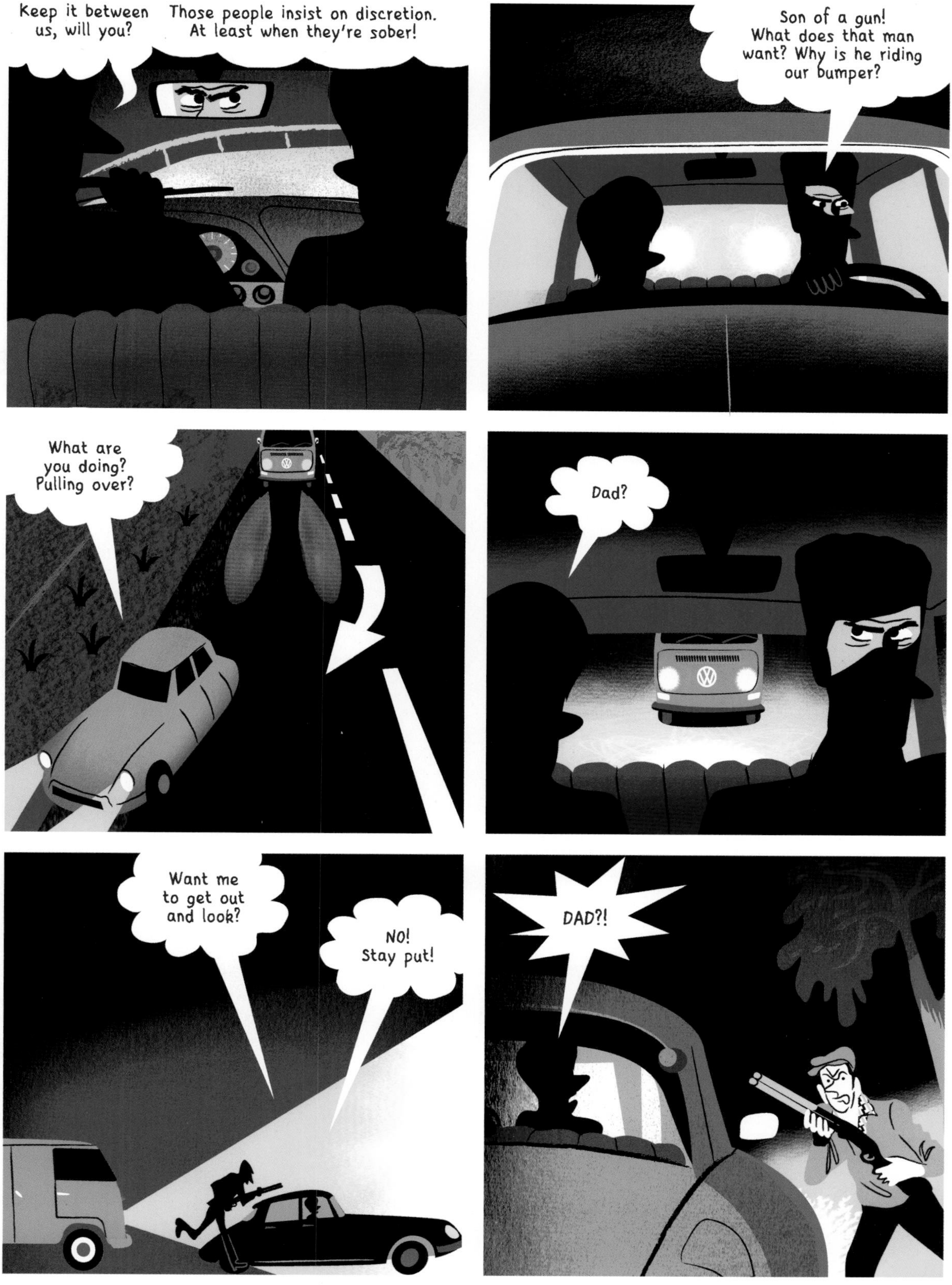
Keep it between us, will you?
Those people insist on discretion. At least when they're sober!
Son of a gun! What does that man want? Why is he riding our bumper?
What are you doing? Pulling over?
Dad?
Want me to get out and look?
NO! Stay put!
DAD?!

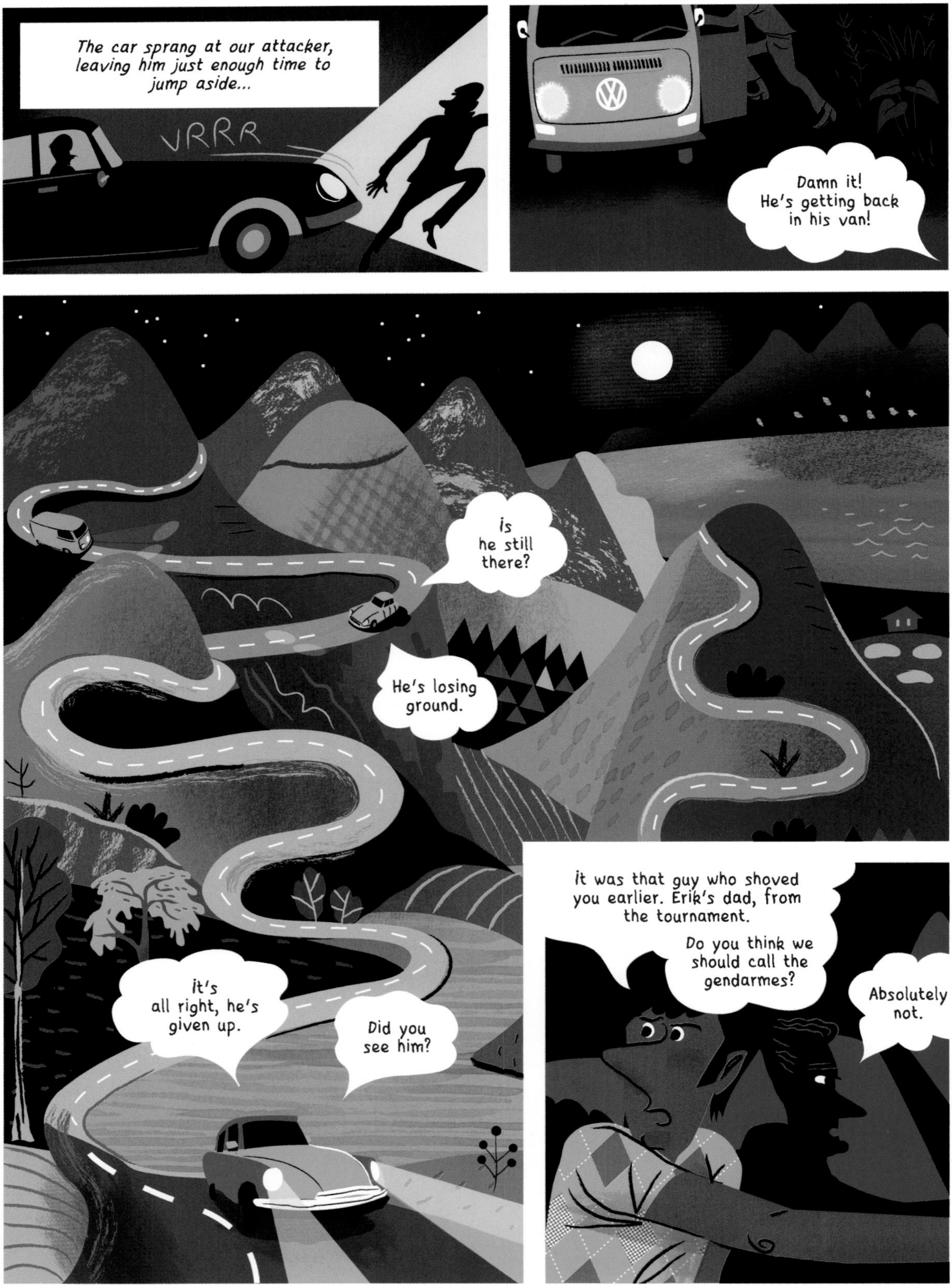
The car sprang at our attacker, leaving him just enough time to jump aside...
VRRR
Damn it! He's getting back in his van!
Is he still there?
He's losing ground.
It's all right, he's given up.
Did you see him?
It was that guy who shoved you earlier. Erik's dad, from the tournament.
Do you think we should call the gendarmes?
Absolutely not.

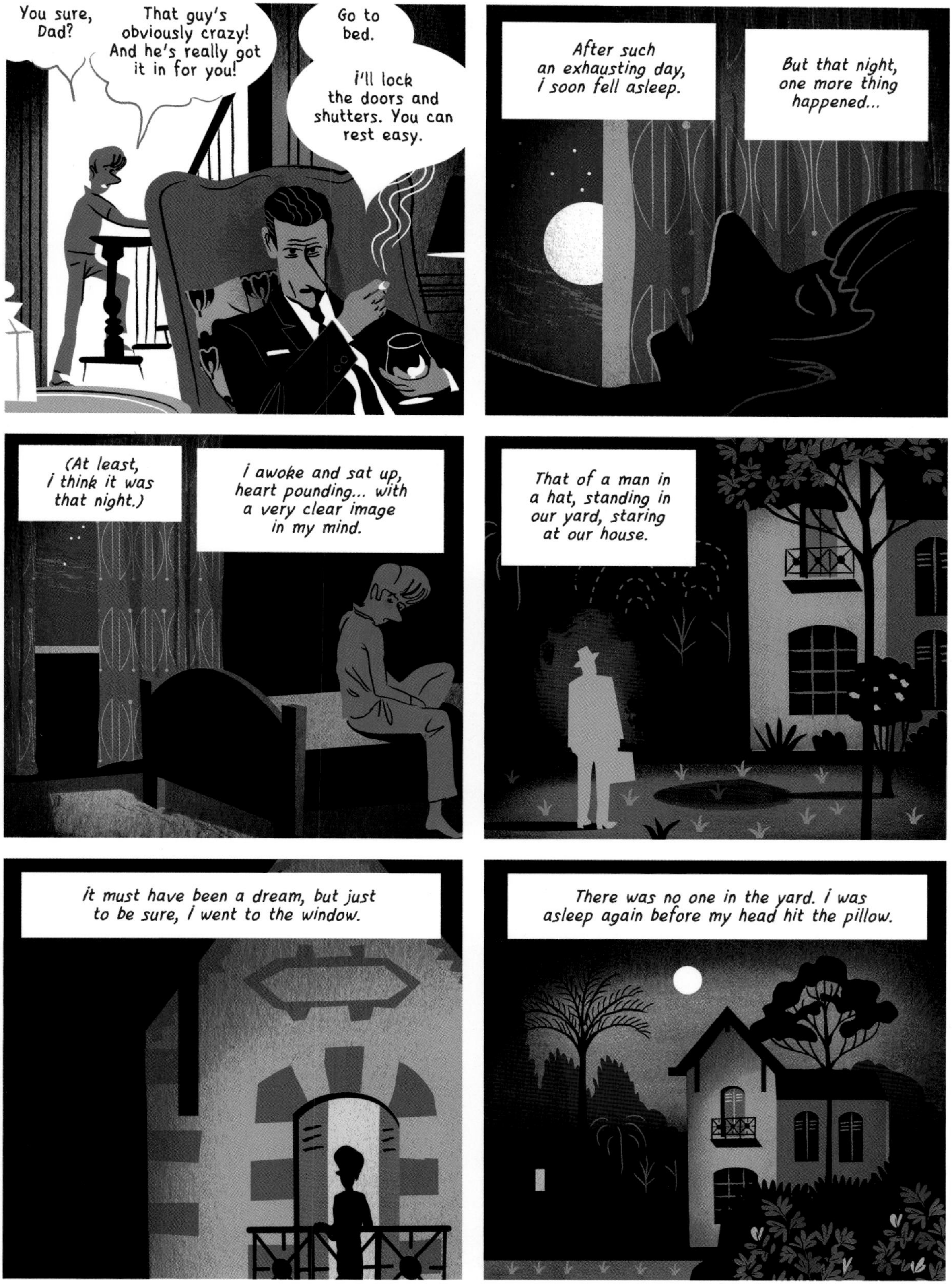
You sure, Dad?
That guy's obviously crazy! And he's really got it in for you!
Go to bed.
i'll lock the doors and shutters. You can rest easy.
After such an exhausting day, i soon fell asleep.
But that night, one more thing happened...
(At least, i think it was that night.)
i awoke and sat up, heart pounding... with a very clear image in my mind.
That of a man in a hat, standing in our yard, staring at our house.
it must have been a dream, but just to be sure, i went to the window.
There was no one in the yard. i was asleep again before my head hit the pillow.

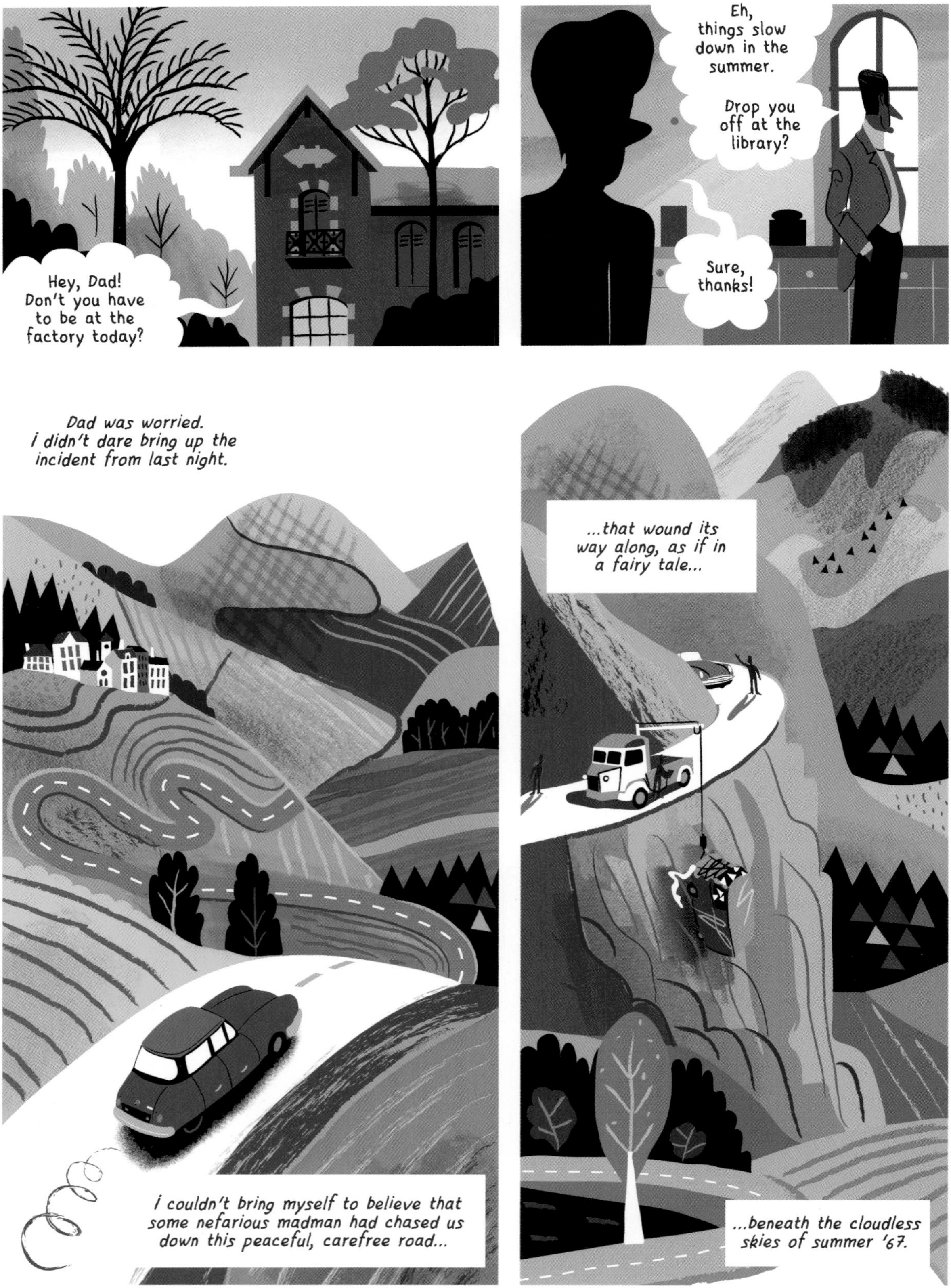
Hey, Dad! Don't you have to be at the factory today?
Eh, things slow down in the summer.
Drop you off at the library?
Sure, thanks!
Dad was worried. I didn't dare bring up the incident from last night.
I couldn't bring myself to believe that some nefarious madman had chased us down this peaceful, carefree road...
...that wound its way along, as if in a fairy tale...
...beneath the cloudless skies of summer '67.

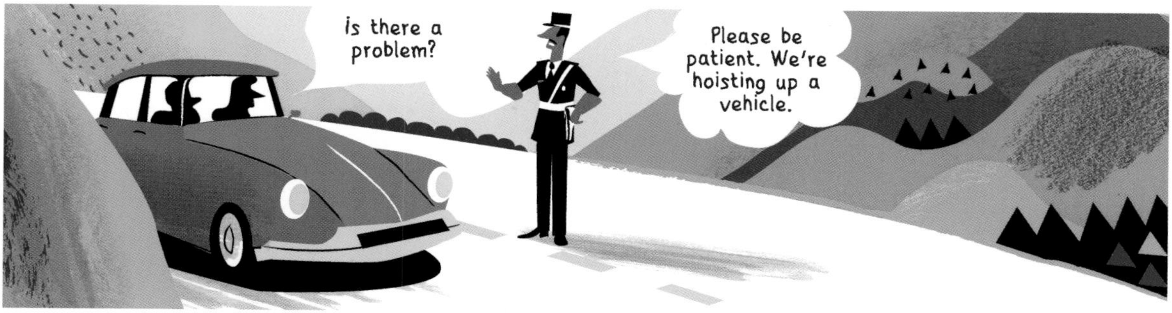
Is there a problem?
Please be patient. We're hoisting up a vehicle.

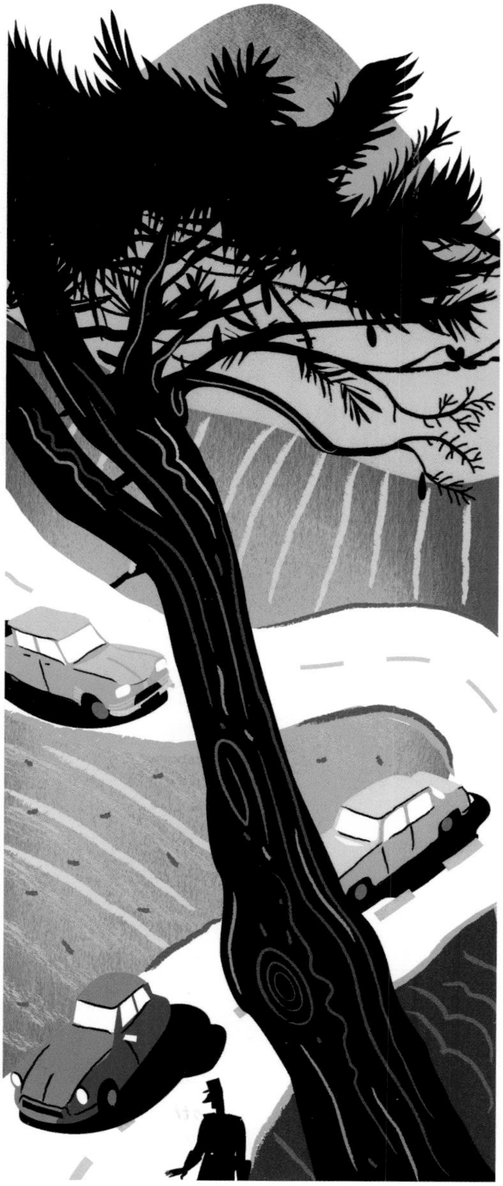

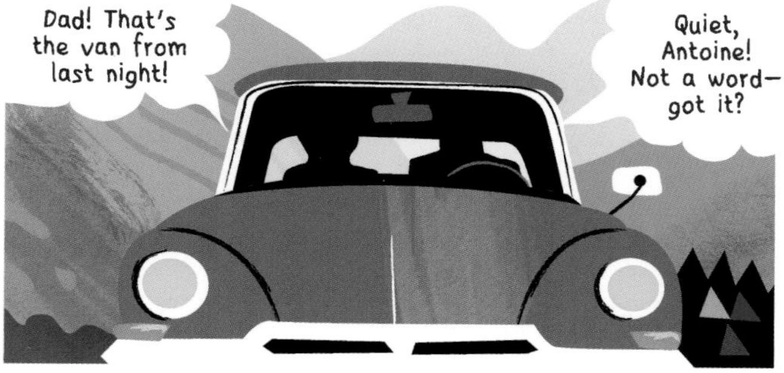
Dad! That's the van from last night!
Quiet, Antoine! Not a word—got it?

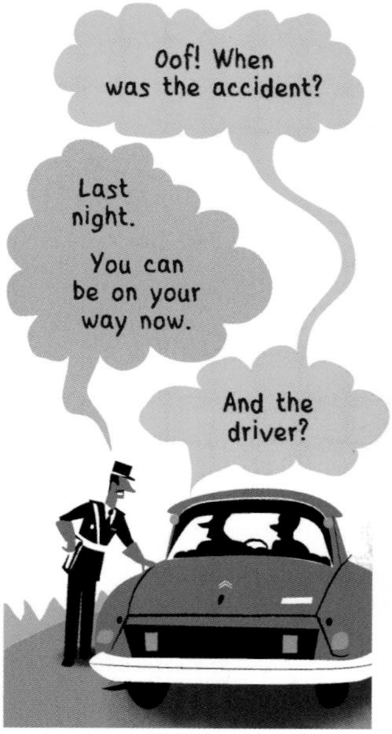
Oof! When was the accident?
Last night.
You can be on your way now.
And the driver?

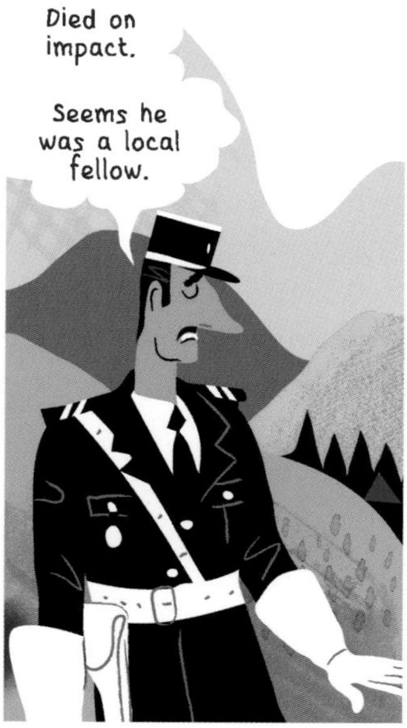
Died on impact.
Seems he was a local fellow.

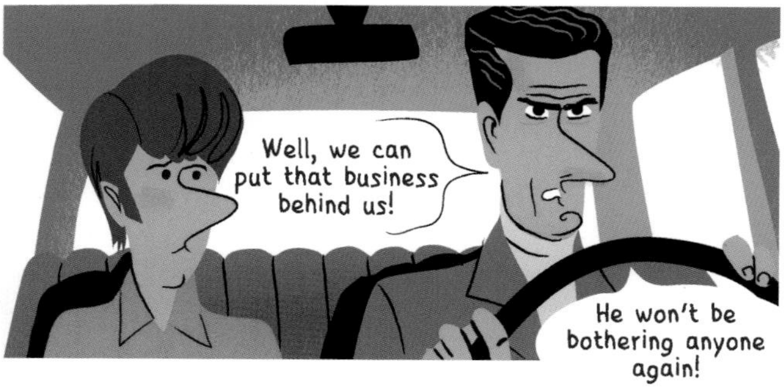
Well, we can put that business behind us!
He won't be bothering anyone again!

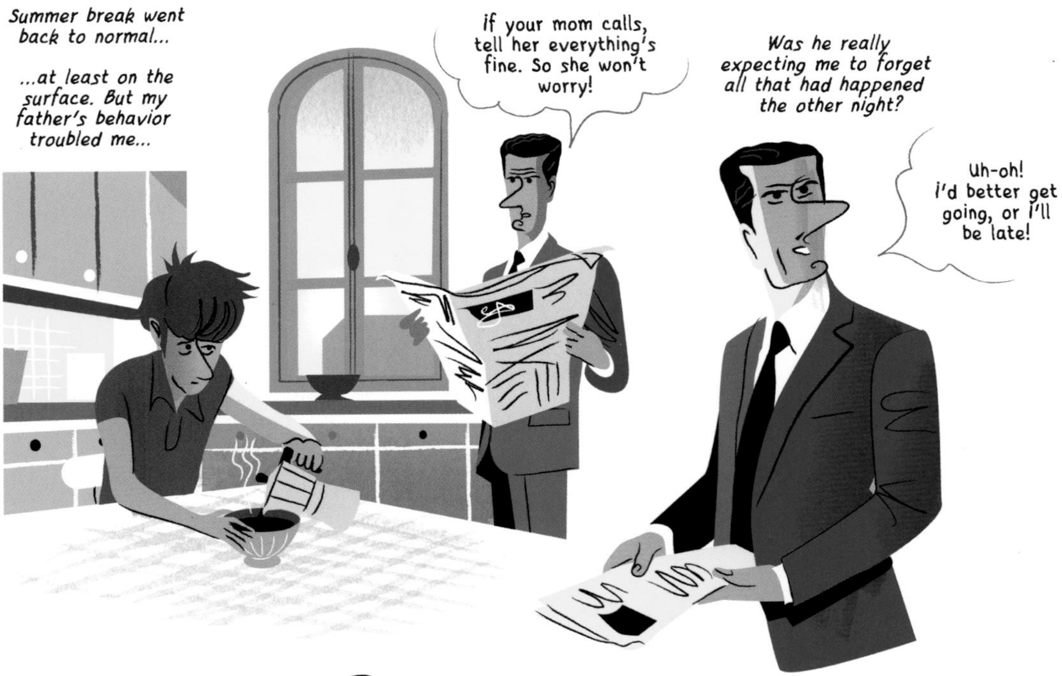
Summer break went back to normal...
...at least on the surface. But my father's behavior troubled me...
If your mom calls, tell her everything's fine. So she won't worry!
Was he really expecting me to forget all that had happened the other night?
Uh-oh! I'd better get going, or I'll be late!

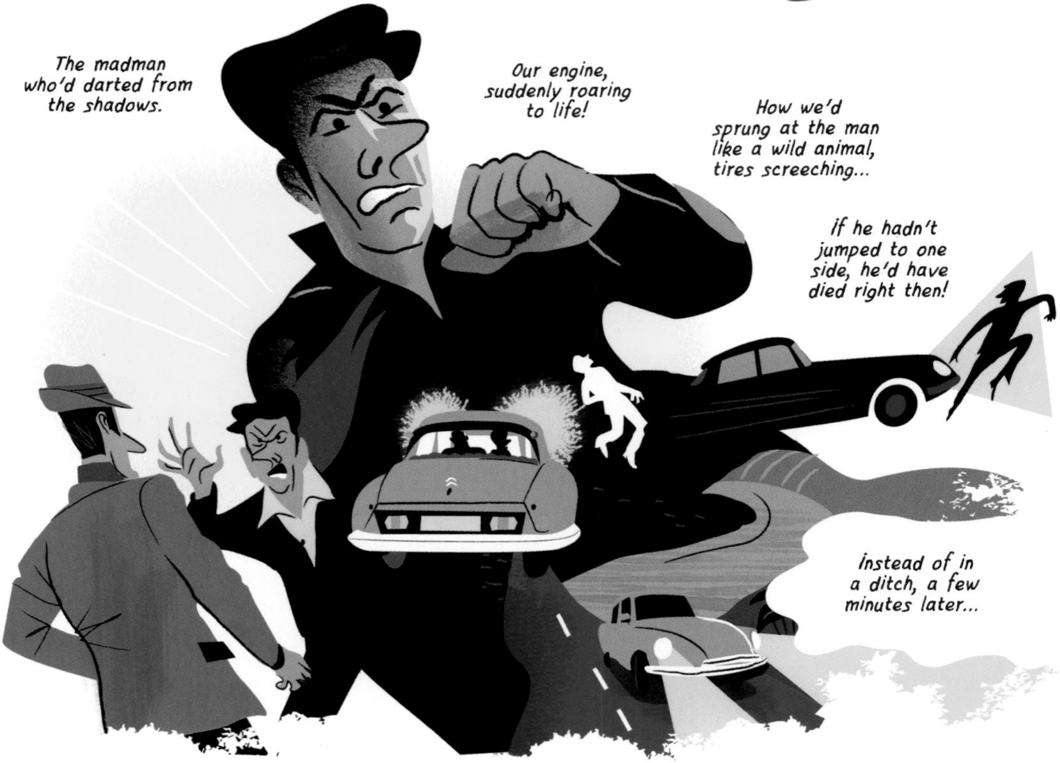
The madman who'd darted from the shadows.
Our engine, suddenly roaring to life!
How we'd sprung at the man like a wild animal, tires screeching...
If he hadn't jumped to one side, he'd have died right then!
Instead of in a ditch, a few minutes later...

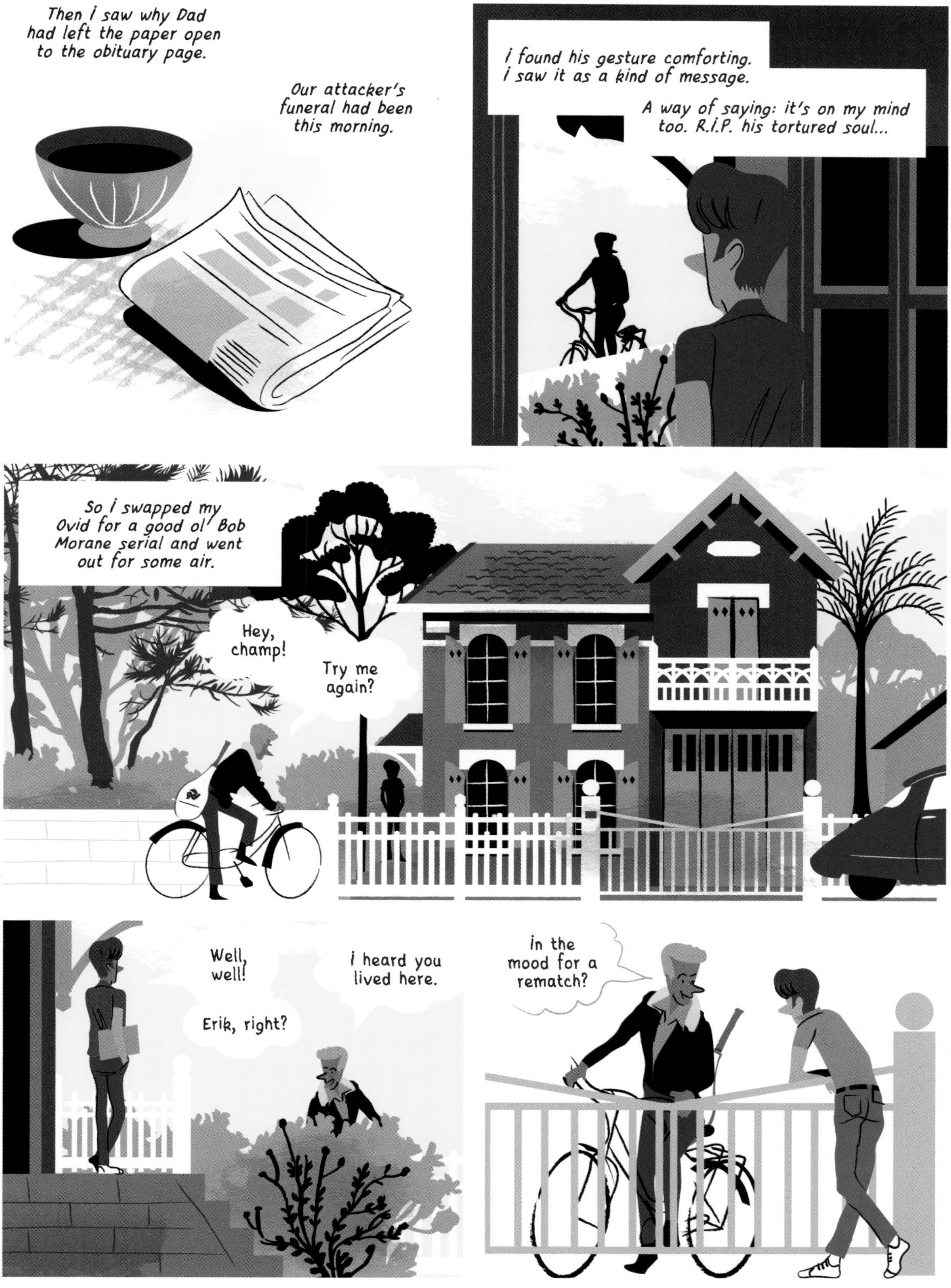
Then I saw why Dad had left the paper open to the obituary page.
Our attacker's funeral had been this morning.
I found his gesture comforting. I saw it as a kind of message.
A way of saying: it's on my mind too. R.I.P. his tortured soul...
So I swapped my Ovid for a good ol' Bob Morane serial and went out for some air.
Hey, champ!
Try me again?
Well, well!
Erik, right?
I heard you lived here.
In the mood for a rematch?

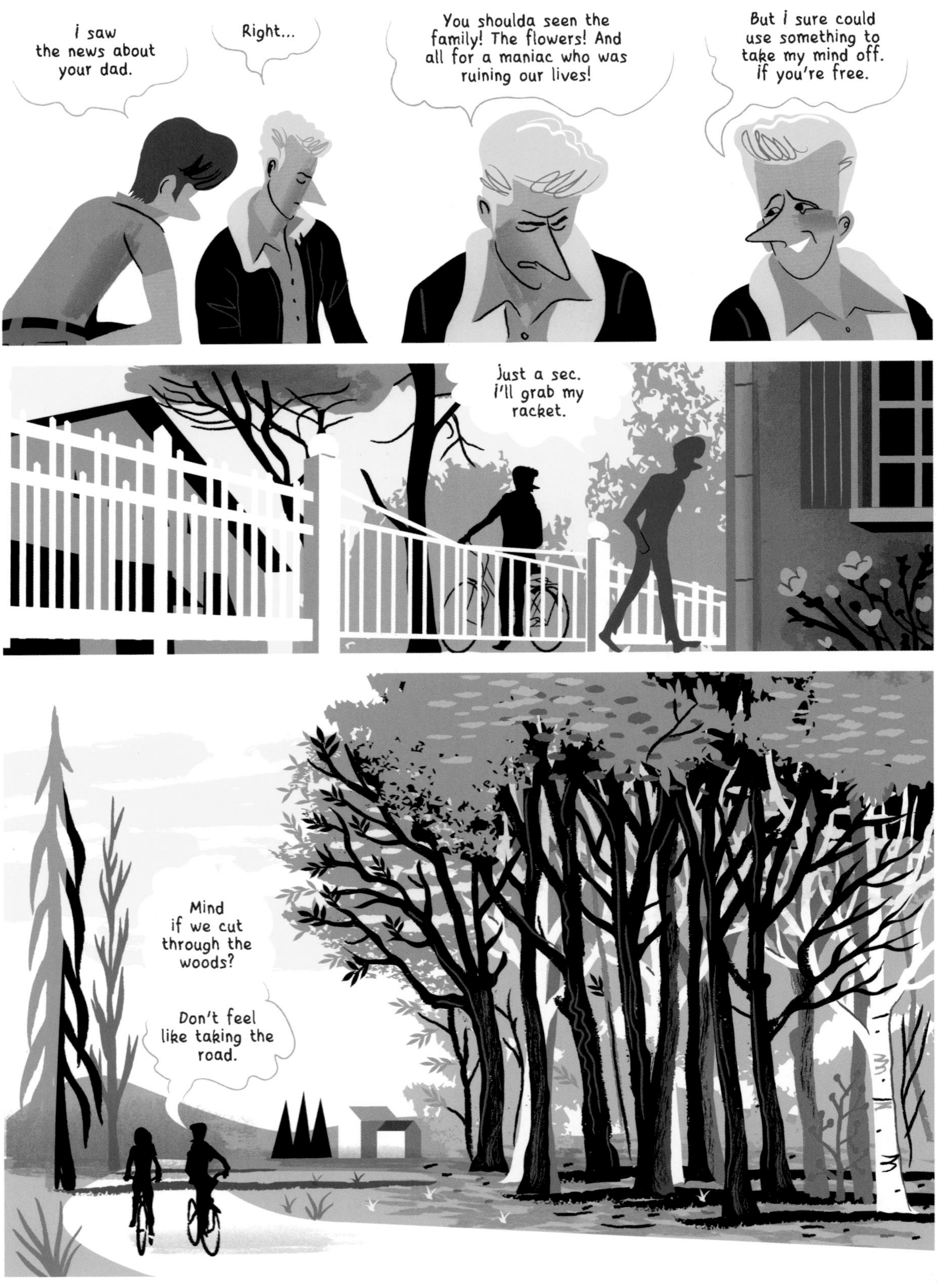
I saw the news about your dad.
Right...
You shoulda seen the family! The flowers! And all for a maniac who was ruining our lives!
But I sure could use something to take my mind off. If you're free.
Just a sec. I'll grab my racket.
Mind if we cut through the woods?
Don't feel like taking the road.

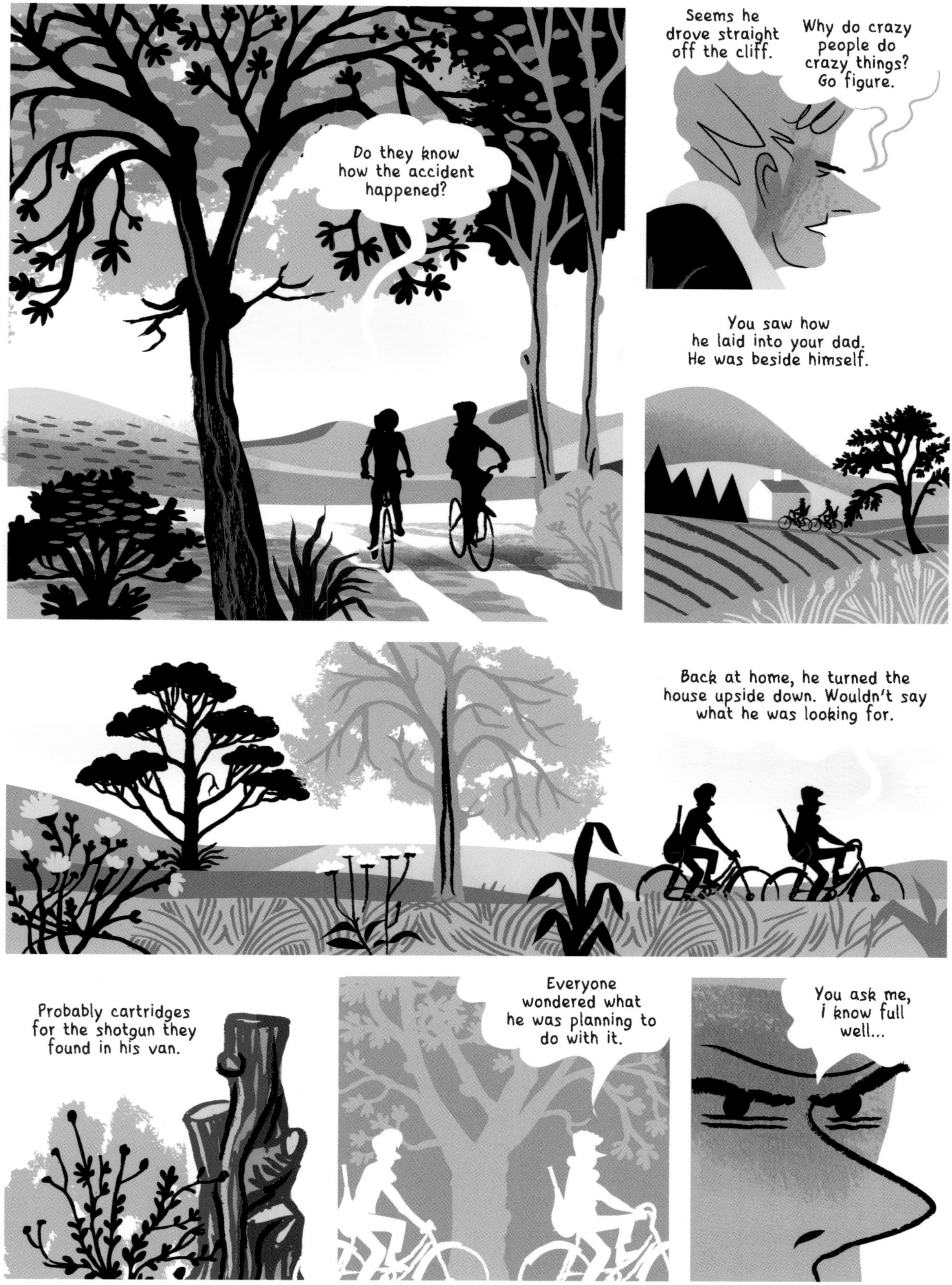
Do they know how the accident happened?
Seems he drove straight off the cliff.
Why do crazy people do crazy things? Go figure.
You saw how he laid into your dad. He was beside himself.
Back at home, he turned the house upside down. Wouldn't say what he was looking for.
Probably cartridges for the shotgun they found in his van.
Everyone wondered what he was planning to do with it.
You ask me, I know full well...

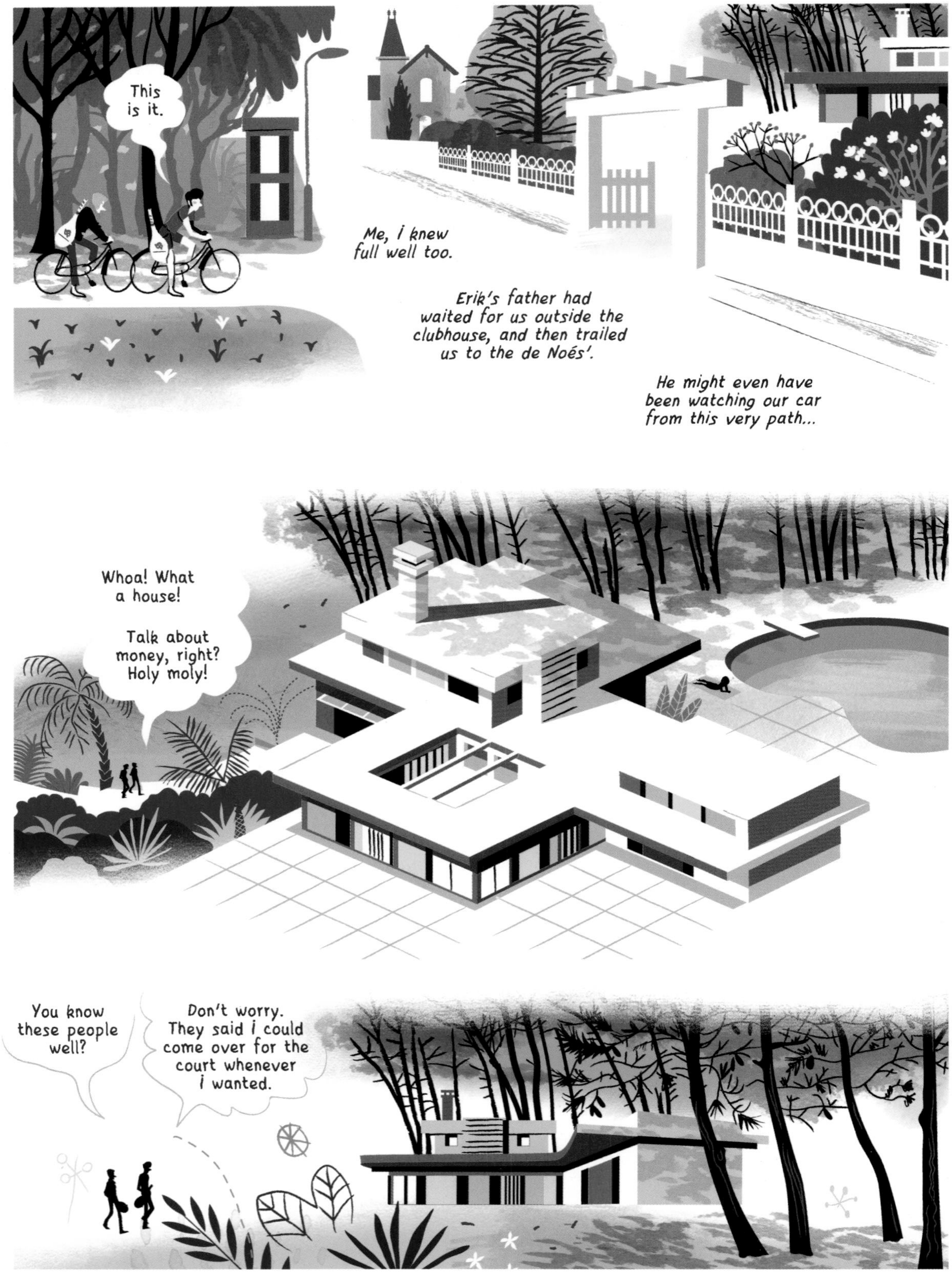
This is it.
Me, I knew full well too.
Erik's father had waited for us outside the clubhouse, and then trailed us to the de Noés'.
He might even have been watching our car from this very path...
Whoa! What a house!
Talk about money, right? Holy moly!
You know these people well?
Don't worry. They said I could come over for the court whenever I wanted.

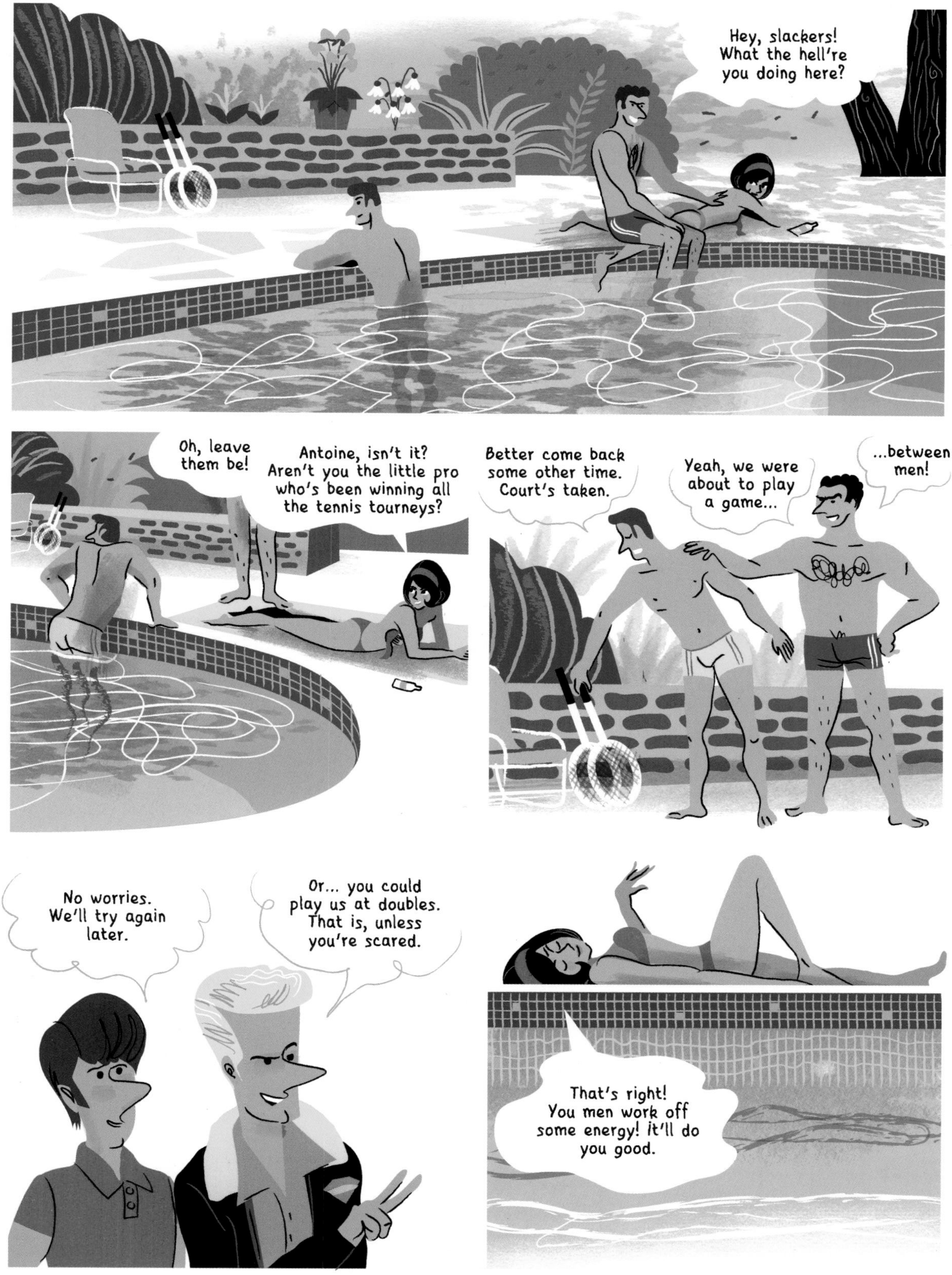
Hey, slackers! What the hell're you doing here?
Oh, leave them be!
Antoine, isn't it? Aren't you the little pro who's been winning all the tennis tourneys?
Better come back some other time. Court's taken.
Yeah, we were about to play a game...
...between men!
No worries. We'll try again later.
Or... you could play us at doubles. That is, unless you're scared.
That's right! You men work off some energy! It'll do you good.

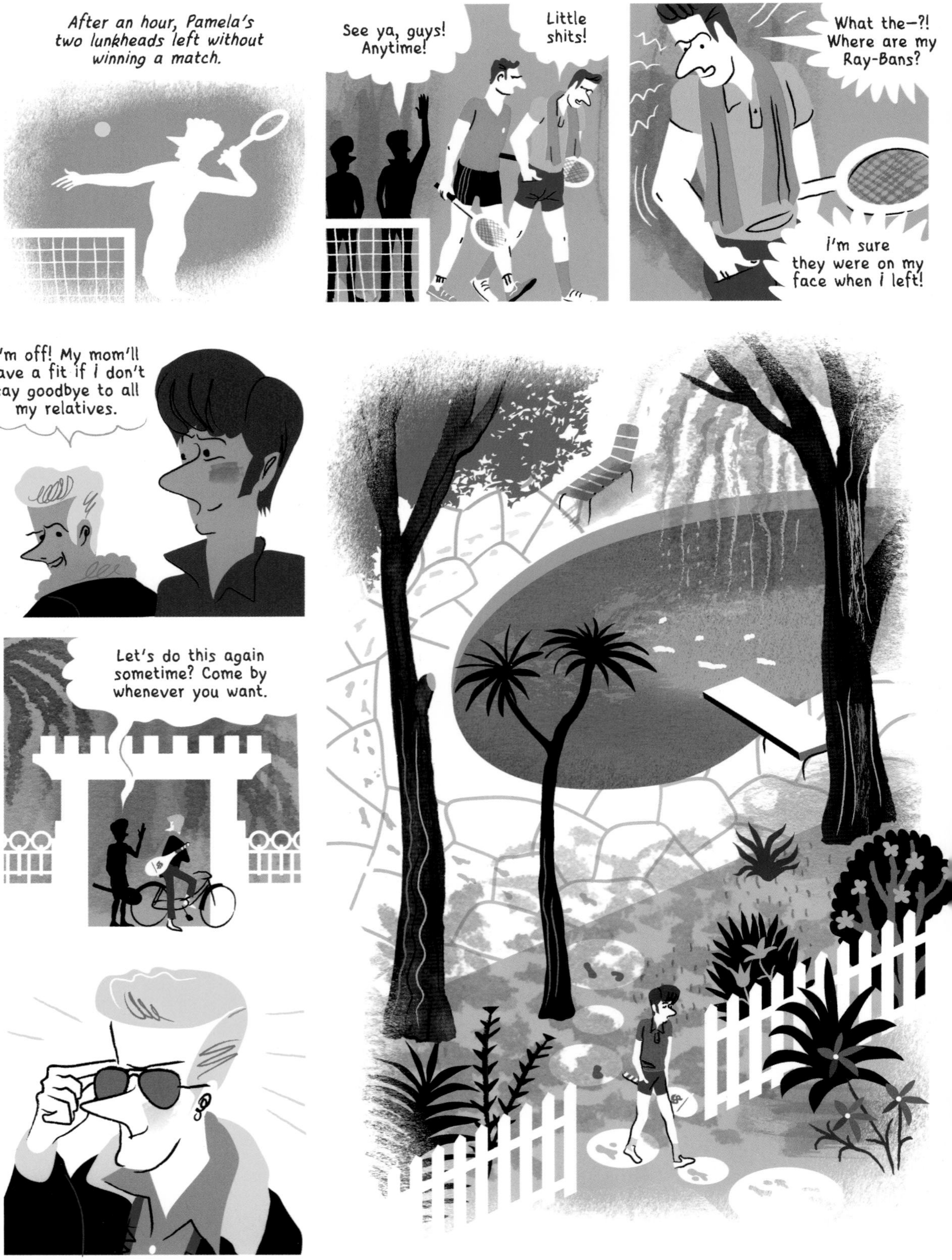

After an hour, Pamela's two lunkheads left without winning a match.
See ya, guys! Anytime!
Little shits!
What the—?! Where are my Ray-Bans?
I'm sure they were on my face when I left!
I'm off! My mom'll have a fit if I don't say goodbye to all my relatives.
Let's do this again sometime? Come by whenever you want.

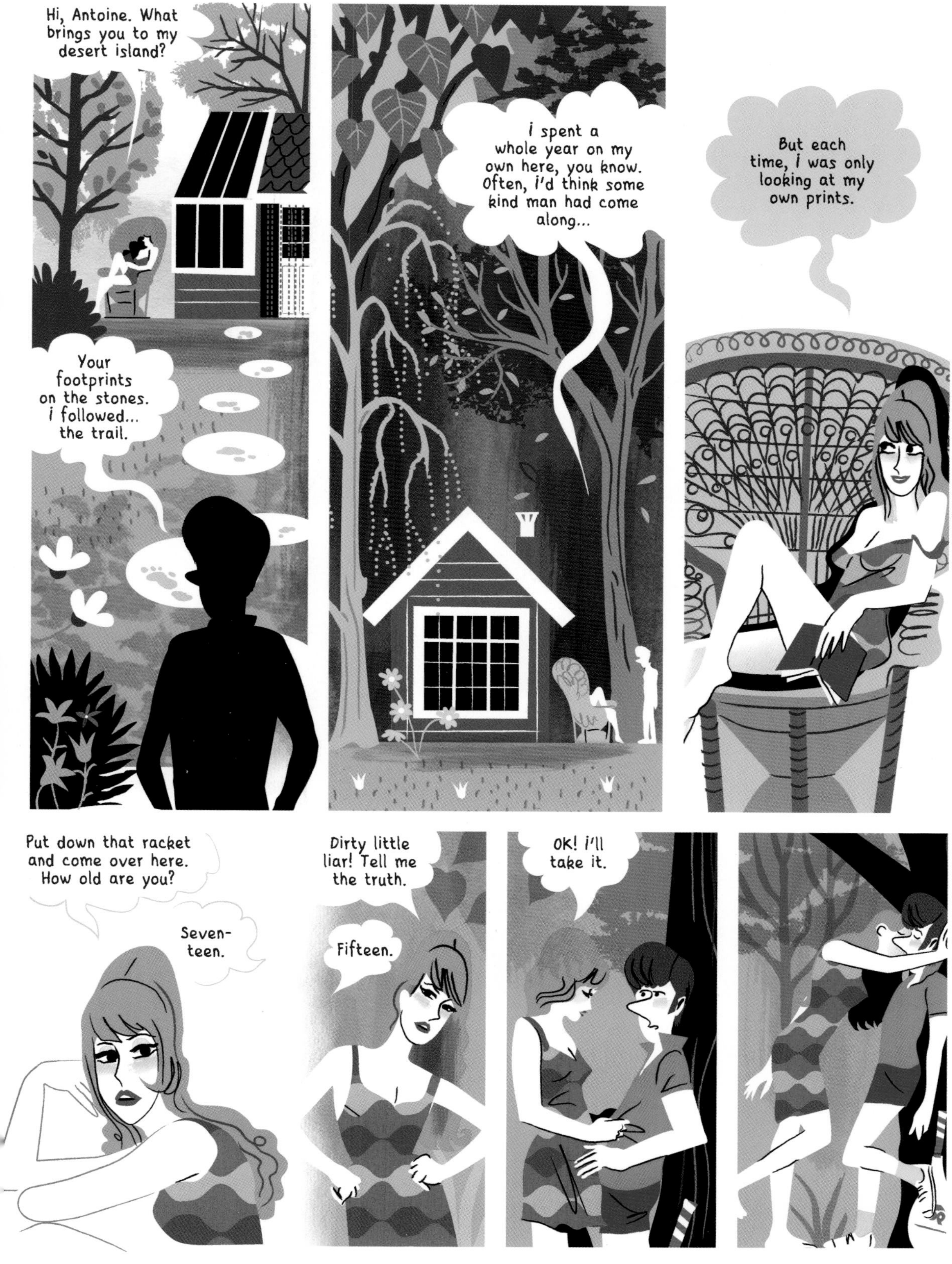
Hi, Antoine. What brings you to my desert island?
Your footprints on the stones. I followed... the trail.
I spent a whole year on my own here, you know. Often, I'd think some kind man had come along...
But each time, I was only looking at my own prints.
Put down that racket and come over here. How old are you?
Seven-teen.
Dirty little liar! Tell me the truth.
Fifteen.
OK! I'll take it.

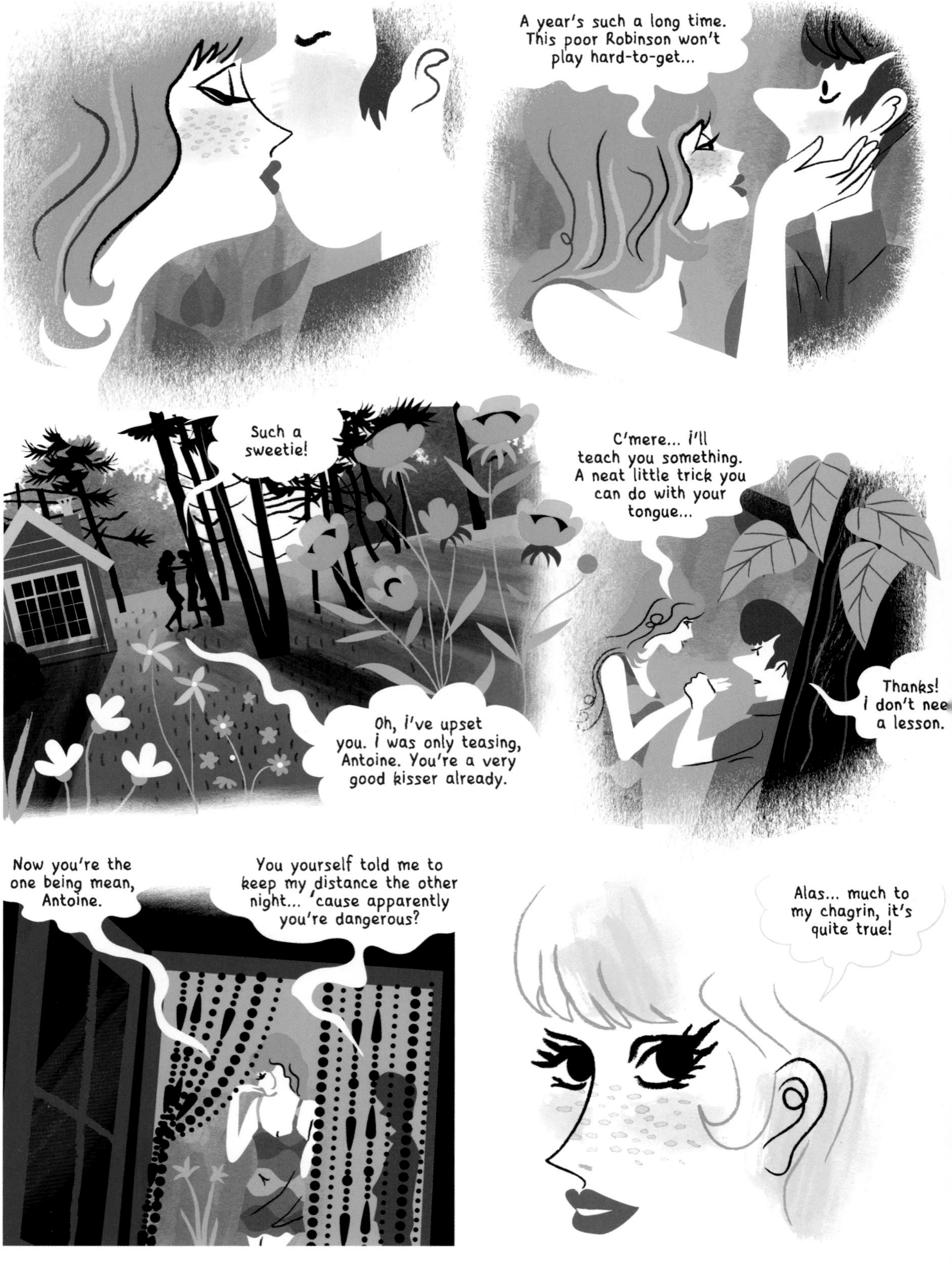
A year's such a long time. This poor Robinson won't play hard-to-get...
Such a sweetie!
Oh, I've upset you. I was only teasing, Antoine. You're a very good kisser already.
C'mere... I'll teach you something. A neat little trick you can do with your tongue...
Thanks! I don't nee a lesson.
Now you're the one being mean, Antoine.
You yourself told me to keep my distance the other night... 'cause apparently you're dangerous?
Alas... much to my chagrin, it's quite true!

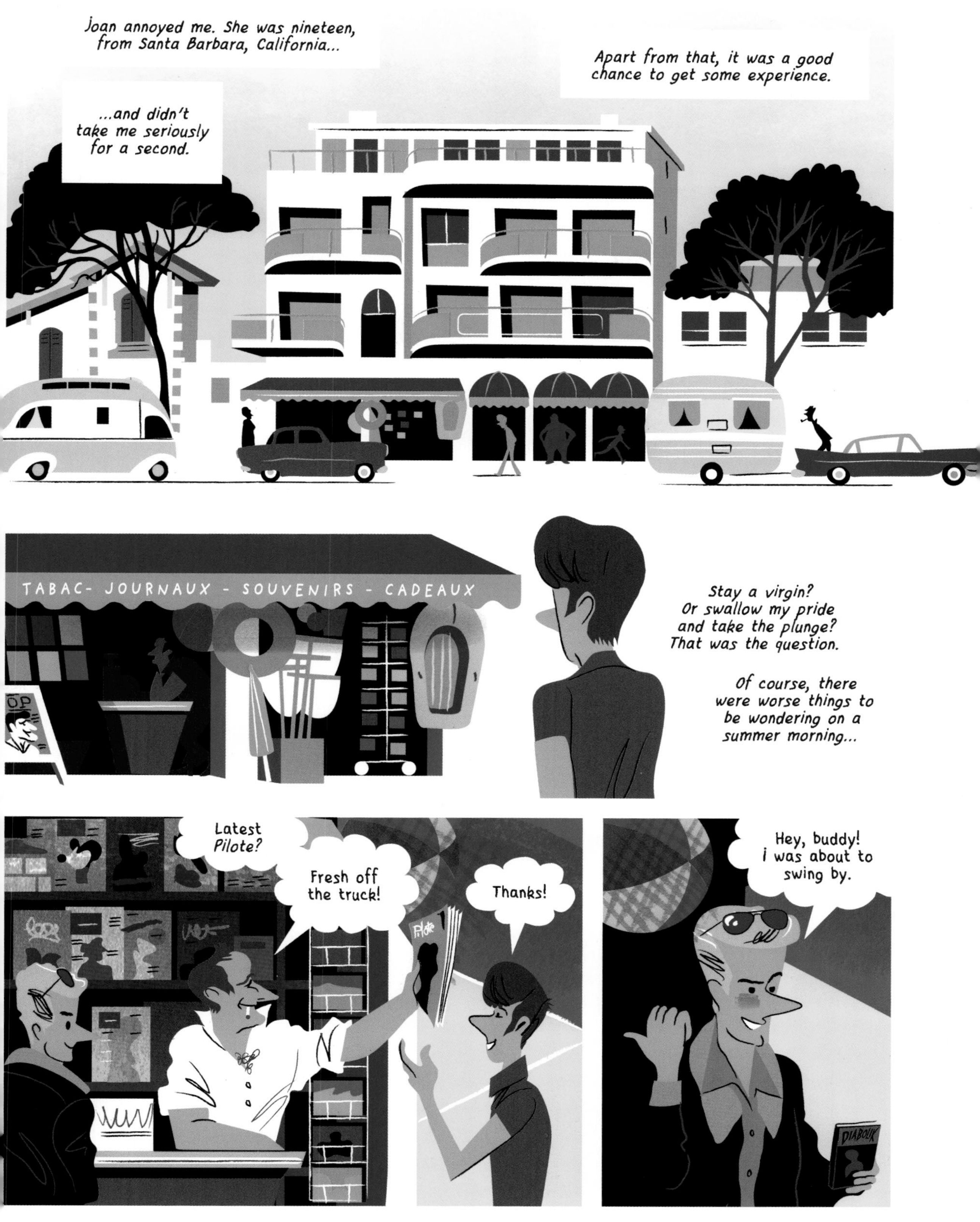
Joan annoyed me. She was nineteen, from Santa Barbara, California...
...and didn't take me seriously for a second.
Apart from that, it was a good chance to get some experience.
TABAC- JOURNAUX - SOUVENIRS - CADEAUX
Stay a virgin? Or swallow my pride and take the plunge? That was the question.
Of course, there were worse things to be wondering on a summer morning...
Latest Pilote?
Fresh off the truck!
Pilote
Thanks!
Hey, buddy! I was about to swing by.
DIABOLIK

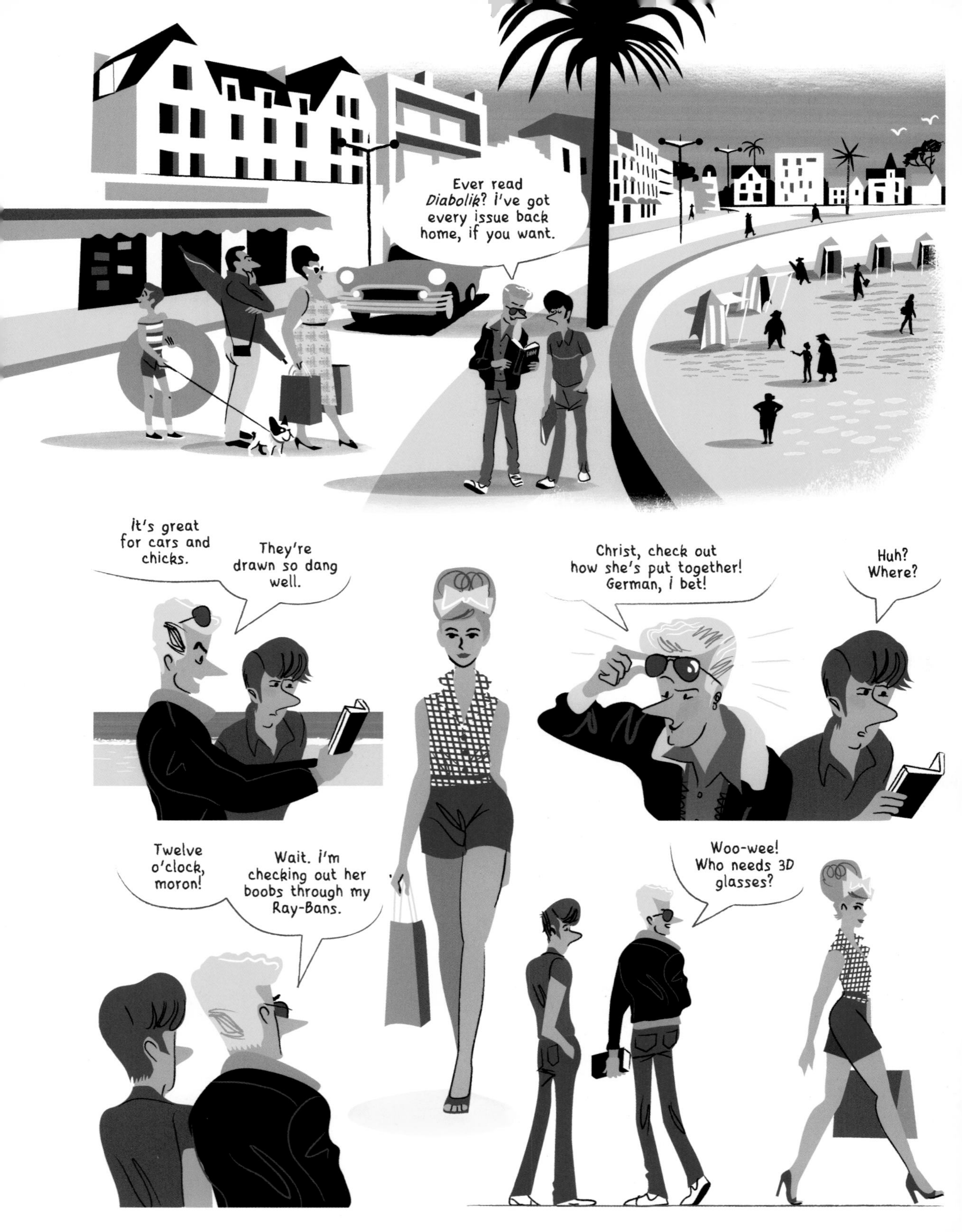

Ever read *Diabolik*? I've got every issue back home, if you want.
It's great for cars and chicks.
They're drawn so dang well.
Christ, check out how she's put together! German, I bet!
Huh? Where?
Twelve o'clock, moron!
Wait. I'm checking out her boobs through my Ray-Bans.
Woo-wee! Who needs 3D glasses?

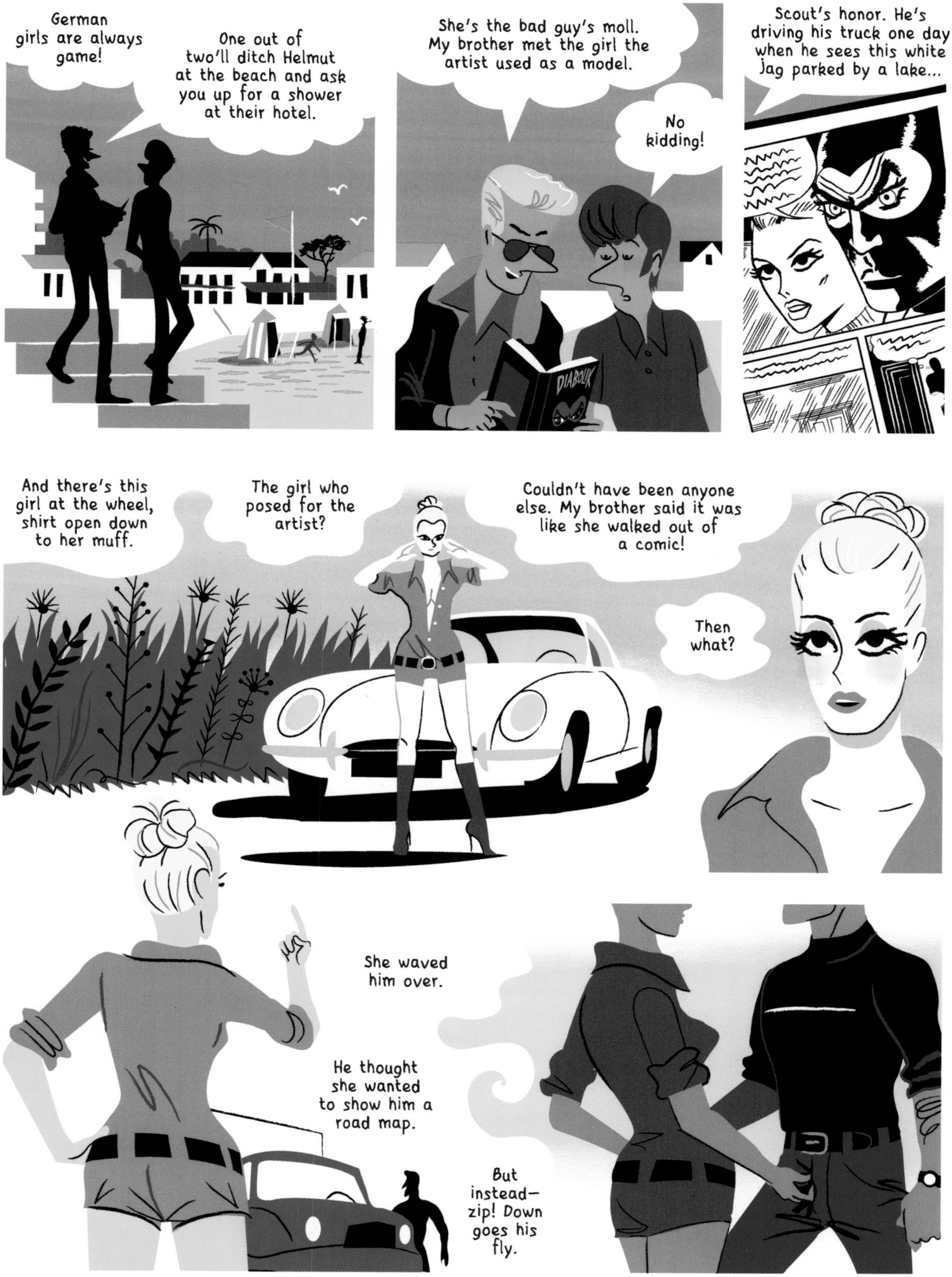
German girls are always game!
One out of two'll ditch Helmut at the beach and ask you up for a shower at their hotel.
She's the bad guy's moll. My brother met the girl the artist used as a model.
DIABOLIK
No kidding!
Scout's honor. He's driving his truck one day when he sees this white Jag parked by a lake...
And there's this girl at the wheel, shirt open down to her muff.
The girl who posed for the artist?
Couldn't have been anyone else. My brother said it was like she walked out of a comic!
Then what?
She waved him over.
He thought she wanted to show him a road map.
But instead— zip! Down goes his fly.

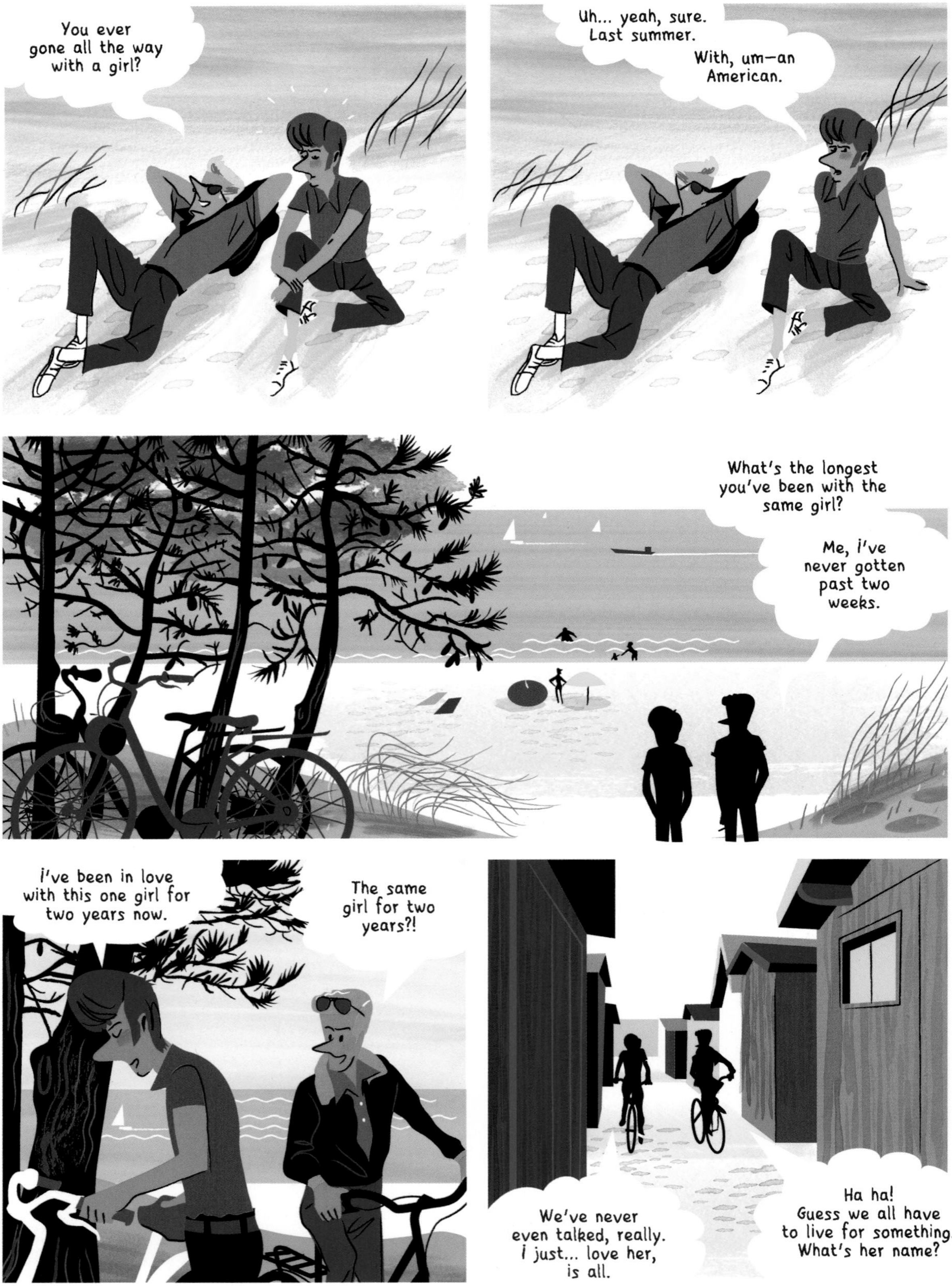
You ever gone all the way with a girl?
Uh... yeah, sure. Last summer.
With, um—an American.
What's the longest you've been with the same girl?
Me, I've never gotten past two weeks.
I've been in love with this one girl for two years now.
The same girl for two years?!
We've never even talked, really. I just... love her, is all.
Ha ha! Guess we all have to live for something. What's her name?

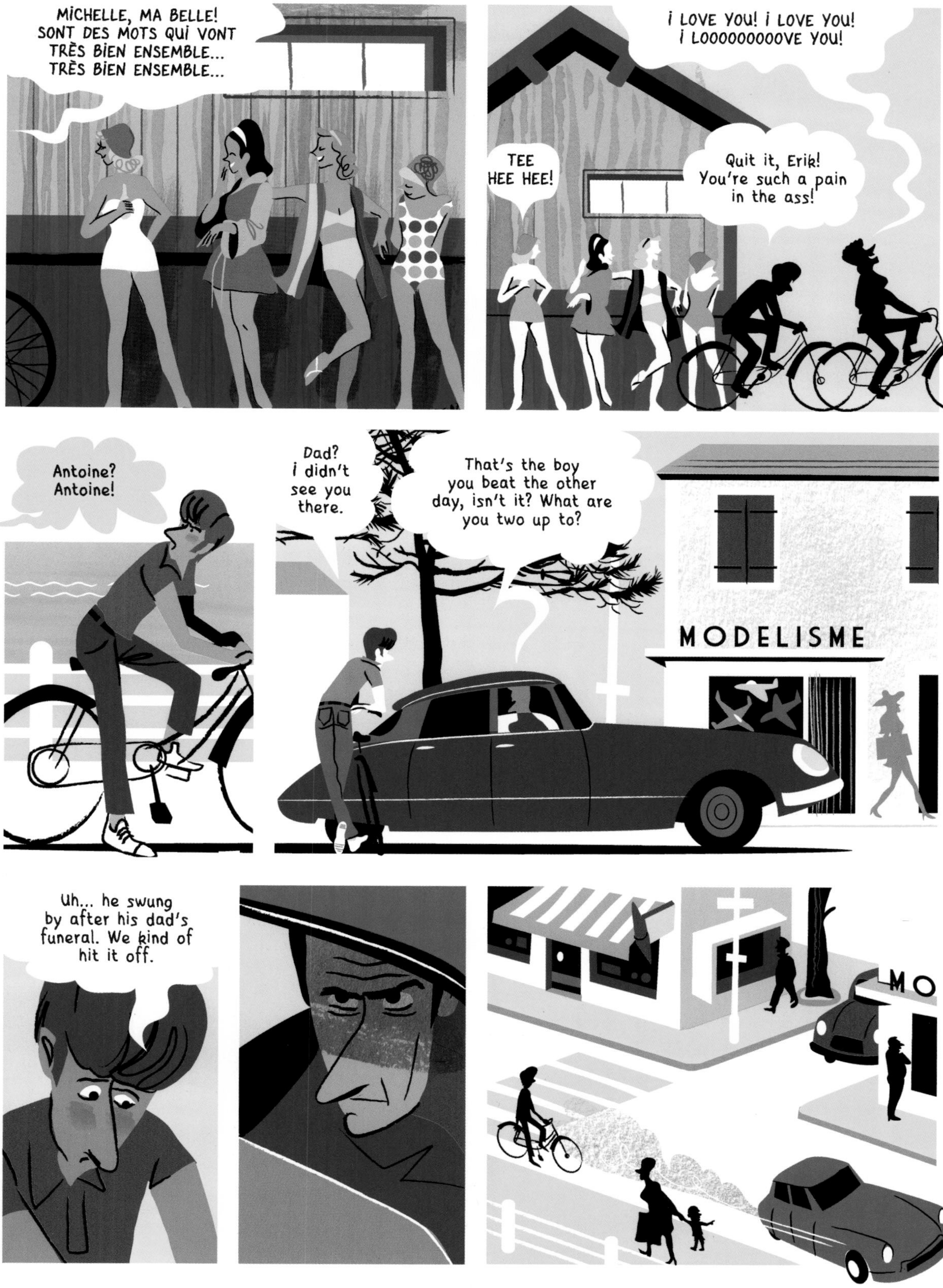
MICHELLE, MA BELLE! SONT DES MOTS QUI VONT TRÈS BIEN ENSEMBLE... TRÈS BIEN ENSEMBLE...
I LOVE YOU! I LOVE YOU! I LOOOOOOOOOVE YOU!
TEE HEE HEE!
Quit it, Erik! You're such a pain in the ass!
Antoine? Antoine!
Dad? I didn't see you there.
That's the boy you beat the other day, isn't it? What are you two up to?
MODELISME
Uh... he swung by after his dad's funeral. We kind of hit it off.
MO

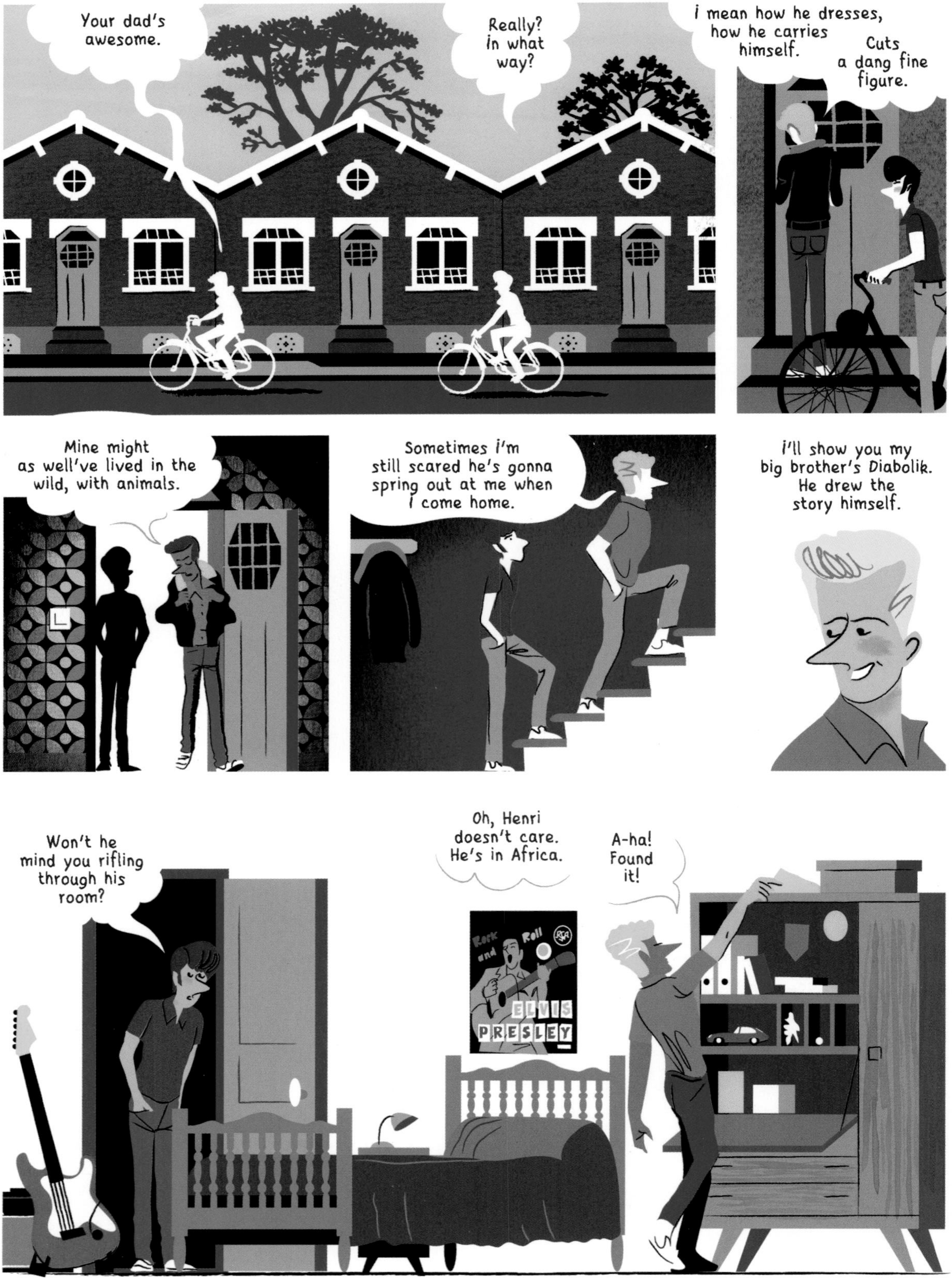
Your dad's awesome.
Really? In what way?
I mean how he dresses, how he carries himself.
Cuts a dang fine figure.
Mine might as well've lived in the wild, with animals.
Sometimes I'm still scared he's gonna spring out at me when I come home.
I'll show you my big brother's Diabolik. He drew the story himself.
Won't he mind you rifling through his room?
Rock and Roll
ELVIS PRESLEY
Oh, Henri doesn't care. He's in Africa.
A-ha! Found it!

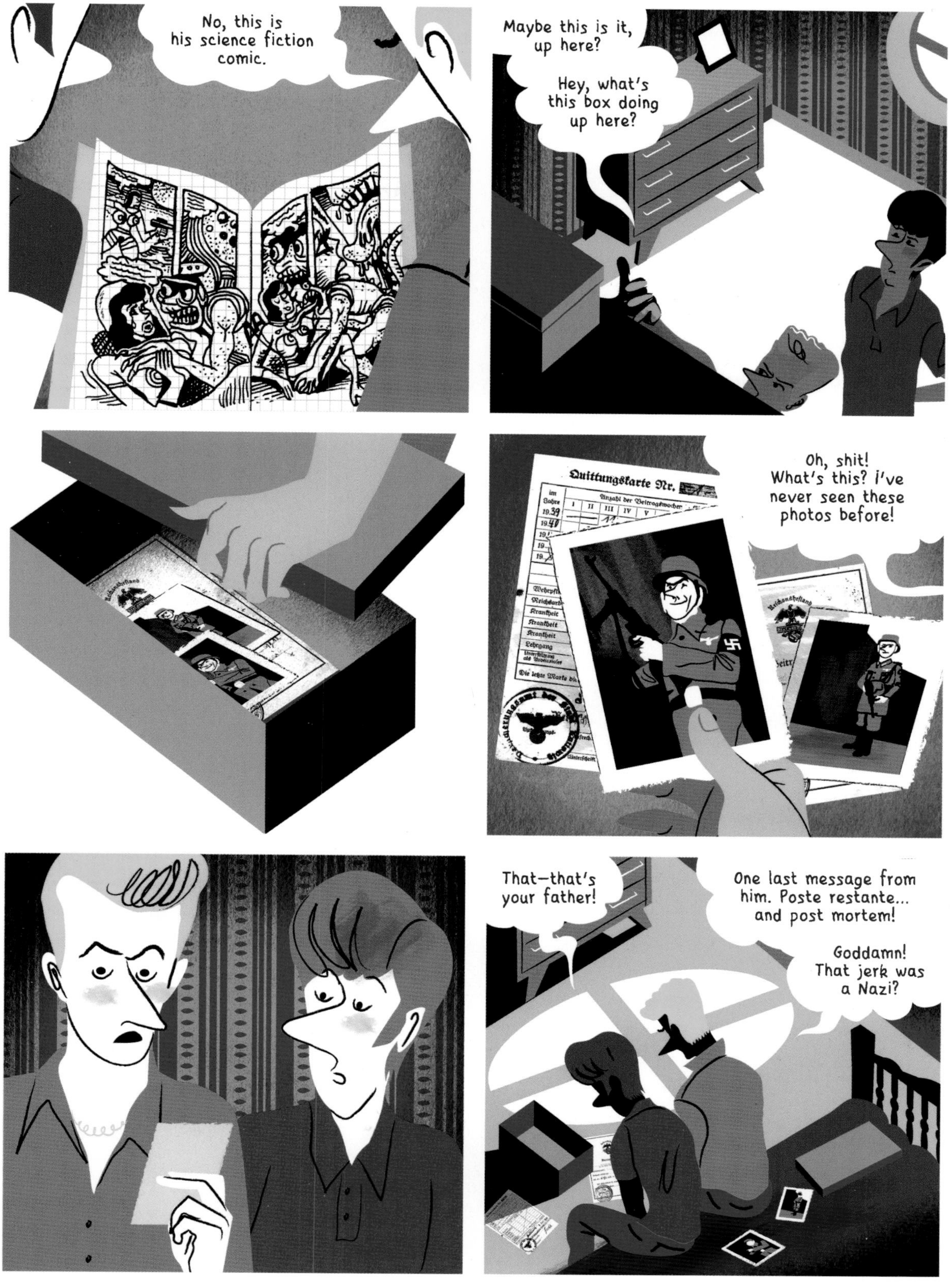
No, this is his science fiction comic.
Maybe this is it, up here?
Hey, what's this box doing up here?
Quittungskarte Nr.
Oh, shit! What's this? I've never seen these photos before!
That—that's your father!
One last message from him. Poste restante... and post mortem!
Goddamn! That jerk was a Nazi?

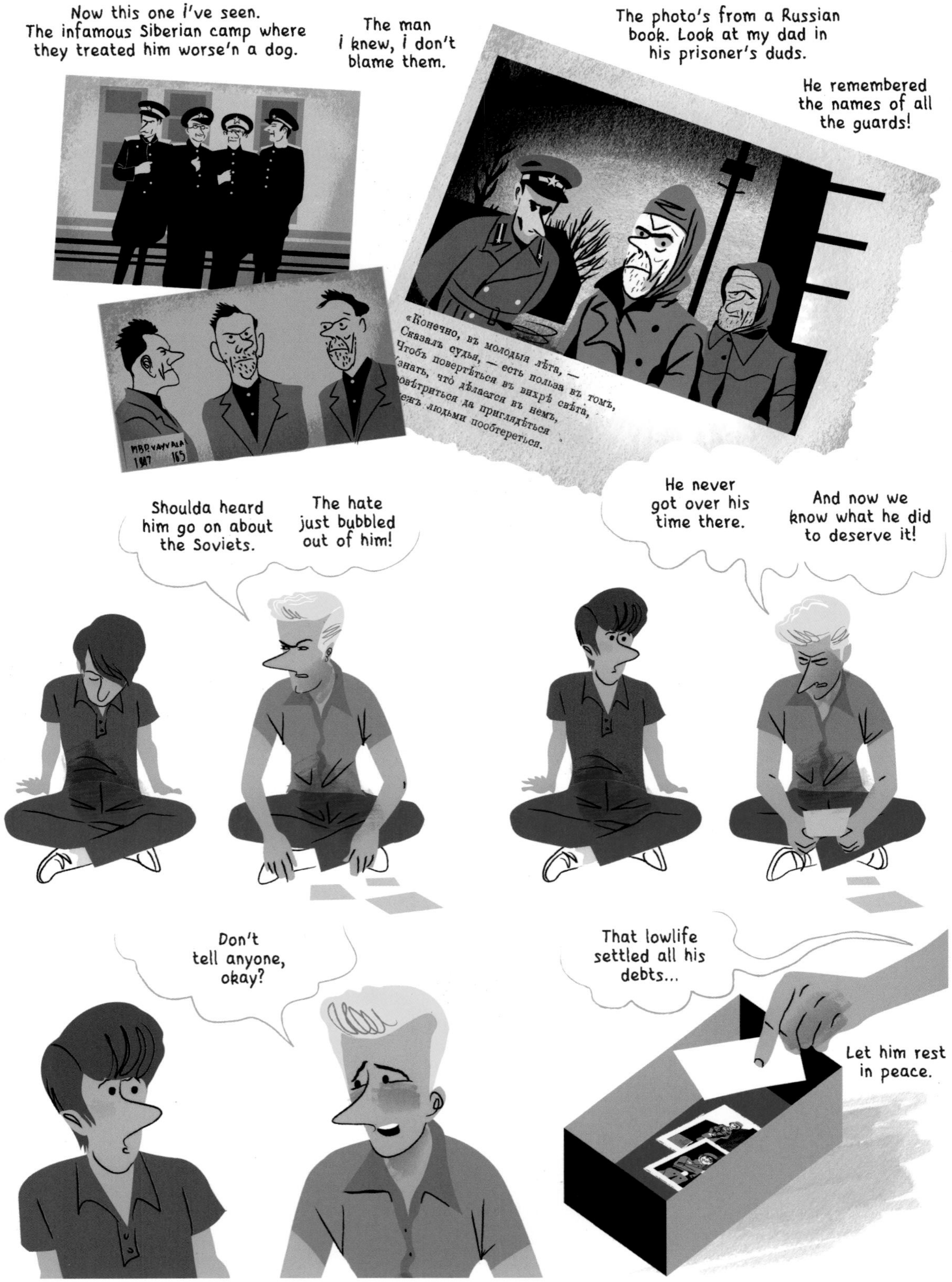
Now this one i've seen. The infamous Siberian camp where they treated him worse'n a dog.
The man i knew, i don't blame them.
The photo's from a Russian book. Look at my dad in his prisoner's duds.
He remembered the names of all the guards!
«Конечно, въ молодыя лѣта, —
Сказалъ судья, — есть польза въ томъ,
Чтобъ повертѣться въ вихрѣ свѣта,
знать, что̀ дѣлается въ немъ,
овѣтриться да приглядѣться
ежъ людьми пообтереться.
Shoulda heard him go on about the Soviets.
The hate just bubbled out of him!
He never got over his time there.
And now we know what he did to deserve it!
Don't tell anyone, okay?
That lowlife settled all his debts...
Let him rest in peace.

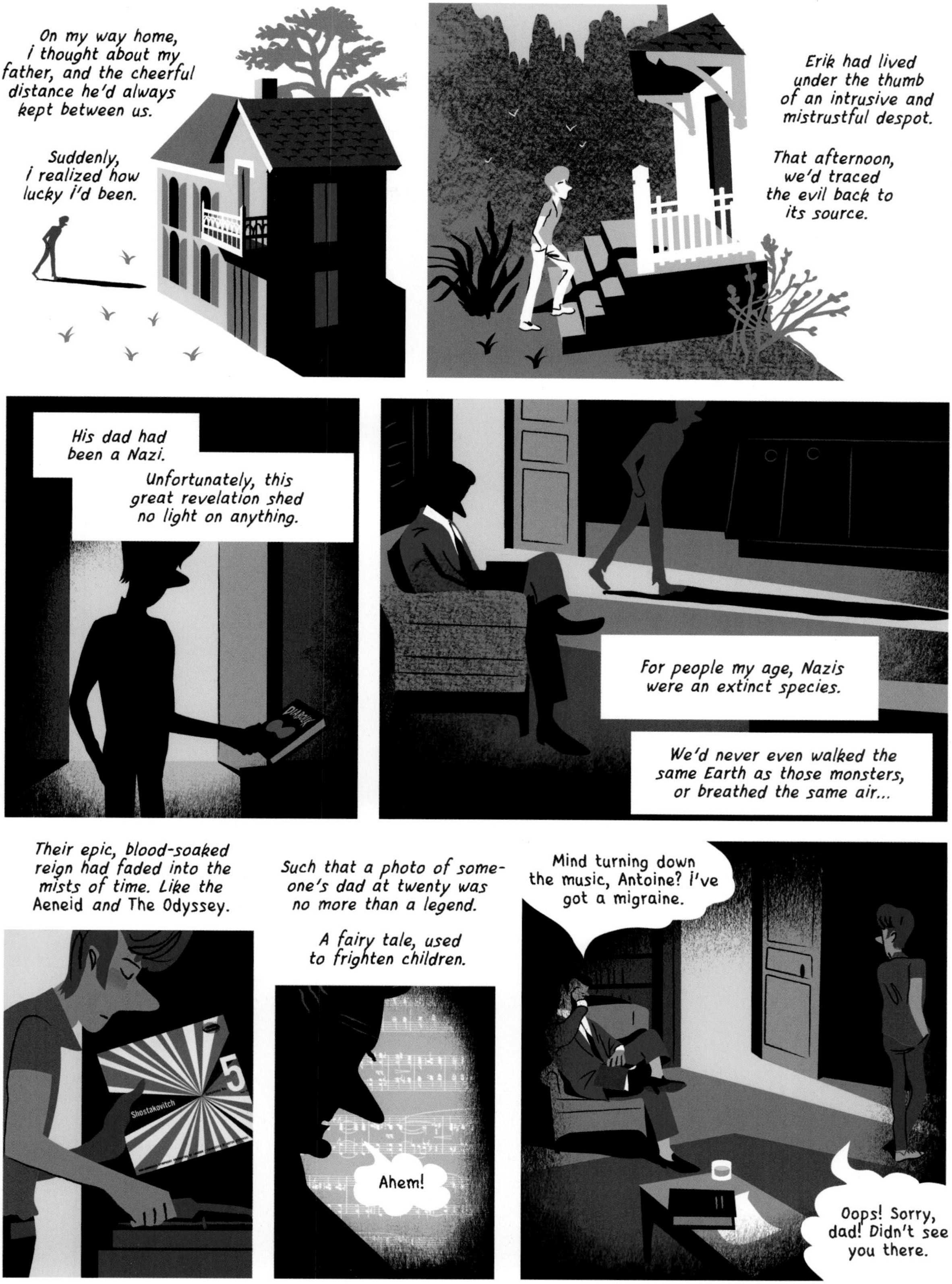

On my way home, i thought about my father, and the cheerful distance he'd always kept between us.
Suddenly, i realized how lucky i'd been.
Erik had lived under the thumb of an intrusive and mistrustful despot.
That afternoon, we'd traced the evil back to its source.
His dad had been a Nazi.
Unfortunately, this great revelation shed no light on anything.
For people my age, Nazis were an extinct species.
We'd never even walked the same Earth as those monsters, or breathed the same air...
Their epic, blood-soaked reign had faded into the mists of time. Like the Aeneid and The Odyssey.
5
Shostakovitch
Such that a photo of some-one's dad at twenty was no more than a legend.
A fairy tale, used to frighten children.
Ahem!
Mind turning down the music, Antoine? i've got a migraine.
Oops! Sorry, dad! Didn't see you there.

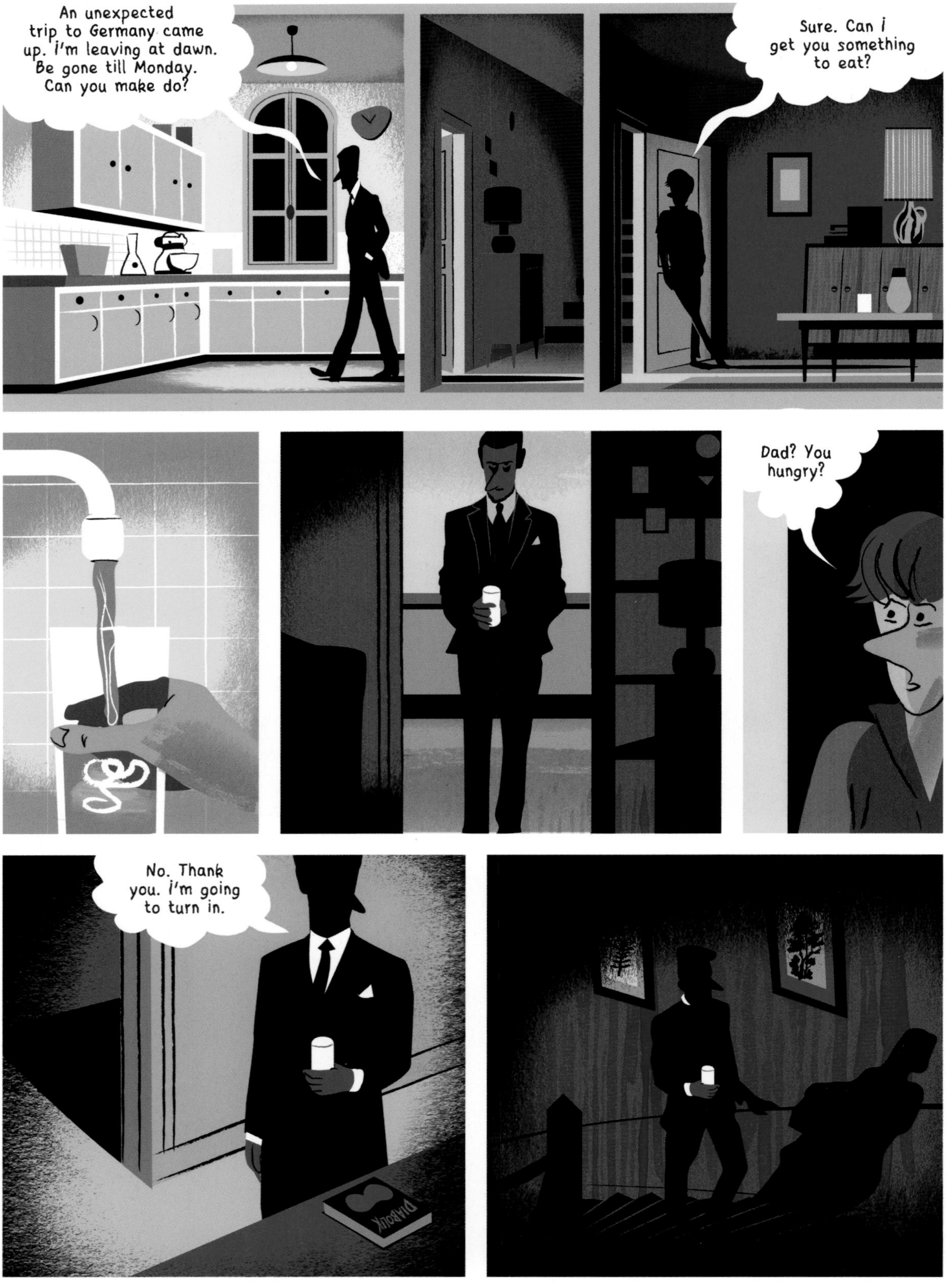
An unexpected trip to Germany came up. I'm leaving at dawn. Be gone till Monday. Can you make do?
Sure. Can I get you something to eat?
Dad? You hungry?
No. Thank you. I'm going to turn in.

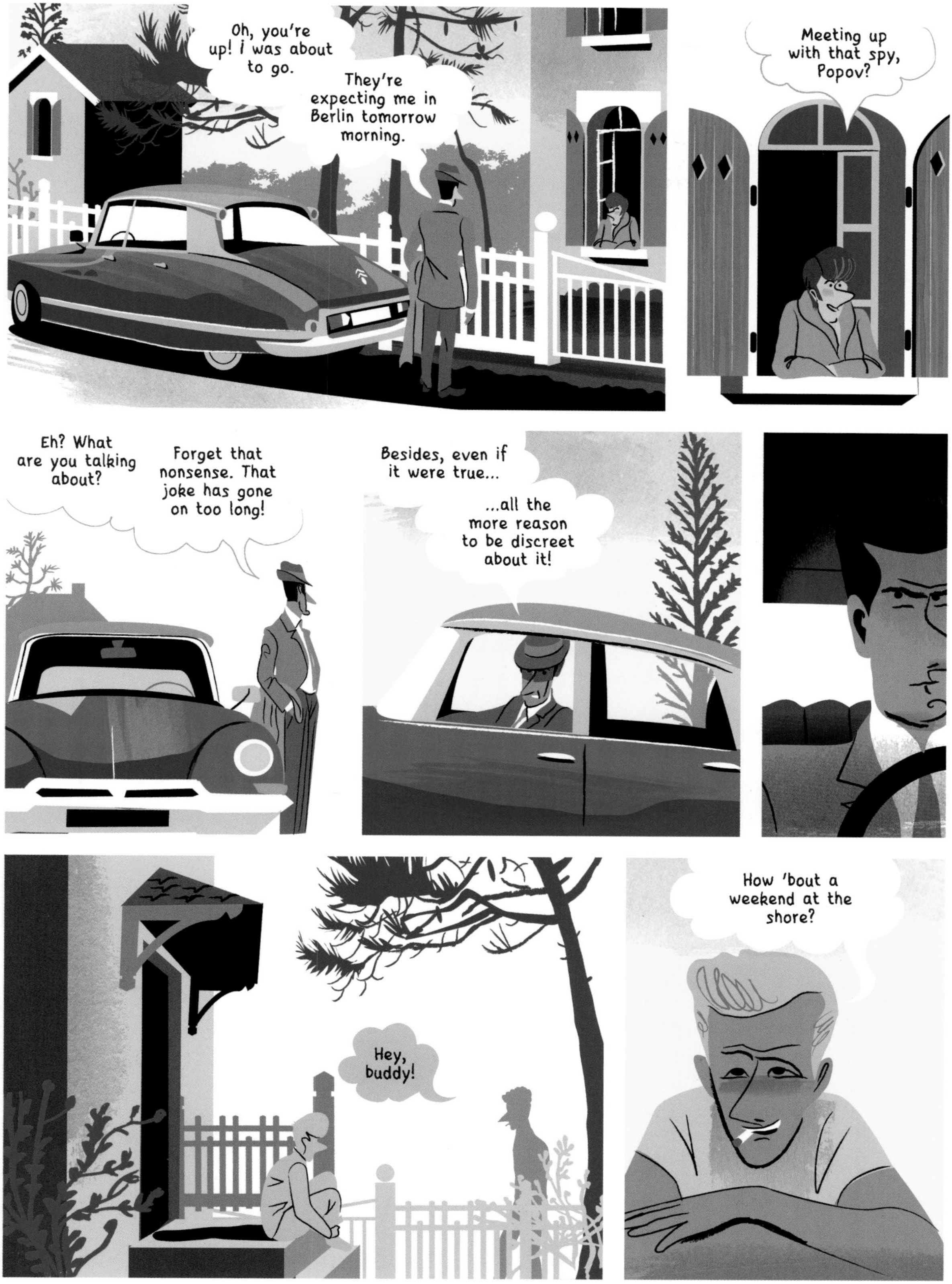
Oh, you're up! I was about to go.
They're expecting me in Berlin tomorrow morning.
Meeting up with that spy, Popov?
Eh? What are you talking about?
Forget that nonsense. That joke has gone on too long!
Besides, even if it were true...
...all the more reason to be discreet about it!
Hey, buddy!
How 'bout a weekend at the shore?

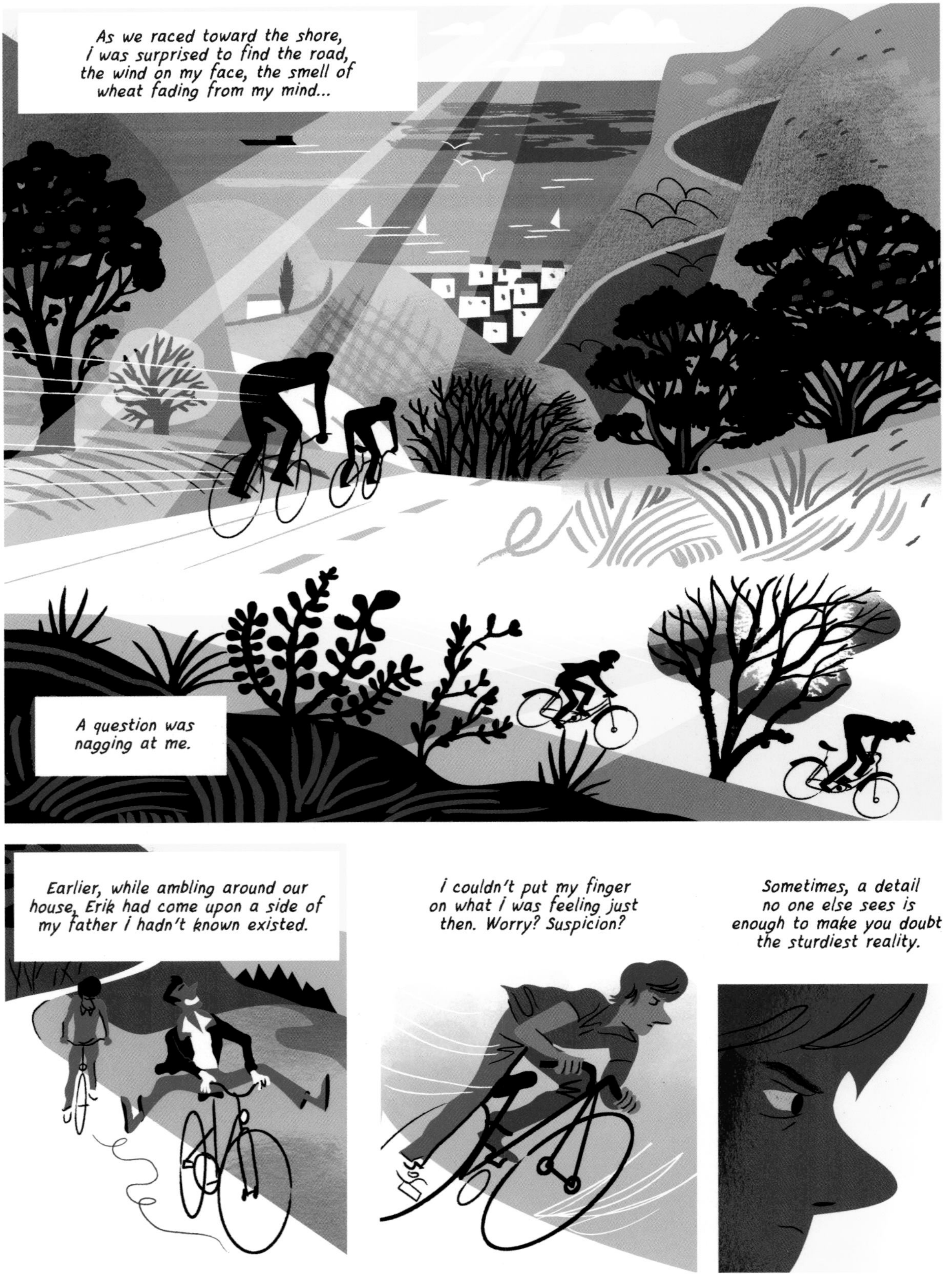
As we raced toward the shore, i was surprised to find the road, the wind on my face, the smell of wheat fading from my mind...
A question was nagging at me.
Earlier, while ambling around our house, Erik had come upon a side of my father i hadn't known existed.
i couldn't put my finger on what i was feeling just then. Worry? Suspicion?
Sometimes, a detail no one else sees is enough to make you doubt the sturdiest reality.

A few hours earlier...

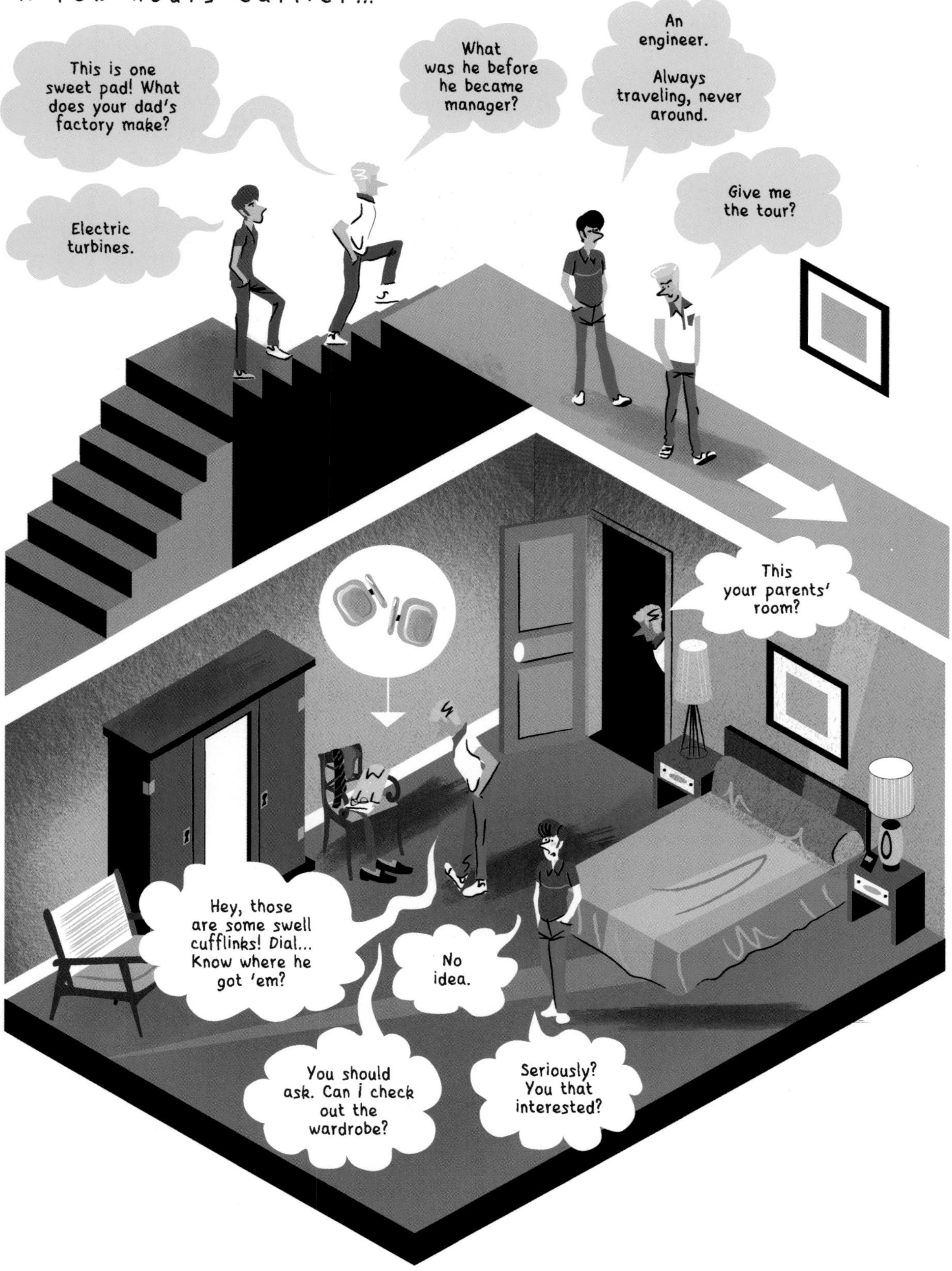
This is one sweet pad! What does your dad's factory make?
Electric turbines.
What was he before he became manager?
An engineer.
Always traveling, never around.
Give me the tour?
This your parents' room?
Hey, those are some swell cufflinks! Dial... Know where he got 'em?
No idea.
You should ask. Can I check out the wardrobe?
Seriously? You that interested?

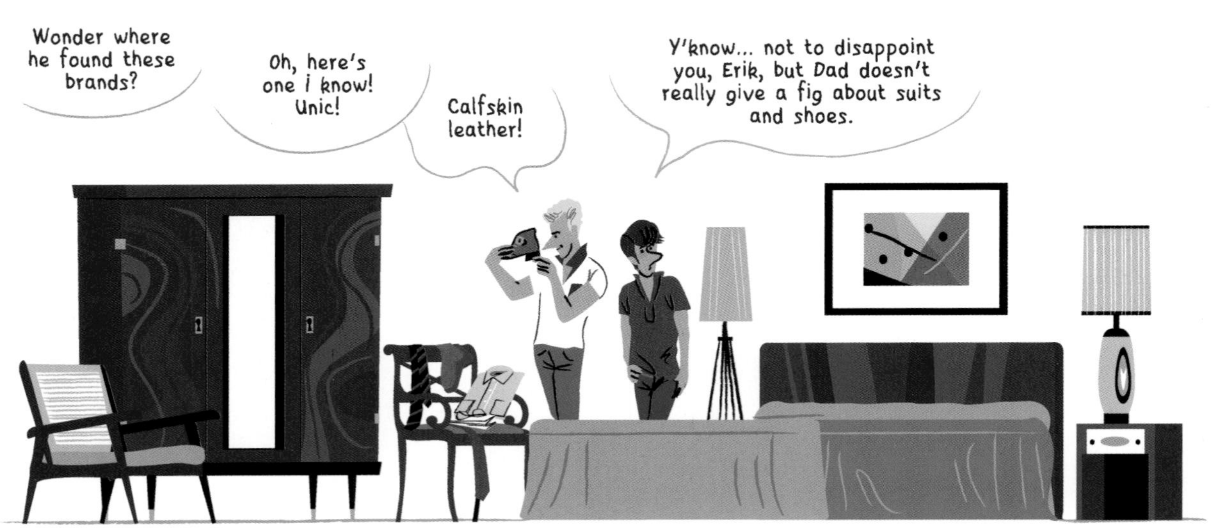
Wonder where he found these brands?
Oh, here's one I know! Unic!
Calfskin leather!
Y'know... not to disappoint you, Erik, but Dad doesn't really give a fig about suits and shoes.

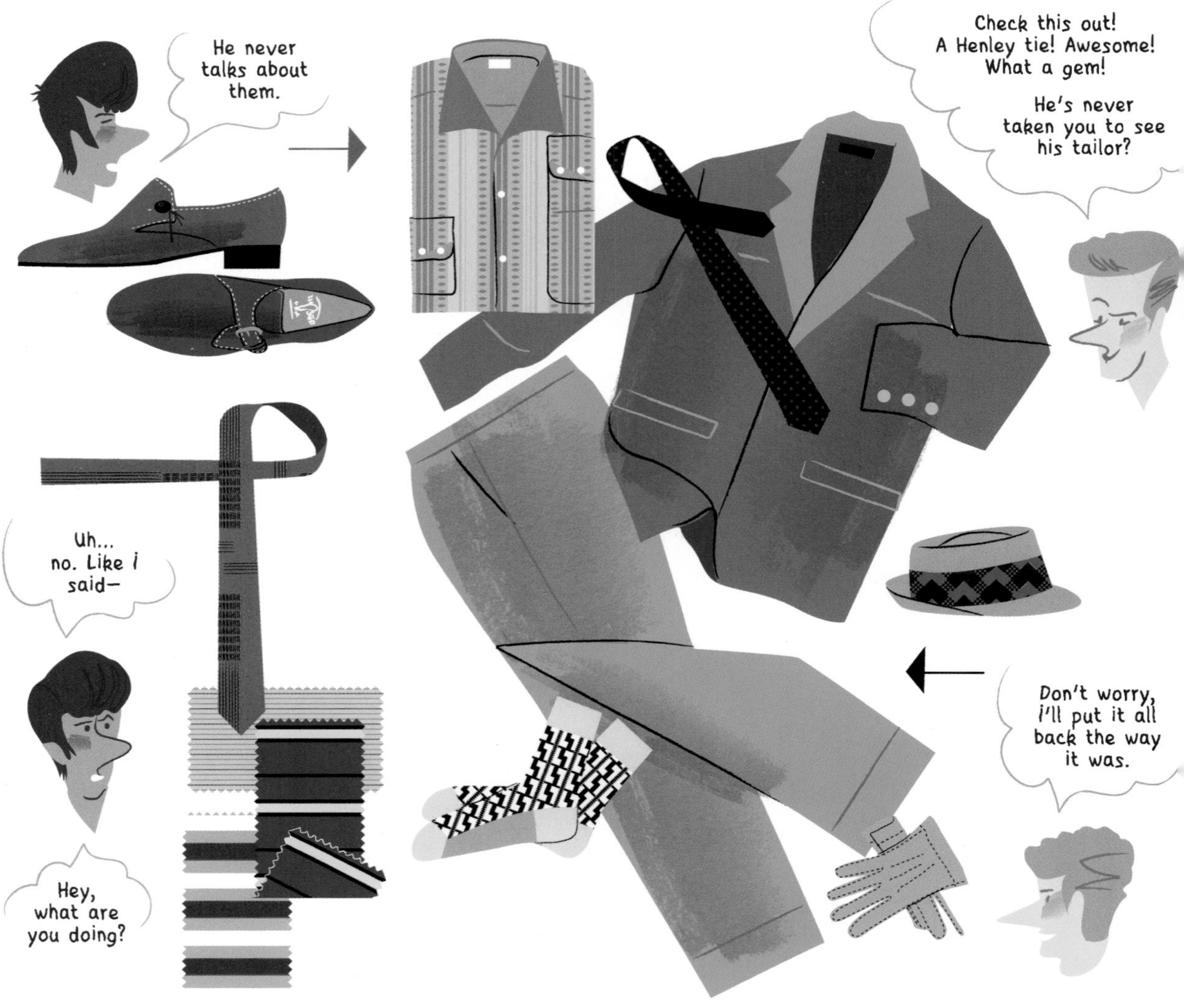
He never talks about them.
Check this out! A Henley tie! Awesome! What a gem!
He's never taken you to see his tailor?
Uh... no. Like I said—
Don't worry, I'll put it all back the way it was.
Hey, what are you doing?

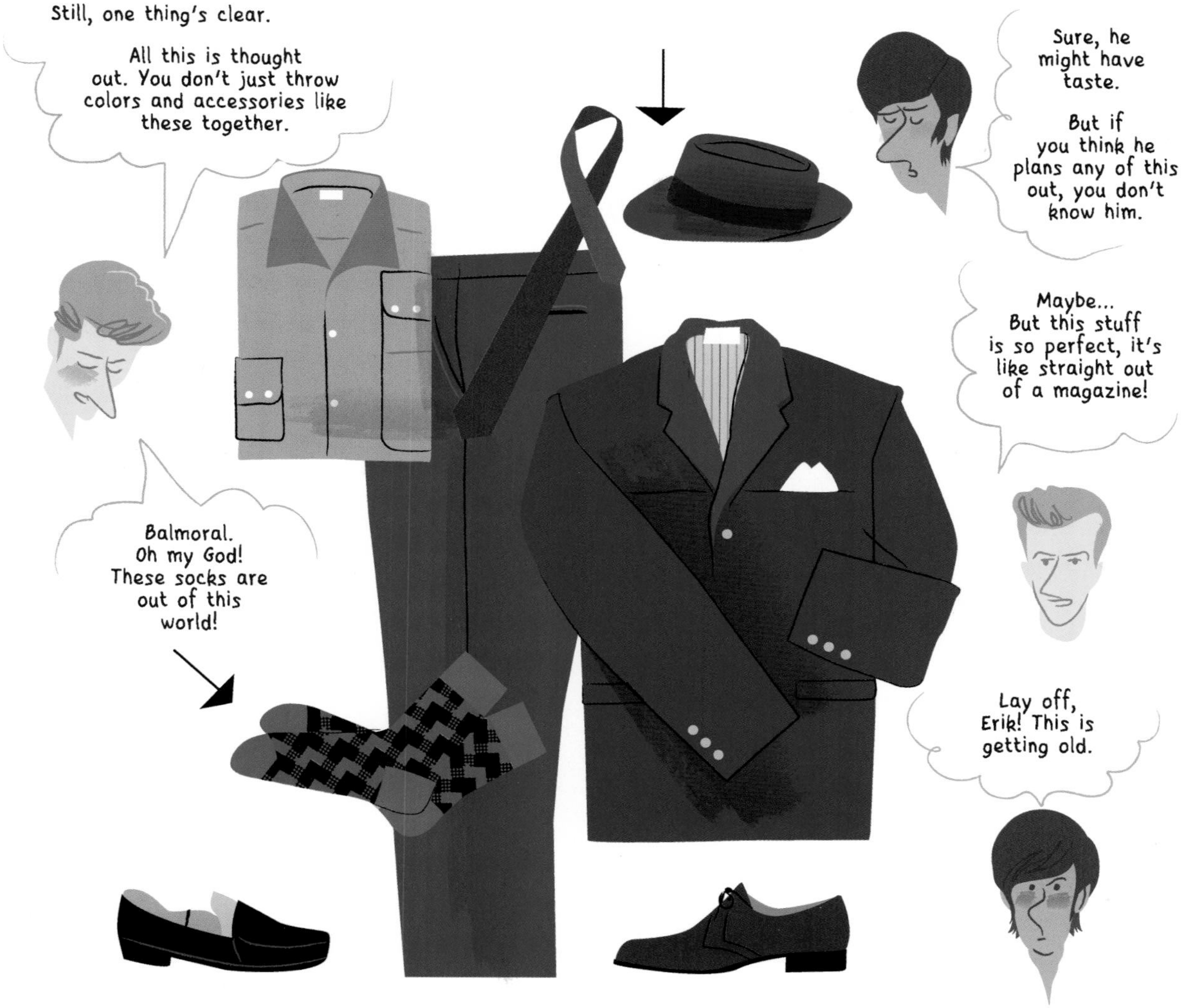
Still, one thing's clear.
All this is thought out. You don't just throw colors and accessories like these together.
Sure, he might have taste.
But if you think he plans any of this out, you don't know him.
Maybe... But this stuff is so perfect, it's like straight out of a magazine!
Balmoral. Oh my God! These socks are out of this world!
Lay off, Erik! This is getting old.

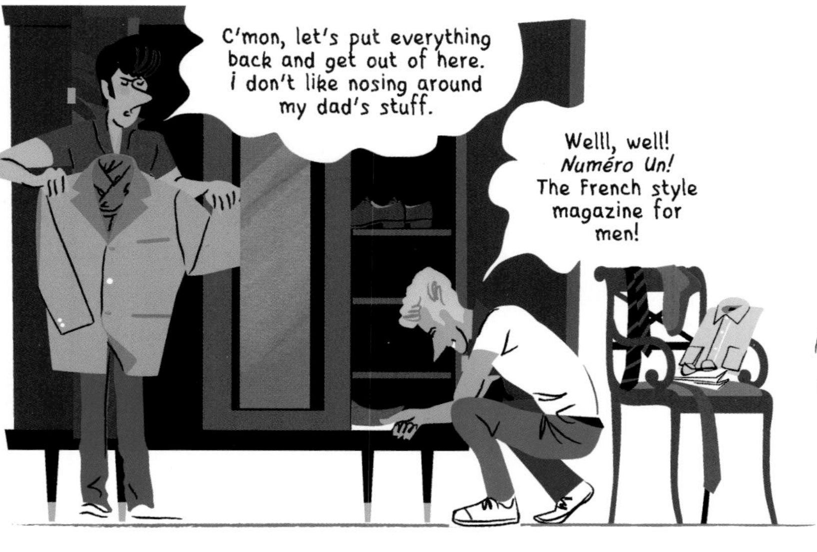
C'mon, let's put everything back and get out of here. I don't like nosing around my dad's stuff.
Welll, well! *Numéro Un!* The French style magazine for men!

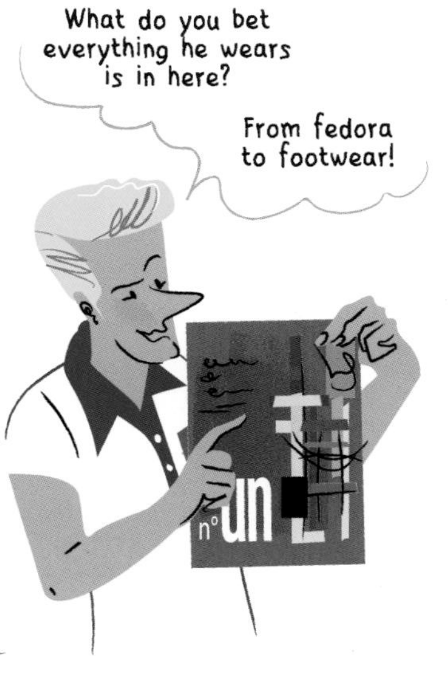
What do you bet everything he wears is in here?
From fedora to footwear!

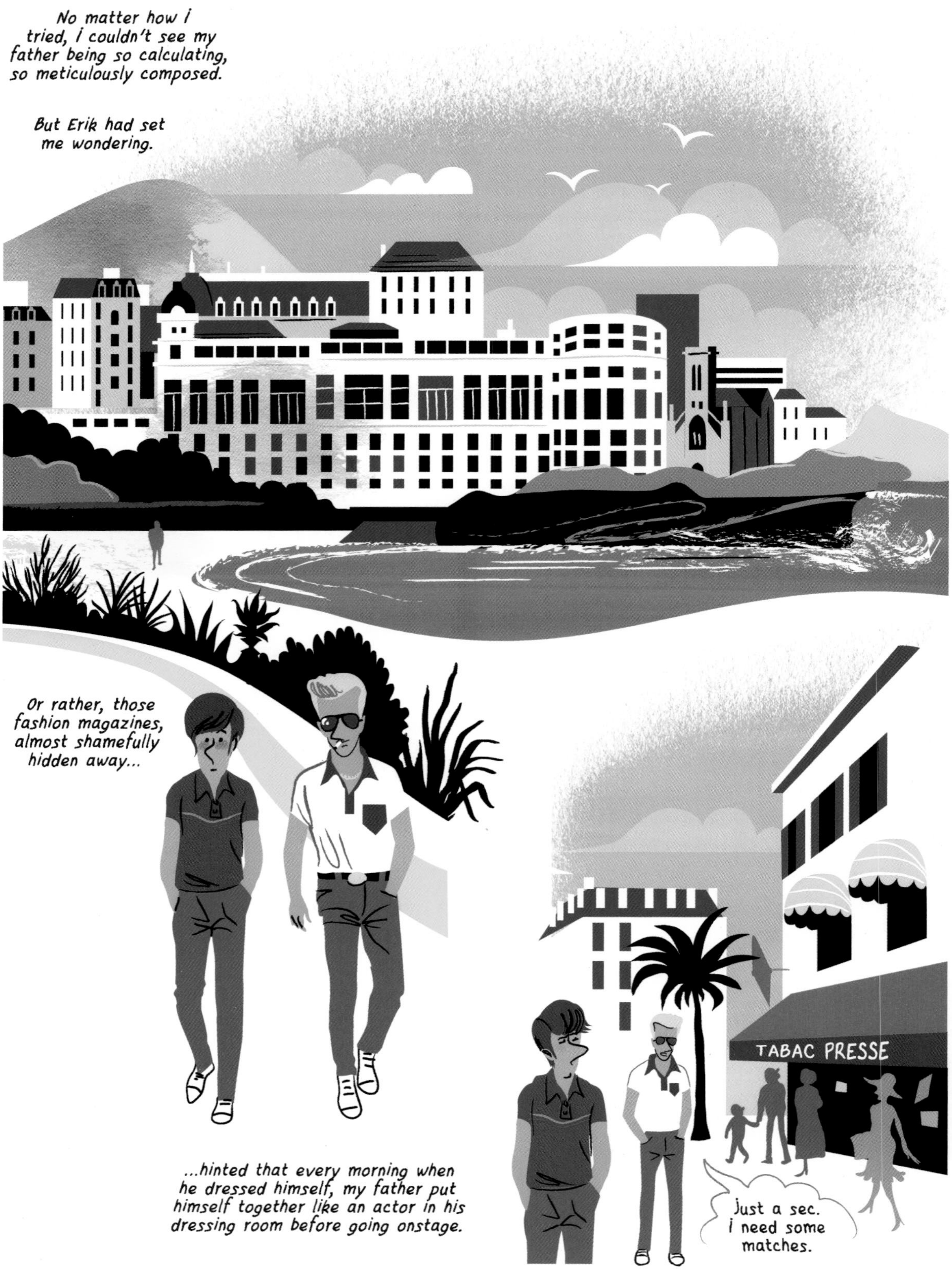
No matter how I tried, I couldn't see my father being so calculating, so meticulously composed.
But Erik had set me wondering.
Or rather, those fashion magazines, almost shamefully hidden away...
...hinted that every morning when he dressed himself, my father put himself together like an actor in his dressing room before going onstage.
TABAC PRESSE
Just a sec. I need some matches.

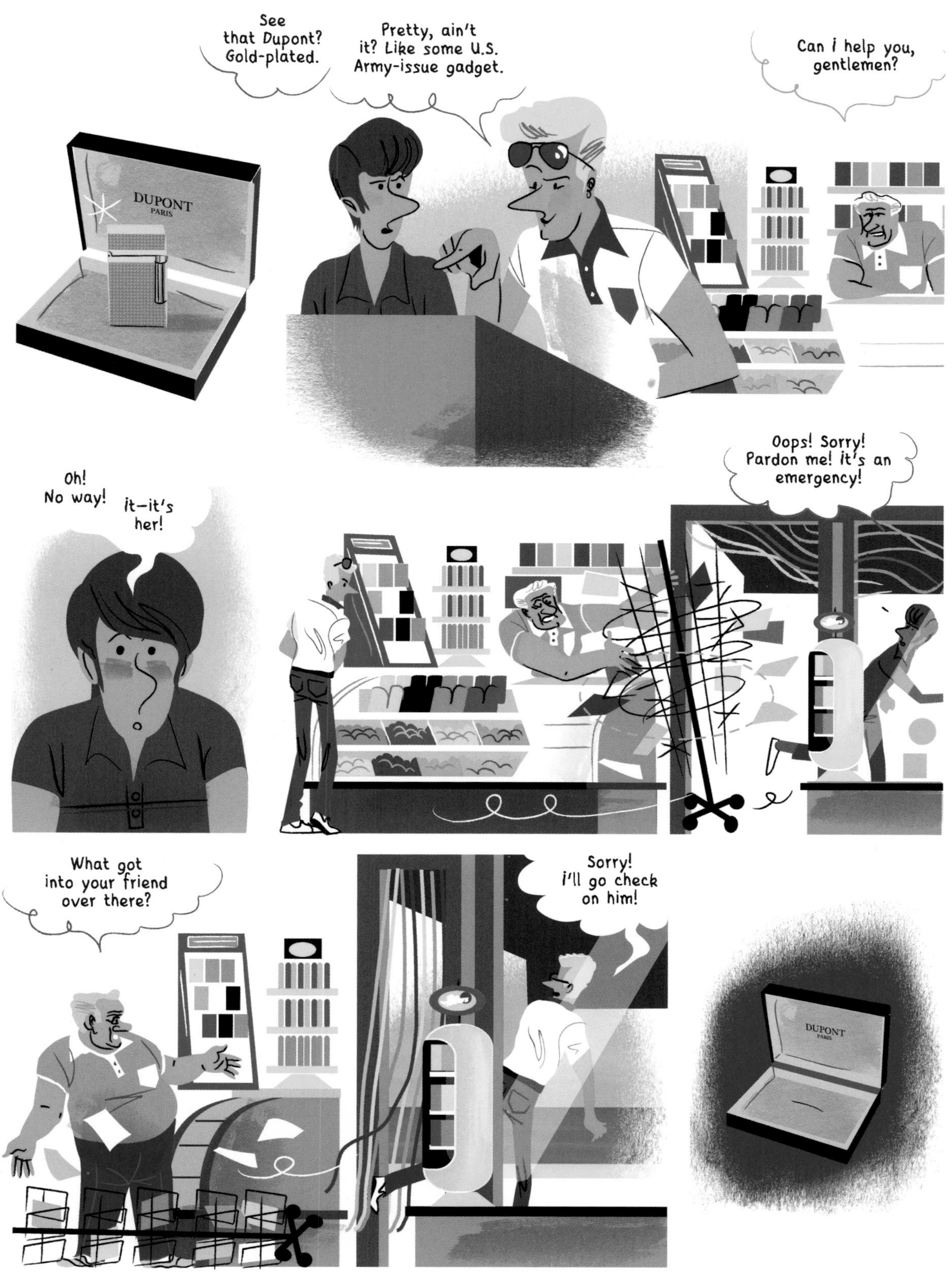
DUPONT
PARIS
See that Dupont? Gold-plated.
Pretty, ain't it? Like some U.S. Army-issue gadget.
Can I help you, gentlemen?
Oh! No way!
It—it's her!
Oops! Sorry! Pardon me! It's an emergency!
What got into your friend over there?
Sorry! I'll go check on him!
DUPONT
PARIS

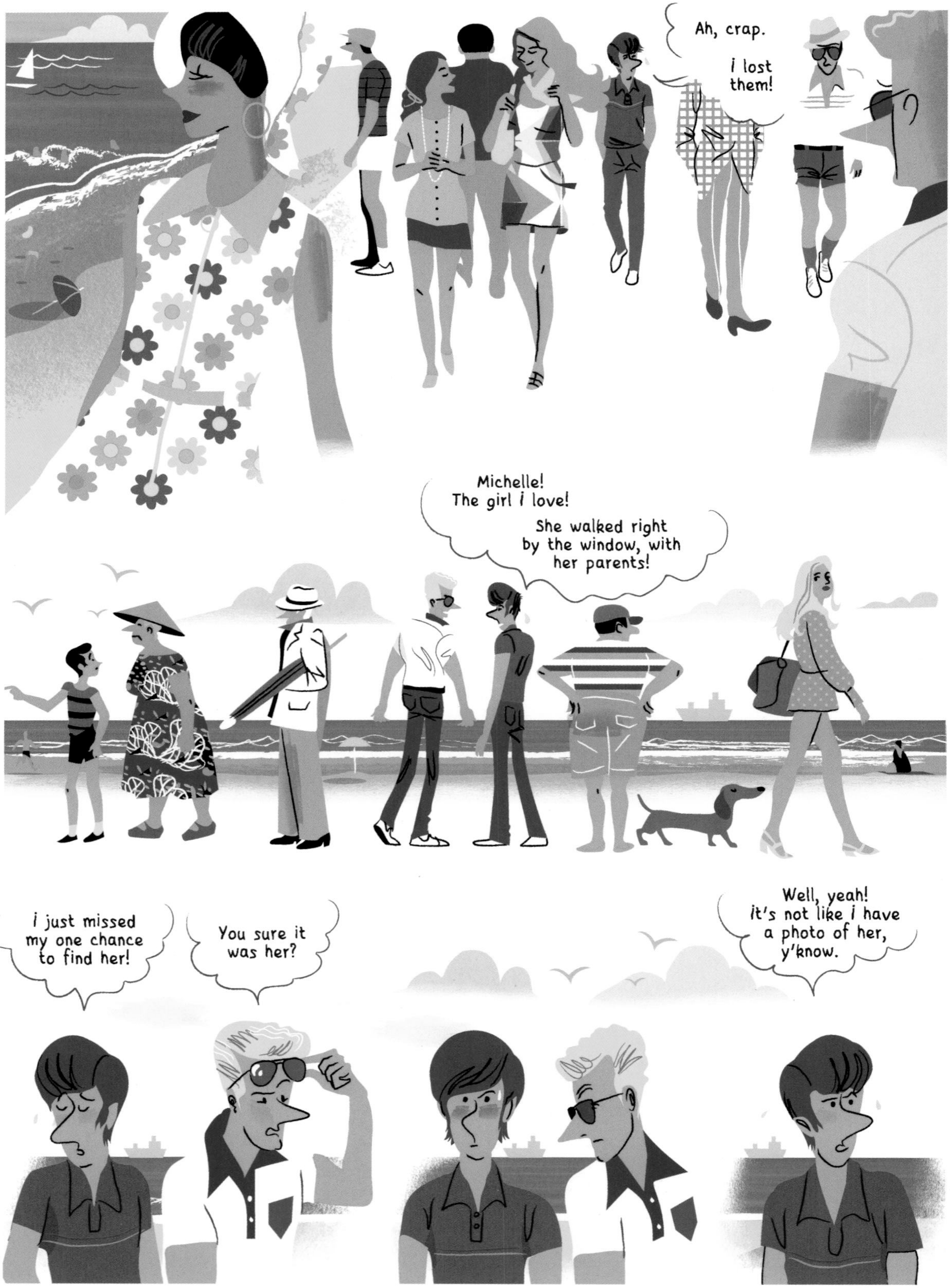
Ah, crap.
i lost them!
Michelle! The girl i love!
She walked right by the window, with her parents!
i just missed my one chance to find her!
You sure it was her?
Well, yeah! it's not like i have a photo of her, y'know.

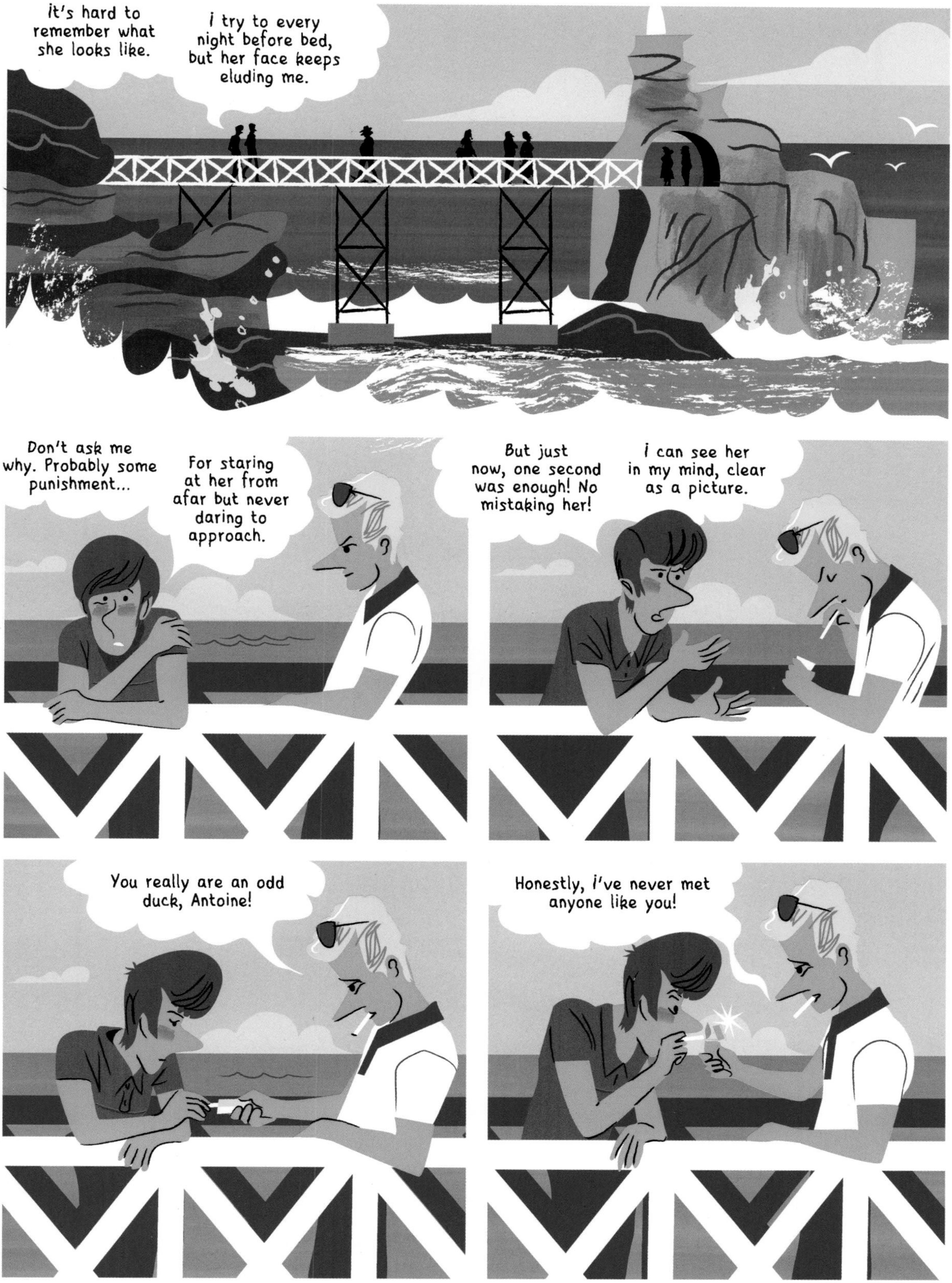
It's hard to remember what she looks like.
I try to every night before bed, but her face keeps eluding me.
Don't ask me why. Probably some punishment...
For staring at her from afar but never daring to approach.
But just now, one second was enough! No mistaking her!
I can see her in my mind, clear as a picture.
You really are an odd duck, Antoine!
Honestly, I've never met anyone like you!

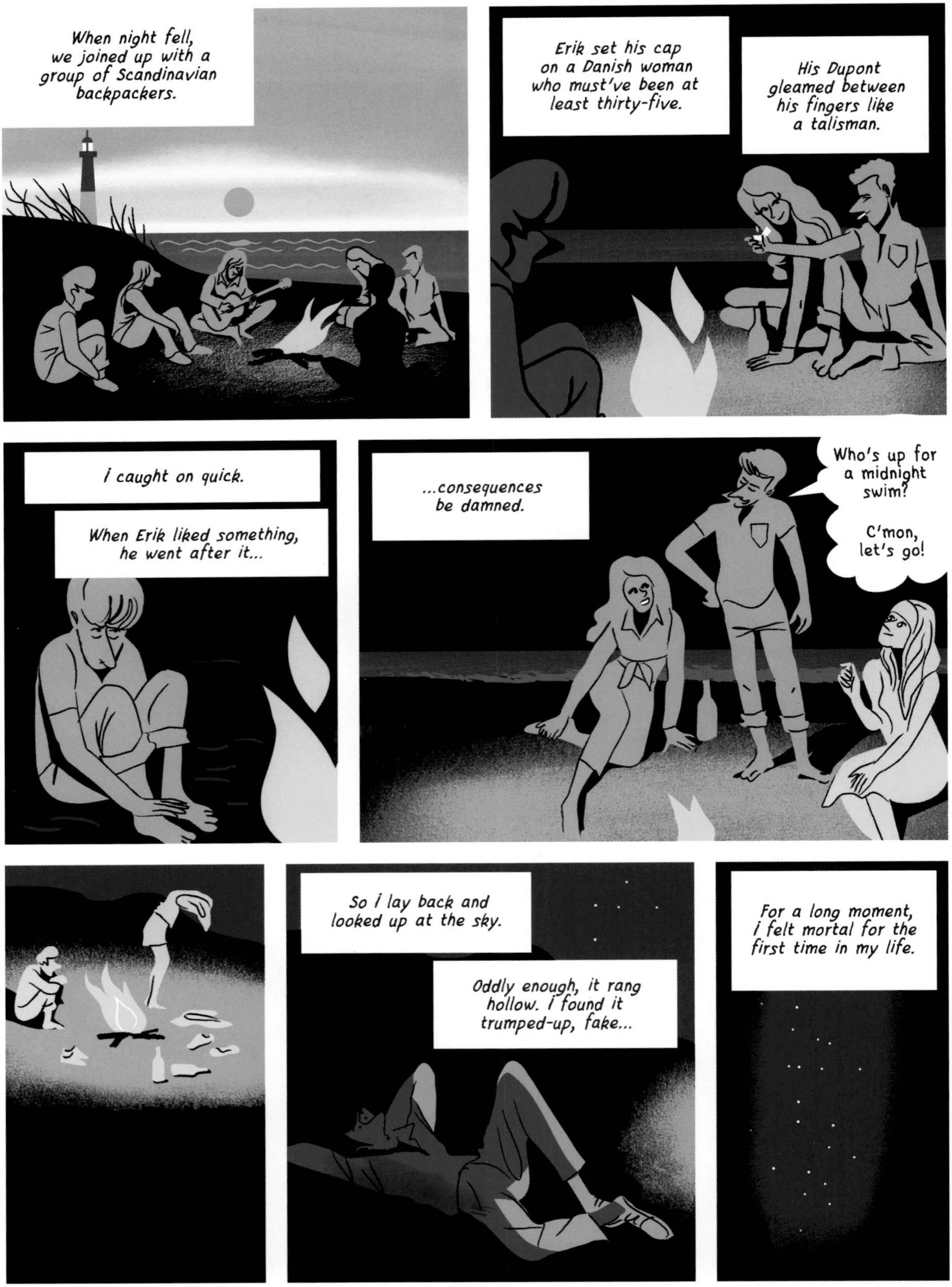
When night fell, we joined up with a group of Scandinavian backpackers.
Erik set his cap on a Danish woman who must've been at least thirty-five.
His Dupont gleamed between his fingers like a talisman.
I caught on quick.
When Erik liked something, he went after it...
...consequences be damned.
Who's up for a midnight swim?
C'mon, let's go!
So I lay back and looked up at the sky.
Oddly enough, it rang hollow. I found it trumped-up, fake...
For a long moment, I felt mortal for the first time in my life.

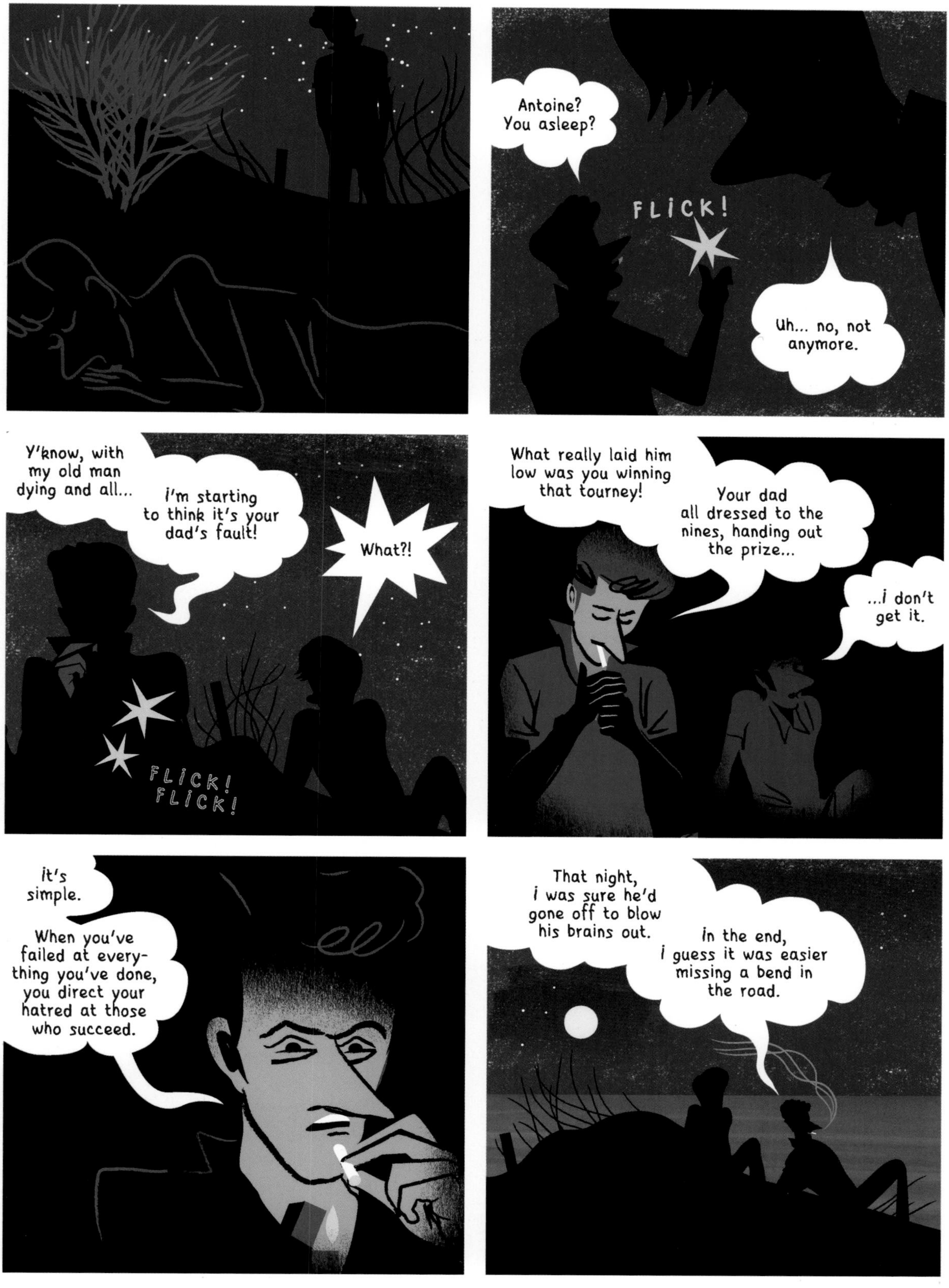
Antoine? You asleep?
FLICK!
Uh... no, not anymore.
Y'know, with my old man dying and all...
i'm starting to think it's your dad's fault!
What?!
FLICK! FLICK!
What really laid him low was you winning that tourney!
Your dad all dressed to the nines, handing out the prize...
...i don't get it.
it's simple.
When you've failed at every-thing you've done, you direct your hatred at those who succeed.
That night, i was sure he'd gone off to blow his brains out.
in the end, i guess it was easier missing a bend in the road.

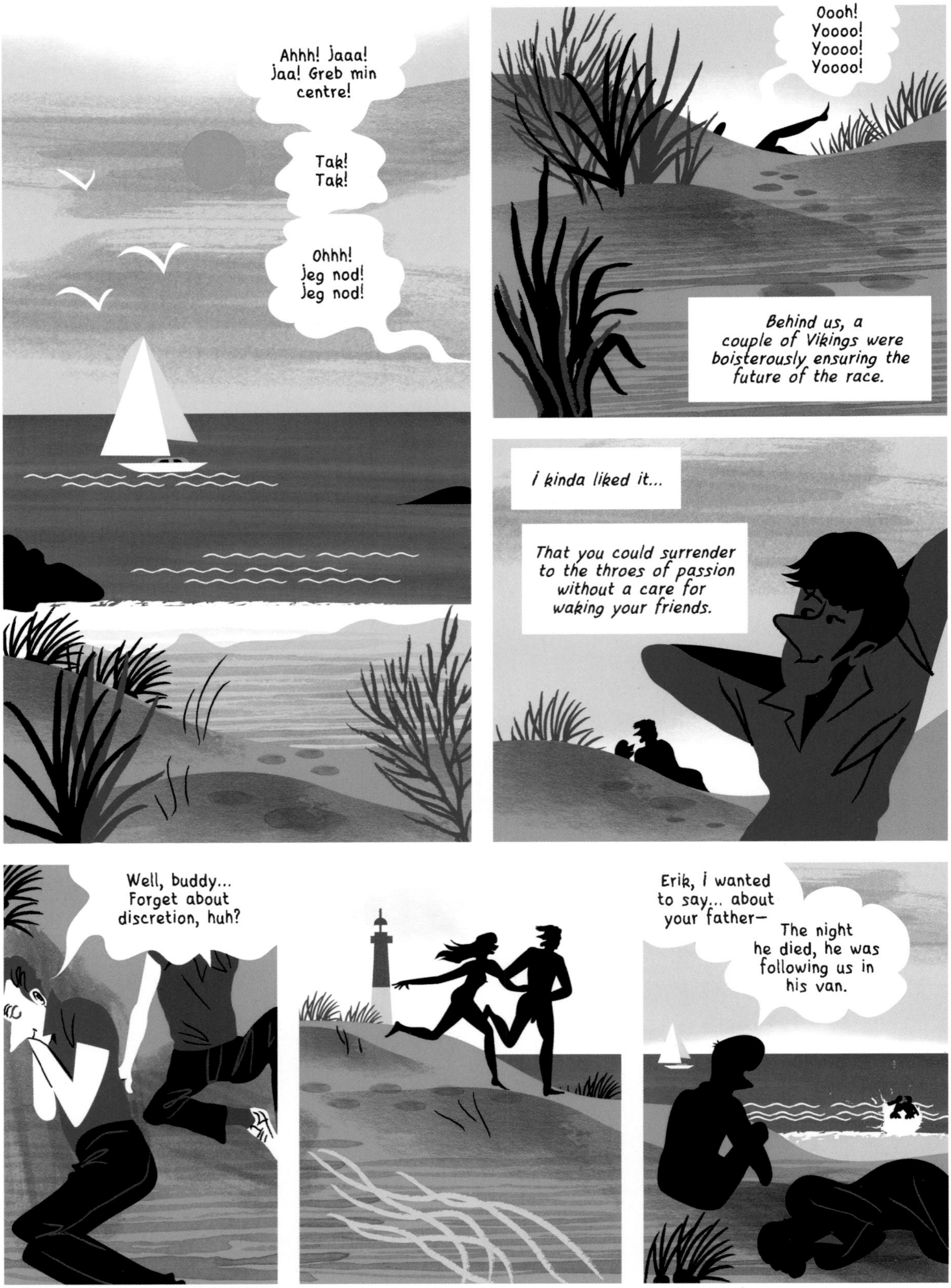
Ahhh! Jaaa! Jaa! Greb min centre!
Tak! Tak!
Ohhh! Jeg nod! Jeg nod!
Oooh! Yoooo! Yoooo! Yoooo!
Behind us, a couple of Vikings were boisterously ensuring the future of the race.
I kinda liked it...
That you could surrender to the throes of passion without a care for waking your friends.
Well, buddy... Forget about discretion, huh?
Erik, I wanted to say... about your father—
The night he died, he was following us in his van.

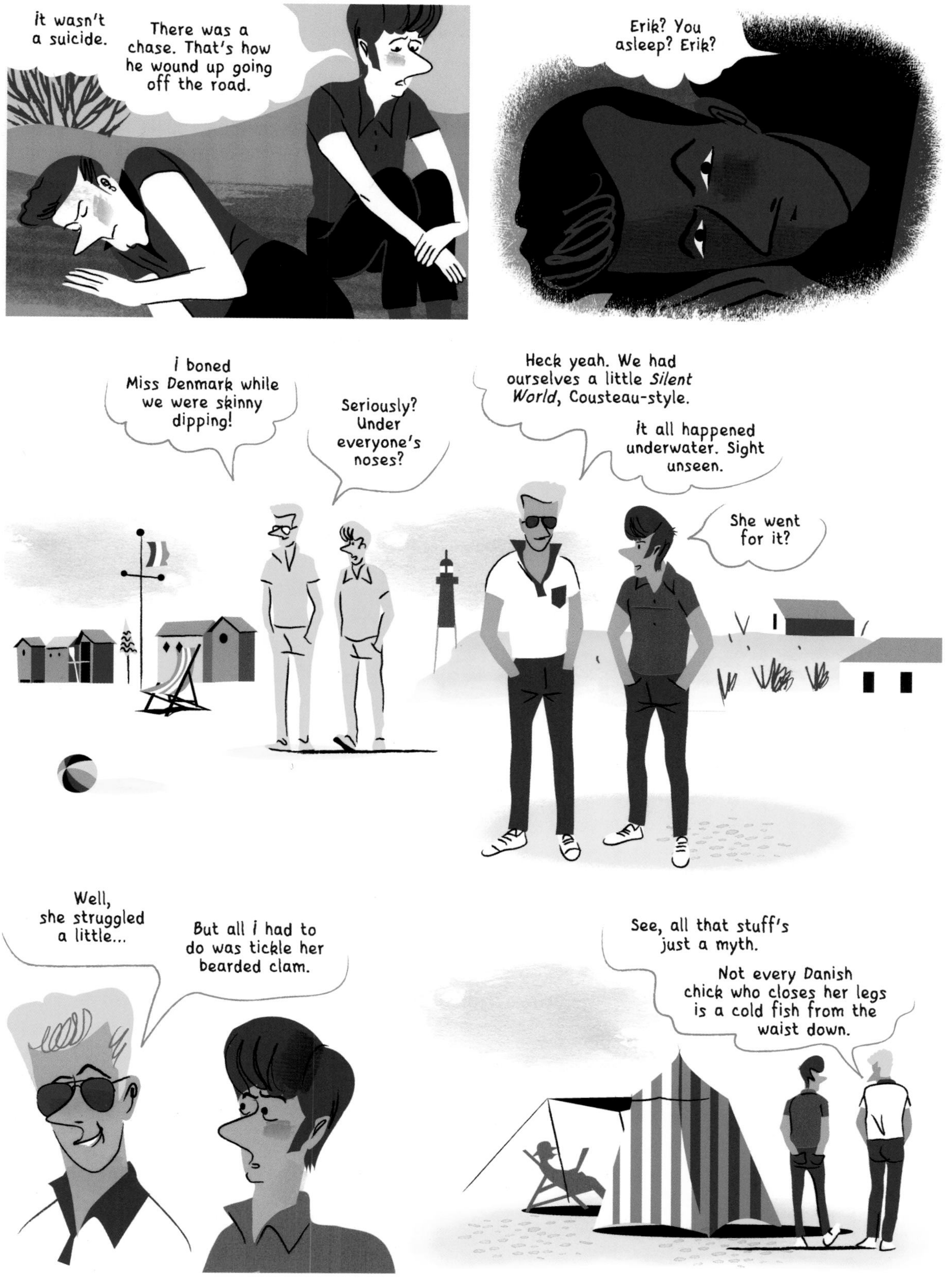
it wasn't a suicide.
There was a chase. That's how he wound up going off the road.
Erik? You asleep? Erik?
i boned Miss Denmark while we were skinny dipping!
Seriously? Under everyone's noses?
Heck yeah. We had ourselves a little *Silent World*, Cousteau-style.
it all happened underwater. Sight unseen.
She went for it?
Well, she struggled a little...
But all i had to do was tickle her bearded clam.
See, all that stuff's just a myth.
Not every Danish chick who closes her legs is a cold fish from the waist down.

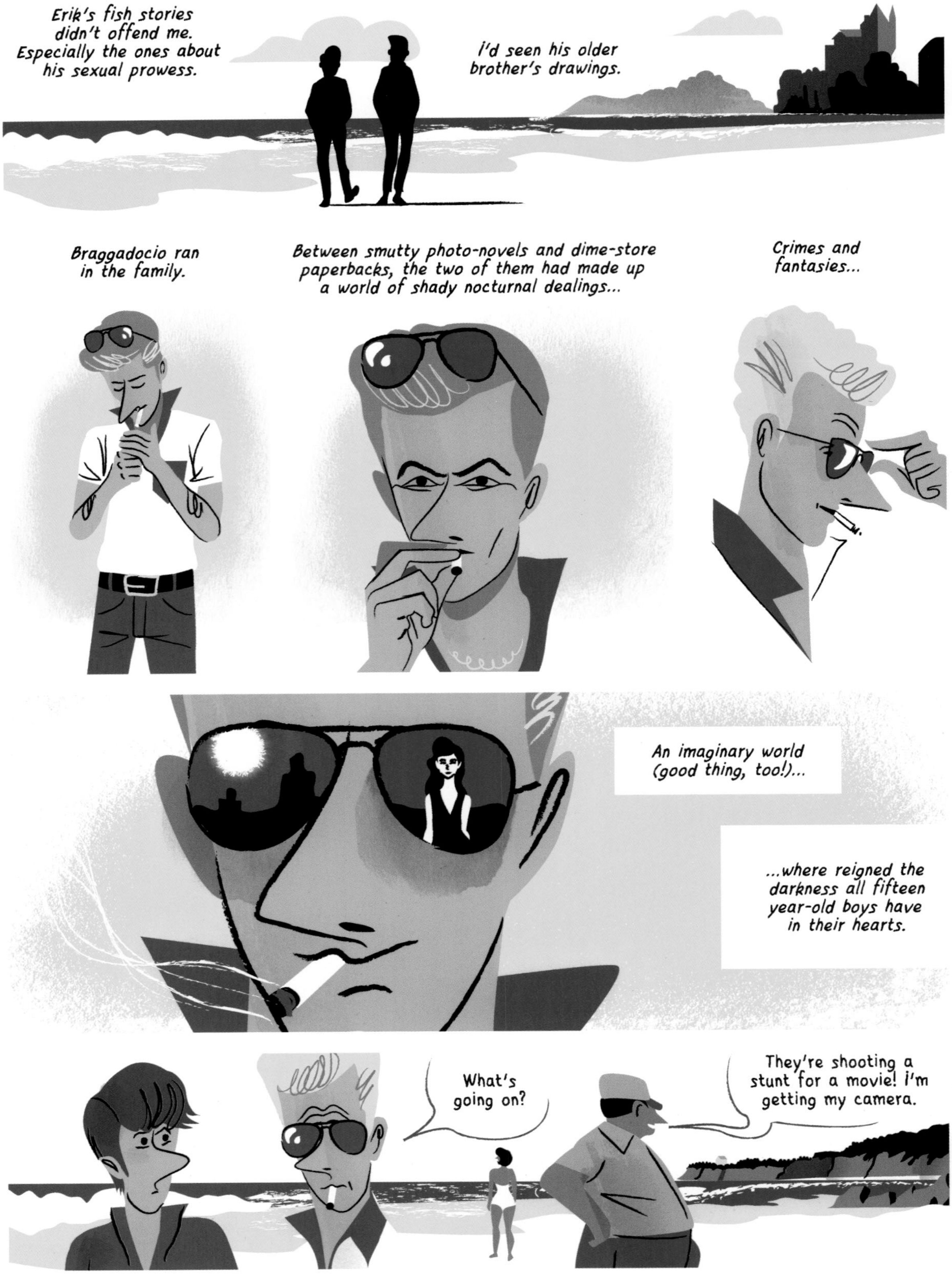
Erik's fish stories didn't offend me. Especially the ones about his sexual prowess.
I'd seen his older brother's drawings.
Braggadocio ran in the family.
Between smutty photo-novels and dime-store paperbacks, the two of them had made up a world of shady nocturnal dealings...
Crimes and fantasies...
An imaginary world (good thing, too!)...
...where reigned the darkness all fifteen year-old boys have in their hearts.
What's going on?
They're shooting a stunt for a movie! I'm getting my camera.

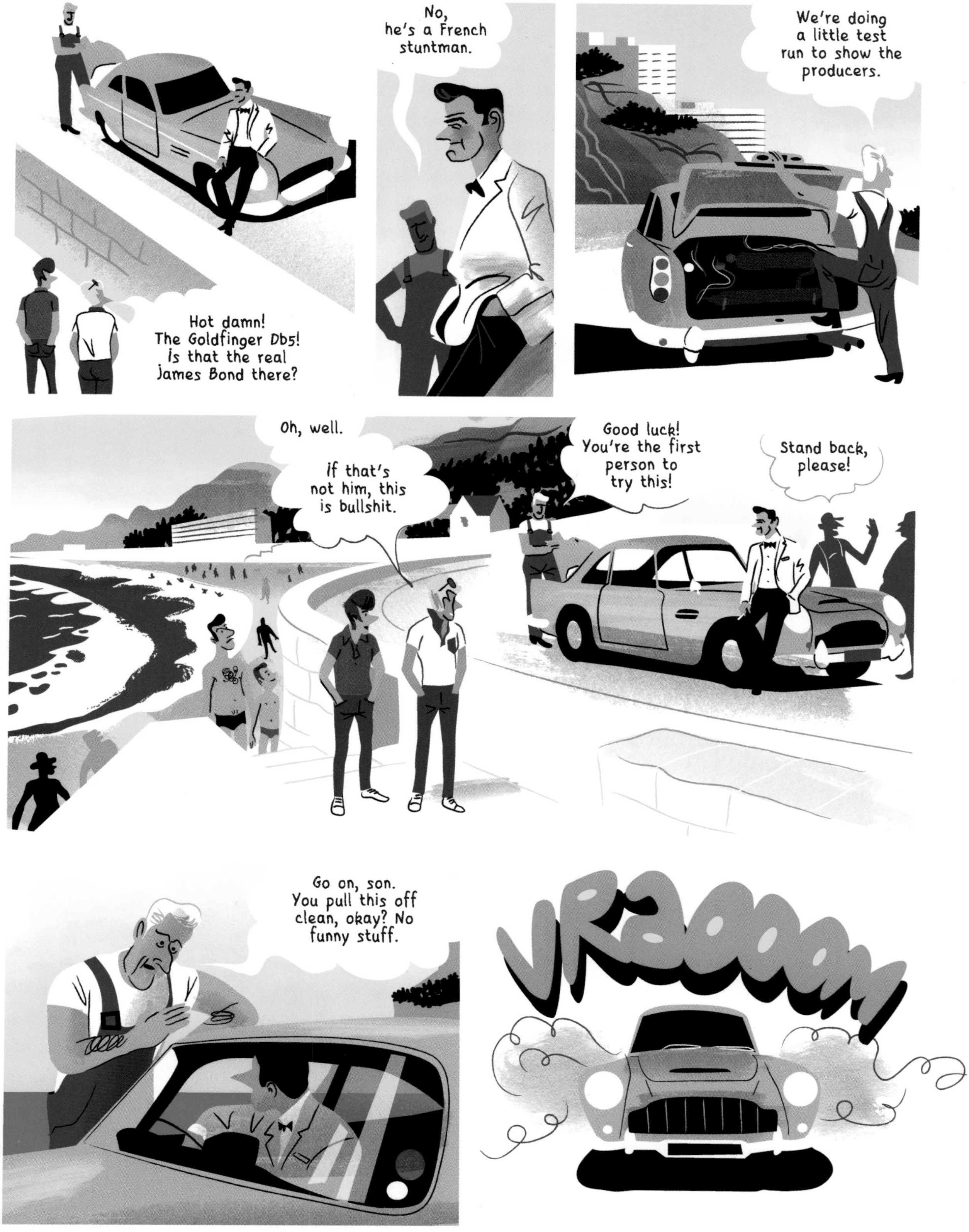
Hot damn! The Goldfinger Db5! Is that the real James Bond there?
No, he's a French stuntman.
We're doing a little test run to show the producers.
Oh, well.
If that's not him, this is bullshit.
Good luck! You're the first person to try this!
Stand back, please!
Go on, son. You pull this off clean, okay? No funny stuff.
VRROOOM

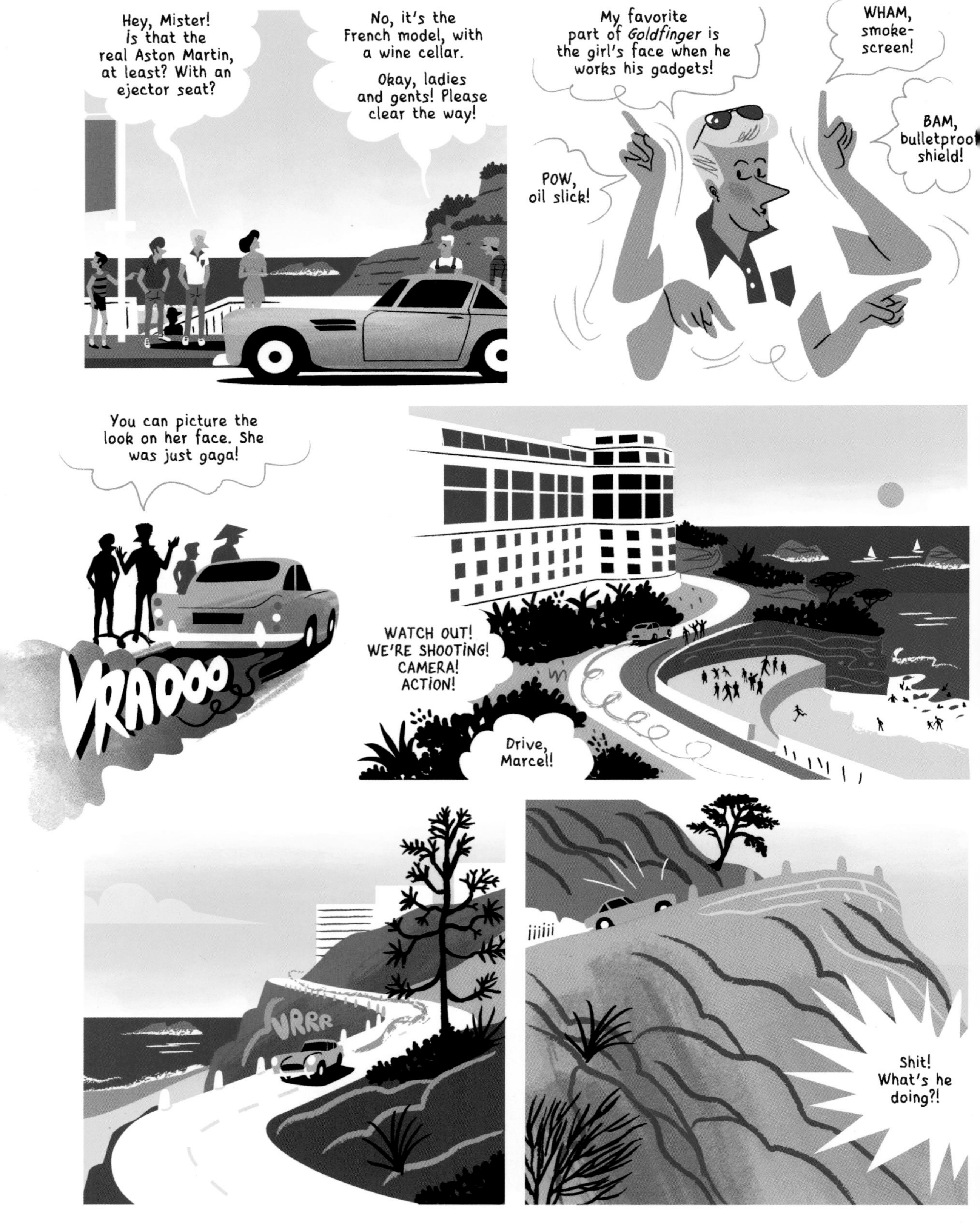
Hey, Mister! is that the real Aston Martin, at least? With an ejector seat?
No, it's the French model, with a wine cellar.
Okay, ladies and gents! Please clear the way!
My favorite part of *Goldfinger* is the girl's face when he works his gadgets!
POW, oil slick!
WHAM, smoke-screen!
BAM, bulletproo shield!
You can picture the look on her face. She was just gaga!
VRAOOO
WATCH OUT! WE'RE SHOOTING! CAMERA! ACTION!
Drive, Marcel!
VRRR
iiiiii
Shit! What's he doing?!

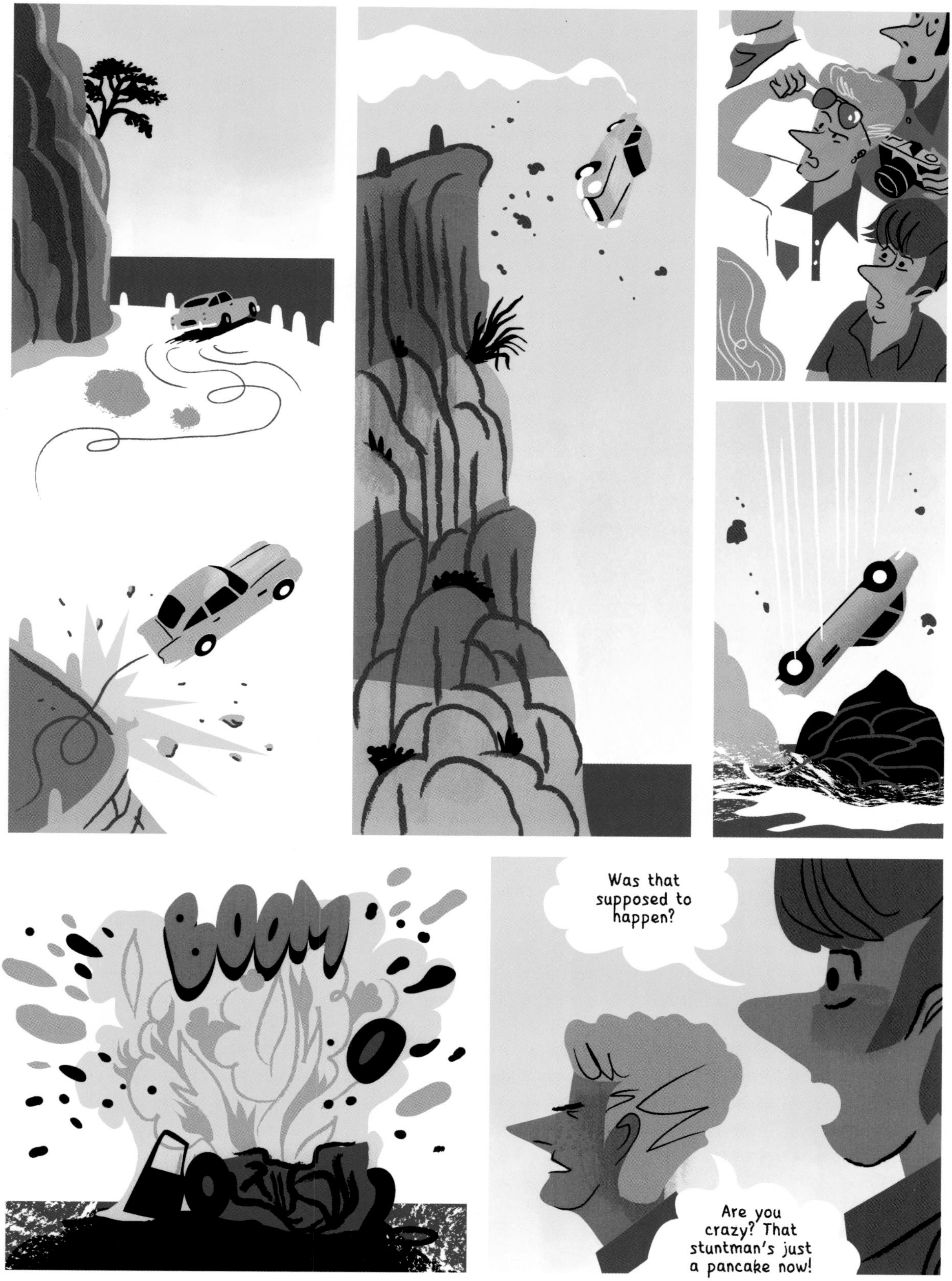
BOOM
Was that supposed to happen?
Are you crazy? That stuntman's just a pancake now!

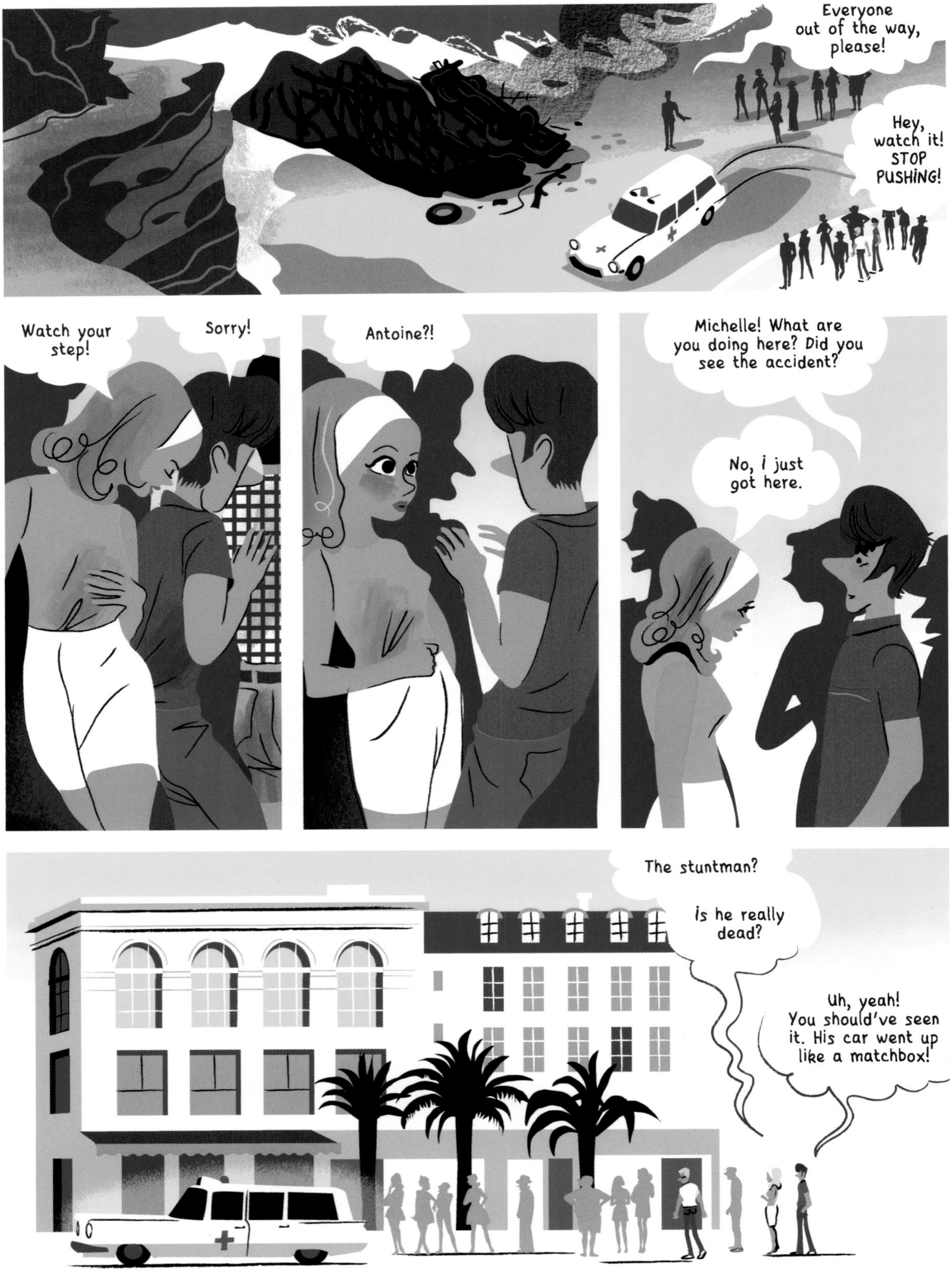
Everyone out of the way, please!
Hey, watch it! STOP PUSHING!
Watch your step!
Sorry!
Antoine?!
Michelle! What are you doing here? Did you see the accident?
No, I just got here.
The stuntman?
Is he really dead?
Uh, yeah! You should've seen it. His car went up like a matchbox!

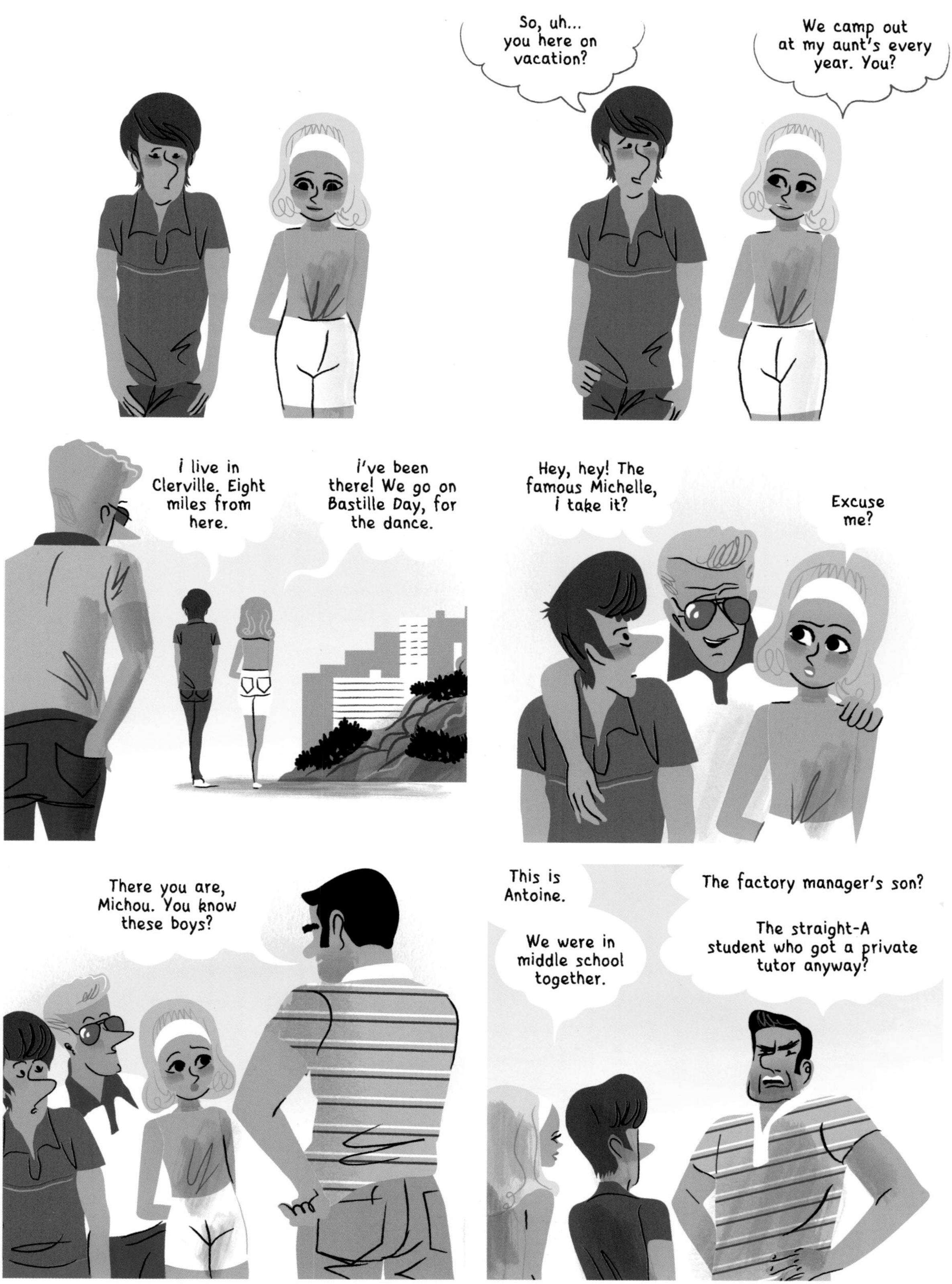
So, uh... you here on vacation?
We camp out at my aunt's every year. You?
I live in Clerville. Eight miles from here.
I've been there! We go on Bastille Day, for the dance.
Hey, hey! The famous Michelle, I take it?
Excuse me?
There you are, Michou. You know these boys?
This is Antoine.
We were in middle school together.
The factory manager's son?
The straight-A student who got a private tutor anyway?

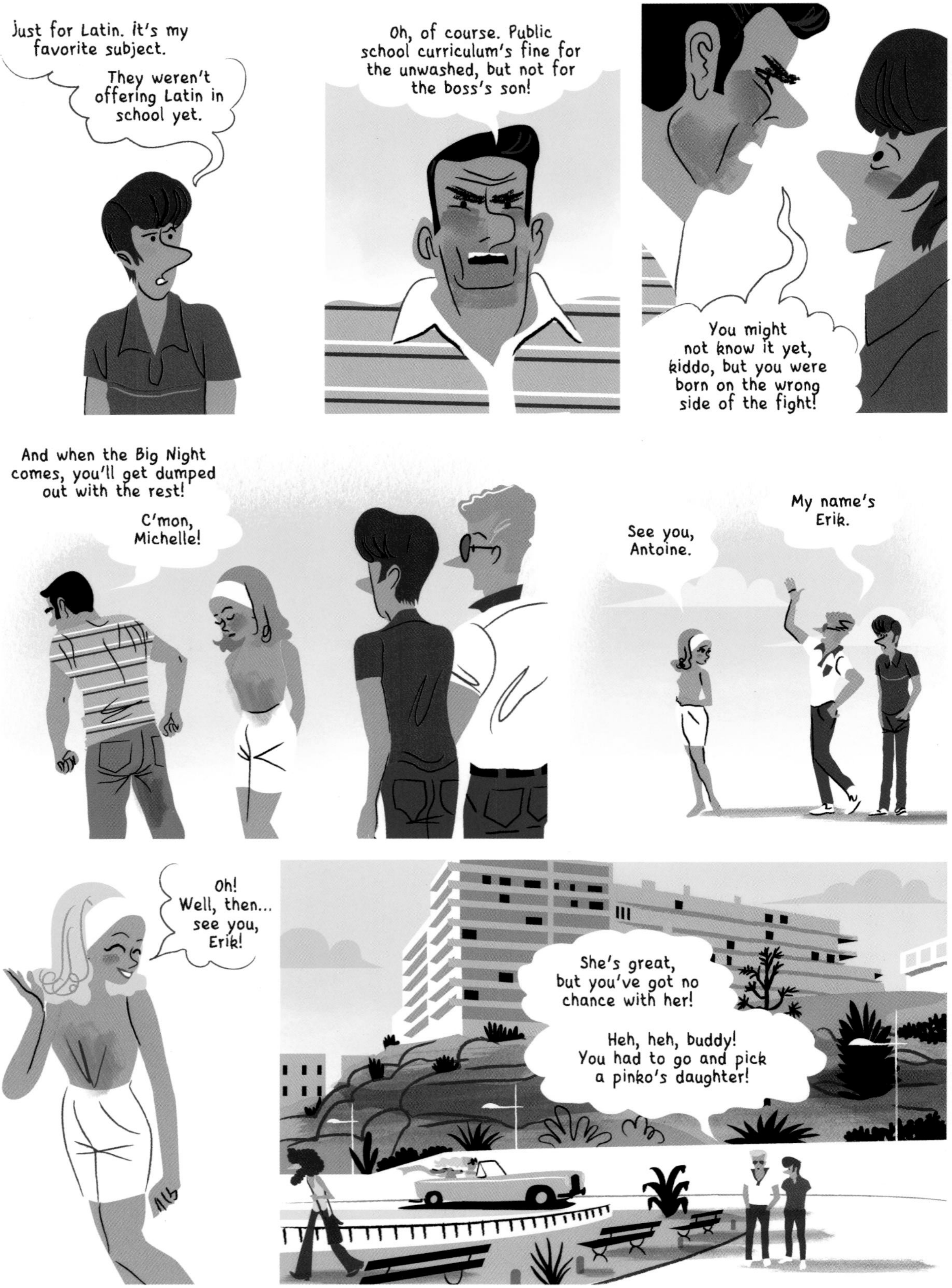
Just for Latin. It's my favorite subject.
They weren't offering Latin in school yet.
Oh, of course. Public school curriculum's fine for the unwashed, but not for the boss's son!
You might not know it yet, kiddo, but you were born on the wrong side of the fight!
And when the Big Night comes, you'll get dumped out with the rest!
C'mon, Michelle!
See you, Antoine.
My name's Erik.
Oh! Well, then... see you, Erik!
She's great, but you've got no chance with her!
Heh, heh, buddy! You had to go and pick a pinko's daughter!

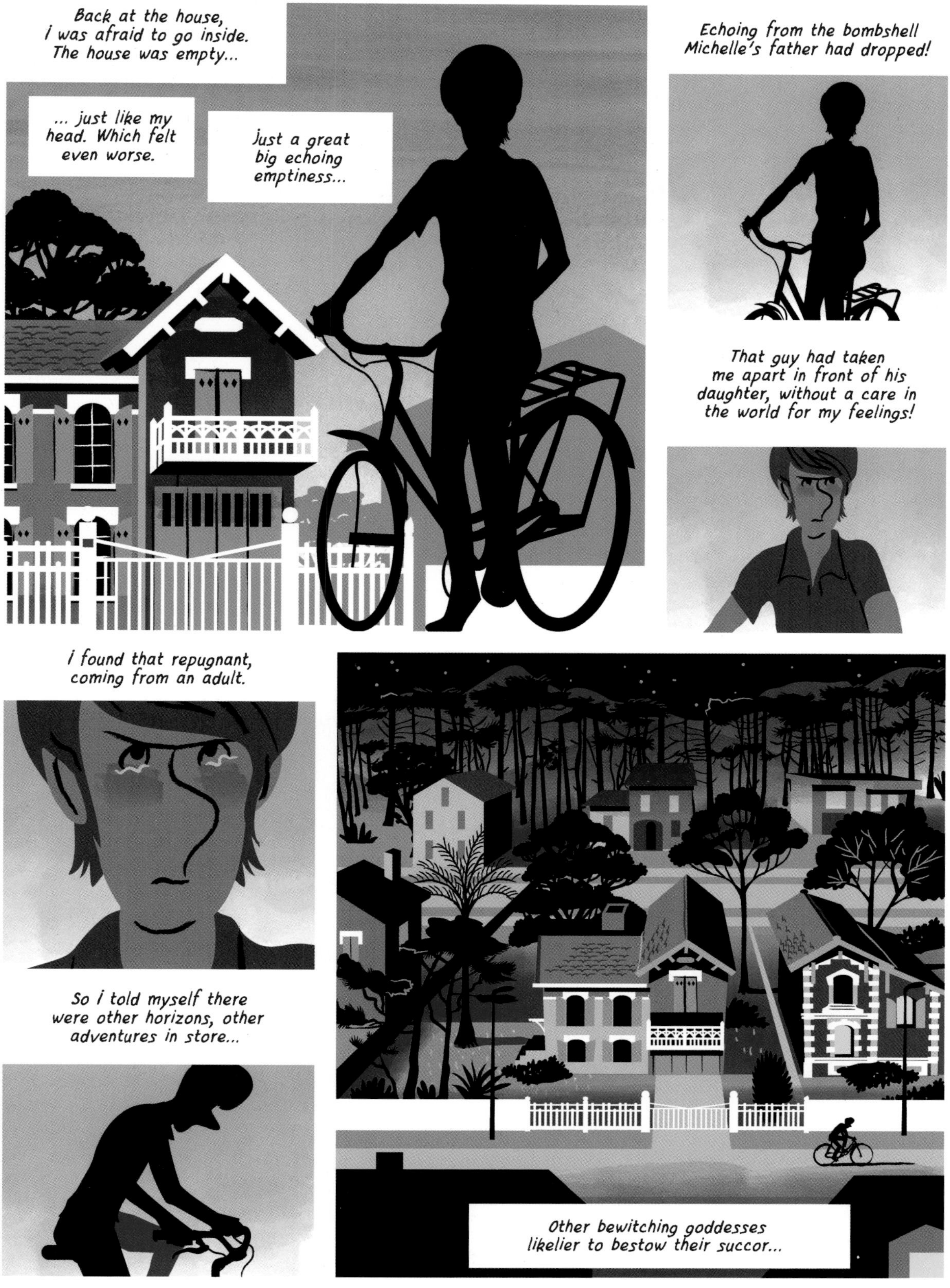
Back at the house, I was afraid to go inside. The house was empty...
... just like my head. Which felt even worse.
Just a great big echoing emptiness...
Echoing from the bombshell Michelle's father had dropped!
That guy had taken me apart in front of his daughter, without a care in the world for my feelings!
I found that repugnant, coming from an adult.
So I told myself there were other horizons, other adventures in store...
Other bewitching goddesses likelier to bestow their succor...

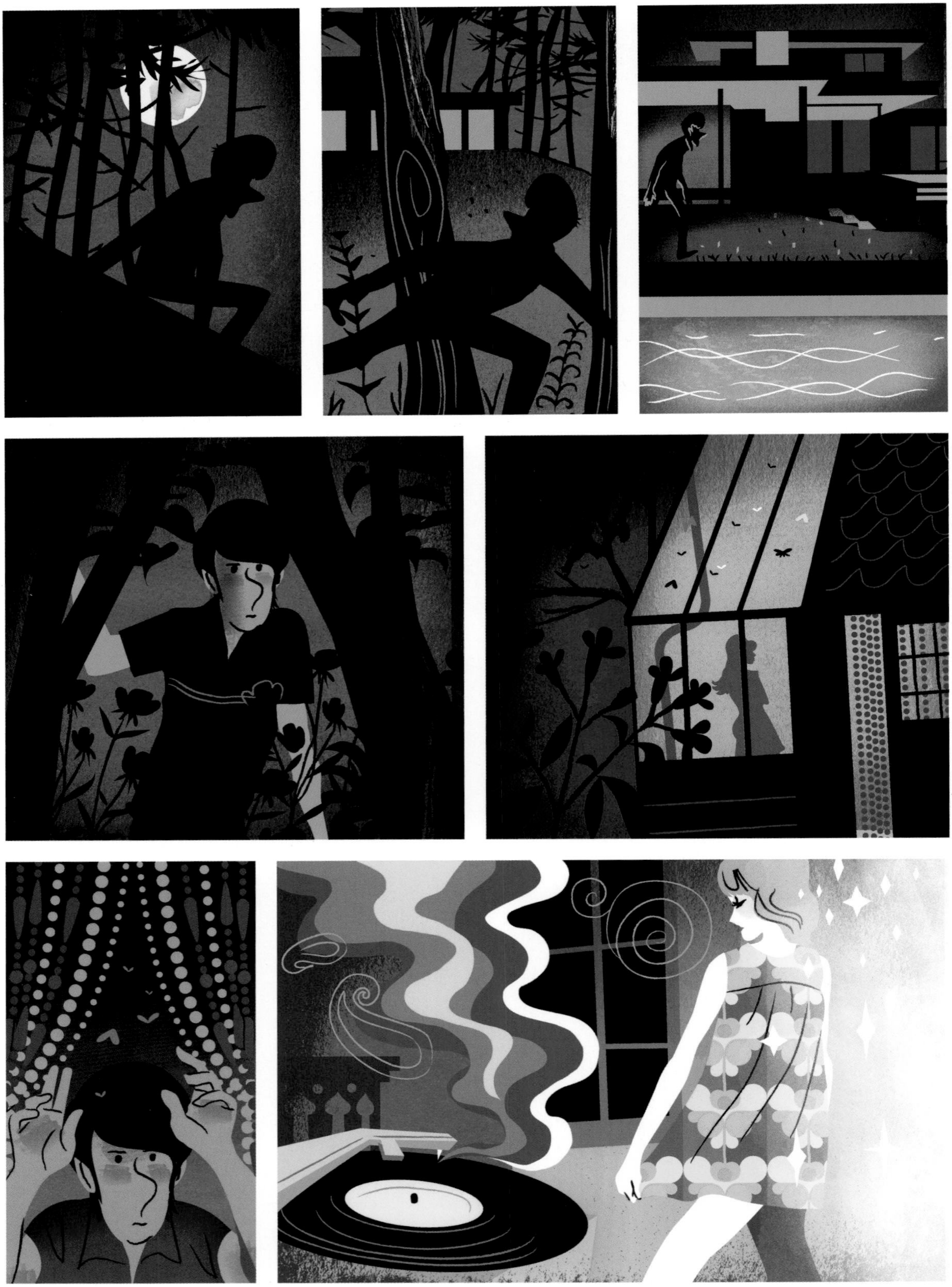

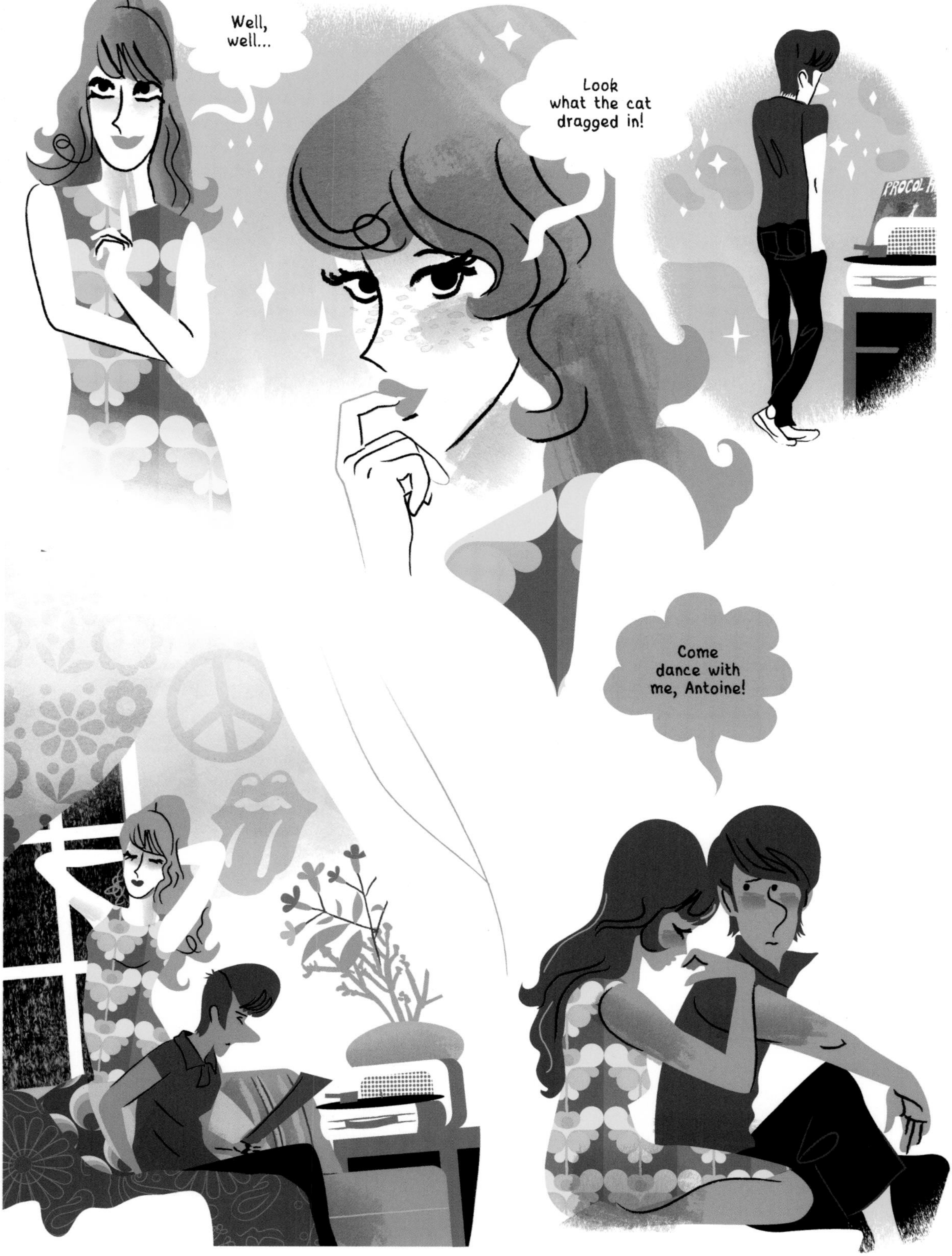
Well, well...
Look what the cat dragged in!
PROCOL H
Come dance with me, Antoine!

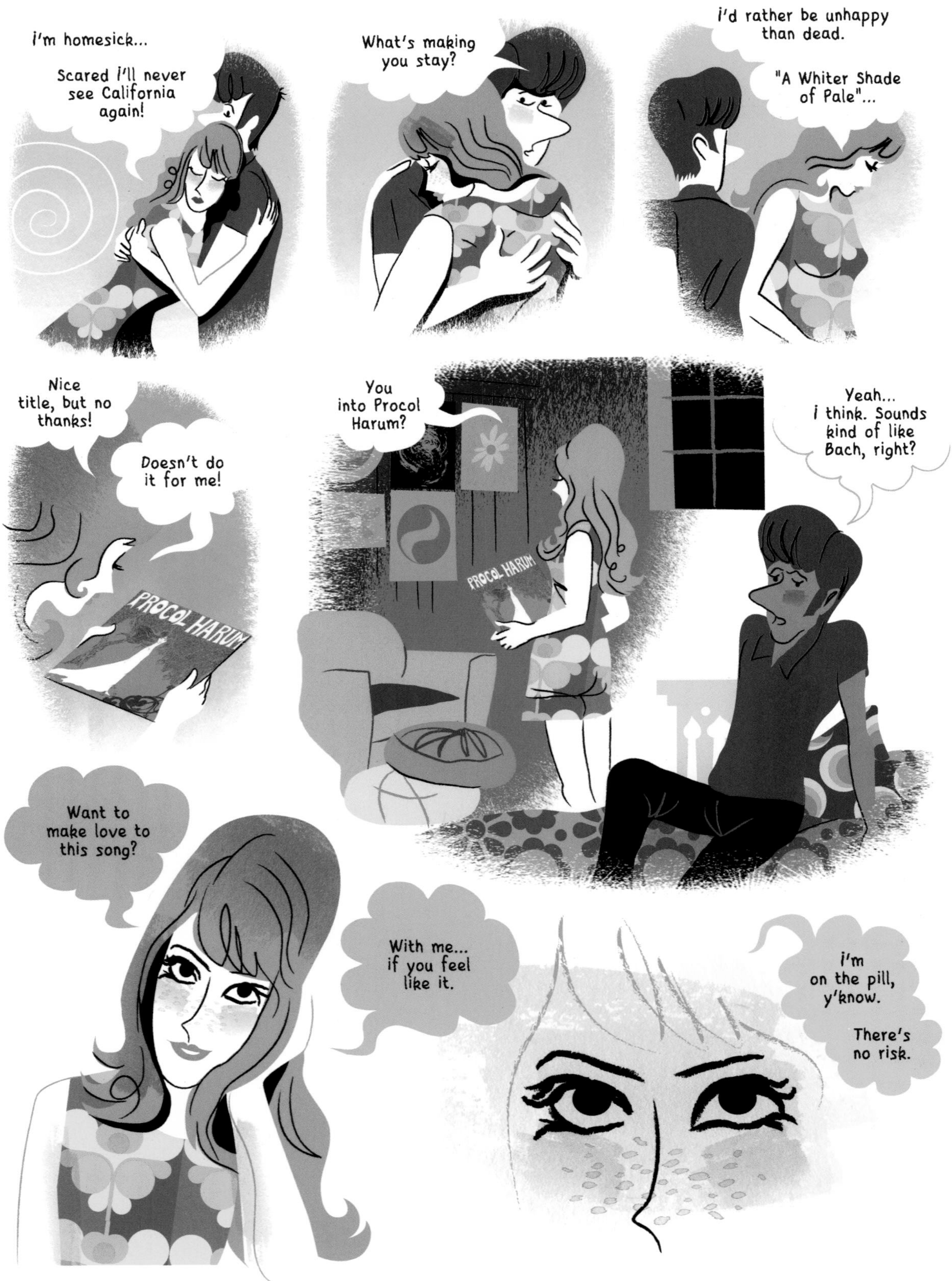
i'm homesick...
Scared i'll never see California again!
What's making you stay?
i'd rather be unhappy than dead.
"A Whiter Shade of Pale"...
Nice title, but no thanks!
Doesn't do it for me!
PROCOL HARUM
You into Procol Harum?
PROCOL HARUM
Yeah... i think. Sounds kind of like Bach, right?
Want to make love to this song?
With me... if you feel like it.
i'm on the pill, y'know.
There's no risk.

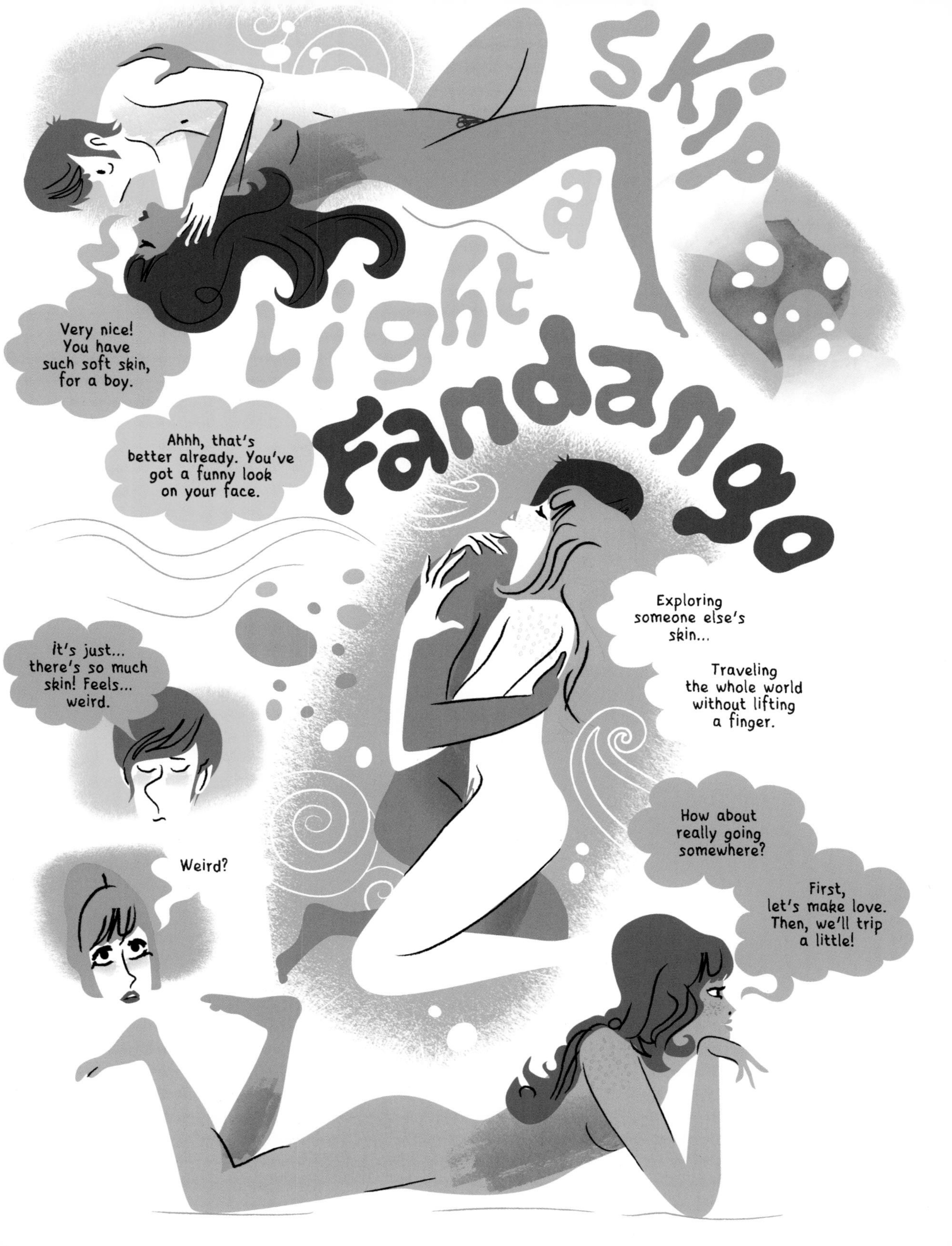
Skip a Light Fandango
Very nice! You have such soft skin, for a boy.
Ahhh, that's better already. You've got a funny look on your face.
Exploring someone else's skin...
Traveling the whole world without lifting a finger.
It's just... there's so much skin! Feels... weird.
How about really going somewhere?
Weird?
First, let's make love. Then, we'll trip a little!

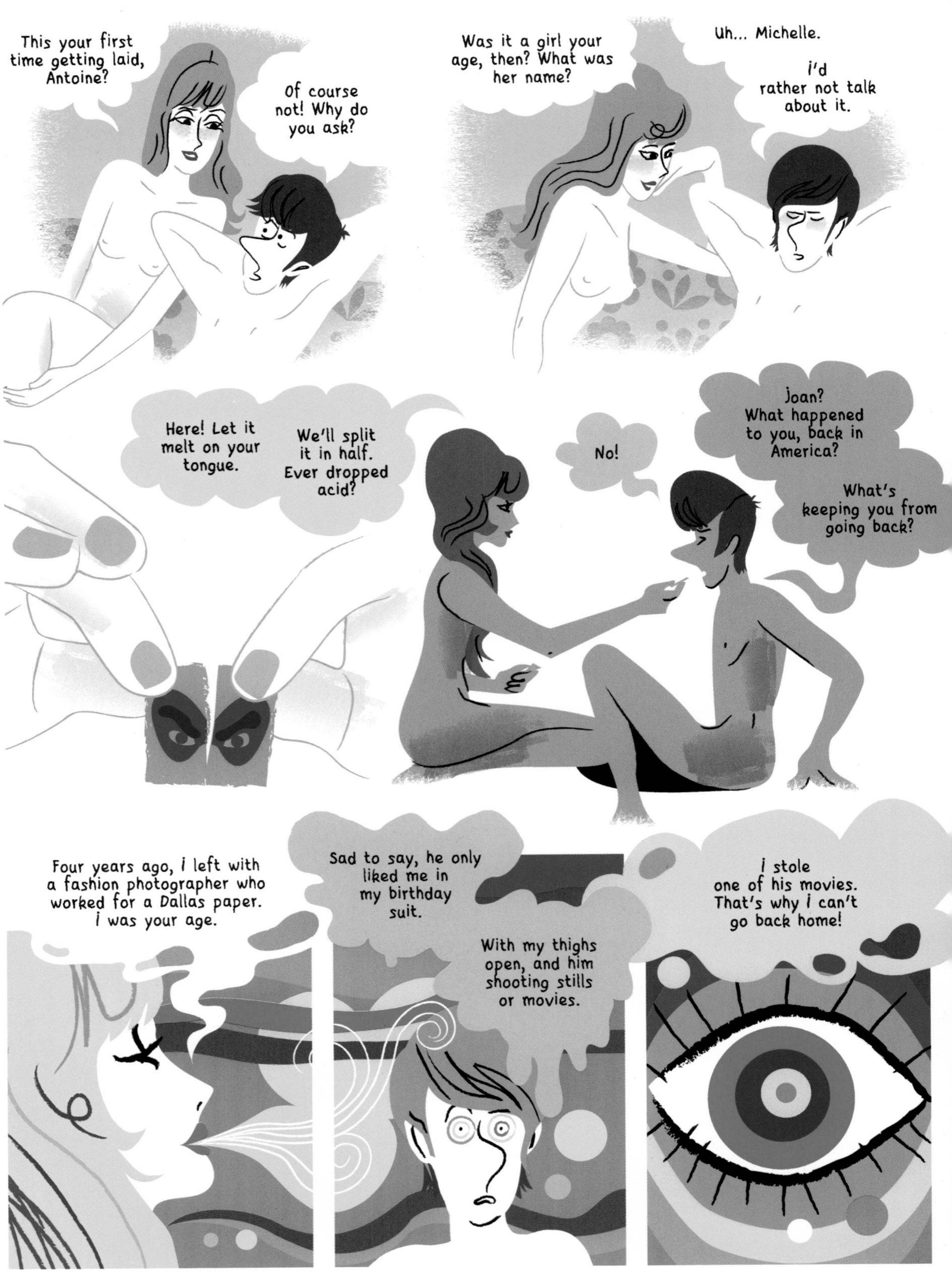
This your first time getting laid, Antoine?
Of course not! Why do you ask?
Was it a girl your age, then? What was her name?
Uh... Michelle.
I'd rather not talk about it.
Here! Let it melt on your tongue.
We'll split it in half. Ever dropped acid?
No!
Joan? What happened to you, back in America?
What's keeping you from going back?
Four years ago, I left with a fashion photographer who worked for a Dallas paper. I was your age.
Sad to say, he only liked me in my birthday suit.
With my thighs open, and him shooting stills or movies.
I stole one of his movies. That's why I can't go back home!

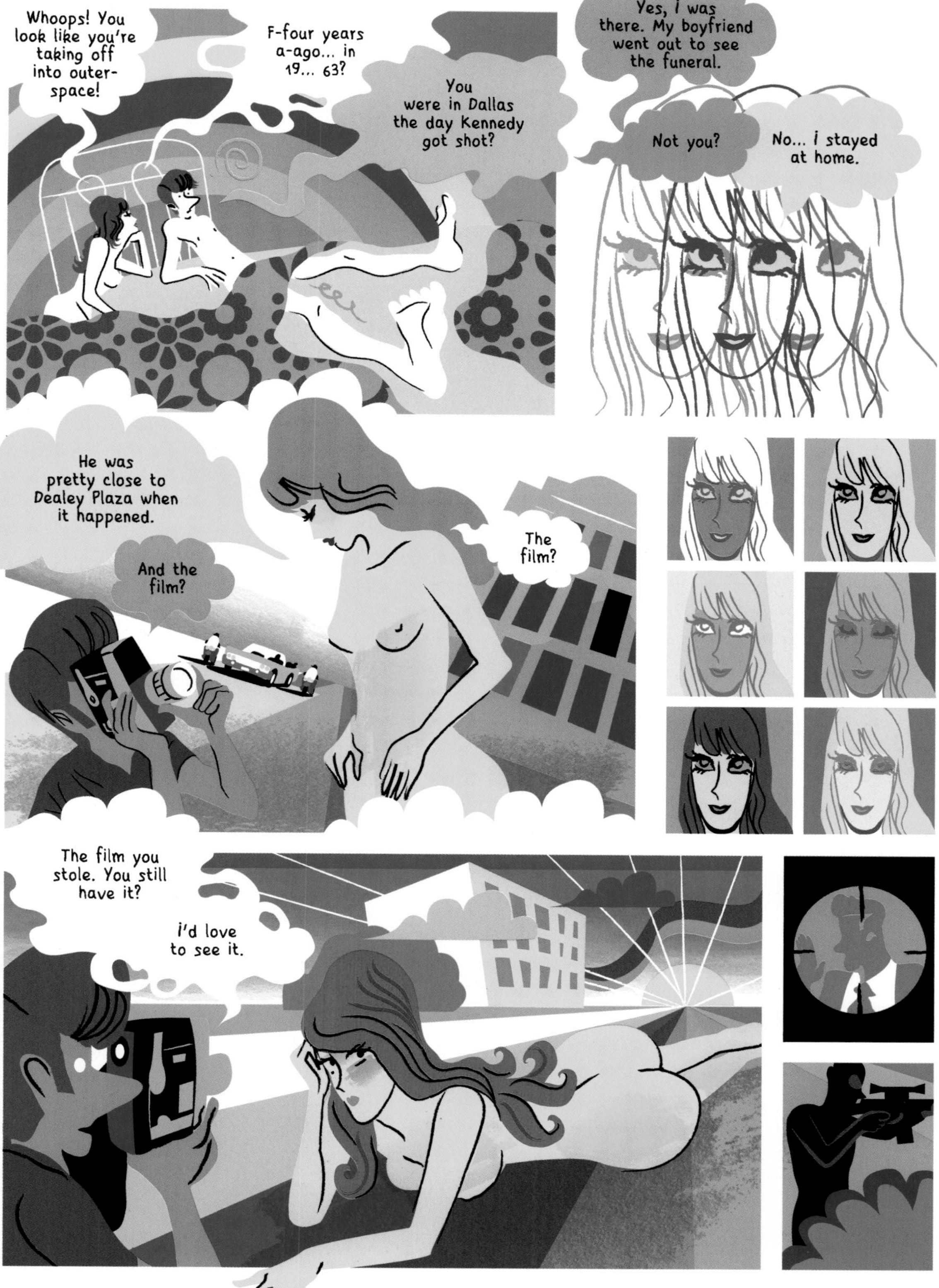
Whoops! You look like you're taking off into outer-space!
F-four years a-ago... in 19... 63?
You were in Dallas the day Kennedy got shot?
Yes, i was there. My boyfriend went out to see the funeral.
Not you?
No... i stayed at home.
He was pretty close to Dealey Plaza when it happened.
And the film?
The film?
The film you stole. You still have it?
i'd love to see it.

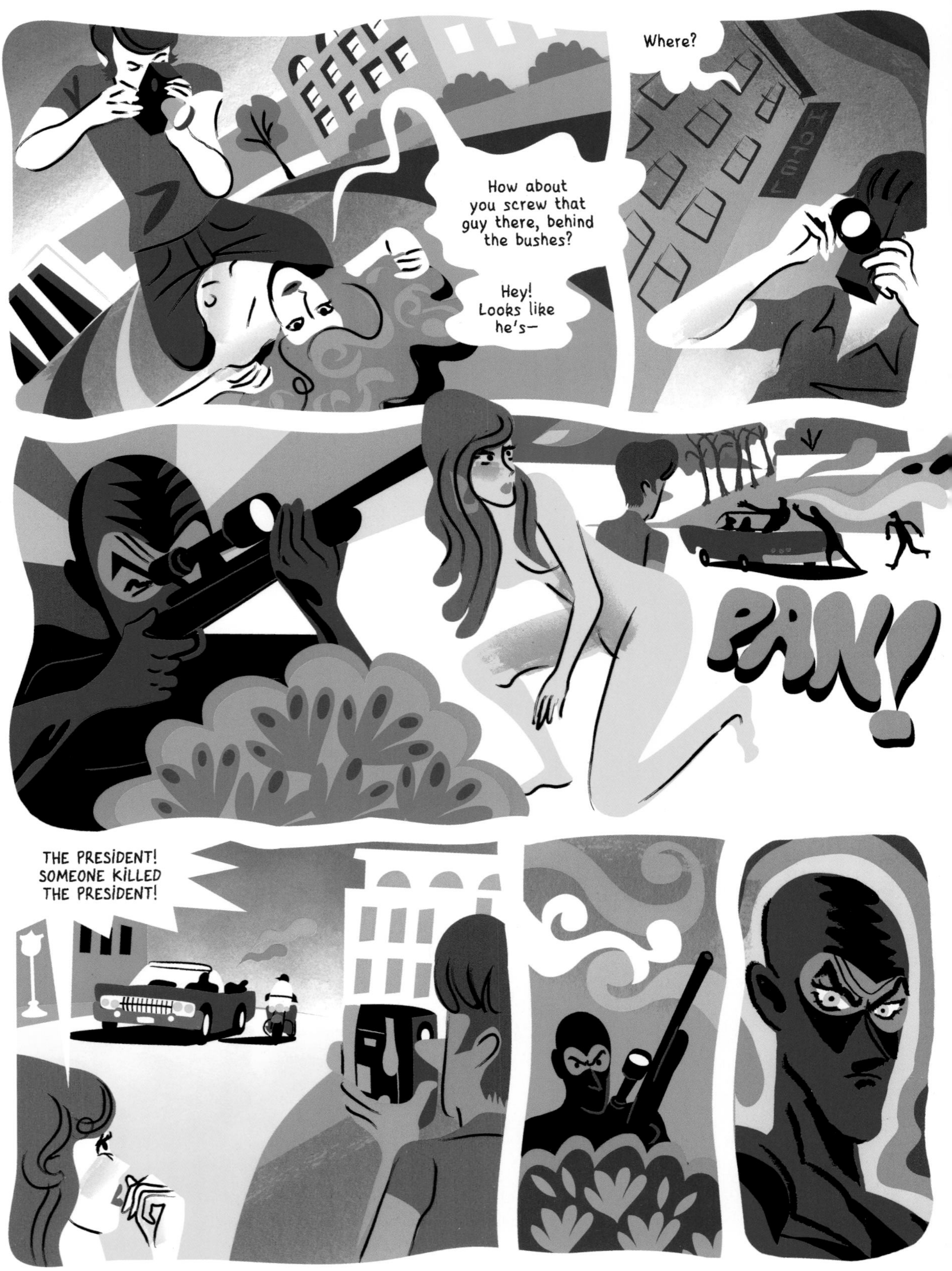
How about you screw that guy there, behind the bushes?
Hey! Looks like he's—
Where?
HOTEL
PAN!
THE PRESIDENT! SOMEONE KILLED THE PRESIDENT!

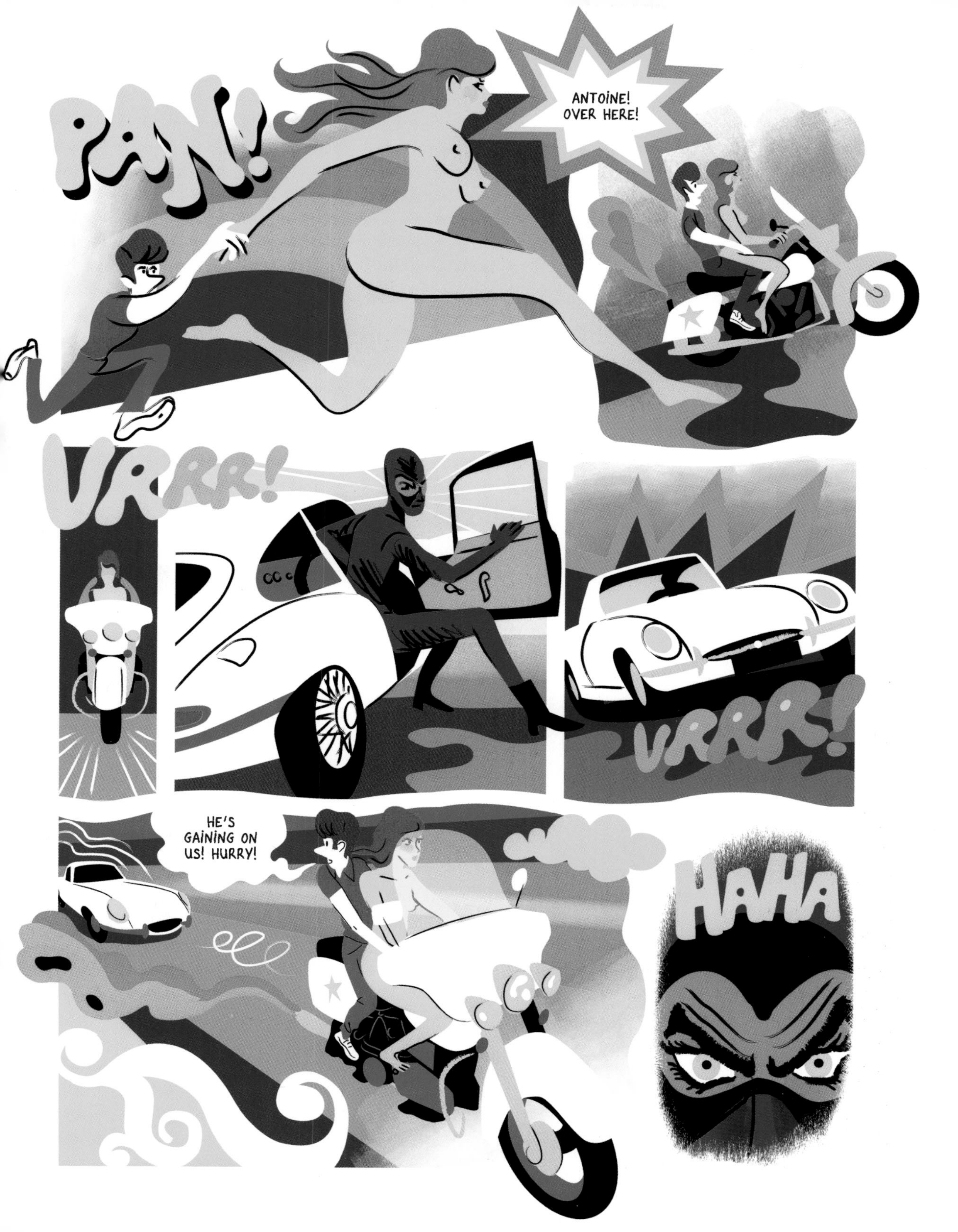
PAN!
ANTOINE! OVER HERE!
VRRR!
VRRR!
HE'S GAINING ON US! HURRY!
HAHA

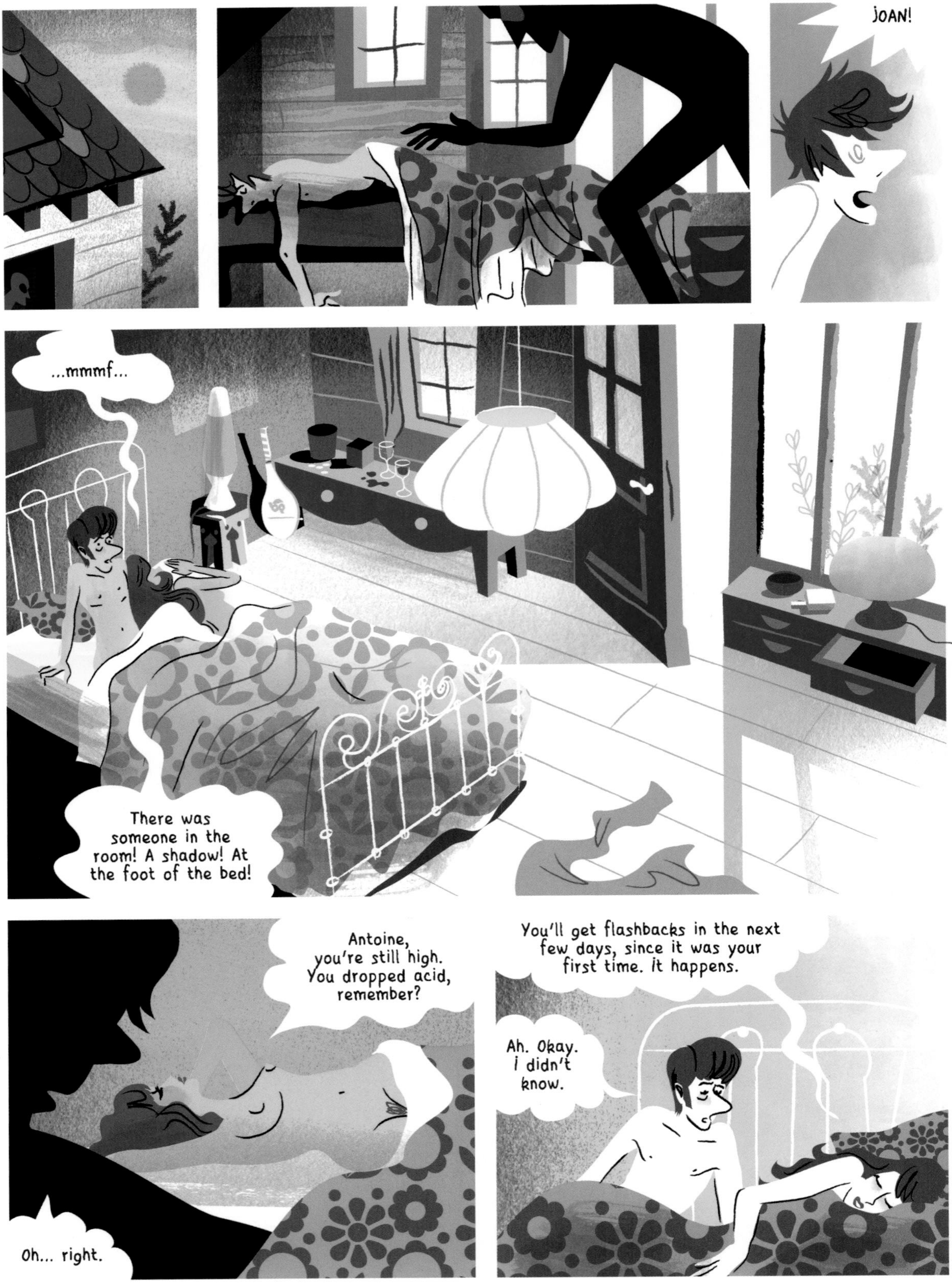
JOAN!
...mmmf...
There was someone in the room! A shadow! At the foot of the bed!
Antoine, you're still high. You dropped acid, remember?
Oh... right.
You'll get flashbacks in the next few days, since it was your first time. It happens.
Ah. Okay. I didn't know.

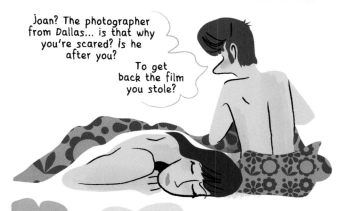

Joan? The photographer from Dallas... is that why you're scared? Is he after you?

To get back the film you stole?

Joan?

No. Actually, he's dead.

That's the part that scares me.

<Oh, my God, you poor baby!> Don't you get it yet?

All that was bullshit!

Don't hate me, but... I can't help lying, Antoine.

I've been filling your head with lies since last night.

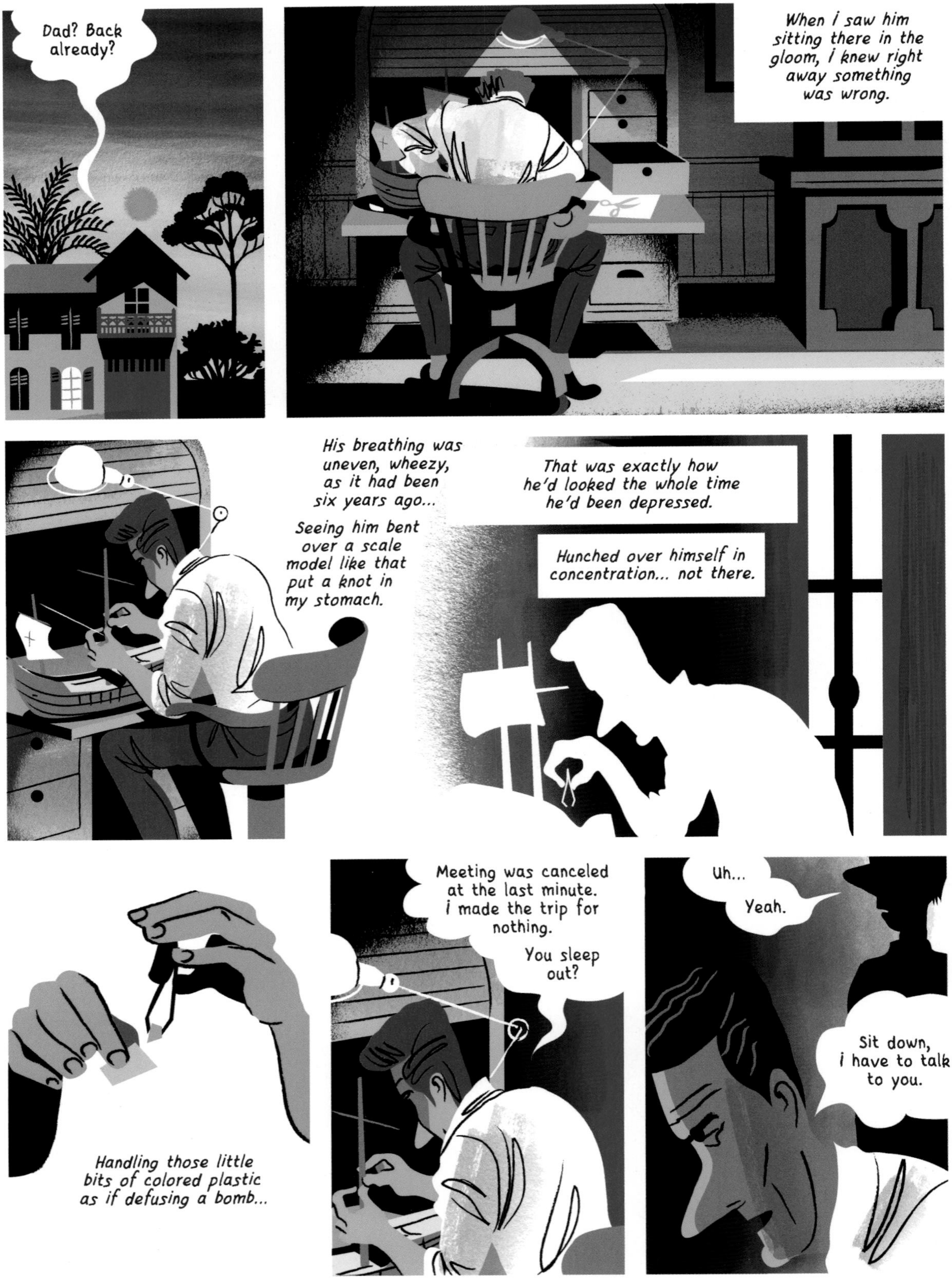
Dad? Back already?
When i saw him sitting there in the gloom, i knew right away something was wrong.
His breathing was uneven, wheezy, as it had been six years ago...
Seeing him bent over a scale model like that put a knot in my stomach.
That was exactly how he'd looked the whole time he'd been depressed.
Hunched over himself in concentration... not there.
Handling those little bits of colored plastic as if defusing a bomb...
Meeting was canceled at the last minute. i made the trip for nothing.
You sleep out?
Uh...
Yeah.
Sit down, i have to talk to you.

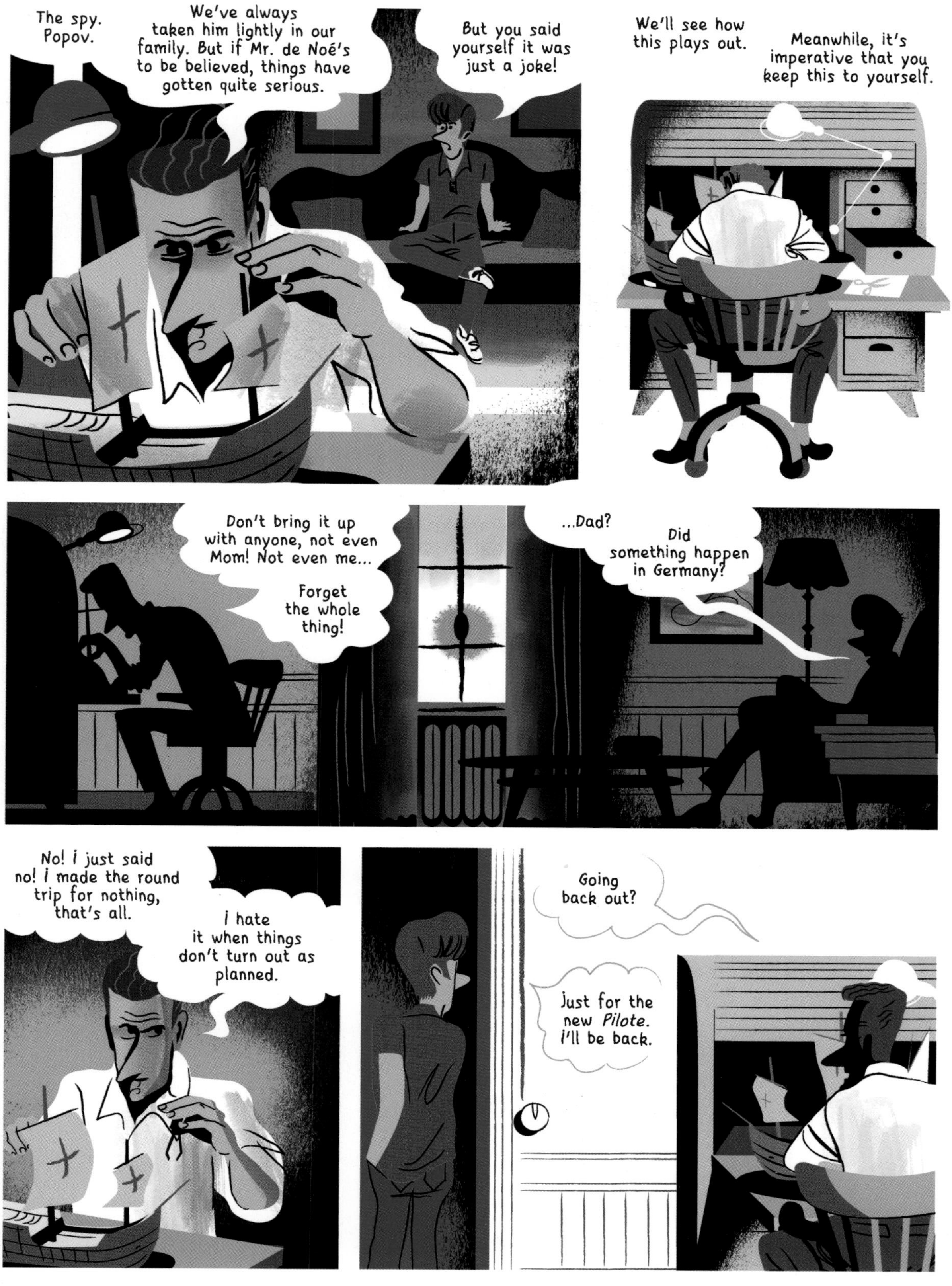
The spy. Popov.
We've always taken him lightly in our family. But if Mr. de Noé's to be believed, things have gotten quite serious.
But you said yourself it was just a joke!
We'll see how this plays out.
Meanwhile, it's imperative that you keep this to yourself.
Don't bring it up with anyone, not even Mom! Not even me...
Forget the whole thing!
...Dad?
Did something happen in Germany?
No! I just said no! I made the round trip for nothing, that's all.
I hate it when things don't turn out as planned.
Going back out?
Just for the new *Pilote*. I'll be back.

When I got to Erik's, I suddenly realized what Joan had meant by a "flashback."

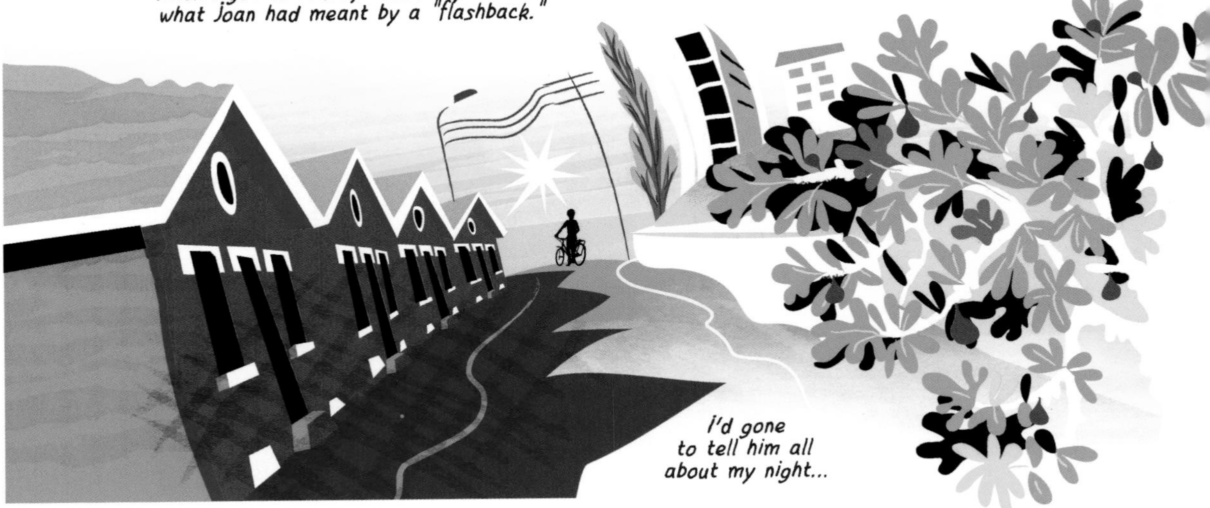
I'd gone to tell him all about my night...

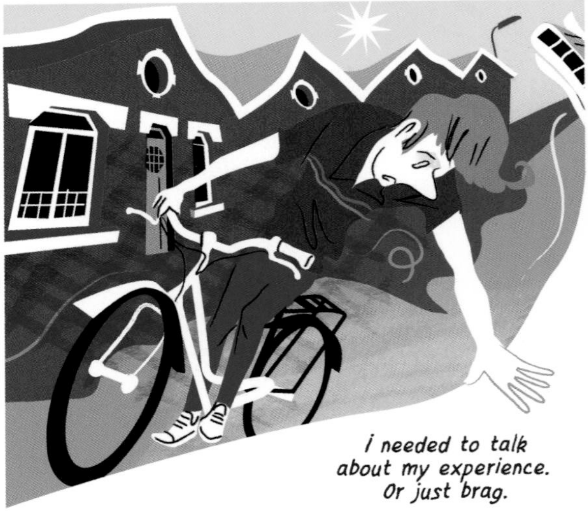
I needed to talk about my experience. Or just brag.

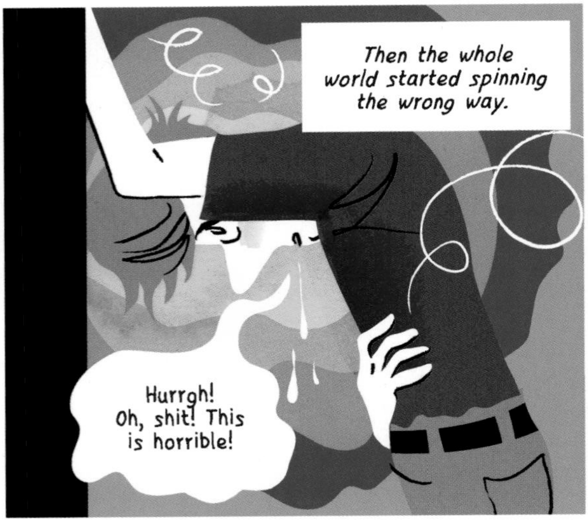
Then the whole world started spinning the wrong way.
Hurrgh! Oh, shit! This is horrible!

The minutes went by...

No one's home... I'll wait till this passes.

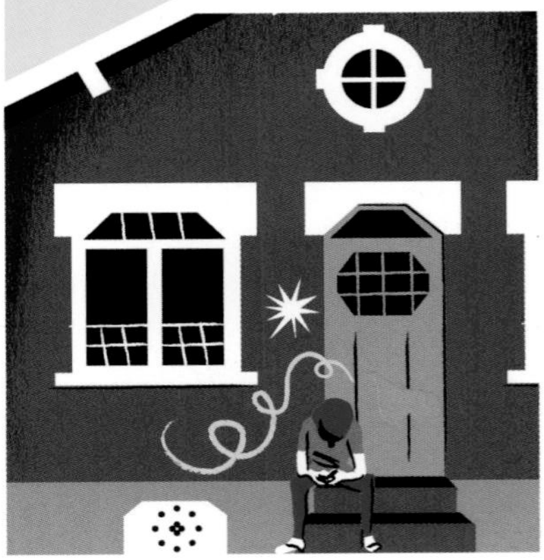

As I left, I felt like a shadow was watching me from his older brother's room.

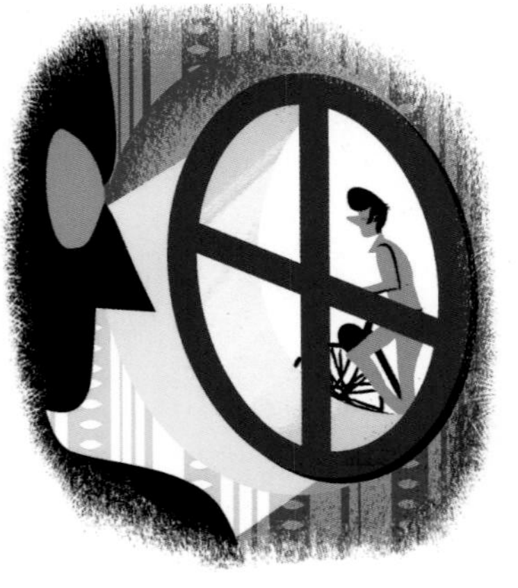

Obviously, I was seeing shadows everywhere.

It was enough to make you wonder how many demons could fit on a single blotter of acid.

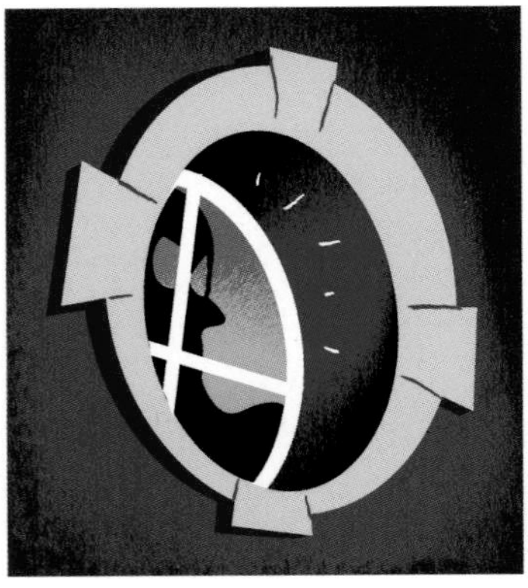

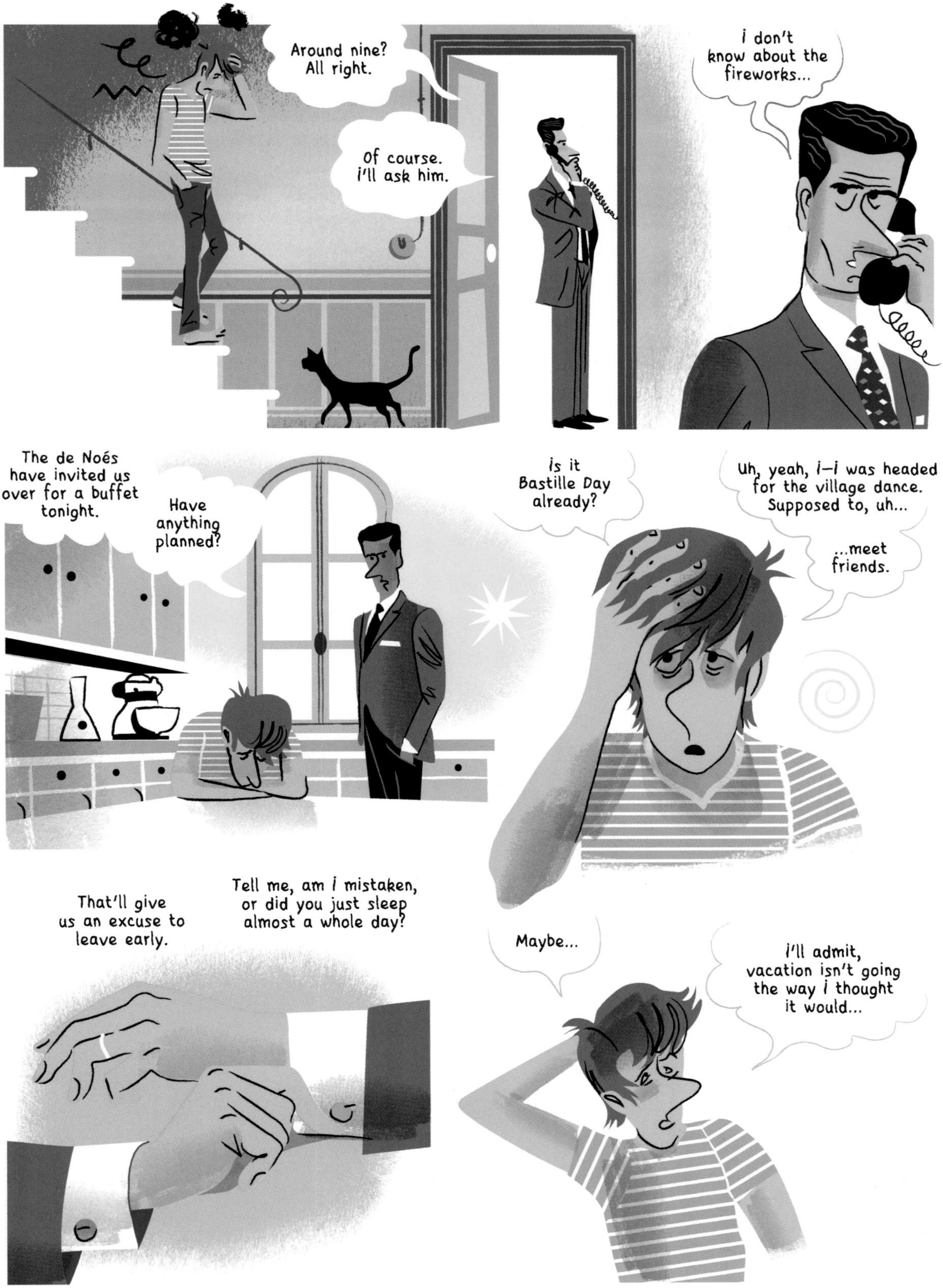

Around nine? All right.
Of course. I'll ask him.
I don't know about the fireworks...
The de Noés have invited us over for a buffet tonight.
Have anything planned?
Is it Bastille Day already?
Uh, yeah, I—I was headed for the village dance. Supposed to, uh...
...meet friends.
That'll give us an excuse to leave early.
Tell me, am I mistaken, or did you just sleep almost a whole day?
Maybe...
I'll admit, vacation isn't going the way I thought it would...

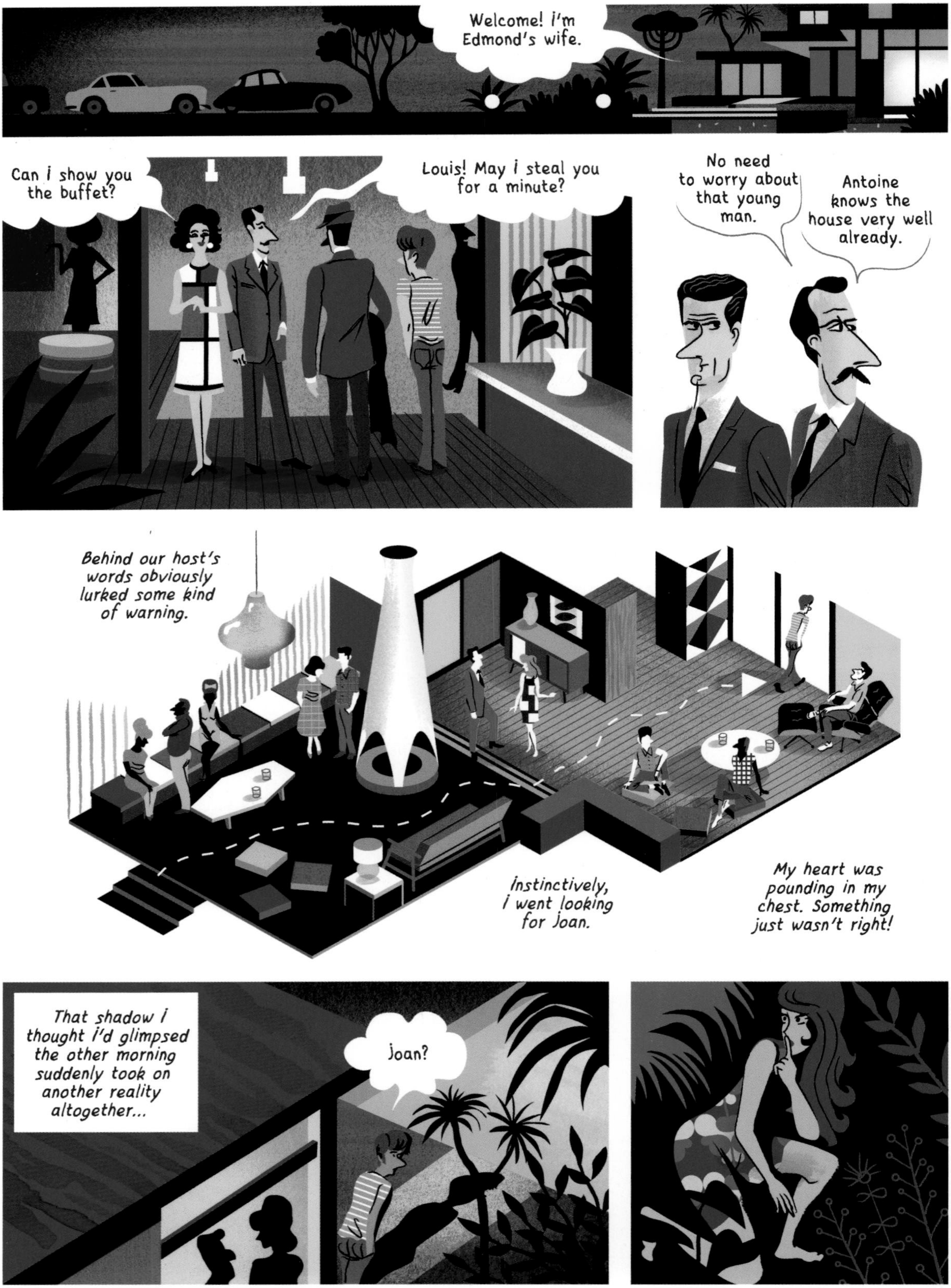
Welcome! I'm Edmond's wife.
Can I show you the buffet?
Louis! May I steal you for a minute?
No need to worry about that young man.
Antoine knows the house very well already.
Behind our host's words obviously lurked some kind of warning.
Instinctively, I went looking for Joan.
My heart was pounding in my chest. Something just wasn't right!
That shadow I thought I'd glimpsed the other morning suddenly took on another reality altogether...
Joan?

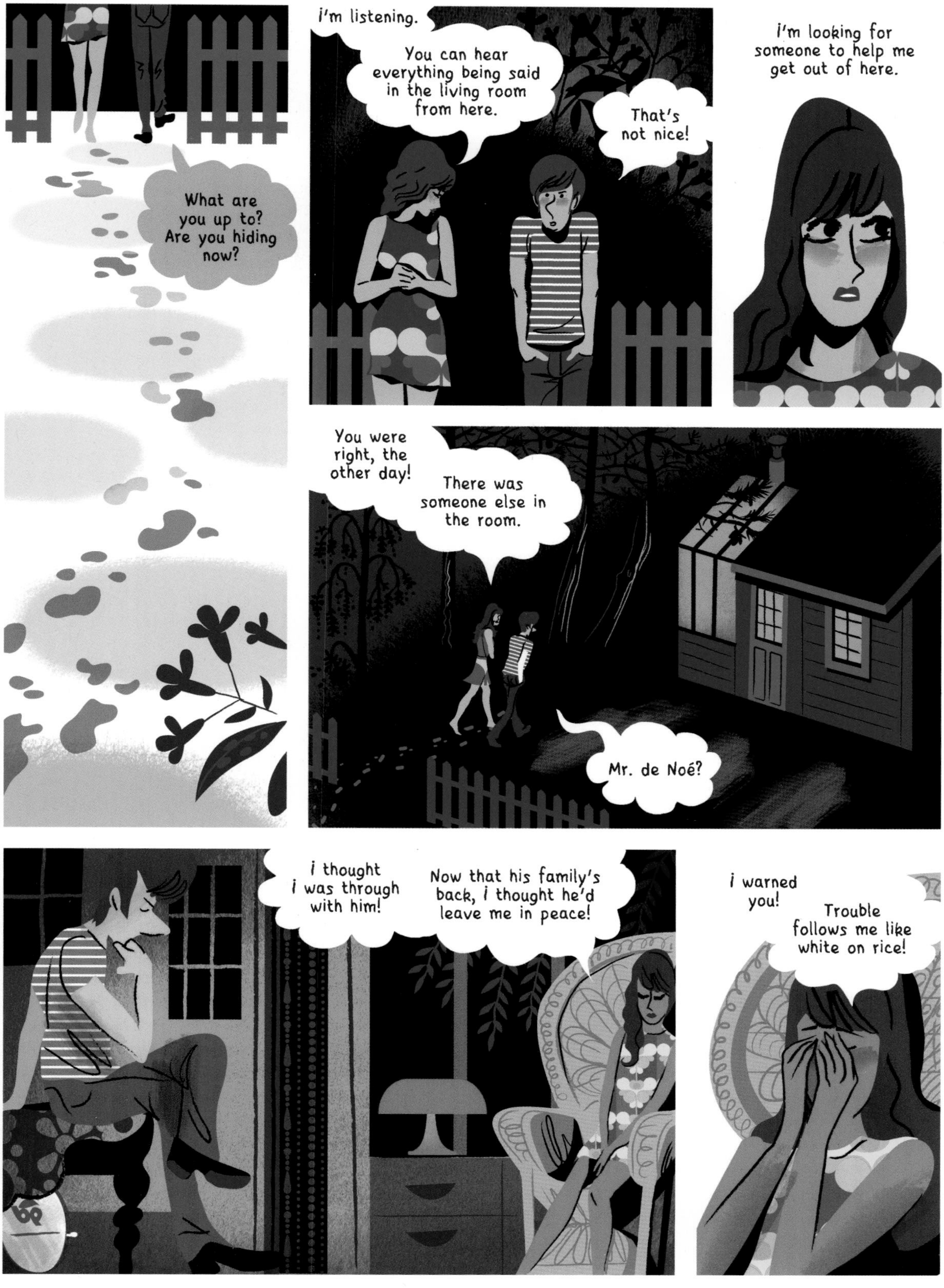
What are you up to? Are you hiding now?
i'm listening.
You can hear everything being said in the living room from here.
That's not nice!
i'm looking for someone to help me get out of here.
You were right, the other day!
There was someone else in the room.
Mr. de Noé?
i thought i was through with him!
Now that his family's back, i thought he'd leave me in peace!
i warned you!
Trouble follows me like white on rice!

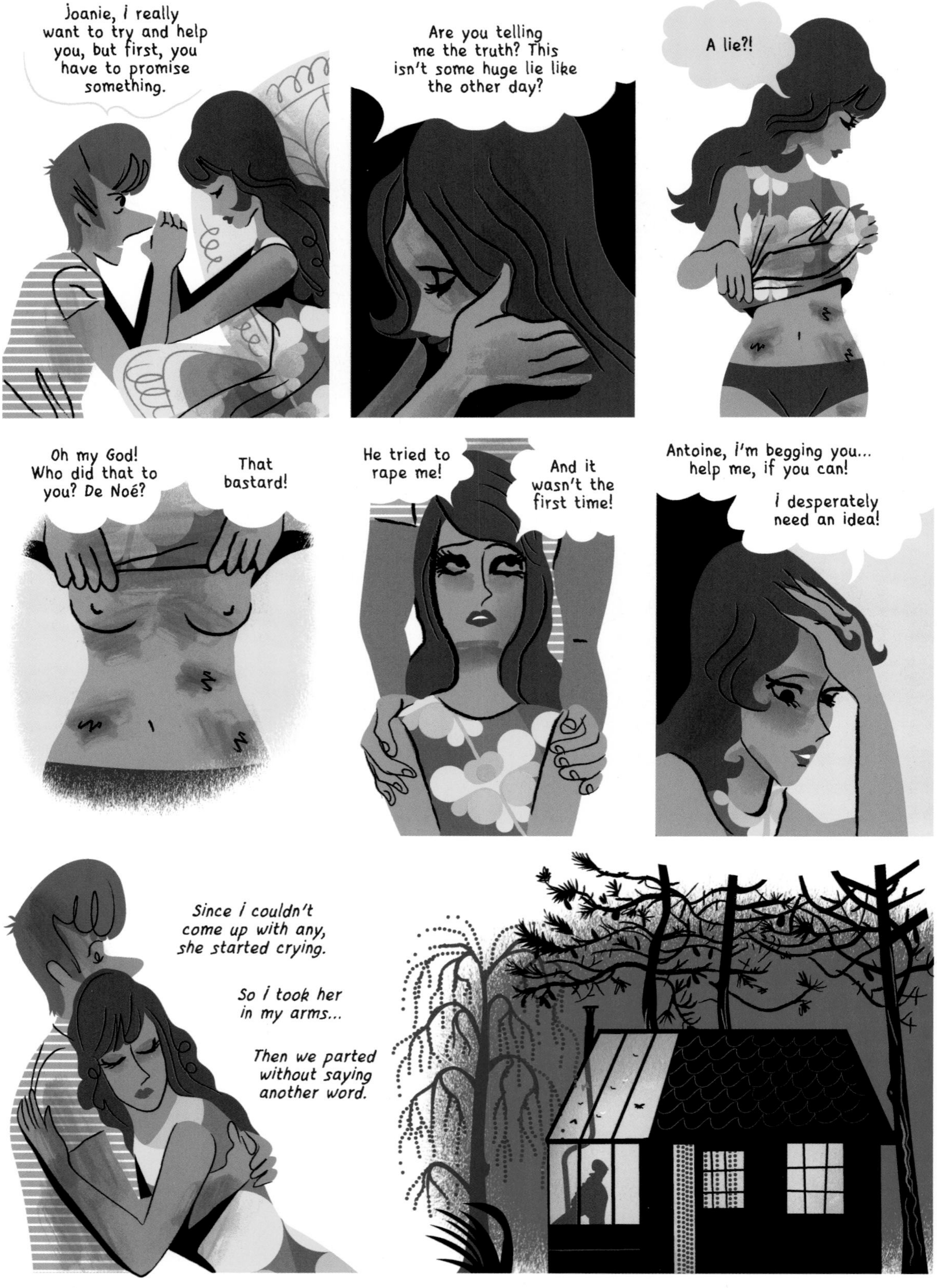
Joanie, I really want to try and help you, but first, you have to promise something.
Are you telling me the truth? This isn't some huge lie like the other day?
A lie?!
Oh my God! Who did that to you? De Noé?
That bastard!
He tried to rape me!
And it wasn't the first time!
Antoine, I'm begging you... help me, if you can!
I desperately need an idea!
Since I couldn't come up with any, she started crying.
So I took her in my arms...
Then we parted without saying another word.

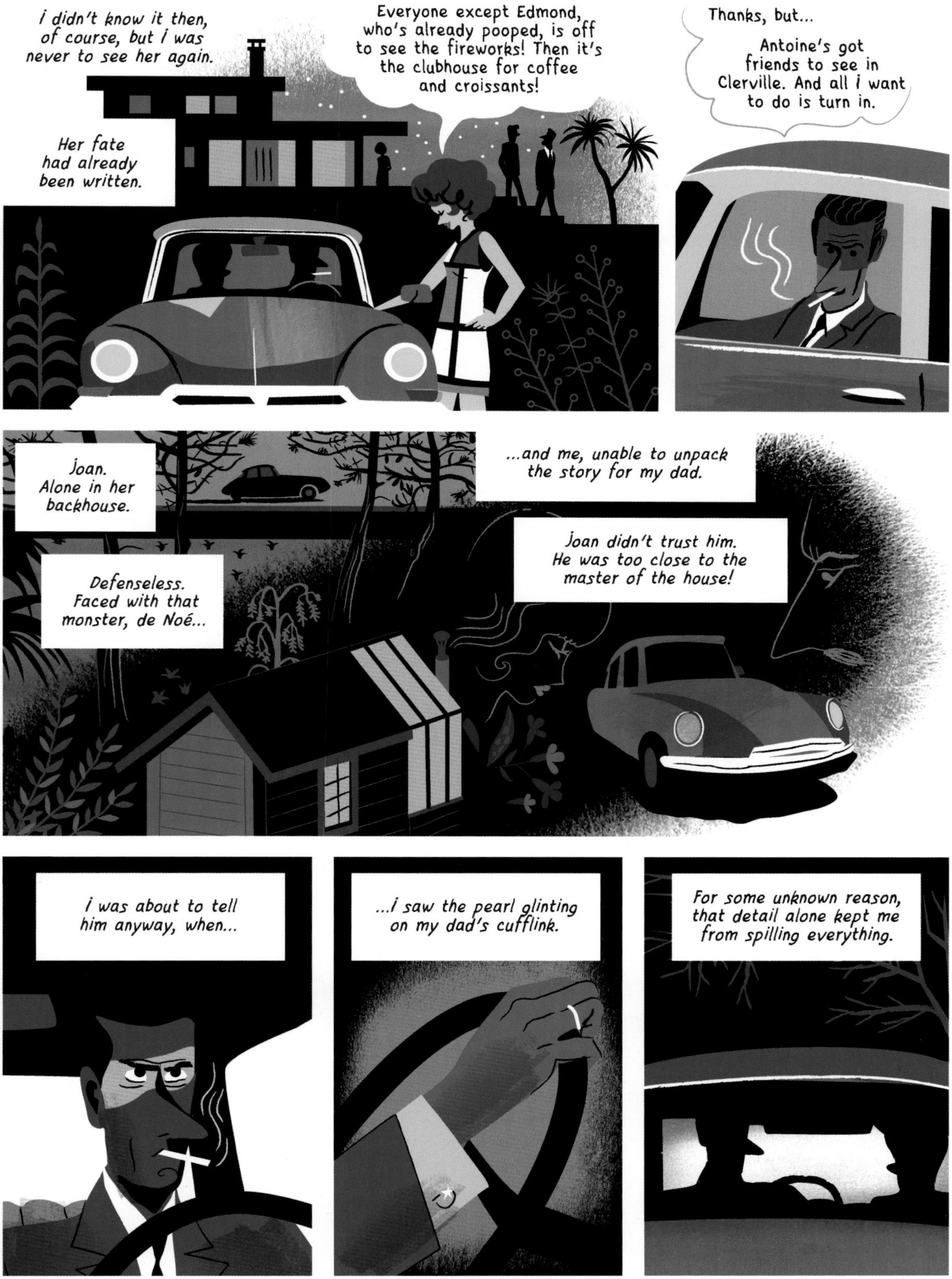
I didn't know it then, of course, but I was never to see her again.
Her fate had already been written.
Everyone except Edmond, who's already pooped, is off to see the fireworks! Then it's the clubhouse for coffee and croissants!
Thanks, but...
Antoine's got friends to see in Clerville. And all I want to do is turn in.
Joan. Alone in her backhouse.
Defenseless. Faced with that monster, de Noé...
...and me, unable to unpack the story for my dad.
Joan didn't trust him. He was too close to the master of the house!
I was about to tell him anyway, when...
...I saw the pearl glinting on my dad's cufflink.
For some unknown reason, that detail alone kept me from spilling everything.

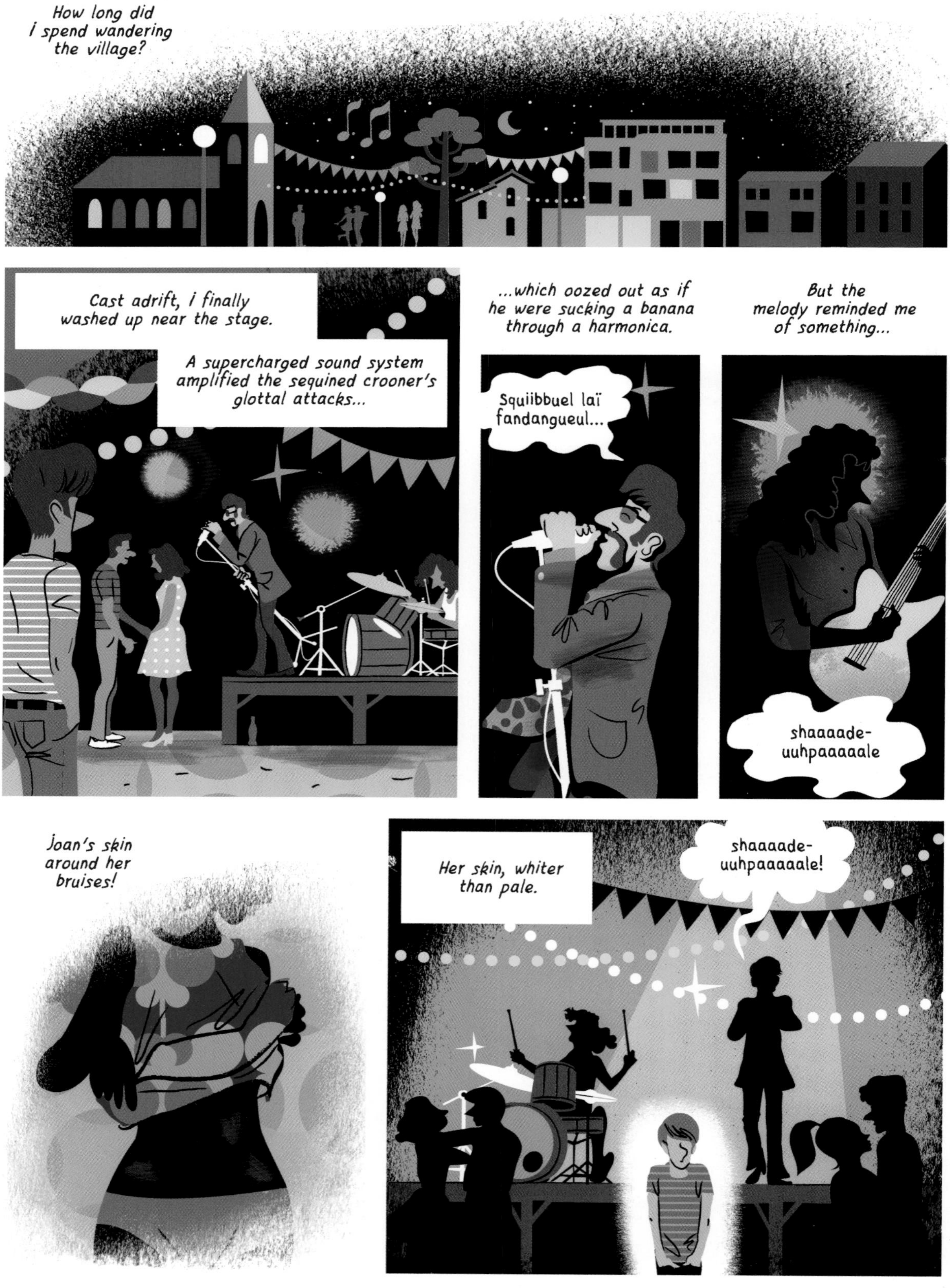
How long did I spend wandering the village?
Cast adrift, I finally washed up near the stage.
A supercharged sound system amplified the sequined crooner's glottal attacks...
...which oozed out as if he were sucking a banana through a harmonica.
Squiibbuel laï fandangueul...
But the melody reminded me of something...
shaaaade-uuhpaaaaale
Joan's skin around her bruises!
Her skin, whiter than pale.
shaaaade-uuhpaaaaale!

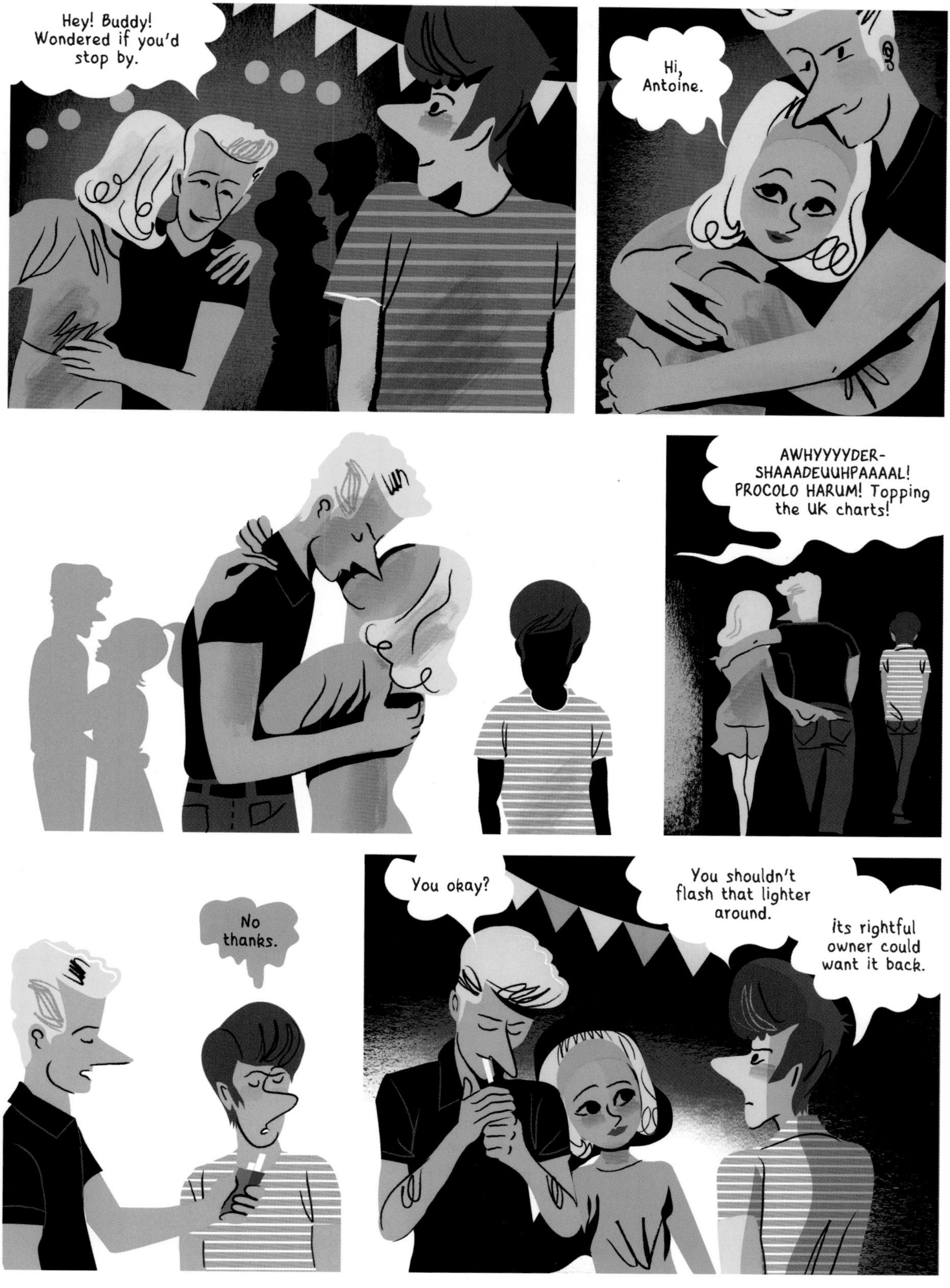
Hey! Buddy! Wondered if you'd stop by.
Hi, Antoine.
AWHYYYYDER-SHAAADEUUHPAAAAL! PROCOLO HARUM! Topping the UK charts!
No thanks.
You okay?
You shouldn't flash that lighter around.
its rightful owner could want it back.

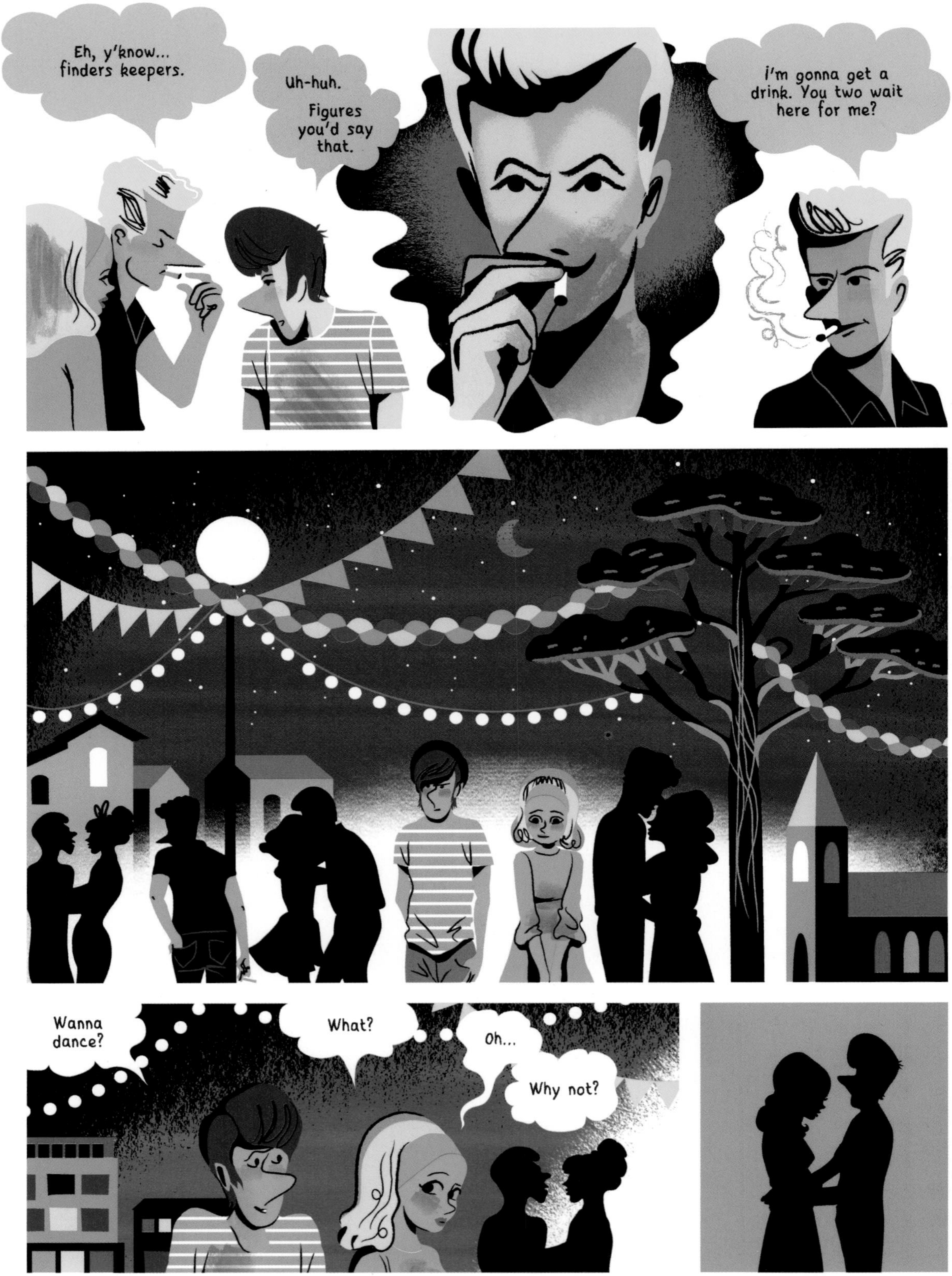

Eh, y'know... finders keepers.
Uh-huh.
Figures you'd say that.
I'm gonna get a drink. You two wait here for me?
Wanna dance?
What?
Oh...
Why not?

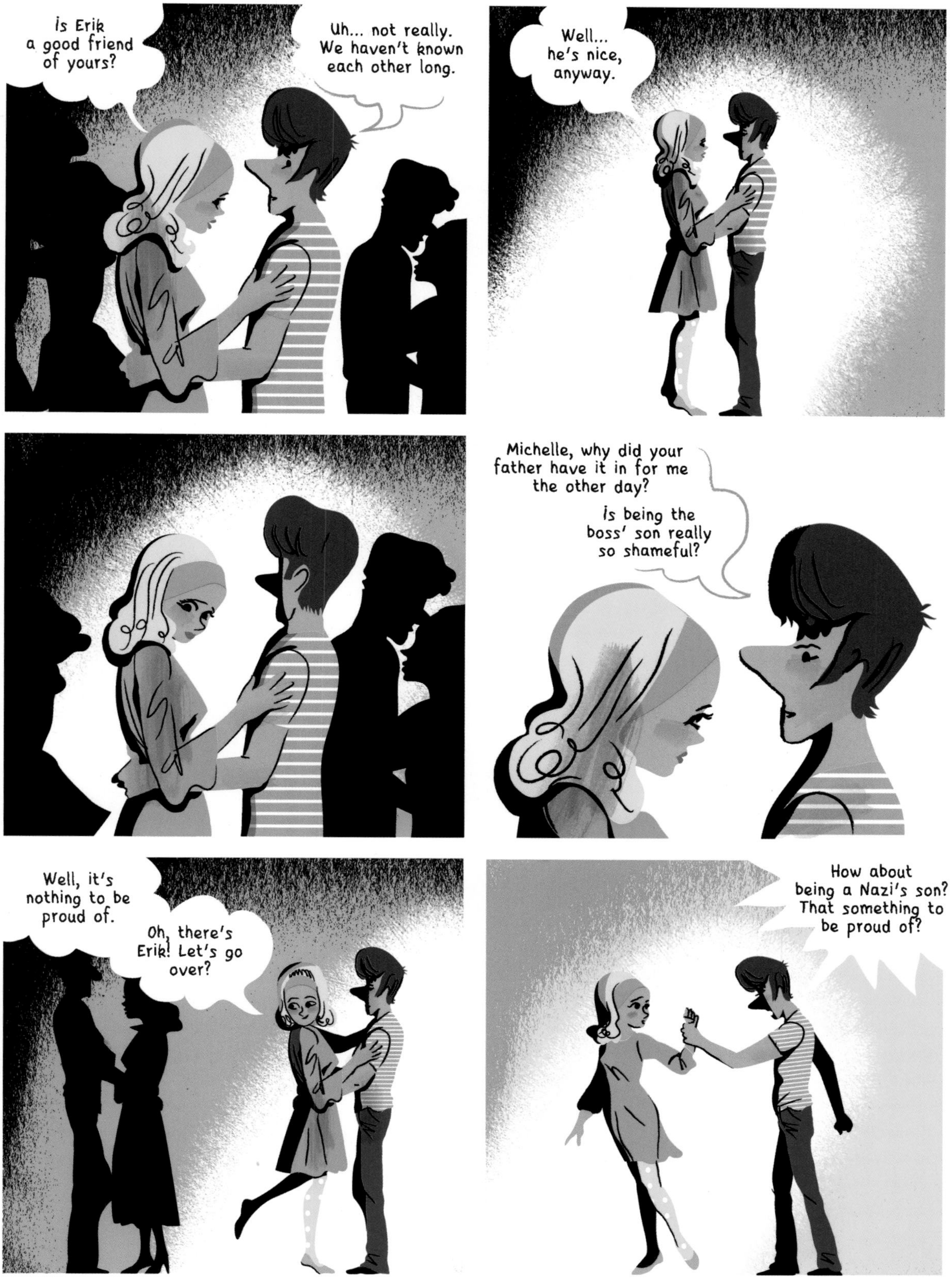
Is Erik a good friend of yours?
Uh... not really. We haven't known each other long.
Well... he's nice, anyway.
Michelle, why did your father have it in for me the other day?
Is being the boss' son really so shameful?
Well, it's nothing to be proud of.
Oh, there's Erik! Let's go over?
How about being a Nazi's son? That something to be proud of?

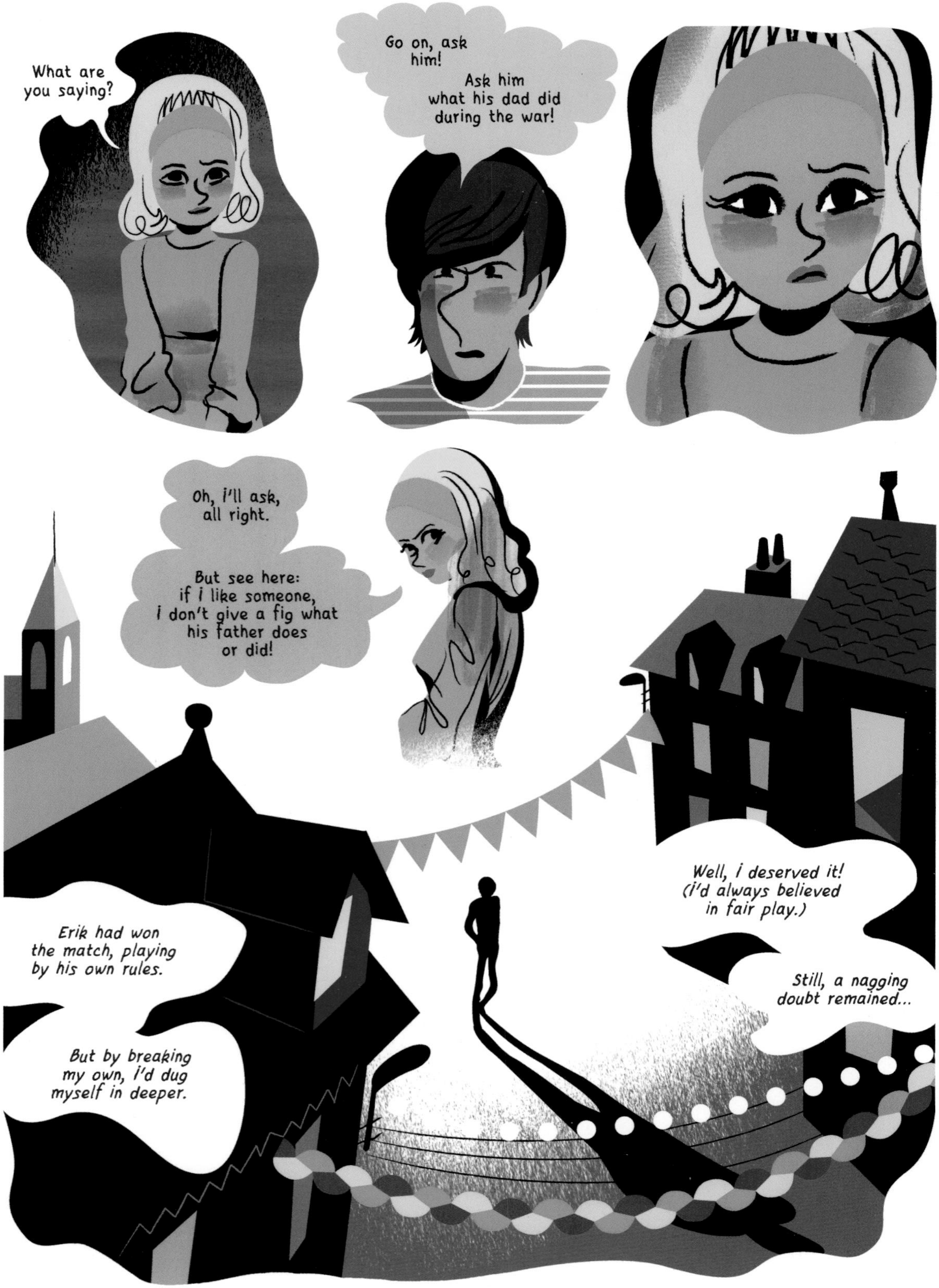
What are you saying?
Go on, ask him!
Ask him what his dad did during the war!
Oh, i'll ask, all right.
But see here: if i like someone, i don't give a fig what his father does or did!
Erik had won the match, playing by his own rules.
But by breaking my own, i'd dug myself in deeper.
Well, i deserved it! (i'd always believed in fair play.)
Still, a nagging doubt remained...

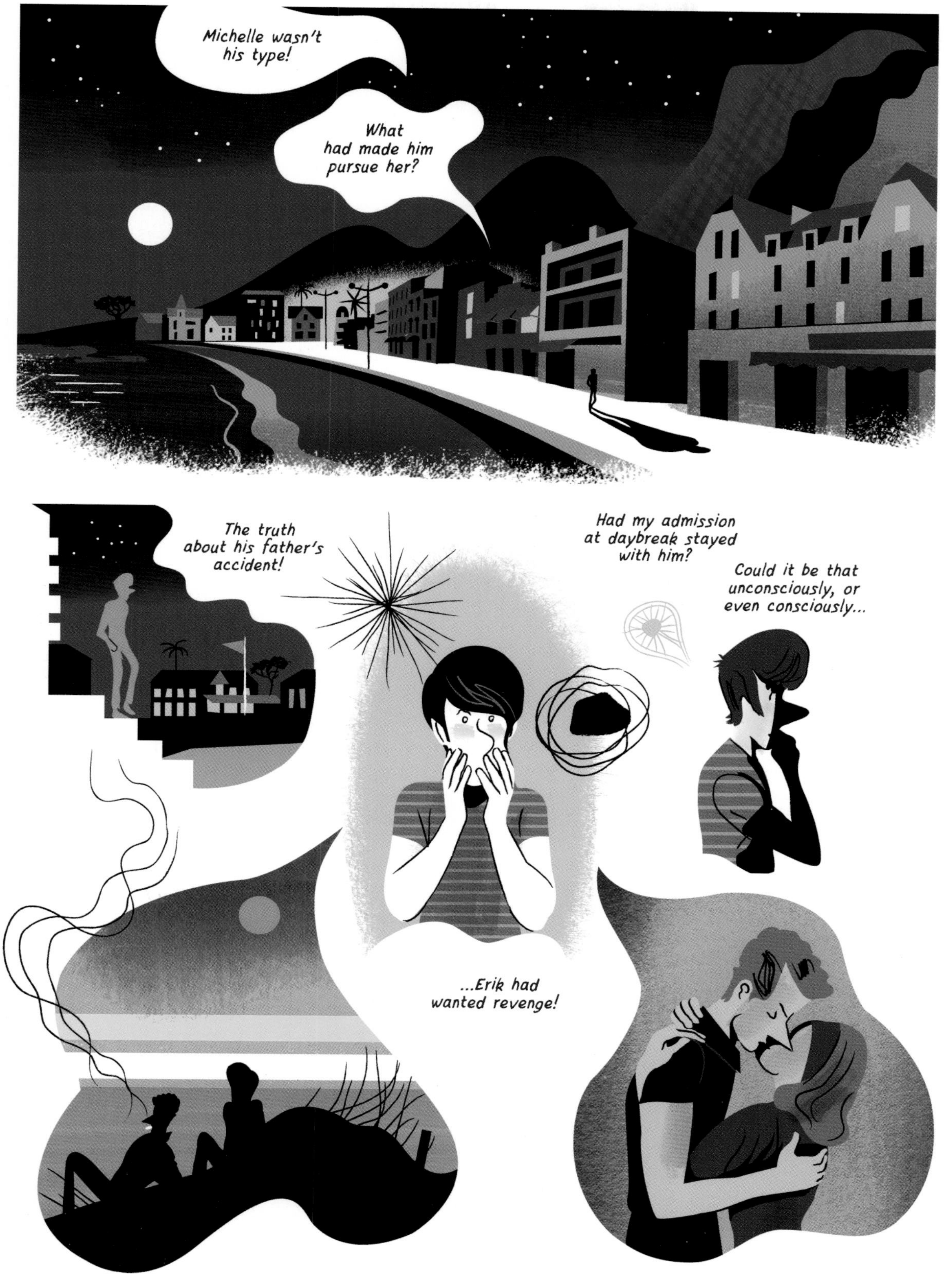
Michelle wasn't his type!
What had made him pursue her?
The truth about his father's accident!
Had my admission at daybreak stayed with him?
Could it be that unconsciously, or even consciously...
...Erik had wanted revenge!

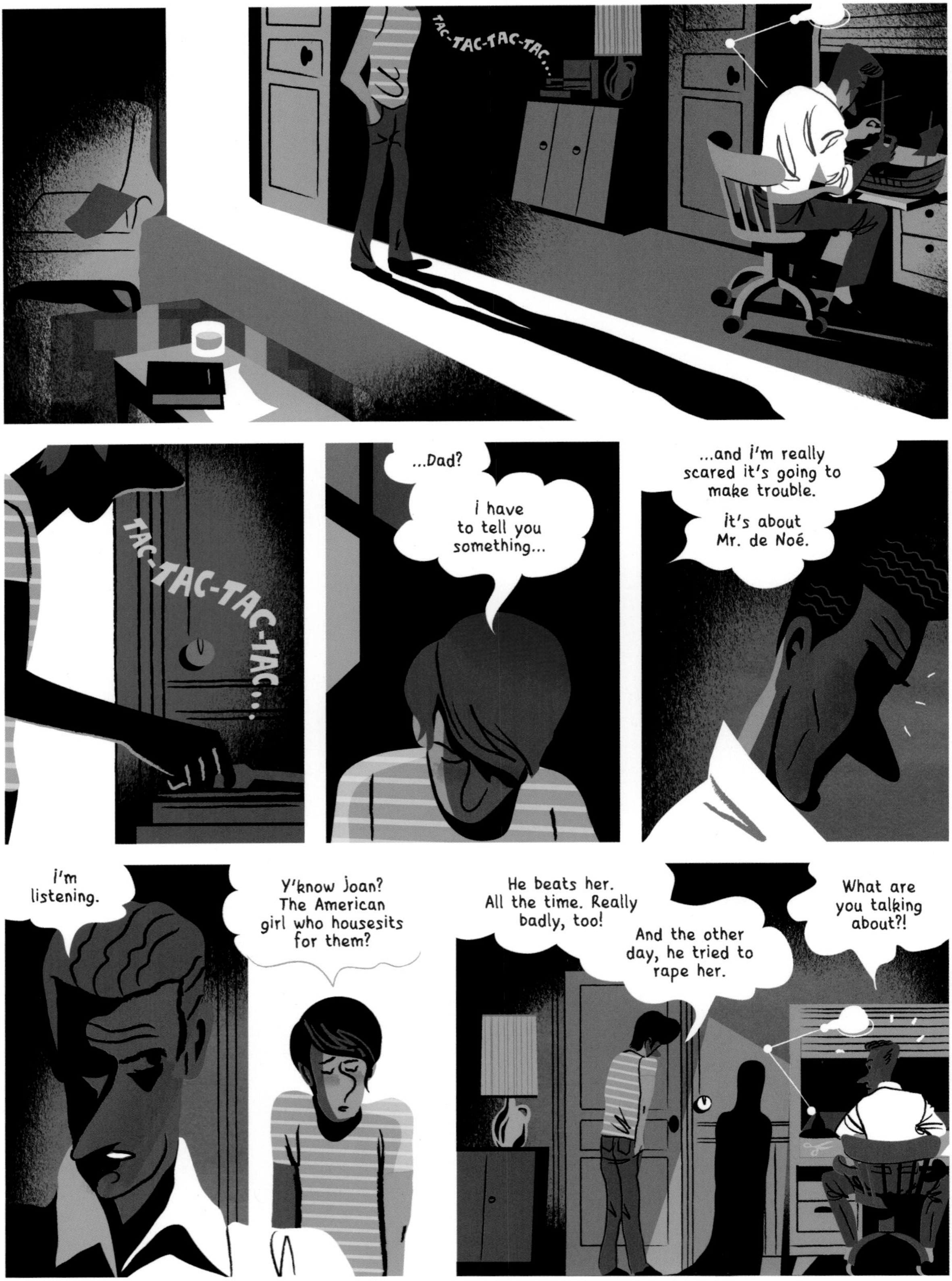
TAC-TAC-TAC-TAC...
TAC-TAC-TAC-TAC...
...Dad?
i have to tell you something...
...and i'm really scared it's going to make trouble.
it's about Mr. de Noé.
i'm listening.
Y'know Joan? The American girl who housesits for them?
He beats her. All the time. Really badly, too!
And the other day, he tried to rape her.
What are you talking about?!

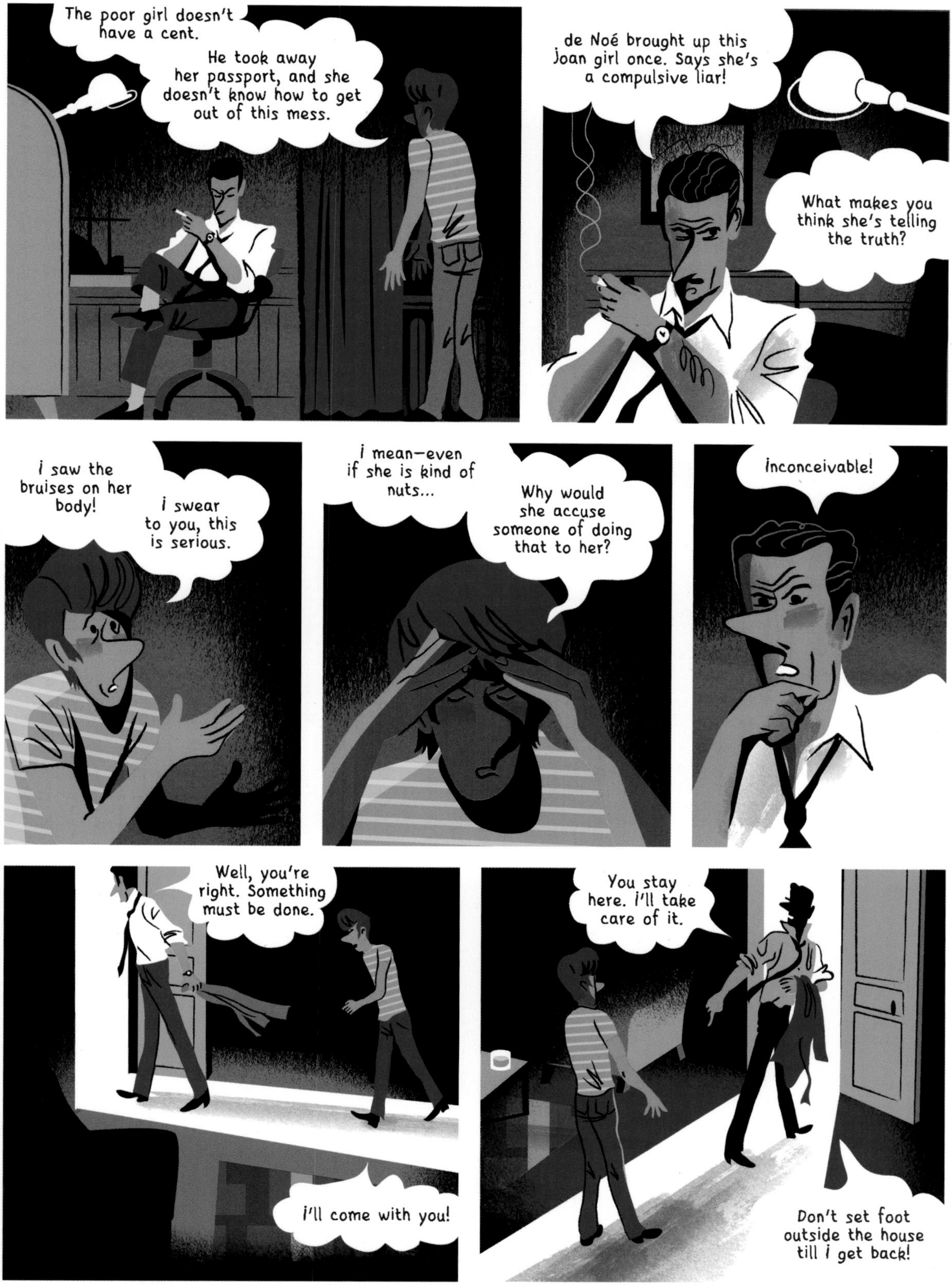
The poor girl doesn't have a cent.
He took away her passport, and she doesn't know how to get out of this mess.
de Noé brought up this Joan girl once. Says she's a compulsive liar!
What makes you think she's telling the truth?
I saw the bruises on her body!
I swear to you, this is serious.
I mean—even if she is kind of nuts...
Why would she accuse someone of doing that to her?
Inconceivable!
Well, you're right. Something must be done.
I'll come with you!
You stay here. I'll take care of it.
Don't set foot outside the house till I get back!

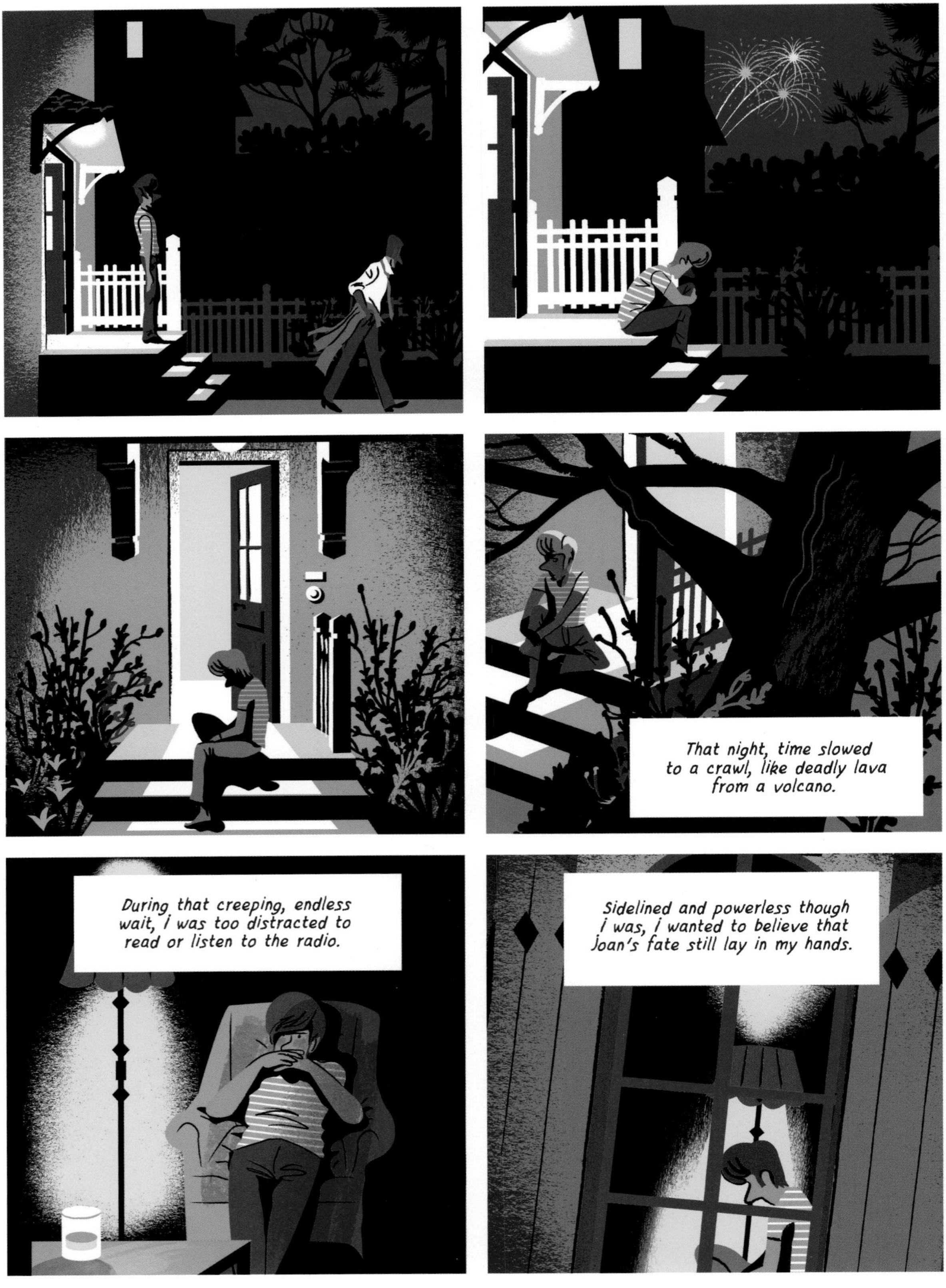
That night, time slowed to a crawl, like deadly lava from a volcano.
During that creeping, endless wait, I was too distracted to read or listen to the radio.
Sidelined and powerless though I was, I wanted to believe that Joan's fate still lay in my hands.

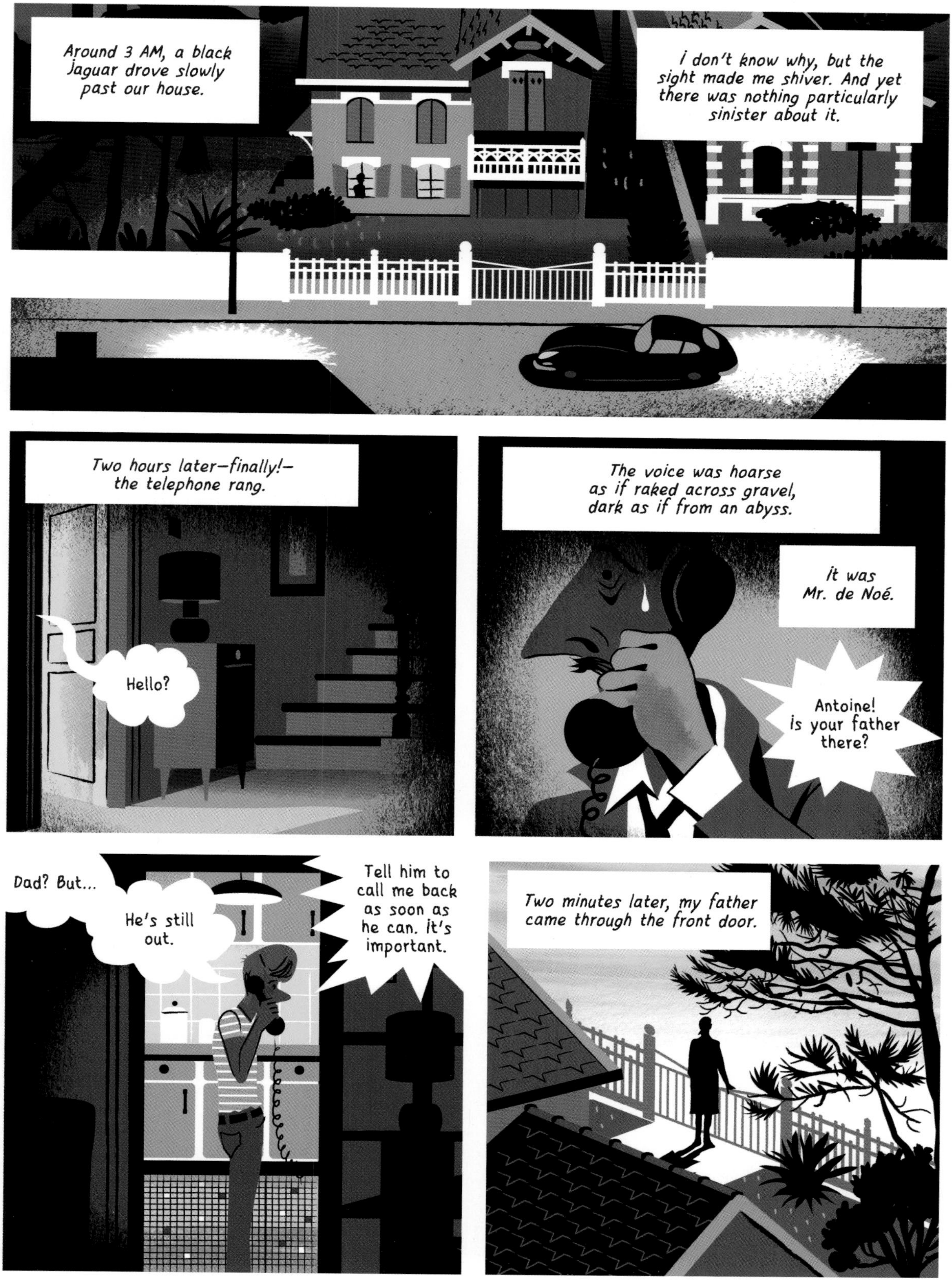
Around 3 AM, a black Jaguar drove slowly past our house.
I don't know why, but the sight made me shiver. And yet there was nothing particularly sinister about it.
Two hours later—finally!— the telephone rang.
Hello?
The voice was hoarse as if raked across gravel, dark as if from an abyss.
It was Mr. de Noé.
Antoine! Is your father there?
Dad? But...
He's still out.
Tell him to call me back as soon as he can. It's important.
Two minutes later, my father came through the front door.

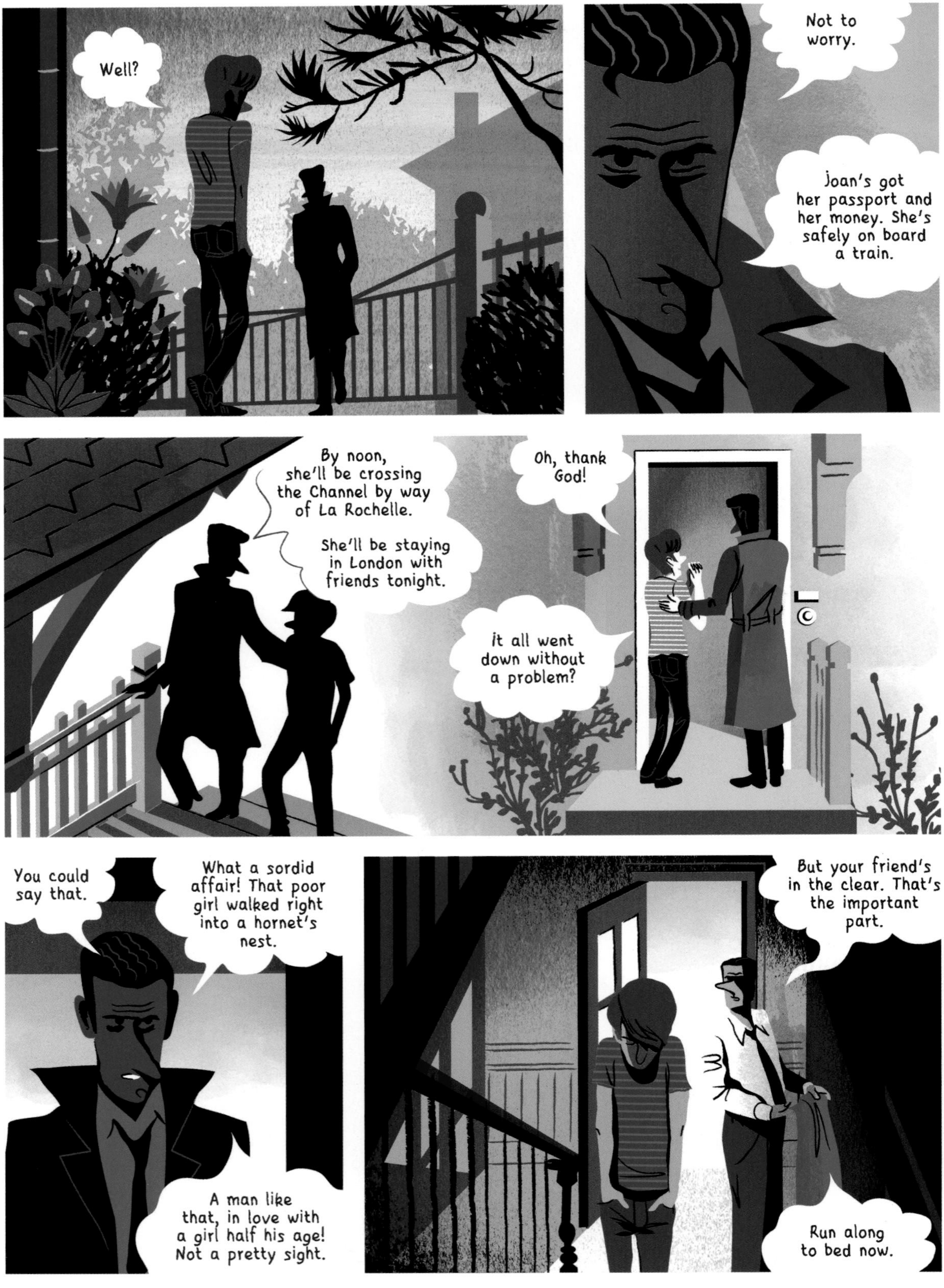

Well?
Not to worry.
Joan's got her passport and her money. She's safely on board a train.
By noon, she'll be crossing the Channel by way of La Rochelle.
She'll be staying in London with friends tonight.
Oh, thank God!
It all went down without a problem?
You could say that.
What a sordid affair! That poor girl walked right into a hornet's nest.
A man like that, in love with a girl half his age! Not a pretty sight.
But your friend's in the clear. That's the important part.
Run along to bed now.

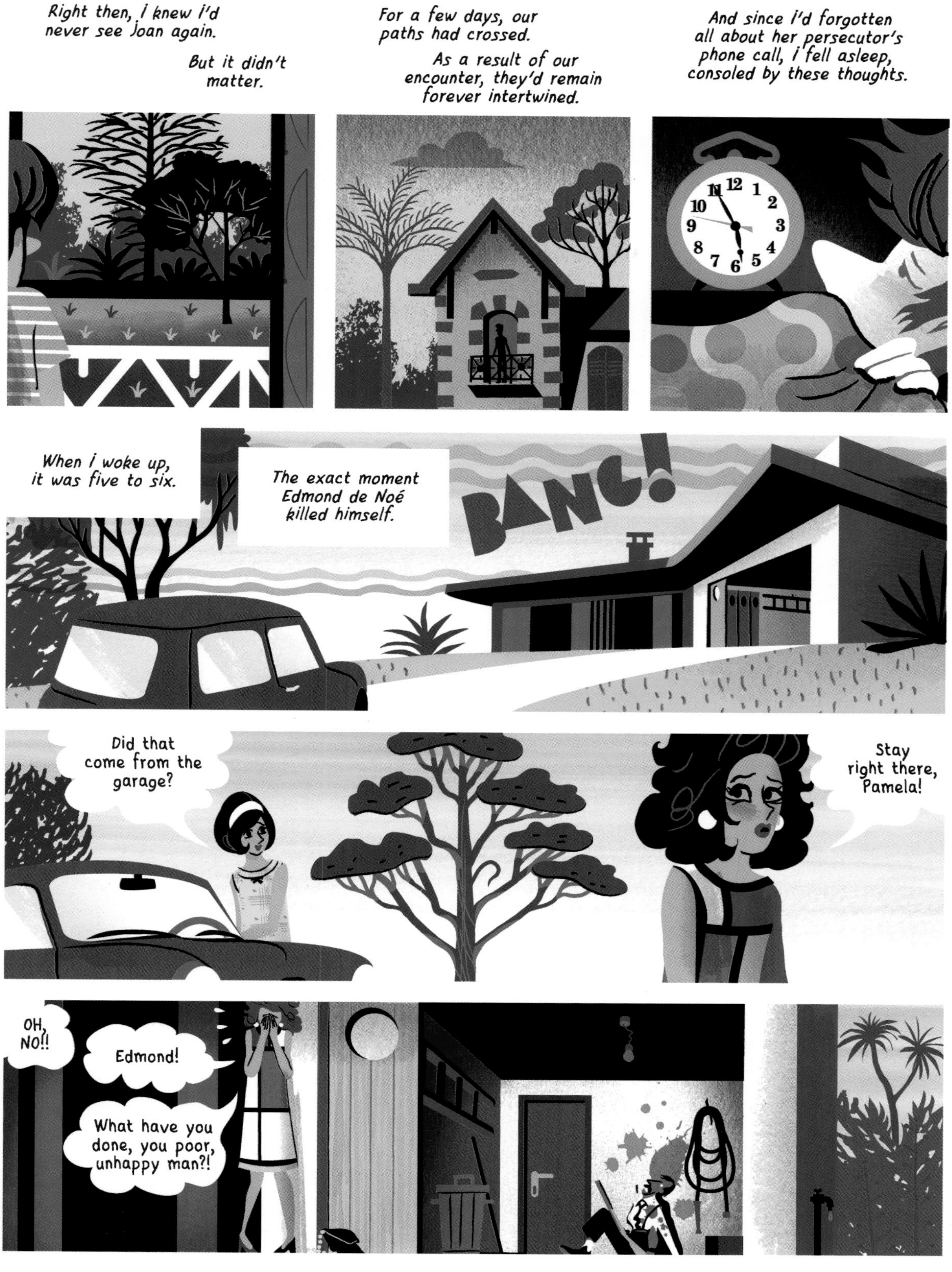
Right then, i knew i'd never see Joan again.
But it didn't matter.
For a few days, our paths had crossed.
As a result of our encounter, they'd remain forever intertwined.
And since i'd forgotten all about her persecutor's phone call, i fell asleep, consoled by these thoughts.
When i woke up, it was five to six.
The exact moment Edmond de Noé killed himself.
BANG!
Did that come from the garage?
Stay right there, Pamela!
OH, NO!!
Edmond!
What have you done, you poor, unhappy man?!

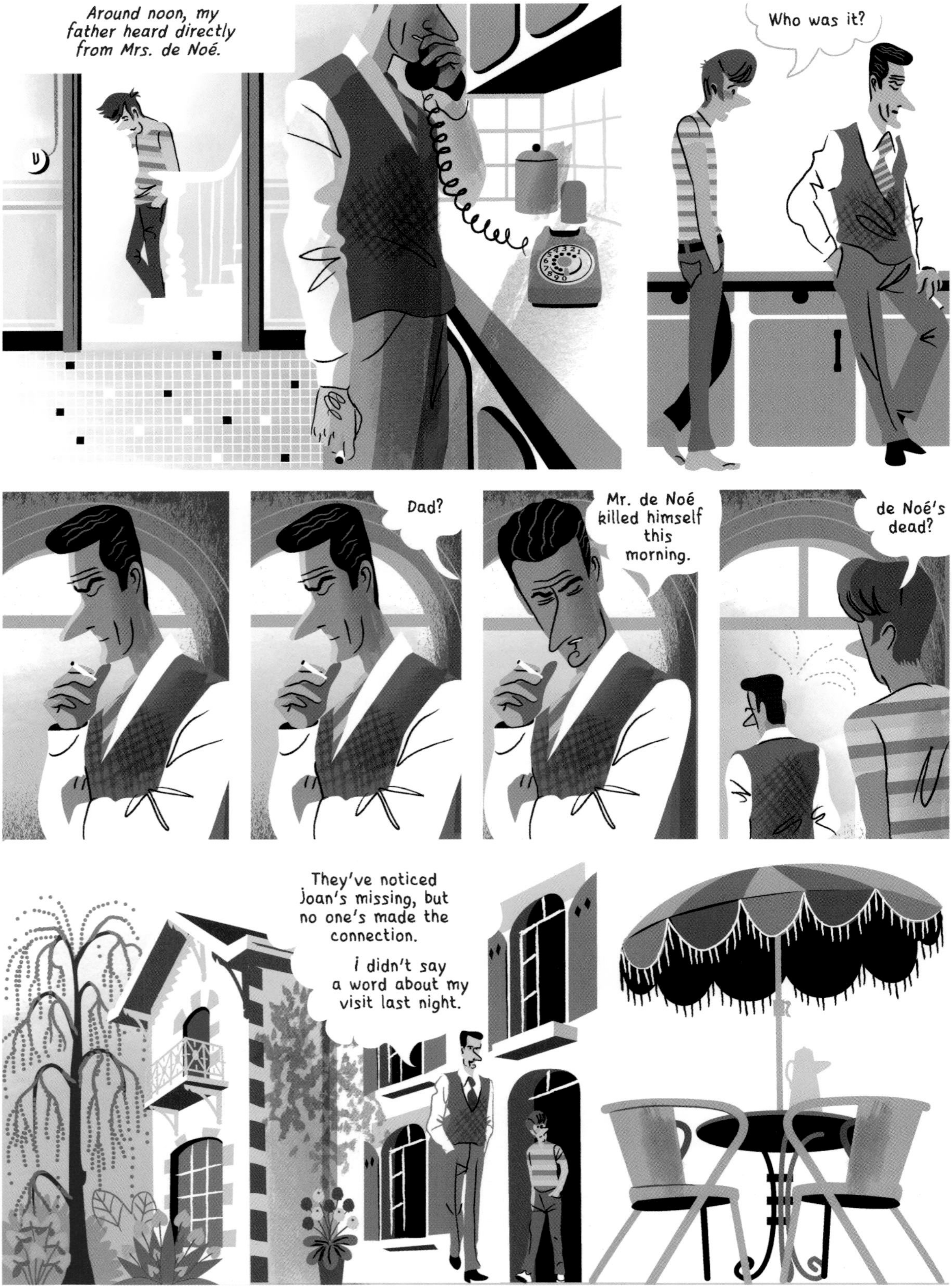
Around noon, my father heard directly from Mrs. de Noé.
Who was it?
Dad?
Mr. de Noé killed himself this morning.
de Noé's dead?
They've noticed Joan's missing, but no one's made the connection.
I didn't say a word about my visit last night.

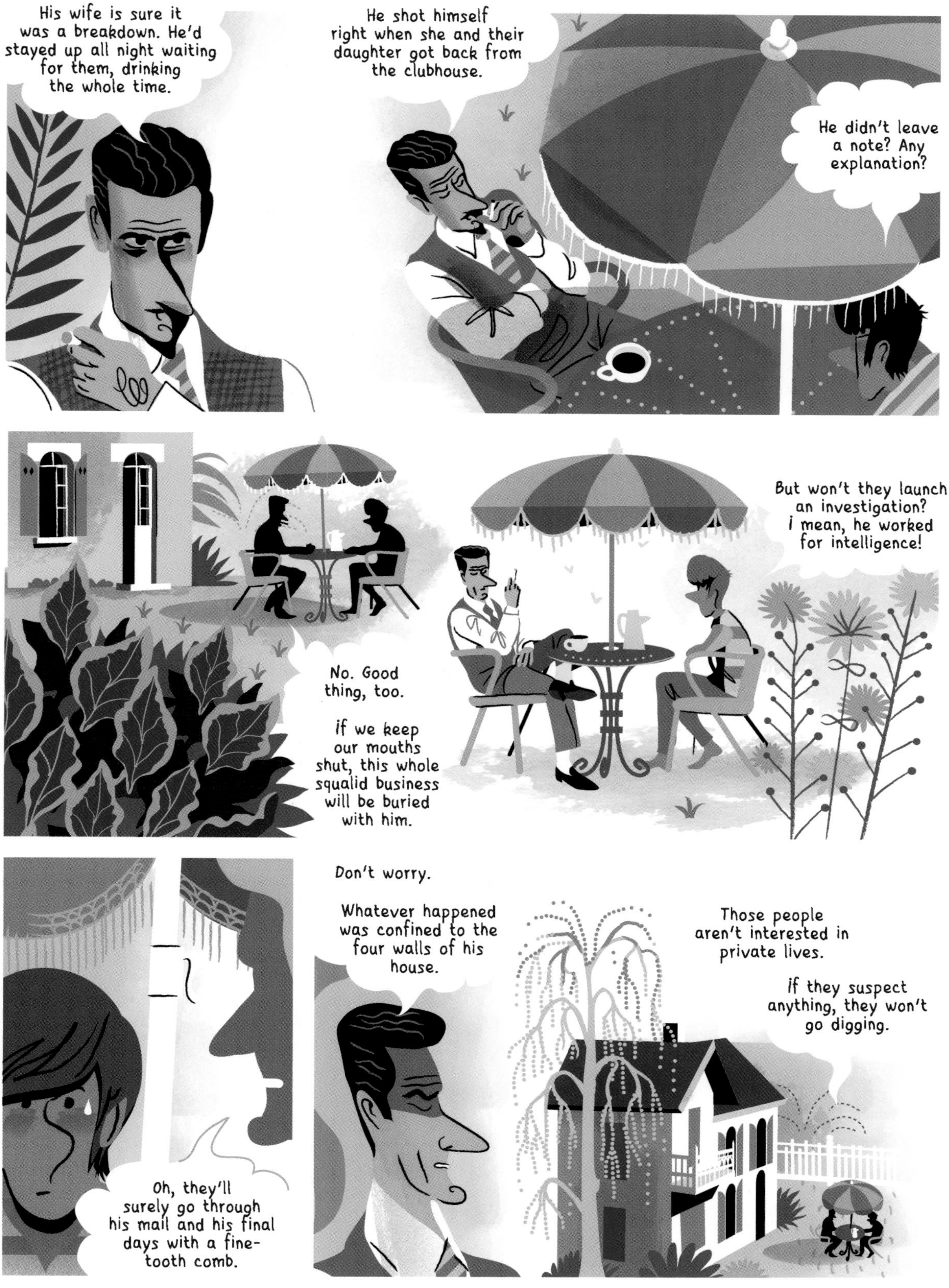
His wife is sure it was a breakdown. He'd stayed up all night waiting for them, drinking the whole time.
He shot himself right when she and their daughter got back from the clubhouse.
He didn't leave a note? Any explanation?
No. Good thing, too.
If we keep our mouths shut, this whole squalid business will be buried with him.
But won't they launch an investigation? I mean, he worked for intelligence!
Oh, they'll surely go through his mail and his final days with a fine-tooth comb.
Don't worry.
Whatever happened was confined to the four walls of his house.
Those people aren't interested in private lives.
If they suspect anything, they won't go digging.

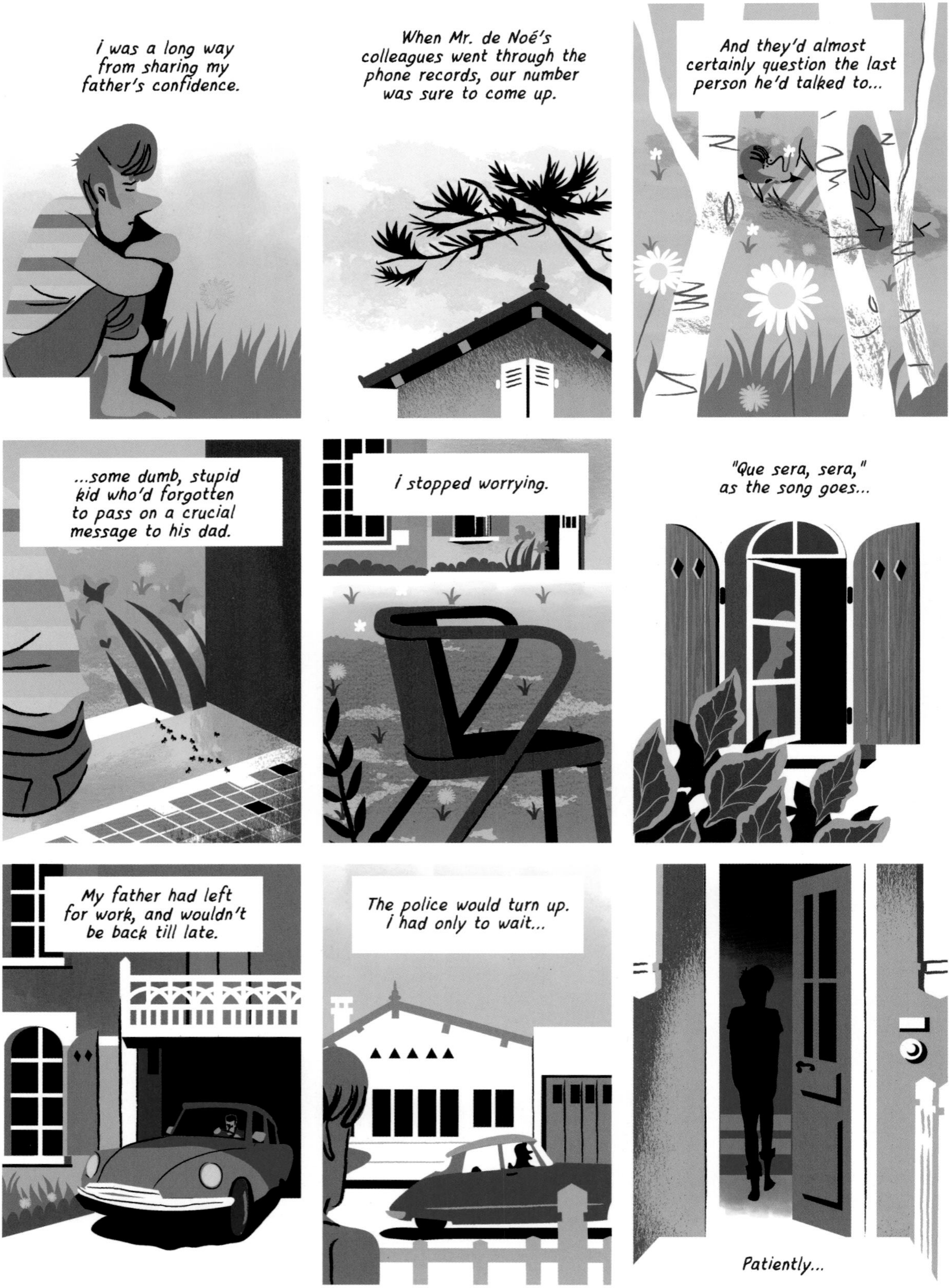

i was a long way from sharing my father's confidence.
When Mr. de Noé's colleagues went through the phone records, our number was sure to come up.
And they'd almost certainly question the last person he'd talked to...
...some dumb, stupid kid who'd forgotten to pass on a crucial message to his dad.
i stopped worrying.
"Que sera, sera," as the song goes...
My father had left for work, and wouldn't be back till late.
The police would turn up. i had only to wait...
Patiently...

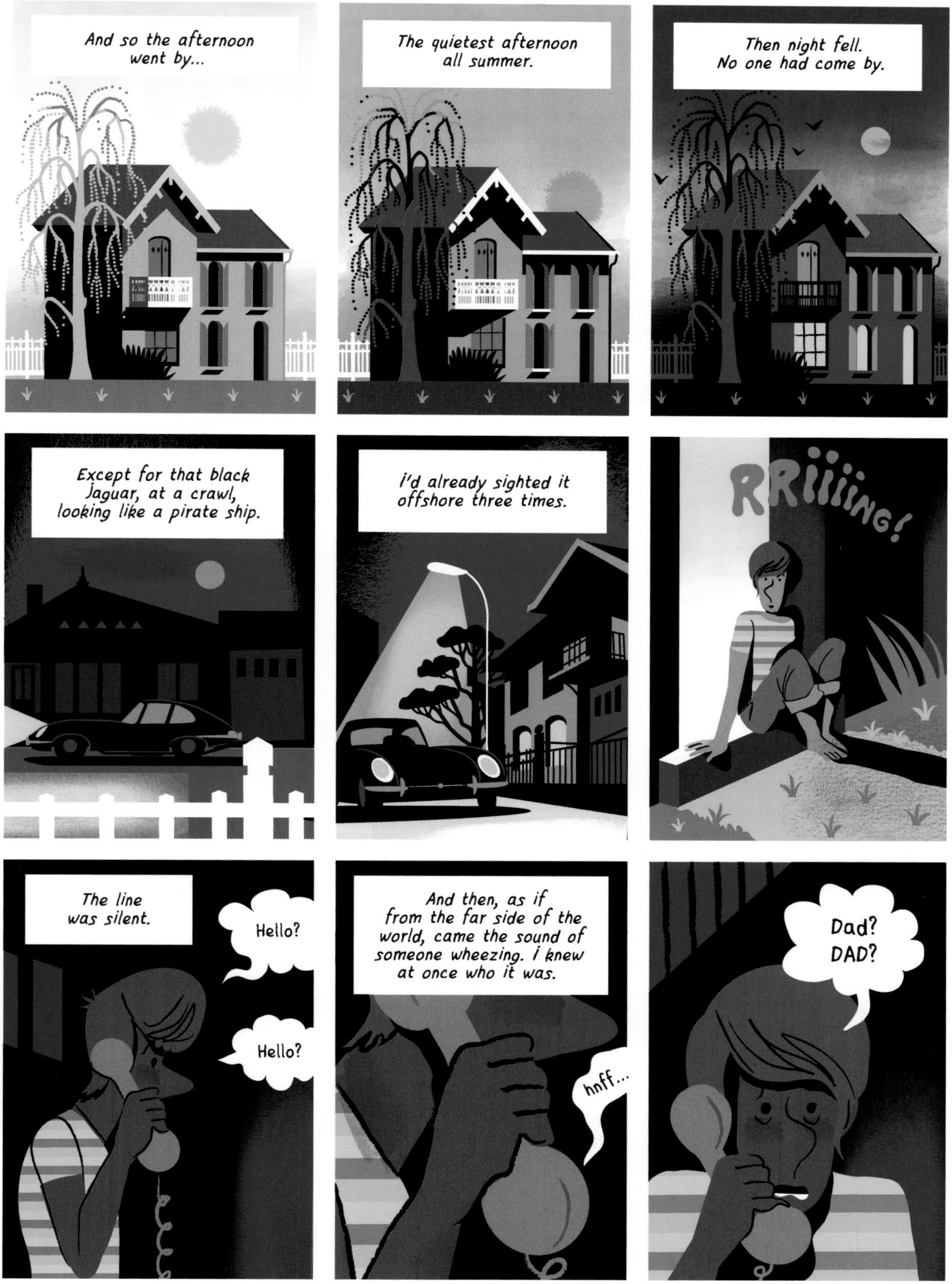

And so the afternoon went by...
The quietest afternoon all summer.
Then night fell. No one had come by.
Except for that black jaguar, at a crawl, looking like a pirate ship.
I'd already sighted it offshore three times.
RRiiiiiNG!
The line was silent.
Hello?
Hello?
And then, as if from the far side of the world, came the sound of someone wheezing. I knew at once who it was.
hnff...
Dad? DAD?

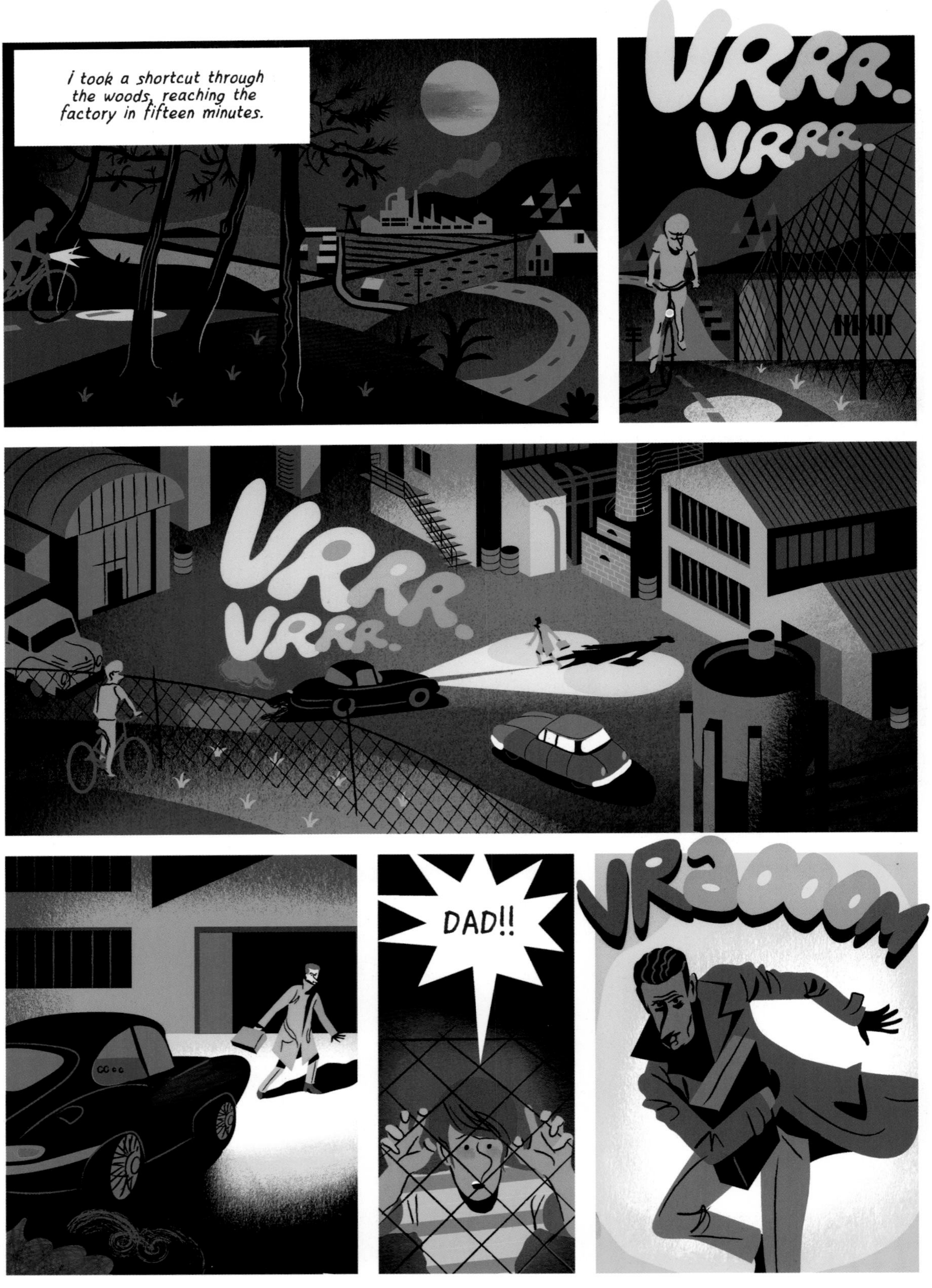
i took a shortcut through the woods, reaching the factory in fifteen minutes.
VRRR. VRRR.
VRRR. VRRR.
DAD!!
VRAOOOM

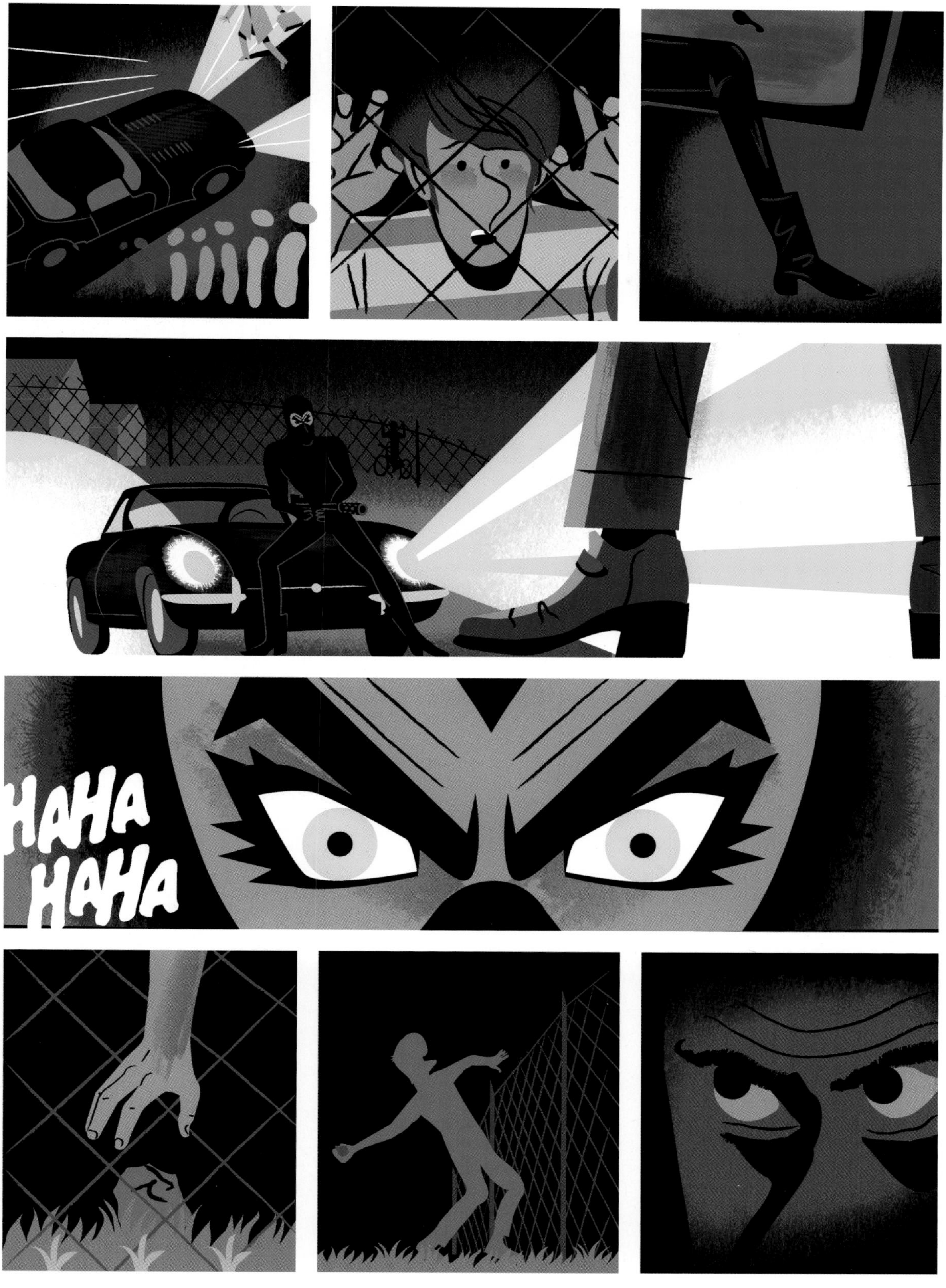
HAHA
HAHA

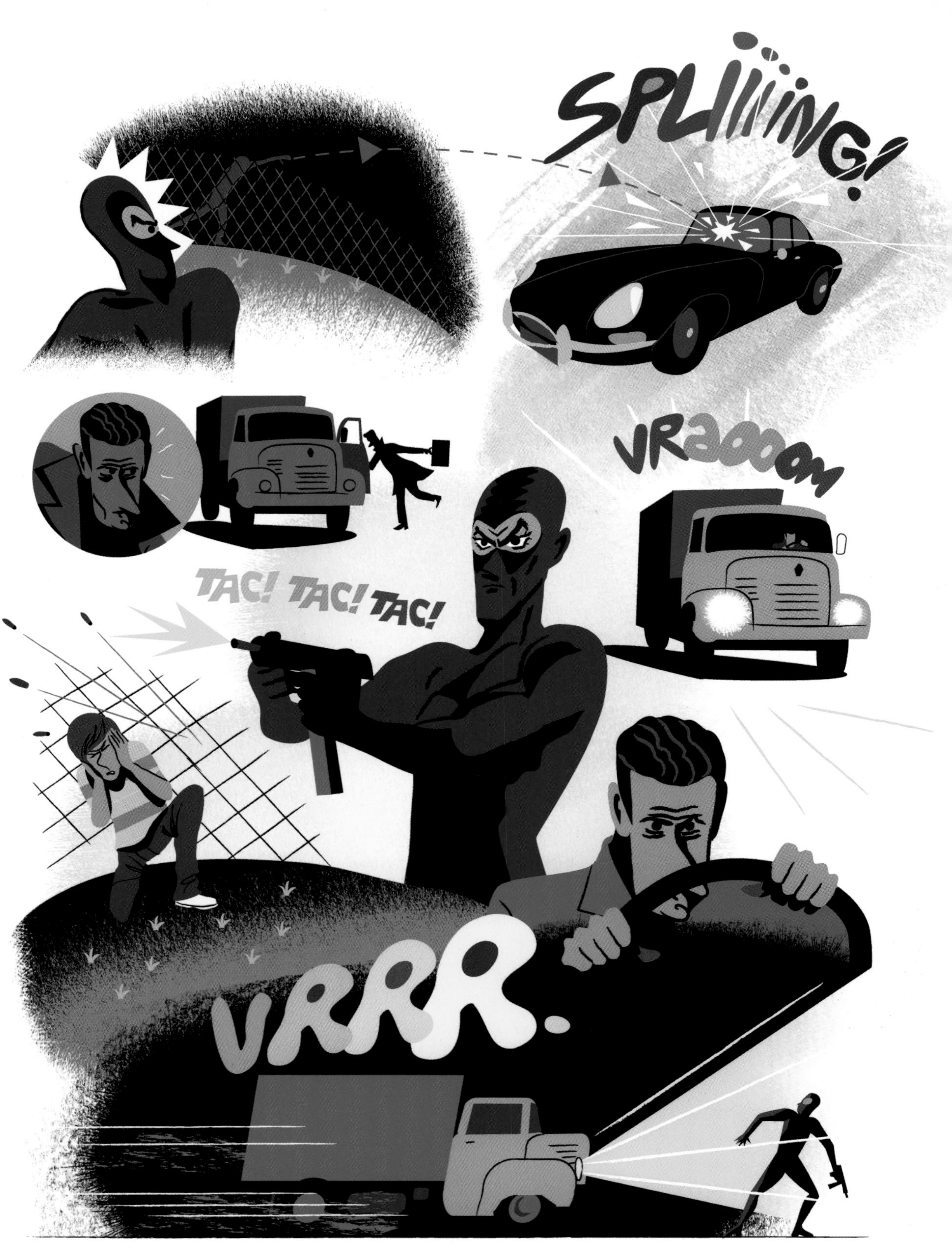
SPLIIING!
VRaOOOM
TAC! TAC! TAC!
VRRR.

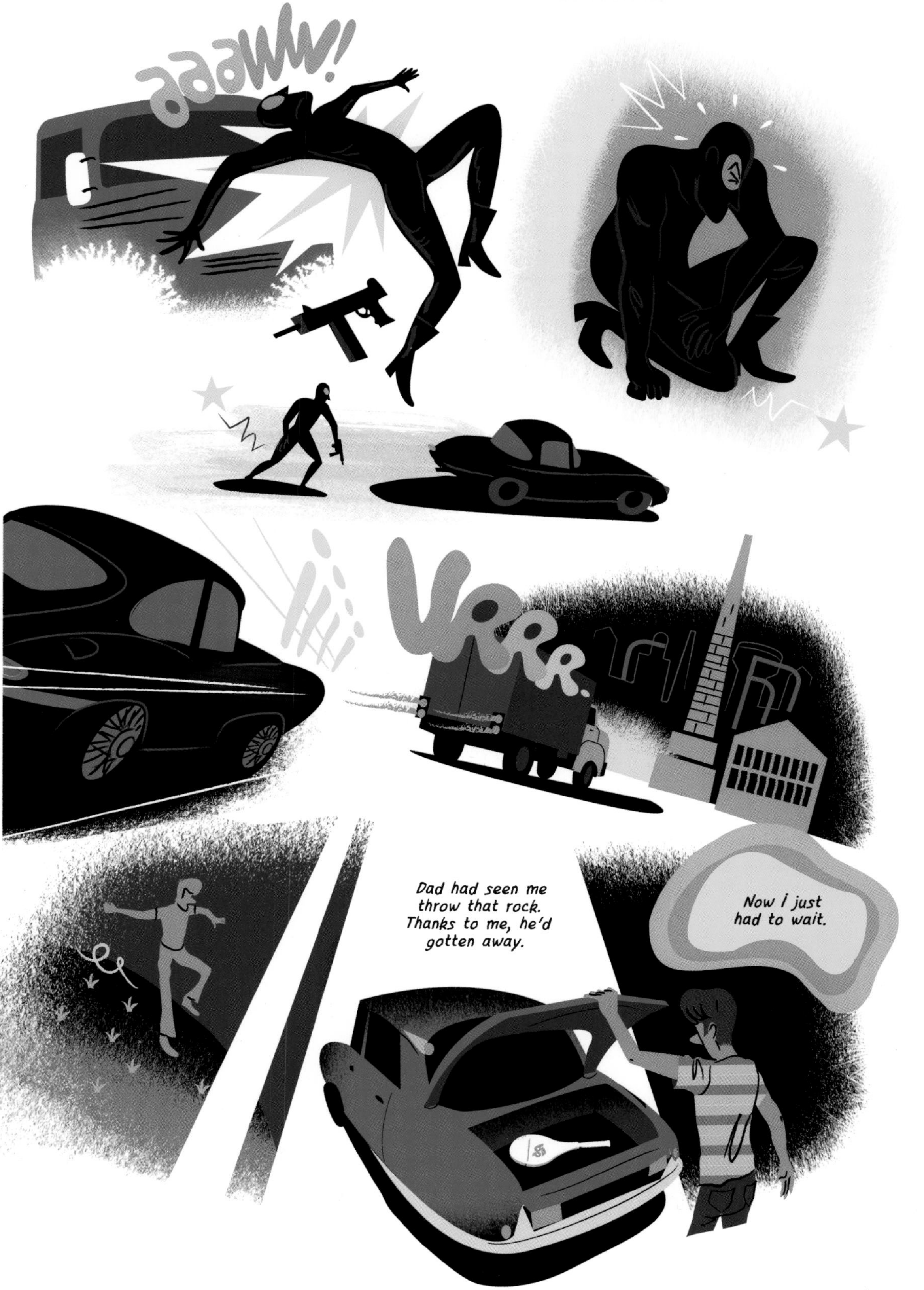
aaawww!
VRRR.
Dad had seen me throw that rock. Thanks to me, he'd gotten away.
Now I just had to wait.

i waited two hours for him to return.

And as the stars glided unperturbed across the dome of the great planetarium...

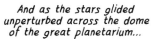

...from a maw of ash and shadow came an insistent whisper: "You'll never see him again!"

And in fact, as i write these lines today, i never have.

S u m m e r   ' 8 7

This is the first time i've ever told anyone this story.

And to be honest, this is where my story must come to an end.

For everything that happened afterward is unimportant.

At the factory, the next two days were filled with worry.

Three days later, my mother and sister came back from Ireland.

The truck? it was found empty, in a field.

Dad? Vanished.

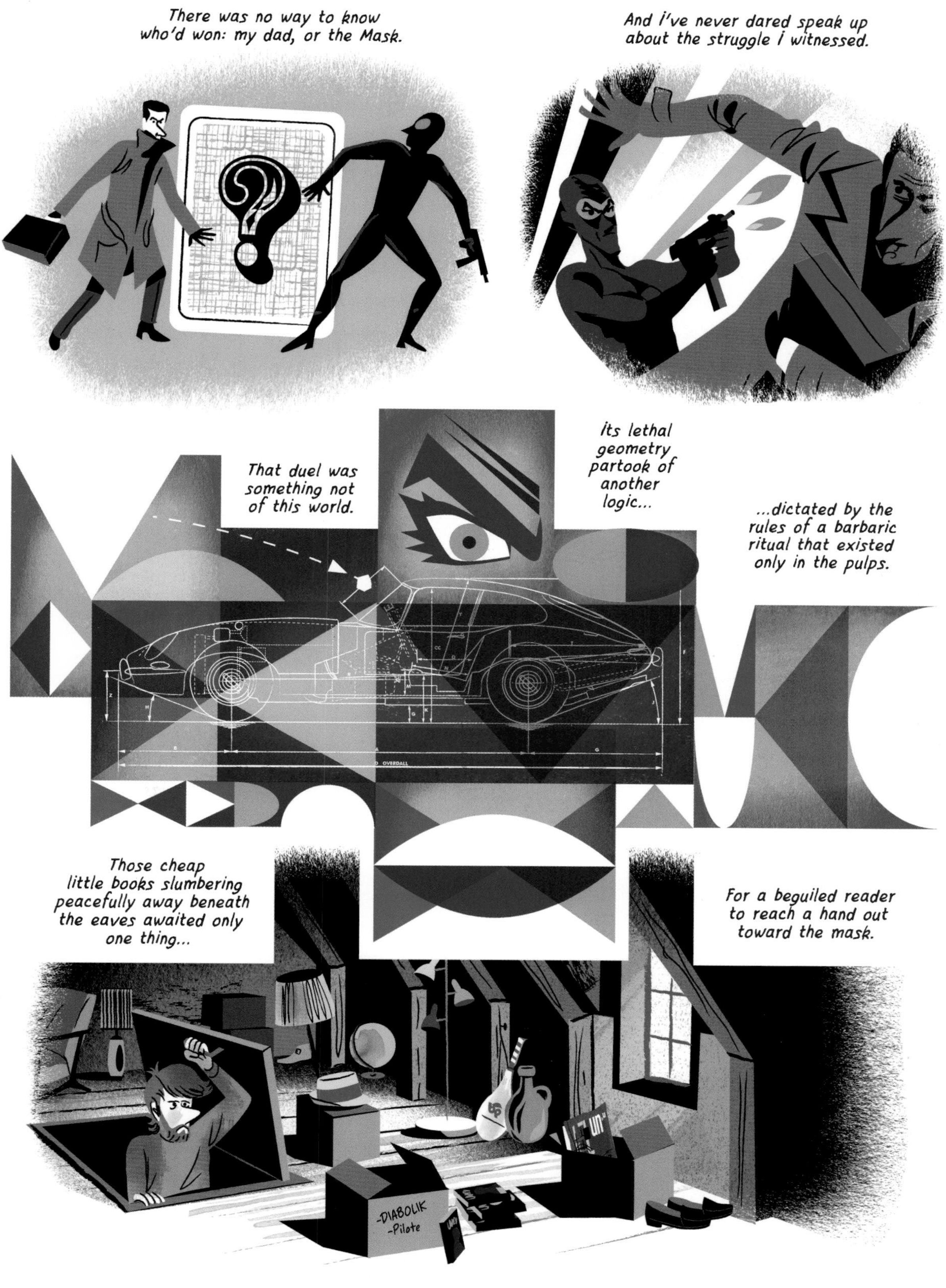
There was no way to know who'd won: my dad, or the Mask.
And i've never dared speak up about the struggle i witnessed.
That duel was something not of this world.
its lethal geometry partook of another logic...
...dictated by the rules of a barbaric ritual that existed only in the pulps.
Those cheap little books slumbering peacefully away beneath the eaves awaited only one thing...
For a beguiled reader to reach a hand out toward the mask.
-DIABOLIK
-Pilote

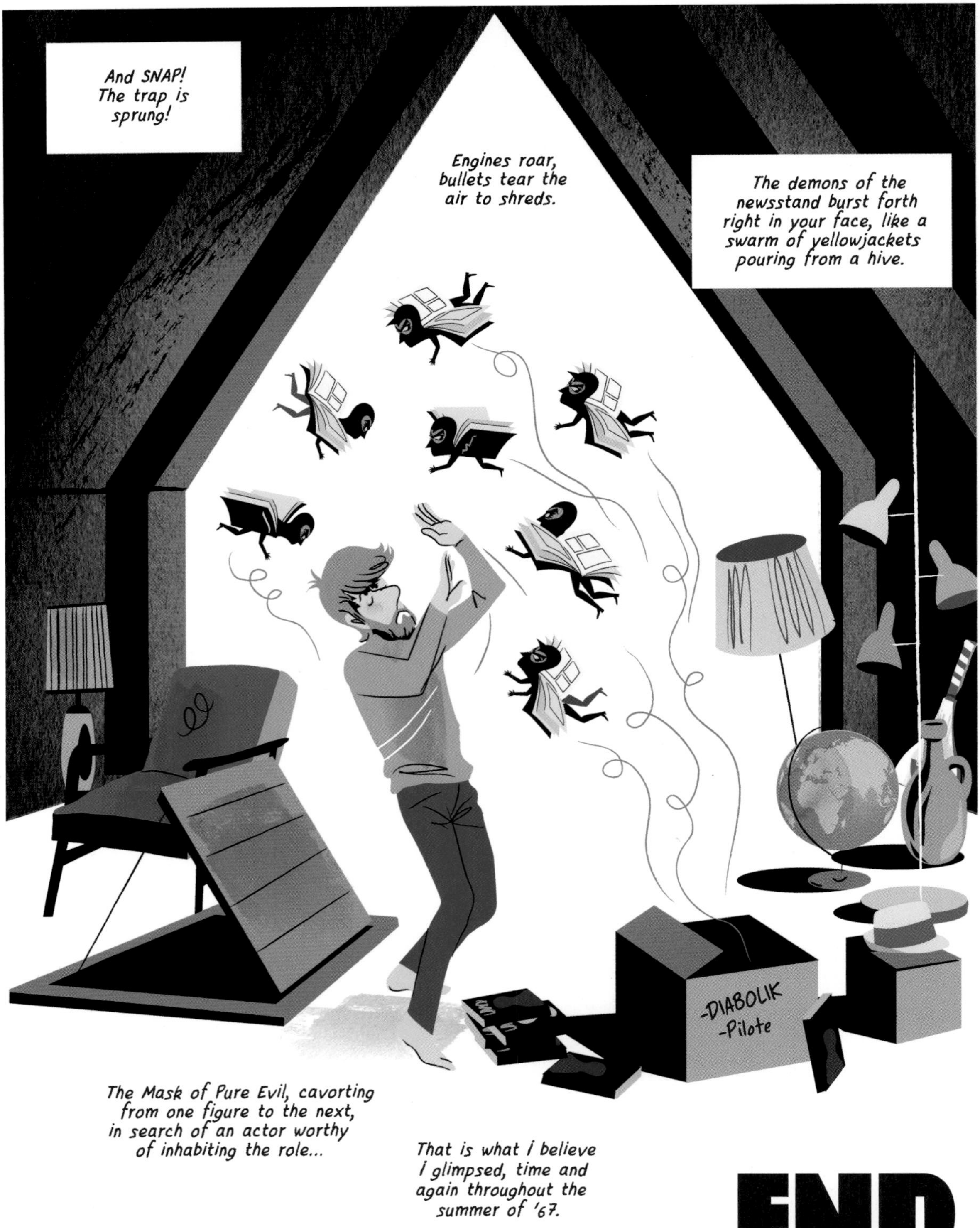
And SNAP! The trap is sprung!
Engines roar, bullets tear the air to shreds.
The demons of the newsstand burst forth right in your face, like a swarm of yellowjackets pouring from a hive.
-DIABOLIK
-Pilote
The Mask of Pure Evil, cavorting from one figure to the next, in search of an actor worthy of inhabiting the role...
That is what I believe I glimpsed, time and again throughout the summer of '67.
END

AFTERWORD

I began writing this book in 1985, seventeen years after the events related herein.

I am still haunted by my father's disappearance. I see shadows no one else sees, and the sound of a telephone ringing makes me nervous: I keep waiting for destiny's fateful summons...

My mother died five years ago. The last time I asked her about Dad's disappearance, she shrugged, as usual, with that pained smile we knew so well.

In March 1985, the news that a body had been found at the bottom of an abandoned well drove me to start work on what would eventually become this book. Early reports in the papers described the skeleton as belonging to someone who had died in the late '60s, most likely as a result of suicide or an accident.

As it so happens, my father and I used to fly model airplanes in a field nearby. He'd often warned me to stay away from that very well.

And so, for a few hours, I believed that his body had been found at last, and the entire summer of '67 flashed before my eyes, like a movie.

Upon further inquiry, I was informed that the body in question was that of a young woman, around twenty years of age. Sometime between 1965 and 1970, she'd died of a broken neck, and she had never been identified. This sad bit of news renewed my desire to go over the puzzle pieces one more time. A need for closure began to grow inside me.

* * *

My sister Nini, who's just read this book in proofs, disapproves of my efforts, and I owe it to myself to pass on her doubts.

According to her, my questions concerning Dad are entirely within the realm of the normal, the kind every fifteen-year-old boy asks now and then—nothing to write a novel about.

Besides, if that masked man had been Evil Incarnate, why had he been limping so pitifully as he got back in his Jaguar?

Allegorical figures that condescend to set foot on this mortal plane hardly let vans run over their toes.

To Nini, the dose of LSD I took obviously explains everything.

Everything, that is, except... Dad's disappearance!

There remains the matter of Mr. de Noé's phone call, of which the Secret Services have no record. Upon examining the phone log, I realized why: the call had been placed from a public phone booth across from his villa.

For a long time, this detail bothered me, though I could never figure out why... until the last words Dad had said the morning he vanished came back to me: "Don't worry. Whatever happened was confined to the four walls of his house. Those people aren't interested in private lives. If they suspect anything, they won't go digging."

But in that case, why did Mr. de Noé call my father from outside the walls of his own house, just before committing suicide?

Antoine Lafarge
Clerville, 1985-1987

PART TWO

THE MASK FALLS

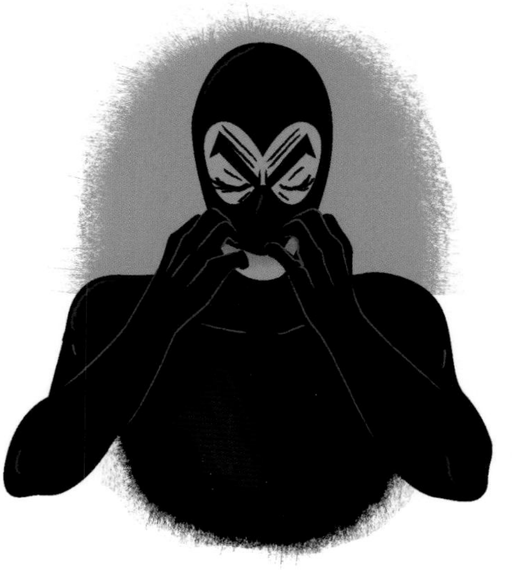

«...The secret of this mask, jumping from one shadow to another, as in search of an actor worthy of embodying...»

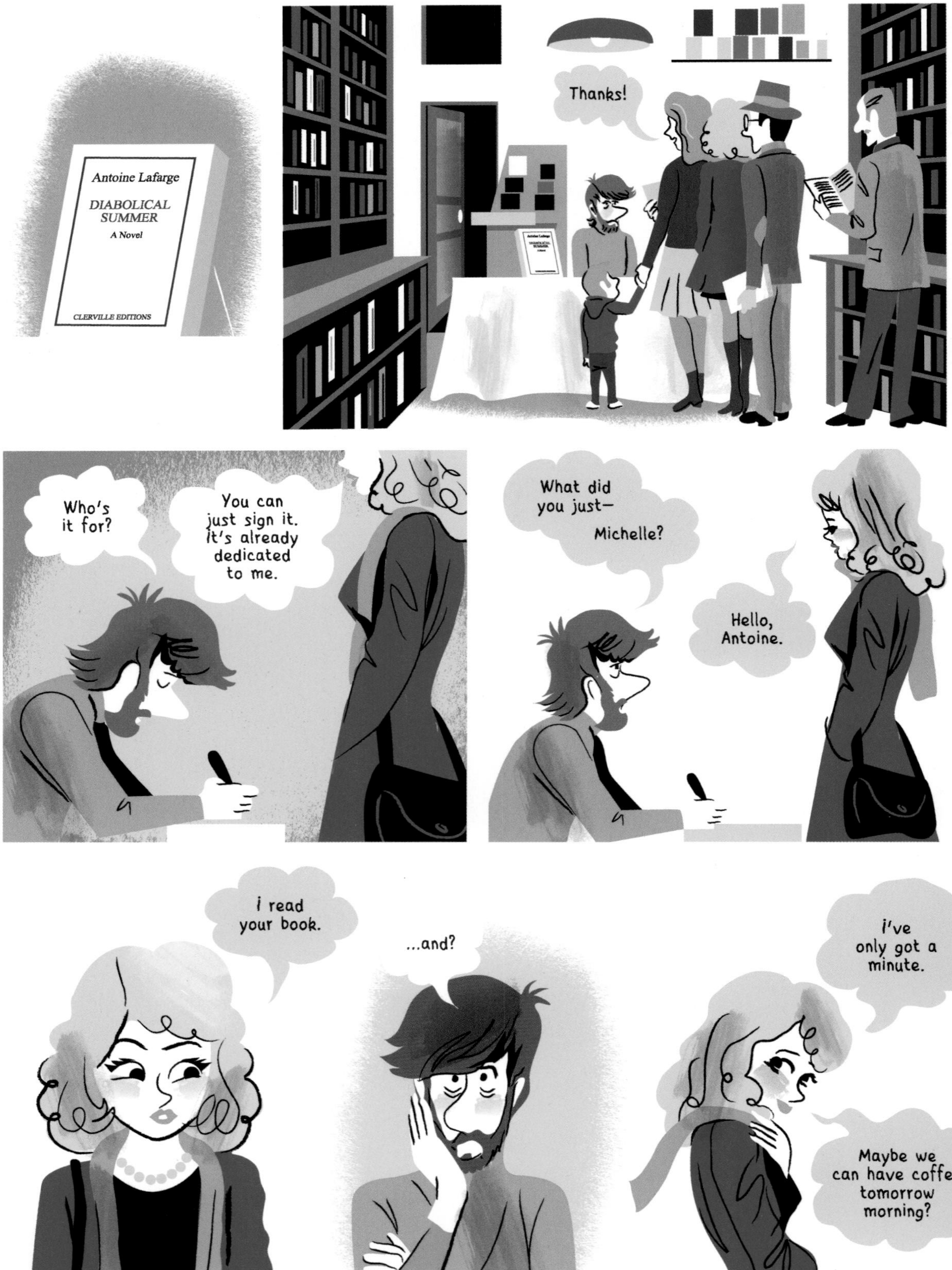

Antoine Lafarge
DIABOLICAL SUMMER
A Novel
CLERVILLE EDITIONS
Thanks!
Who's it for?
You can just sign it. it's already dedicated to me.
What did you just—
Michelle?
Hello, Antoine.
i read your book.
...and?
i've only got a minute.
Maybe we can have coffee tomorrow morning?

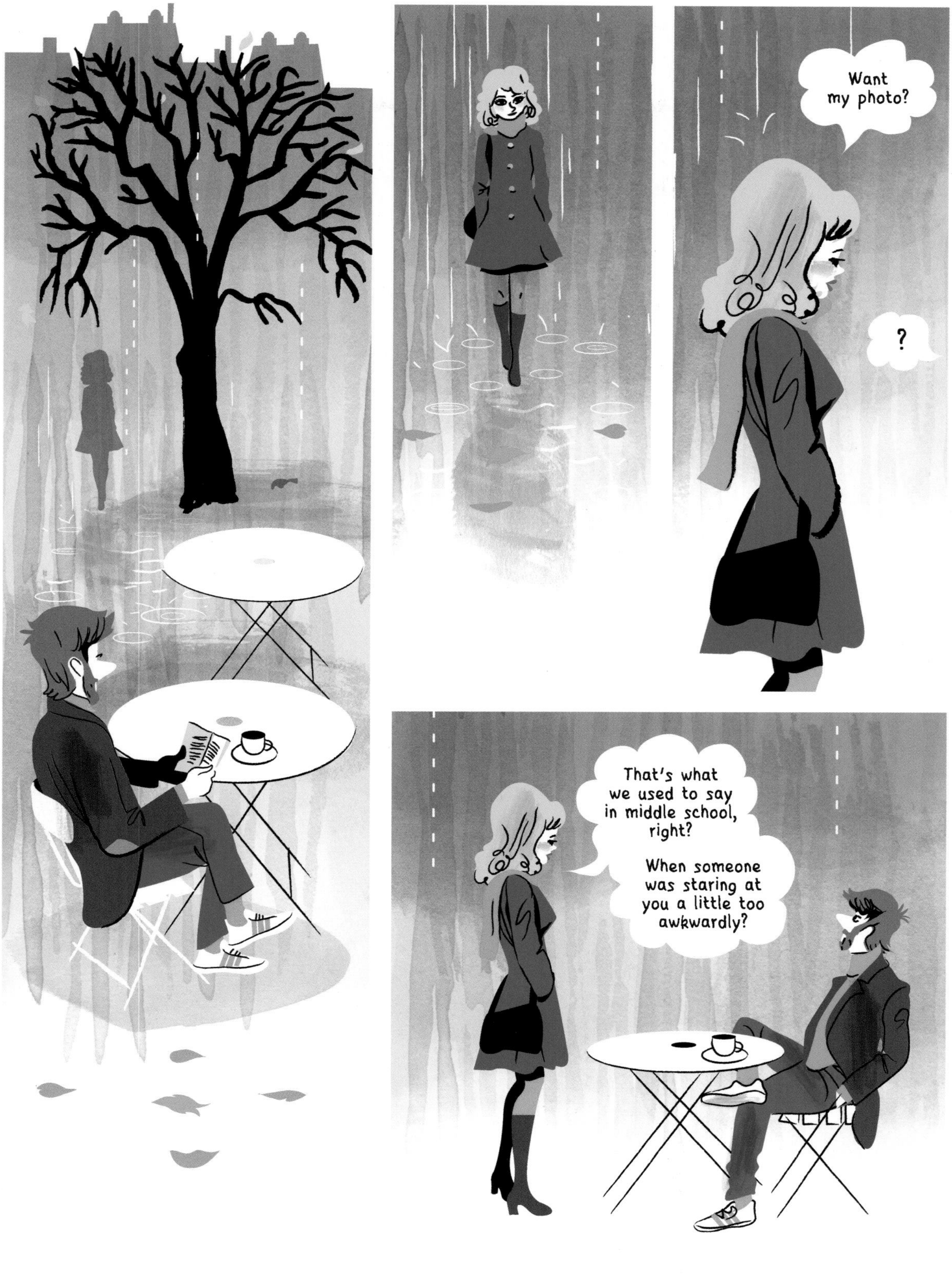
Want my photo?
?
That's what we used to say in middle school, right?
When someone was staring at you a little too awkwardly?

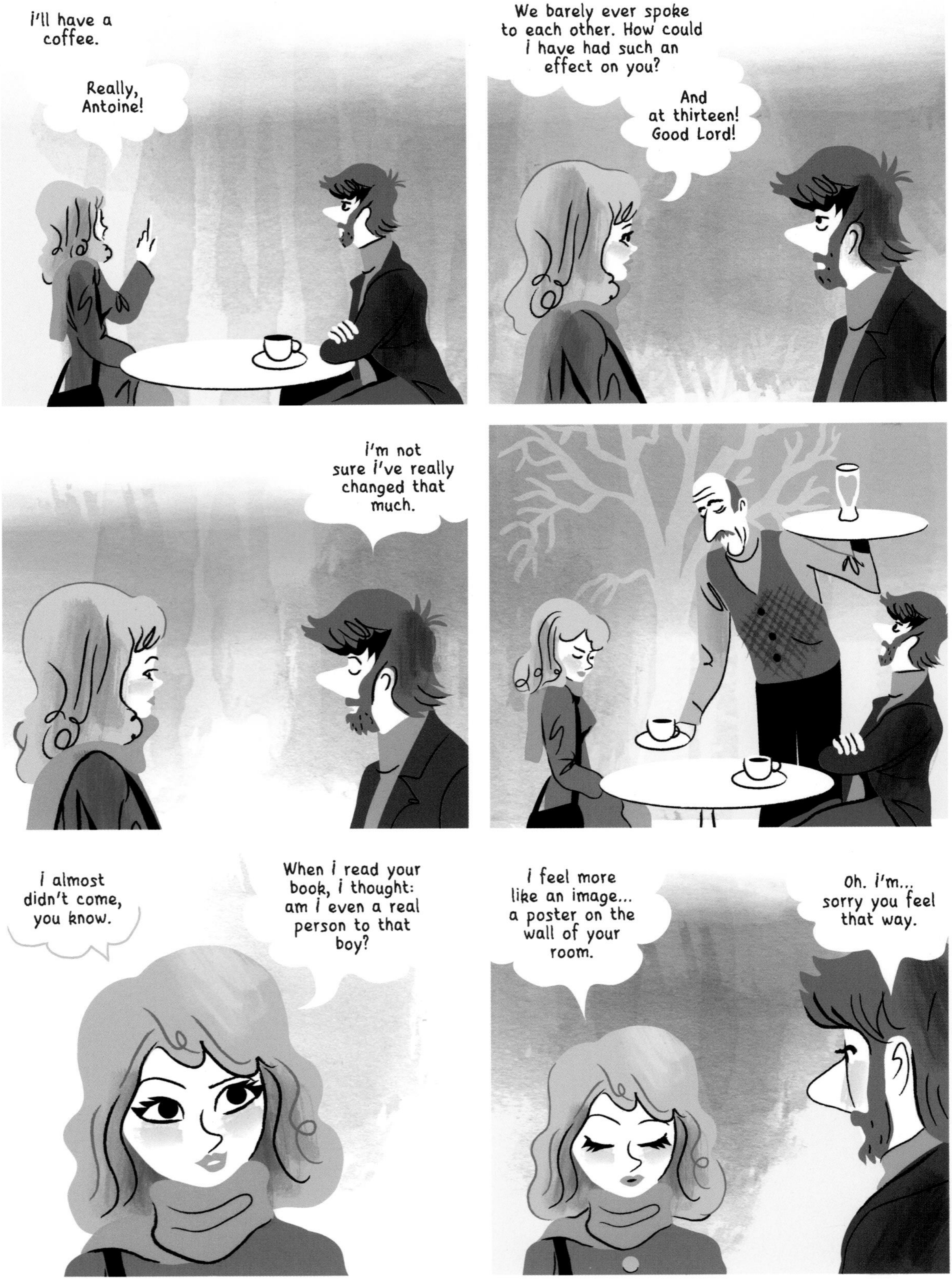
I'll have a coffee.
Really, Antoine!
We barely ever spoke to each other. How could I have had such an effect on you?
And at thirteen! Good Lord!
I'm not sure I've really changed that much.
I almost didn't come, you know.
When I read your book, I thought: am I even a real person to that boy?
I feel more like an image... a poster on the wall of your room.
Oh. I'm... sorry you feel that way.

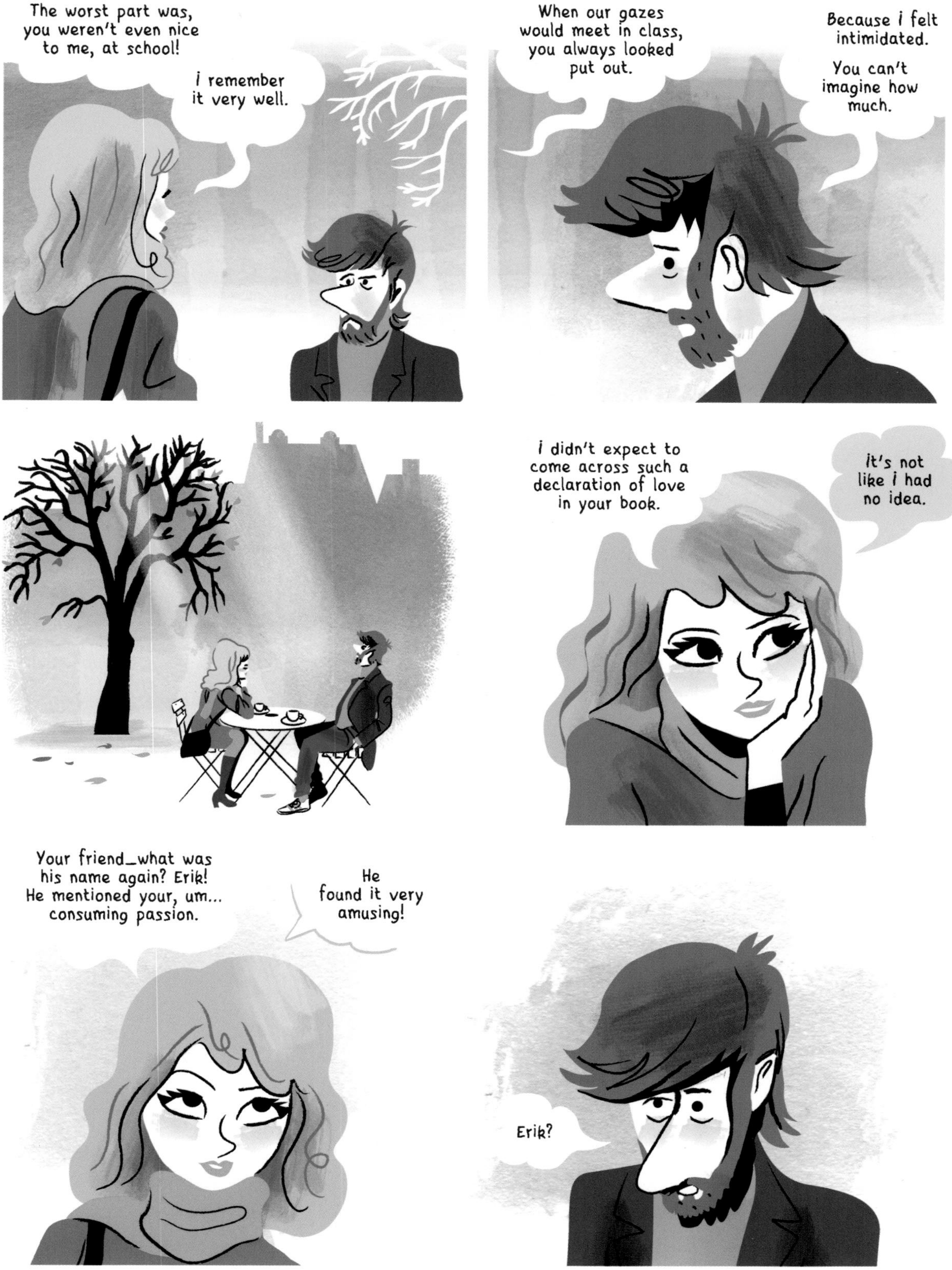
The worst part was, you weren't even nice to me, at school!
I remember it very well.
When our gazes would meet in class, you always looked put out.
Because I felt intimidated.
You can't imagine how much.
I didn't expect to come across such a declaration of love in your book.
It's not like I had no idea.
Your friend_what was his name again? Erik! He mentioned your, um... consuming passion.
He found it very amusing!
Erik?

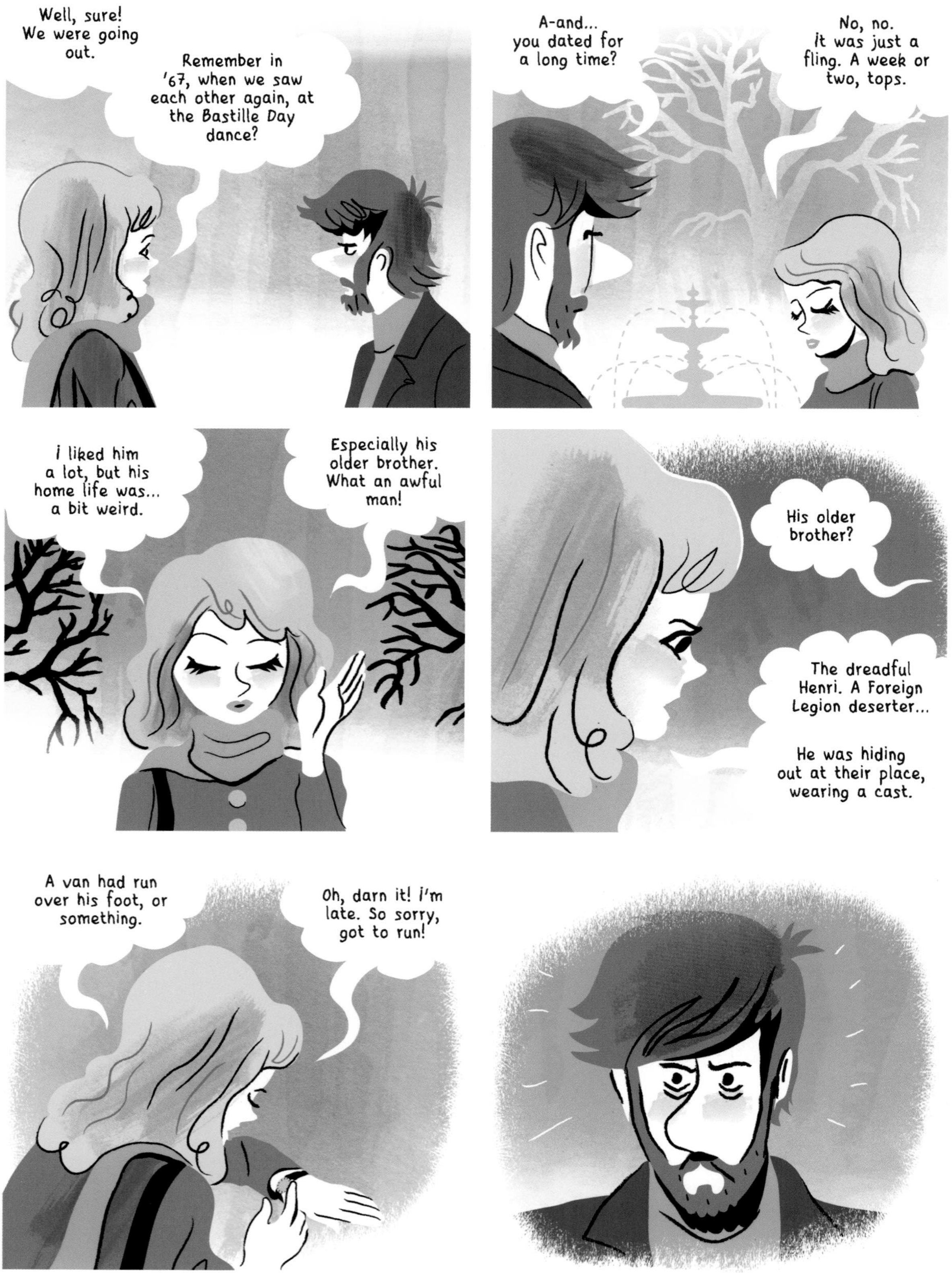
Well, sure! We were going out.
Remember in '67, when we saw each other again, at the Bastille Day dance?
A-and... you dated for a long time?
No, no. It was just a fling. A week or two, tops.
I liked him a lot, but his home life was... a bit weird.
Especially his older brother. What an awful man!
His older brother?
The dreadful Henri. A Foreign Legion deserter...
He was hiding out at their place, wearing a cast.
A van had run over his foot, or something.
Oh, darn it! I'm late. So sorry, got to run!

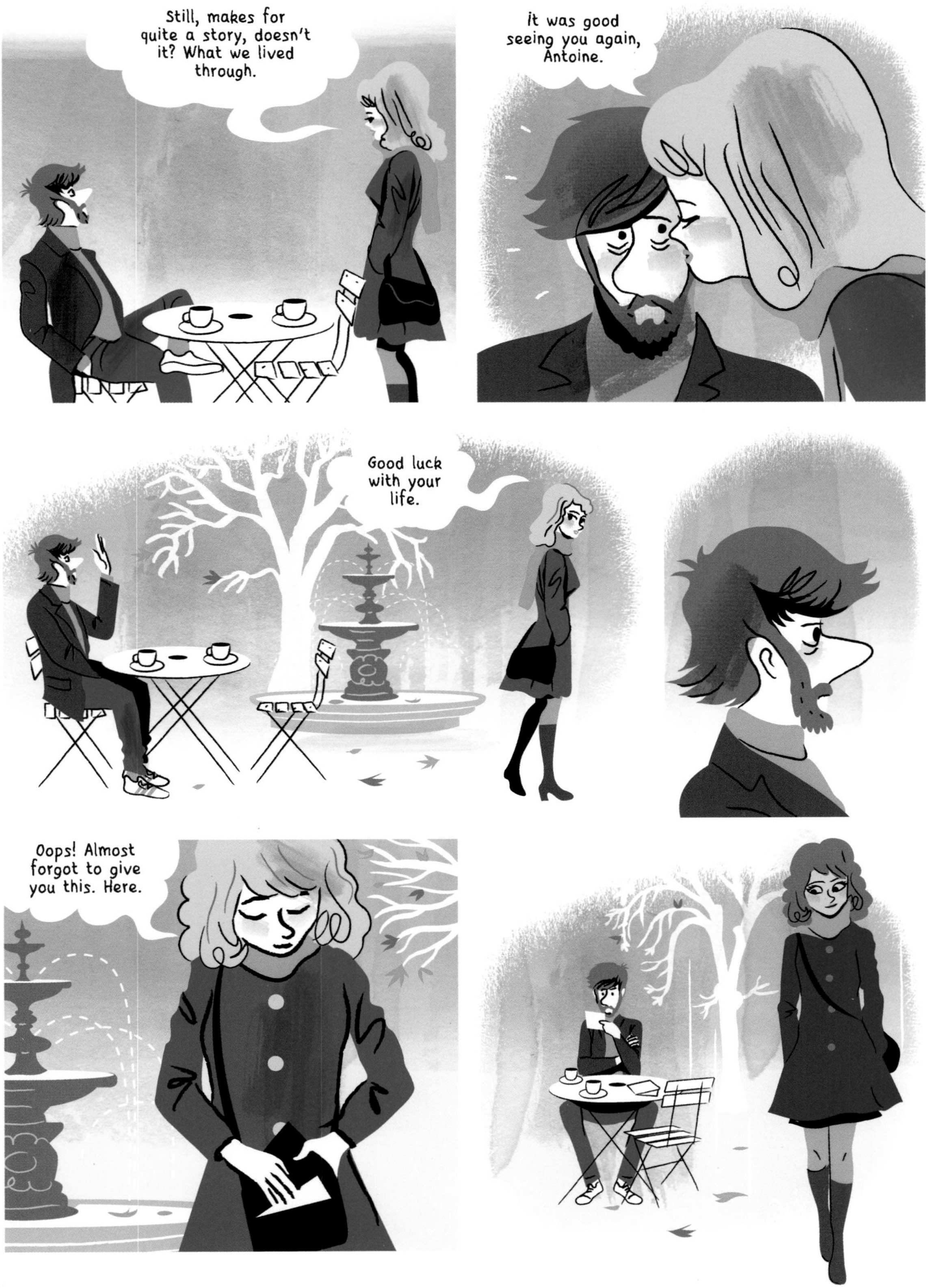
Still, makes for quite a story, doesn't it? What we lived through.
It was good seeing you again, Antoine.
Good luck with your life.
Oops! Almost forgot to give you this. Here.

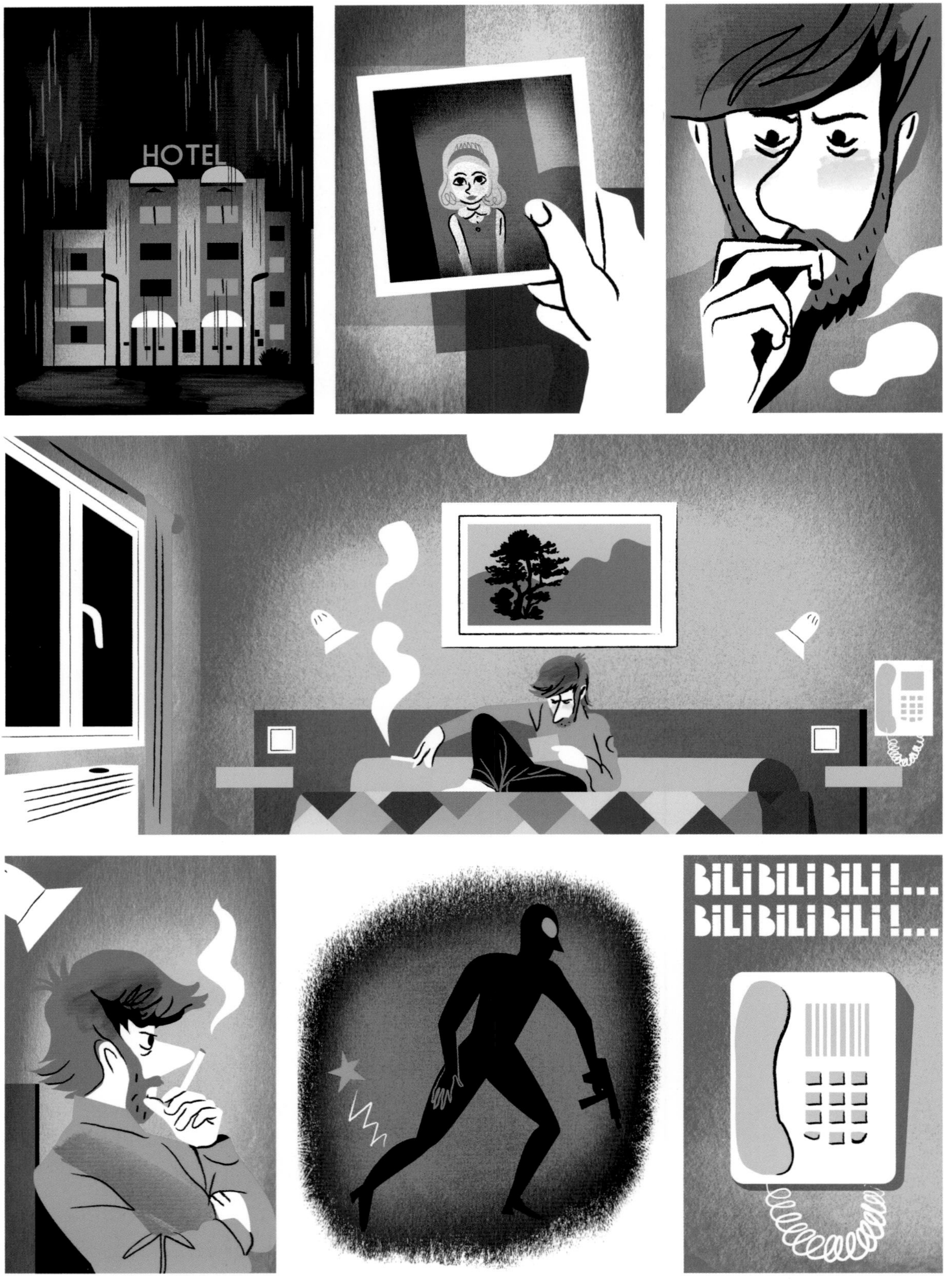
HOTEL
BiLi BiLi BiLi !...
BiLi BiLi BiLi !...

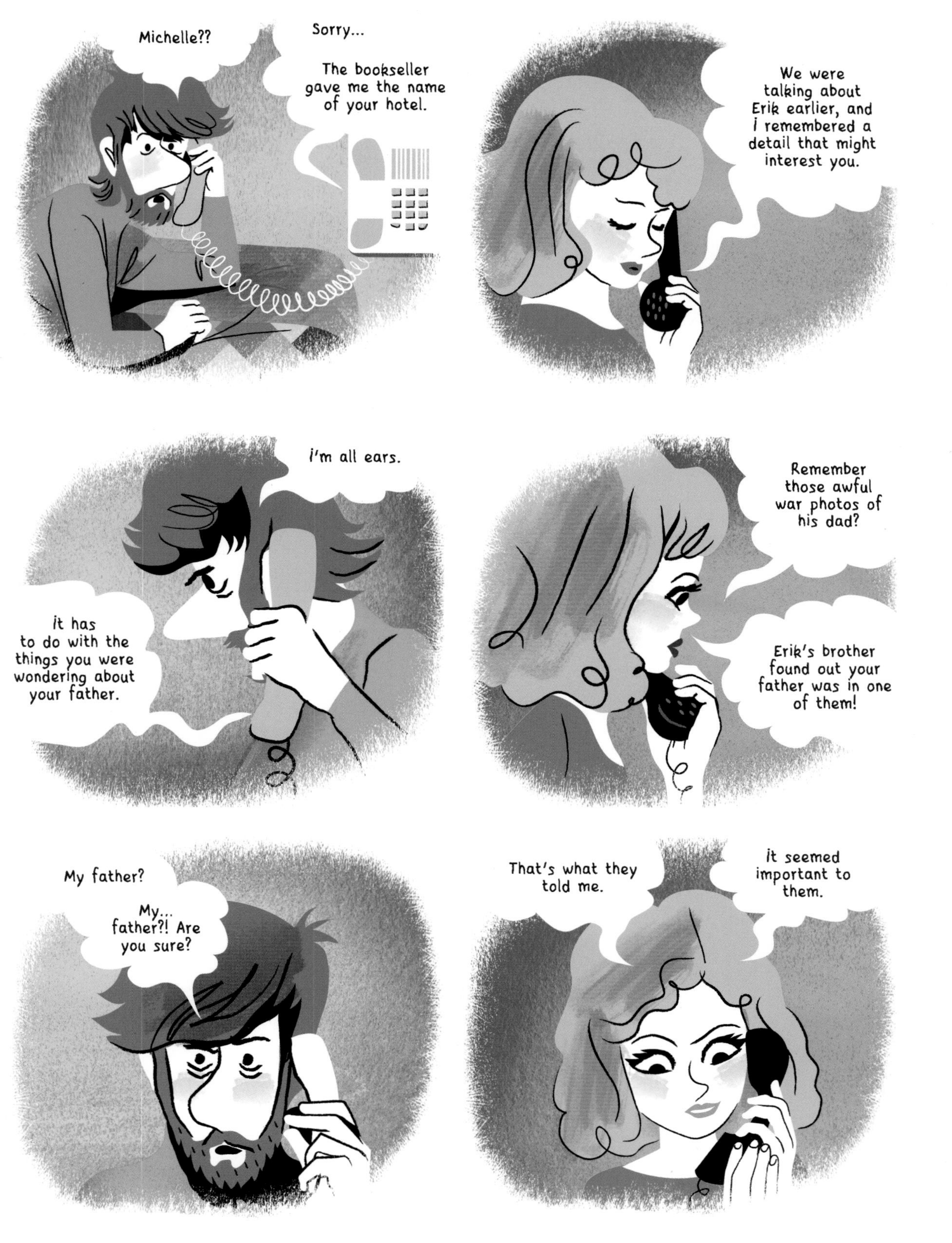
Michelle??
Sorry...
The bookseller gave me the name of your hotel.
We were talking about Erik earlier, and I remembered a detail that might interest you.
I'm all ears.
It has to do with the things you were wondering about your father.
Remember those awful war photos of his dad?
Erik's brother found out your father was in one of them!
My father?
My... father?! Are you sure?
That's what they told me.
It seemed important to them.

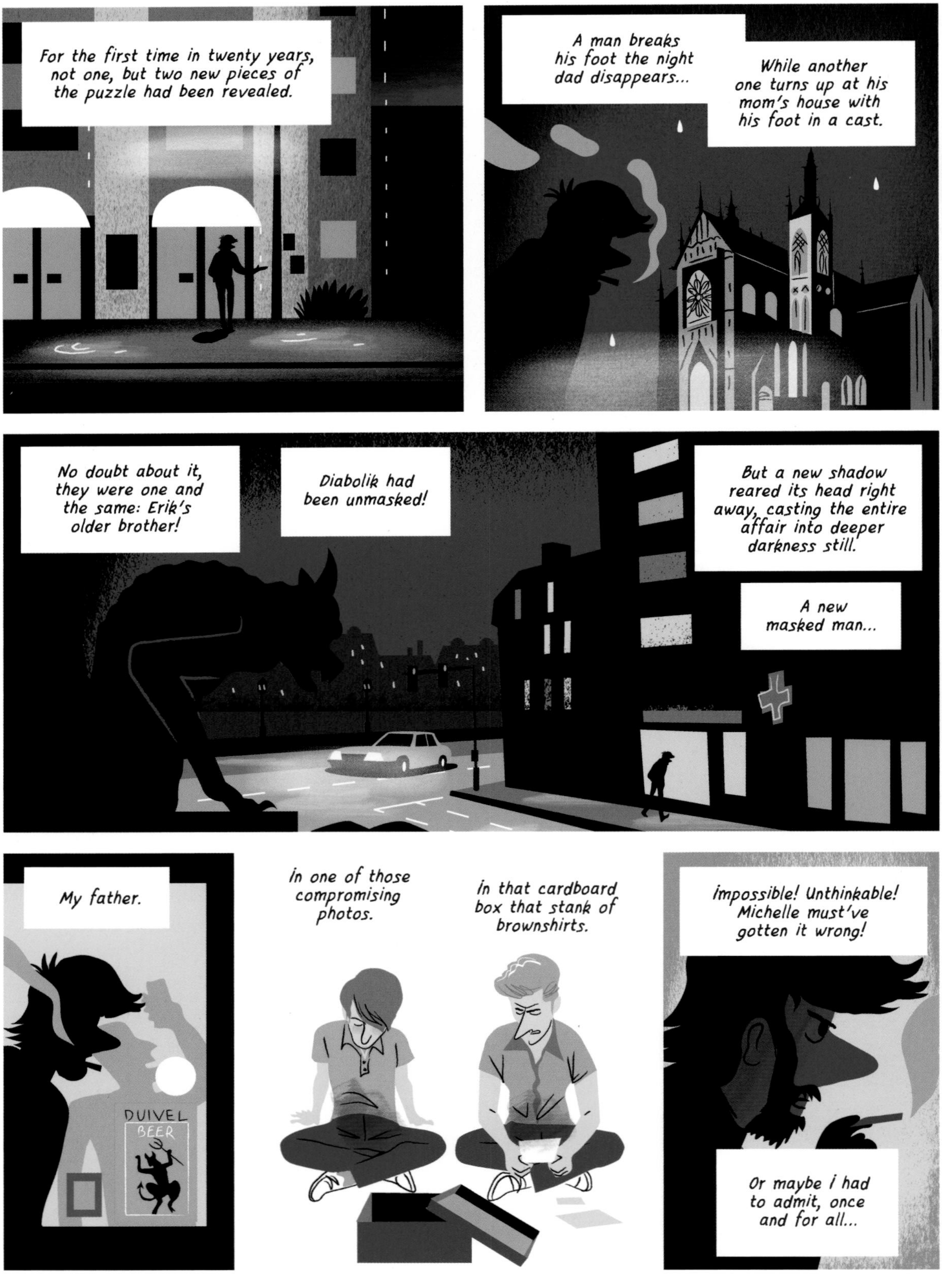
For the first time in twenty years, not one, but two new pieces of the puzzle had been revealed.
A man breaks his foot the night dad disappears...
While another one turns up at his mom's house with his foot in a cast.
No doubt about it, they were one and the same: Erik's older brother!
Diabolik had been unmasked!
But a new shadow reared its head right away, casting the entire affair into deeper darkness still.
A new masked man...
My father.
DUIVEL
BEER
In one of those compromising photos.
In that cardboard box that stank of brownshirts.
Impossible! Unthinkable! Michelle must've gotten it wrong!
Or maybe I had to admit, once and for all...

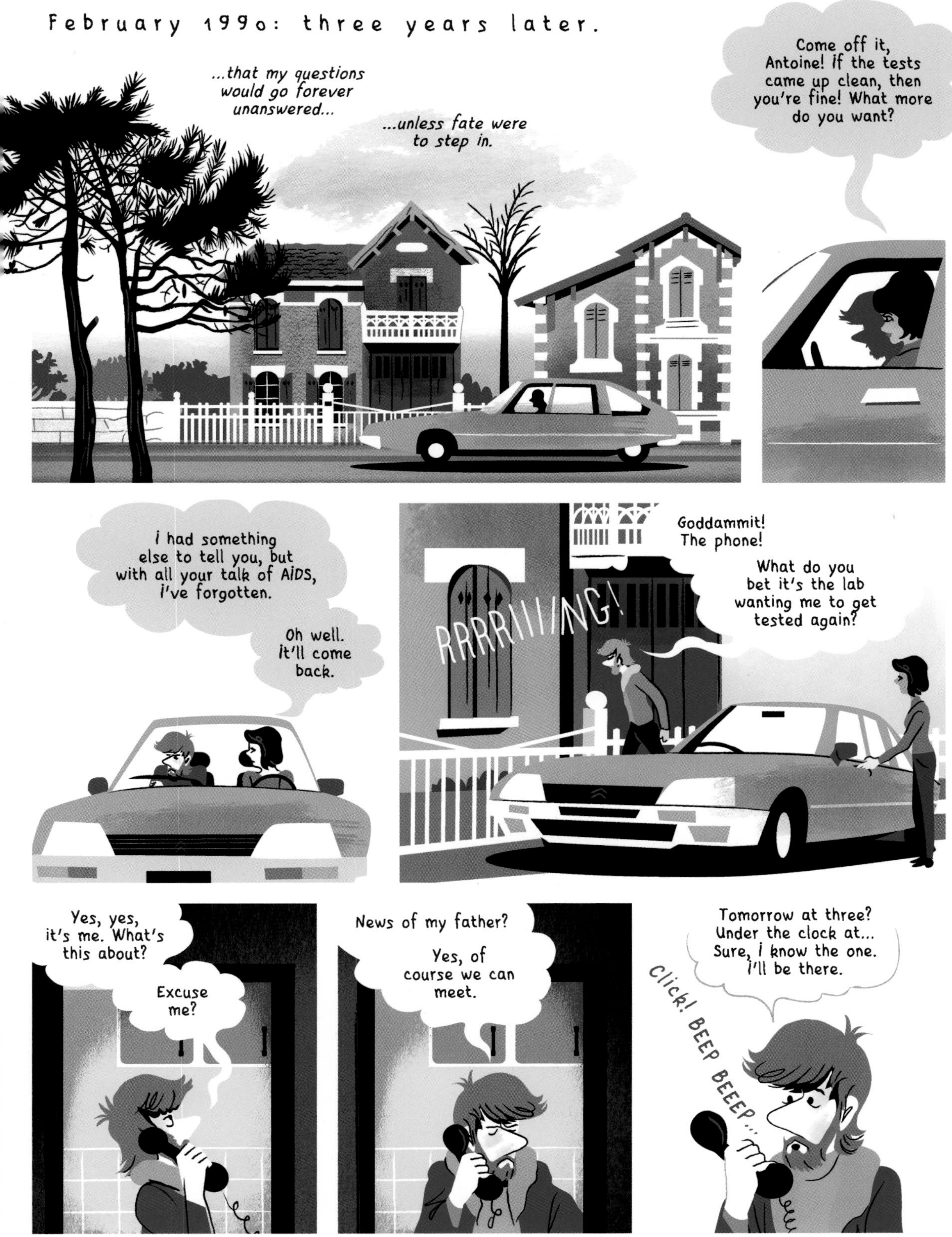
February 1990: three years later.
...that my questions would go forever unanswered...
...unless fate were to step in.
Come off it, Antoine! If the tests came up clean, then you're fine! What more do you want?
I had something else to tell you, but with all your talk of AIDS, I've forgotten.
Oh well. It'll come back.
RRRRIIIING!
Goddammit! The phone!
What do you bet it's the lab wanting me to get tested again?
Yes, yes, it's me. What's this about?
Excuse me?
News of my father?
Yes, of course we can meet.
Tomorrow at three? Under the clock at... Sure, I know the one. I'll be there.
Click! BEEP BEEEP...

The next night...

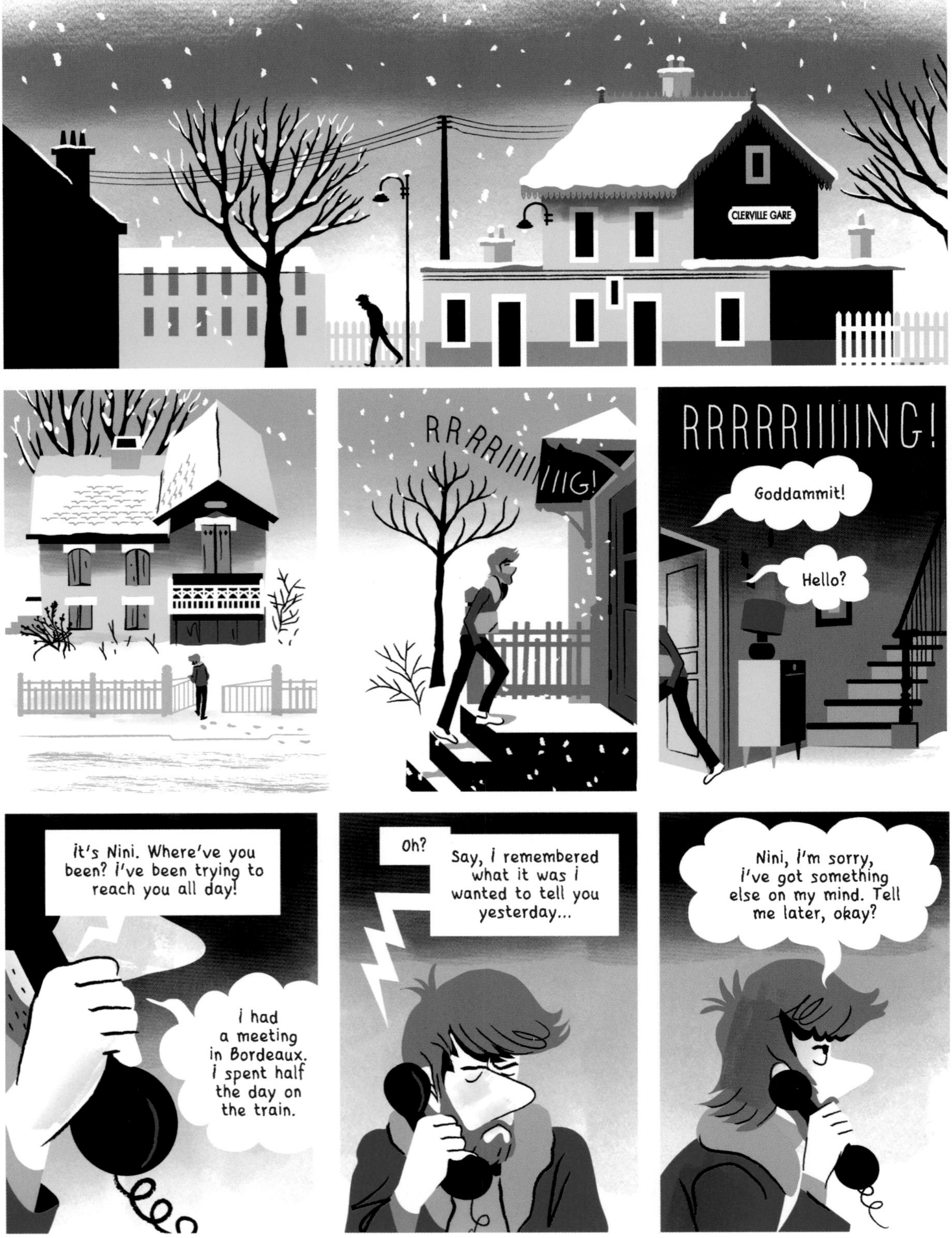
CLERVILLE GARE
RRRRIIIIIIIG!
RRRRRIIIIING!
Goddammit!
Hello?
it's Nini. Where've you been? i've been trying to reach you all day!
i had a meeting in Bordeaux. i spent half the day on the train.
Oh?
Say, i remembered what it was i wanted to tell you yesterday...
Nini, i'm sorry, i've got something else on my mind. Tell me later, okay?

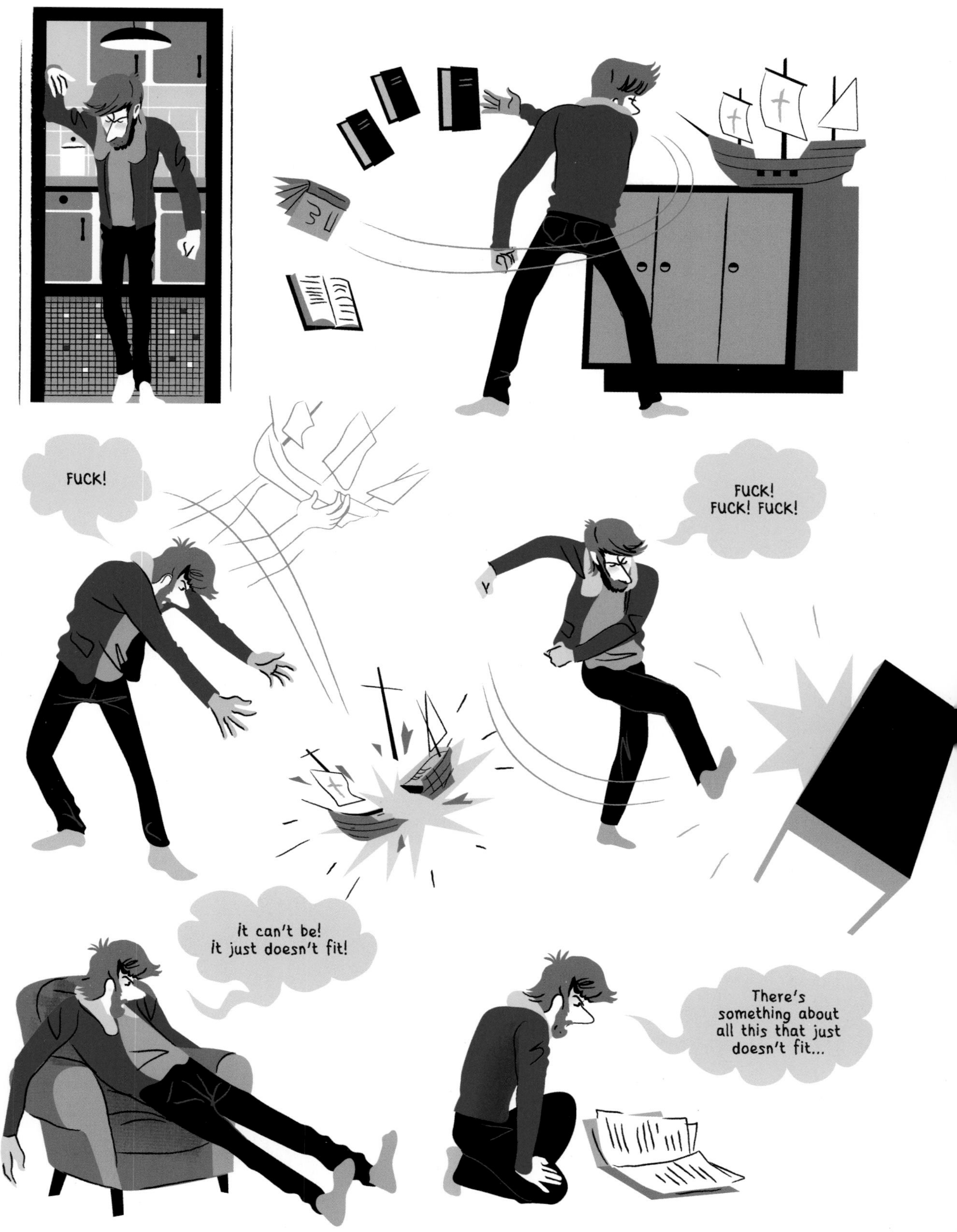
FUCK!
FUCK! FUCK! FUCK!
It can't be! It just doesn't fit!
There's something about all this that just doesn't fit...

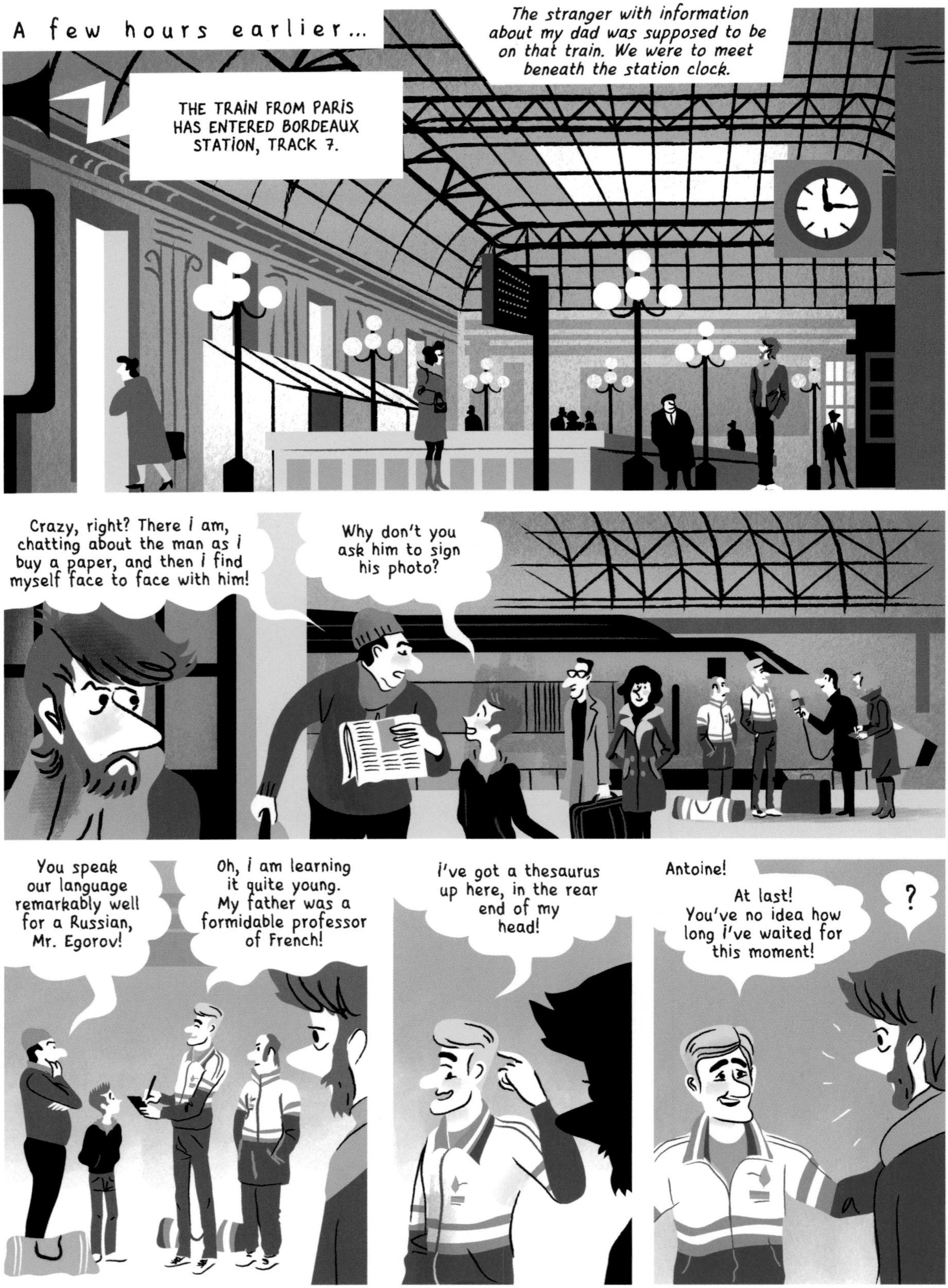
A few hours earlier...
THE TRAIN FROM PARIS HAS ENTERED BORDEAUX STATION, TRACK 7.
The stranger with information about my dad was supposed to be on that train. We were to meet beneath the station clock.
Crazy, right? There I am, chatting about the man as I buy a paper, and then I find myself face to face with him!
Why don't you ask him to sign his photo?
You speak our language remarkably well for a Russian, Mr. Egorov!
Oh, I am learning it quite young. My father was a formidable professor of French!
I've got a thesaurus up here, in the rear end of my head!
Antoine!
At last! You've no idea how long I've waited for this moment!
?

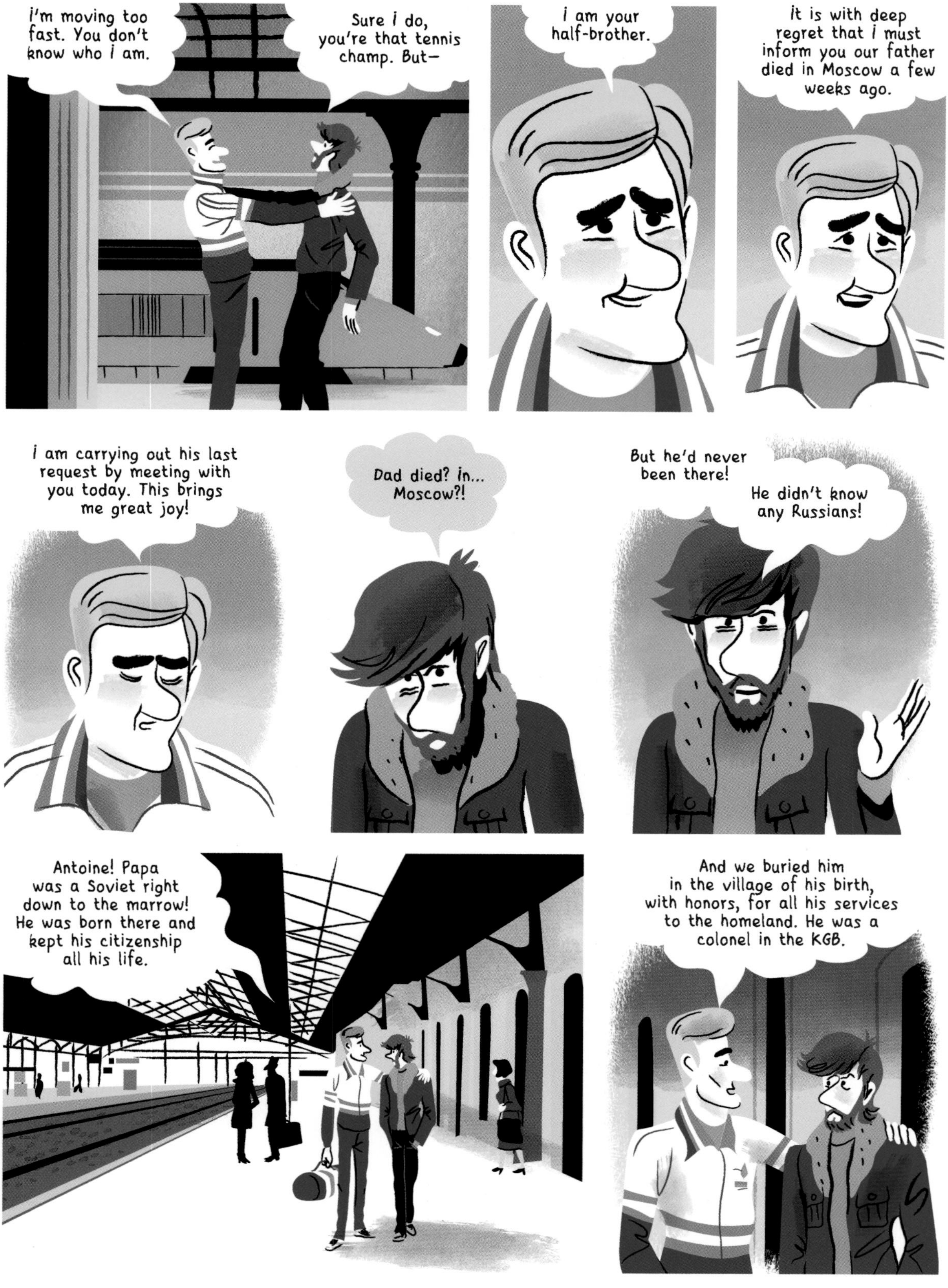
I'm moving too fast. You don't know who I am.
Sure I do, you're that tennis champ. But—
I am your half-brother.
It is with deep regret that I must inform you our father died in Moscow a few weeks ago.
I am carrying out his last request by meeting with you today. This brings me great joy!
Dad died? In... Moscow?!
But he'd never been there!
He didn't know any Russians!
Antoine! Papa was a Soviet right down to the marrow! He was born there and kept his citizenship all his life.
And we buried him in the village of his birth, with honors, for all his services to the homeland. He was a colonel in the KGB.

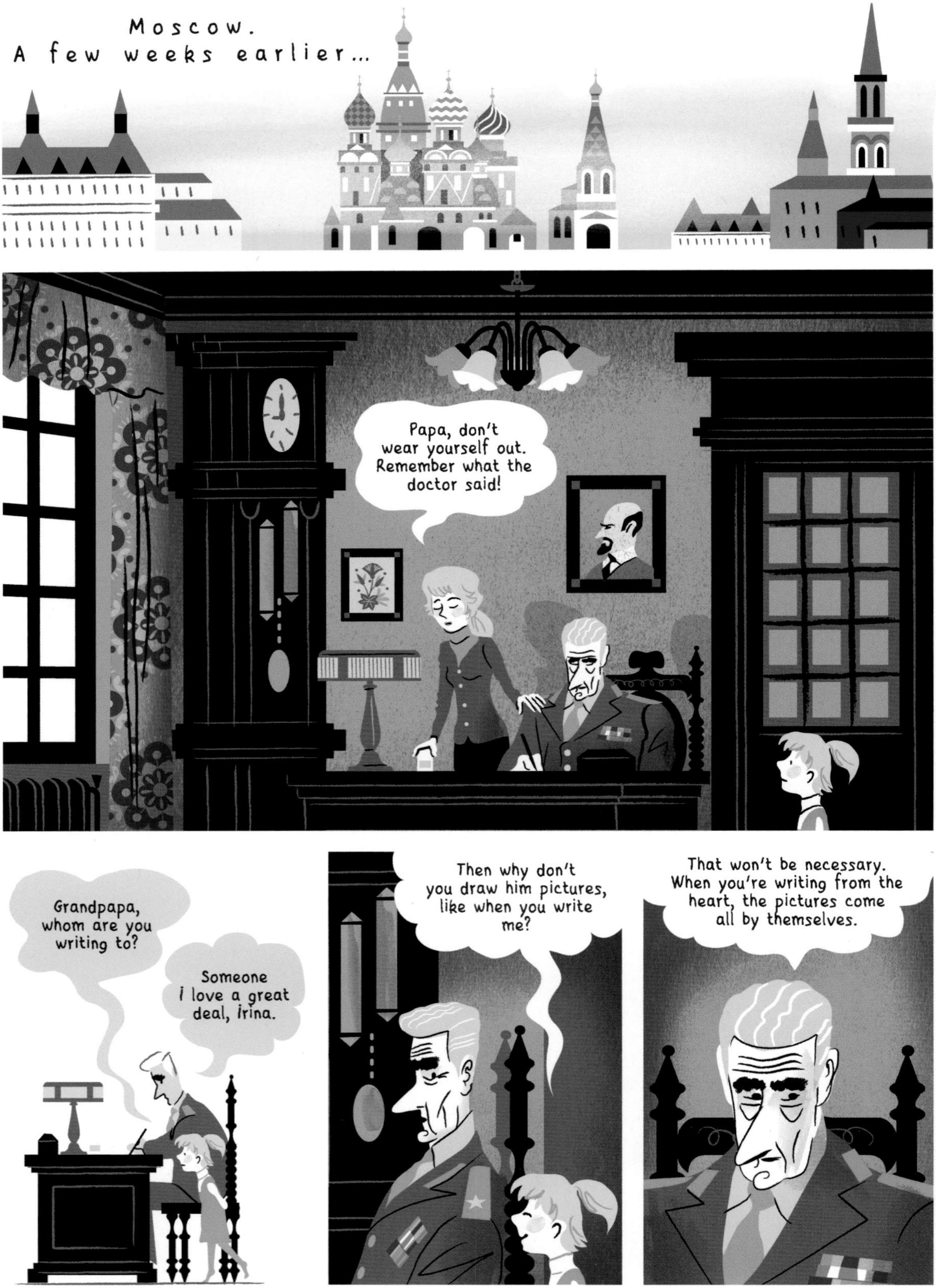
Moscow.
A few weeks earlier...
Papa, don't wear yourself out. Remember what the doctor said!
Grandpapa, whom are you writing to?
Someone I love a great deal, Irina.
Then why don't you draw him pictures, like when you write me?
That won't be necessary. When you're writing from the heart, the pictures come all by themselves.

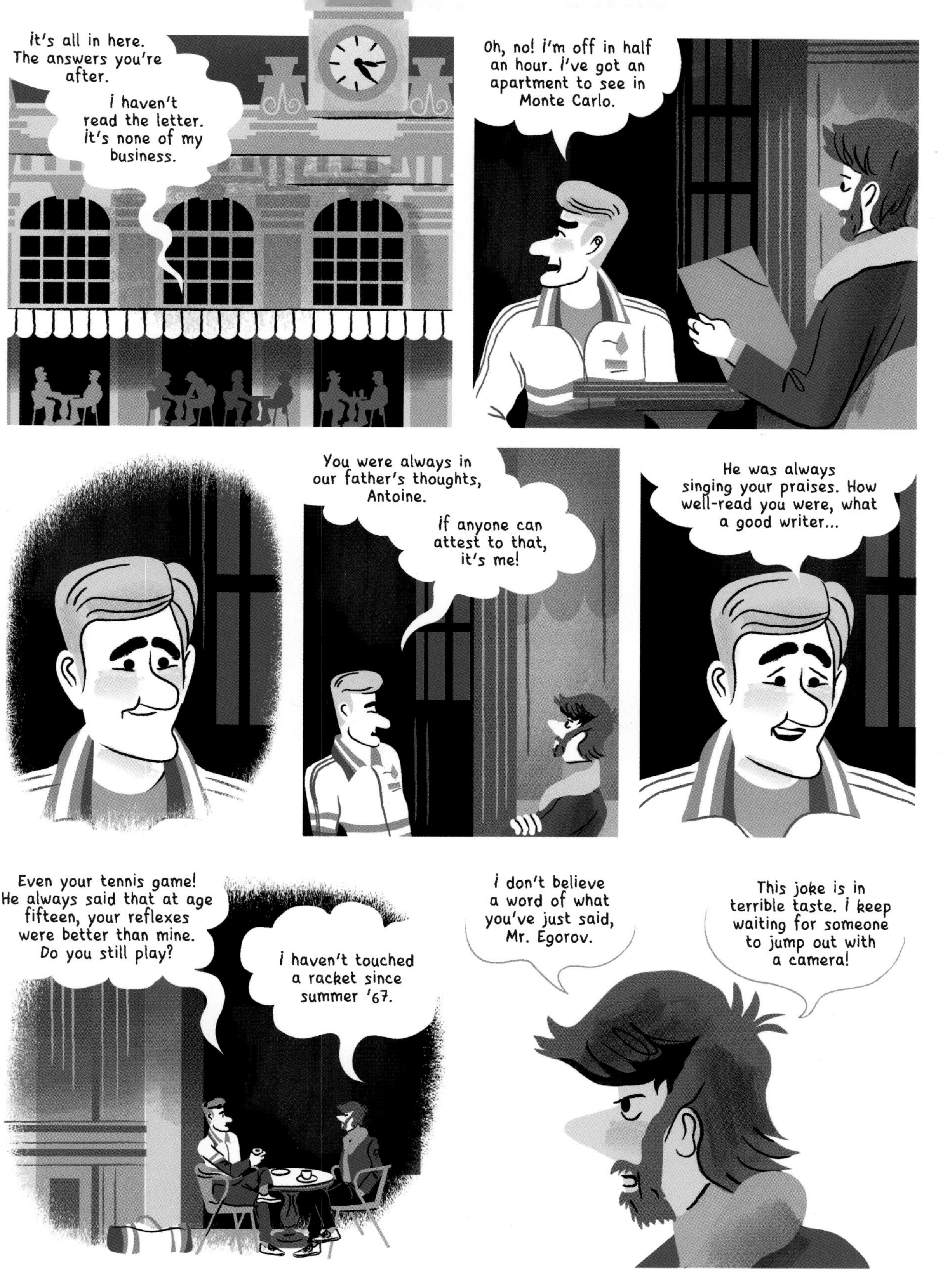

it's all in here. The answers you're after.
i haven't read the letter. it's none of my business.
Oh, no! i'm off in half an hour. i've got an apartment to see in Monte Carlo.
You were always in our father's thoughts, Antoine.
if anyone can attest to that, it's me!
He was always singing your praises. How well-read you were, what a good writer...
Even your tennis game! He always said that at age fifteen, your reflexes were better than mine. Do you still play?
i haven't touched a racket since summer '67.
i don't believe a word of what you've just said, Mr. Egorov.
This joke is in terrible taste. i keep waiting for someone to jump out with a camera!

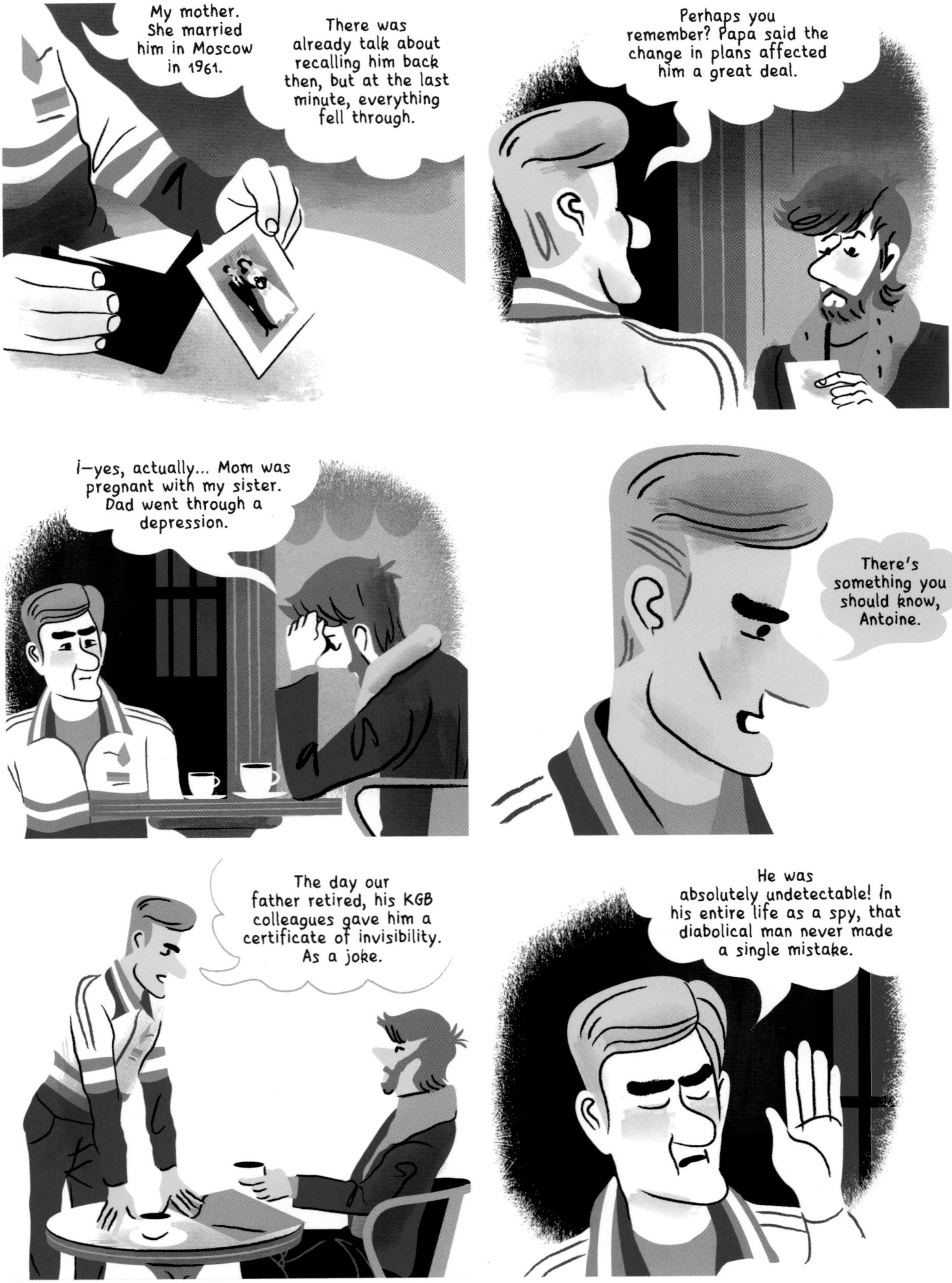
My mother. She married him in Moscow in 1961.
There was already talk about recalling him back then, but at the last minute, everything fell through.
Perhaps you remember? Papa said the change in plans affected him a great deal.
I—yes, actually... Mom was pregnant with my sister. Dad went through a depression.
There's something you should know, Antoine.
The day our father retired, his KGB colleagues gave him a certificate of invisibility. As a joke.
He was absolutely undetectable! In his entire life as a spy, that diabolical man never made a single mistake.

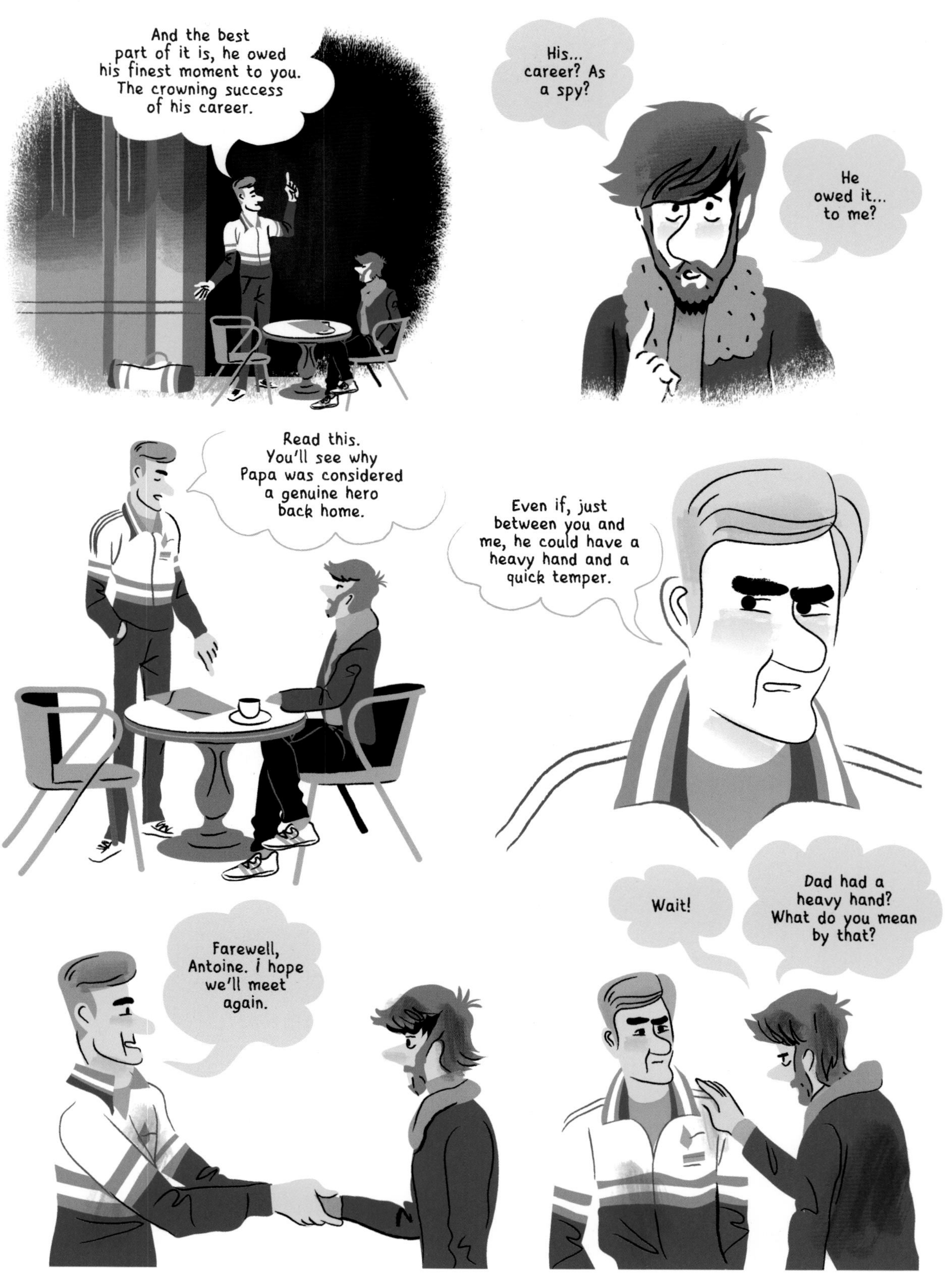
And the best part of it is, he owed his finest moment to you. The crowning success of his career.
His... career? As a spy?
He owed it... to me?
Read this. You'll see why Papa was considered a genuine hero back home.
Even if, just between you and me, he could have a heavy hand and a quick temper.
Farewell, Antoine. I hope we'll meet again.
Wait!
Dad had a heavy hand? What do you mean by that?

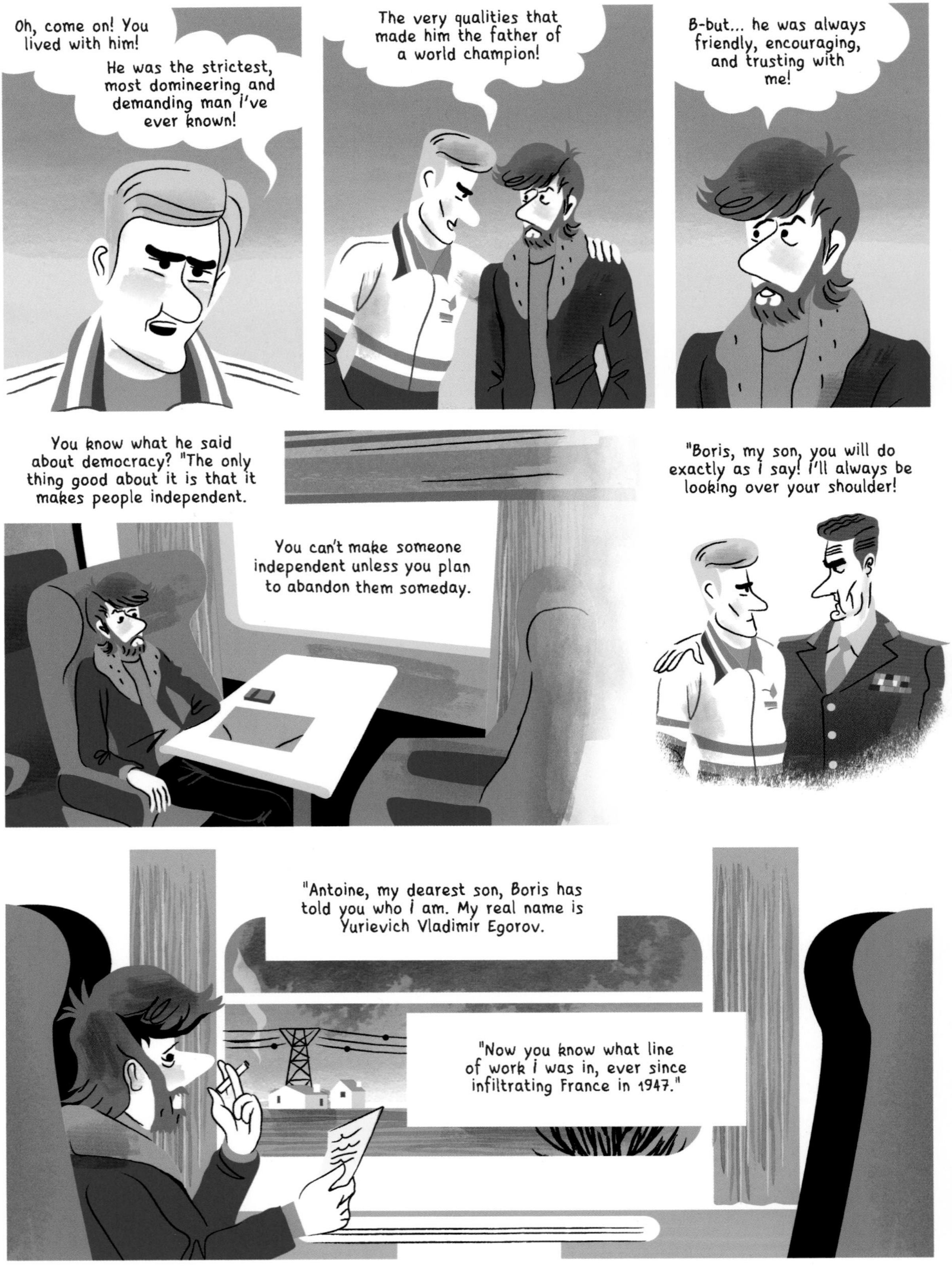

Oh, come on! You lived with him!
He was the strictest, most domineering and demanding man I've ever known!
The very qualities that made him the father of a world champion!
B-but... he was always friendly, encouraging, and trusting with me!
You know what he said about democracy? "The only thing good about it is that it makes people independent.
You can't make someone independent unless you plan to abandon them someday.
"Boris, my son, you will do exactly as I say! I'll always be looking over your shoulder!
"Antoine, my dearest son, Boris has told you who I am. My real name is Yurievich Vladimir Egorov.
"Now you know what line of work I was in, ever since infiltrating France in 1947."

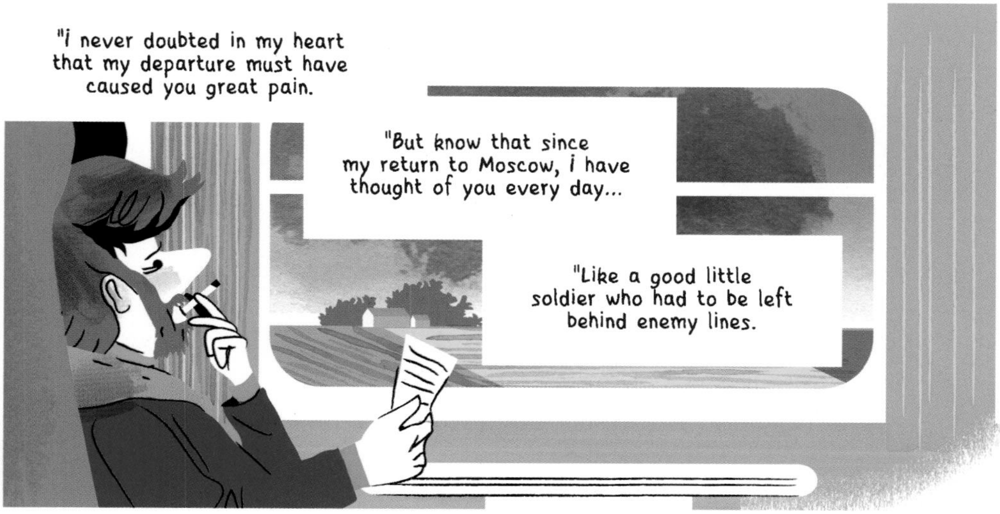
"I never doubted in my heart that my departure must have caused you great pain.
"But know that since my return to Moscow, I have thought of you every day...
"Like a good little soldier who had to be left behind enemy lines.

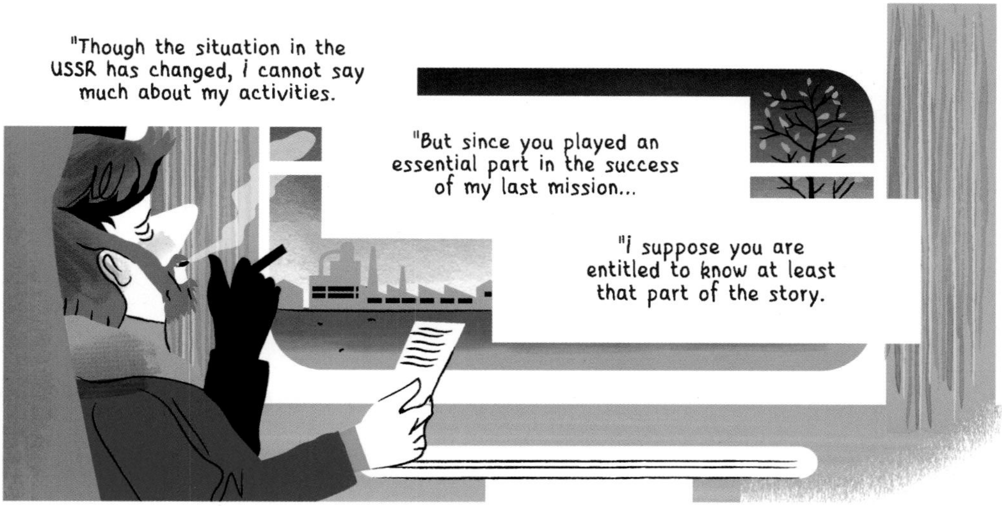
"Though the situation in the USSR has changed, I cannot say much about my activities.
"But since you played an essential part in the success of my last mission...
"I suppose you are entitled to know at least that part of the story.

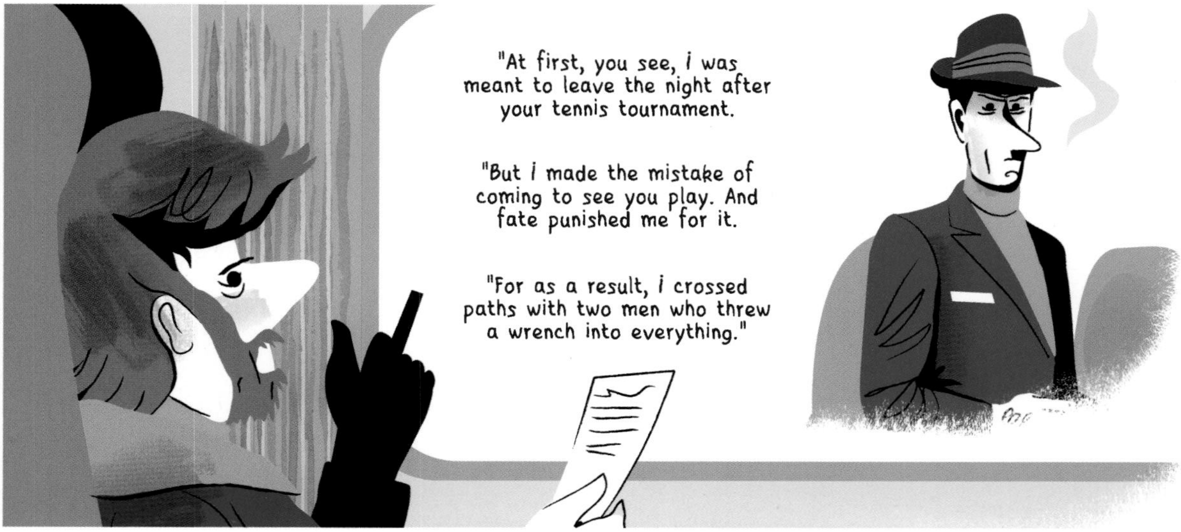
"At first, you see, I was meant to leave the night after your tennis tournament.
"But I made the mistake of coming to see you play. And fate punished me for it.
"For as a result, I crossed paths with two men who threw a wrench into everything."

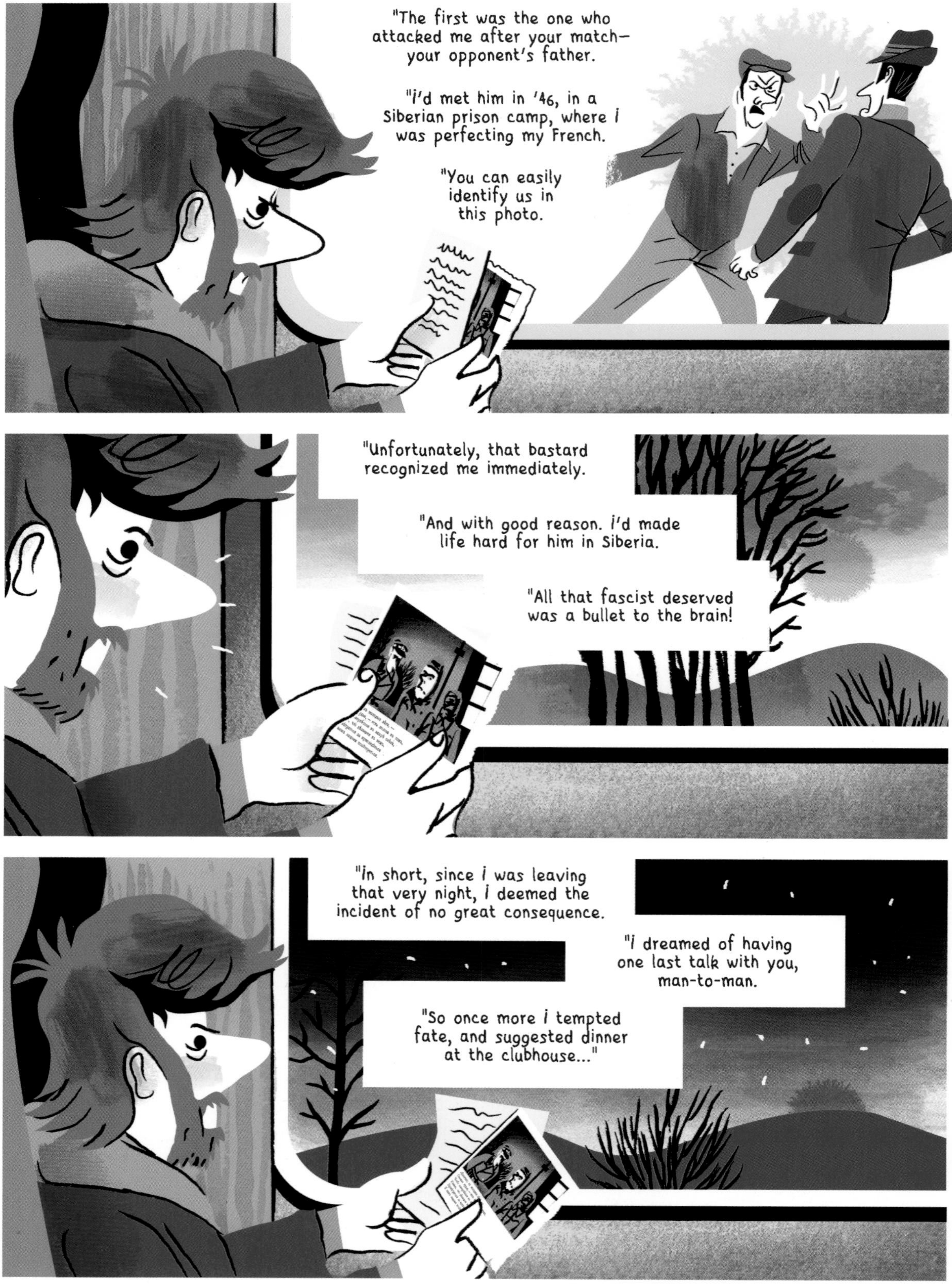
"The first was the one who attacked me after your match—your opponent's father.
"I'd met him in '46, in a Siberian prison camp, where I was perfecting my French.
"You can easily identify us in this photo.
"Unfortunately, that bastard recognized me immediately.
"And with good reason. I'd made life hard for him in Siberia.
"All that fascist deserved was a bullet to the brain!
"In short, since I was leaving that very night, I deemed the incident of no great consequence.
"I dreamed of having one last talk with you, man-to-man.
"So once more I tempted fate, and suggested dinner at the clubhouse..."

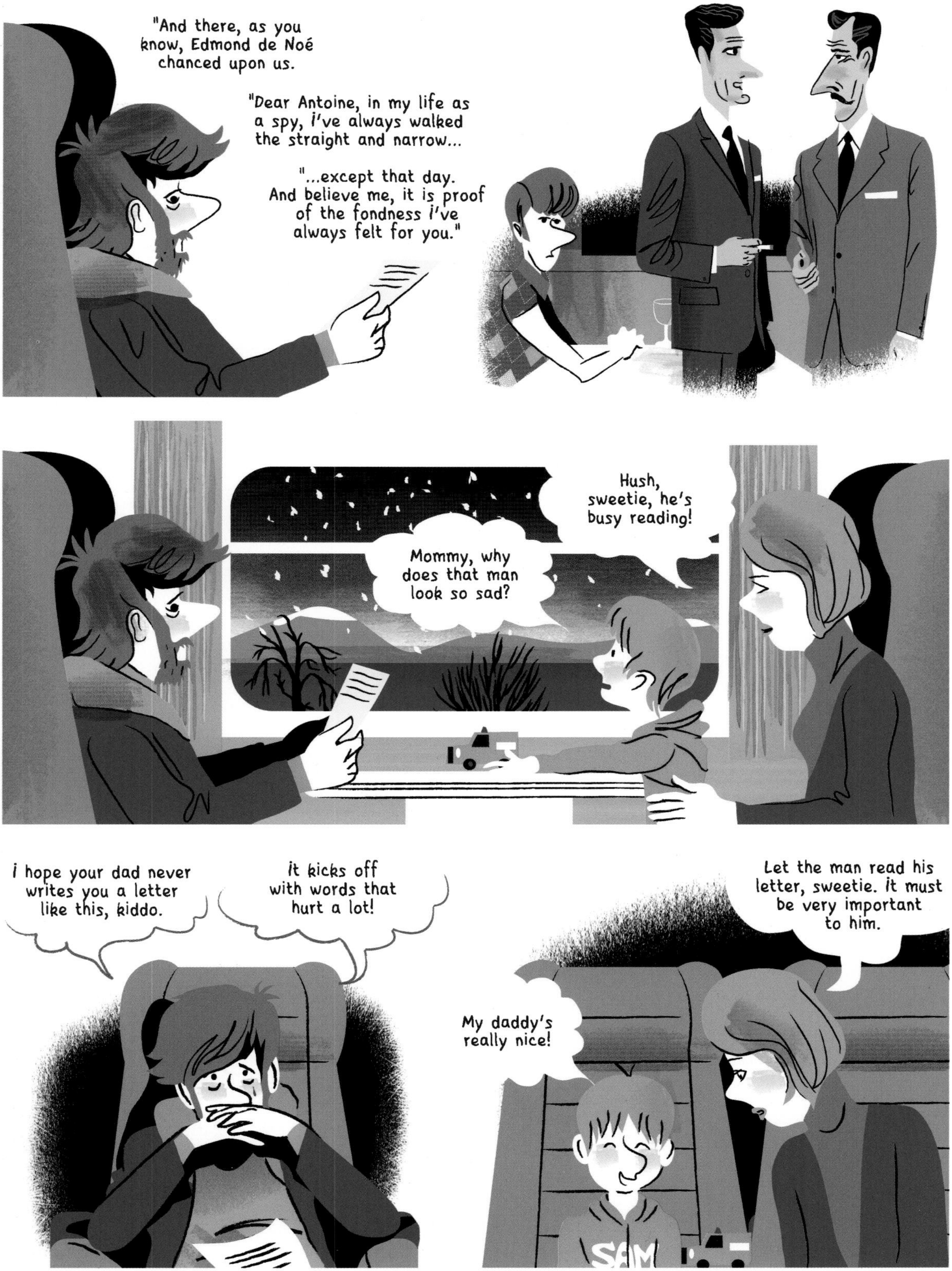
"And there, as you know, Edmond de Noé chanced upon us.
"Dear Antoine, in my life as a spy, I've always walked the straight and narrow...
"...except that day. And believe me, it is proof of the fondness I've always felt for you."
Hush, sweetie, he's busy reading!
Mommy, why does that man look so sad?
I hope your dad never writes you a letter like this, kiddo.
It kicks off with words that hurt a lot!
Let the man read his letter, sweetie. It must be very important to him.
My daddy's really nice!
SAM

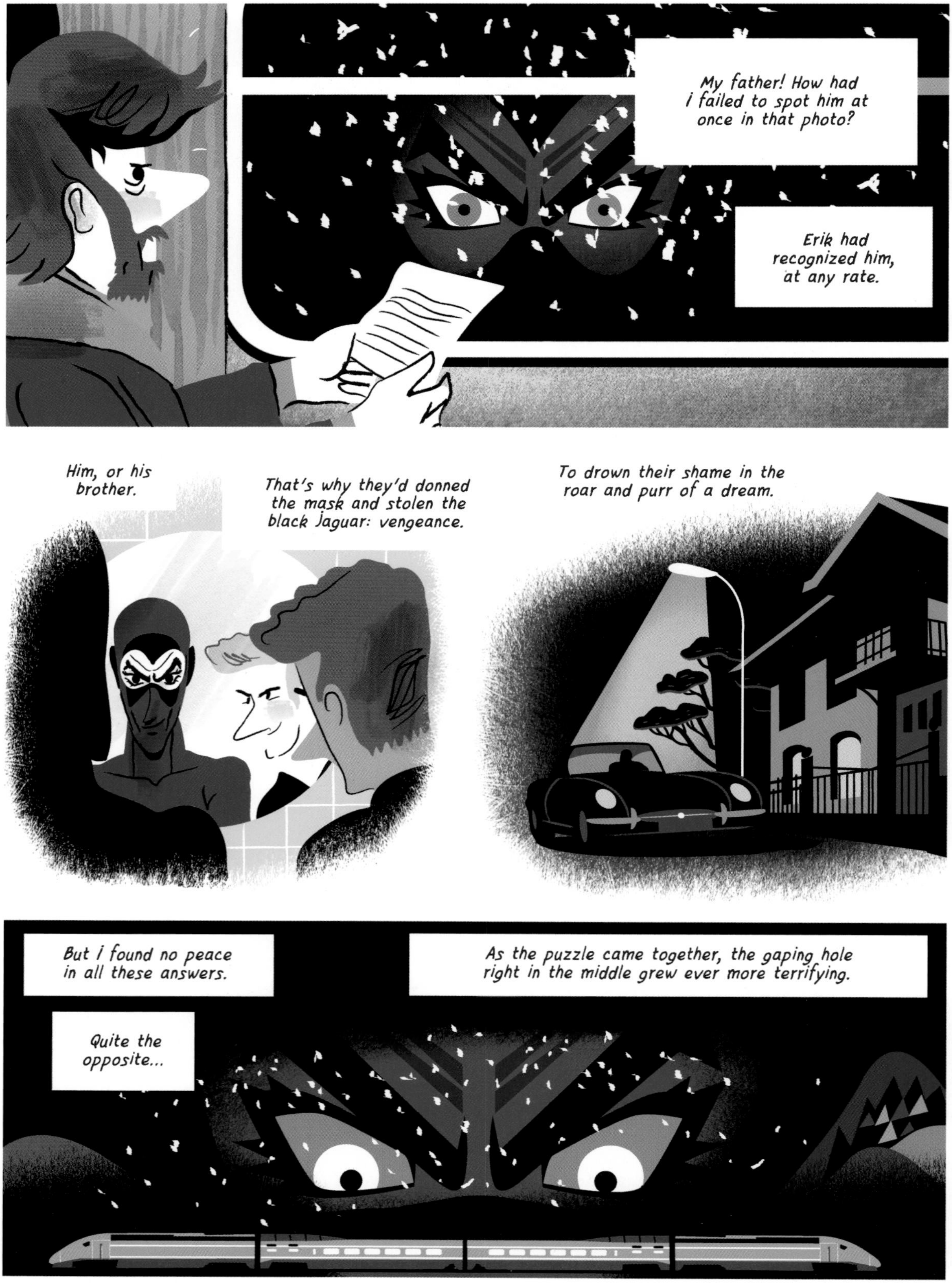
My father! How had i failed to spot him at once in that photo?
Erik had recognized him, at any rate.
Him, or his brother.
That's why they'd donned the mask and stolen the black Jaguar: vengeance.
To drown their shame in the roar and purr of a dream.
But i found no peace in all these answers.
As the puzzle came together, the gaping hole right in the middle grew ever more terrifying.
Quite the opposite...

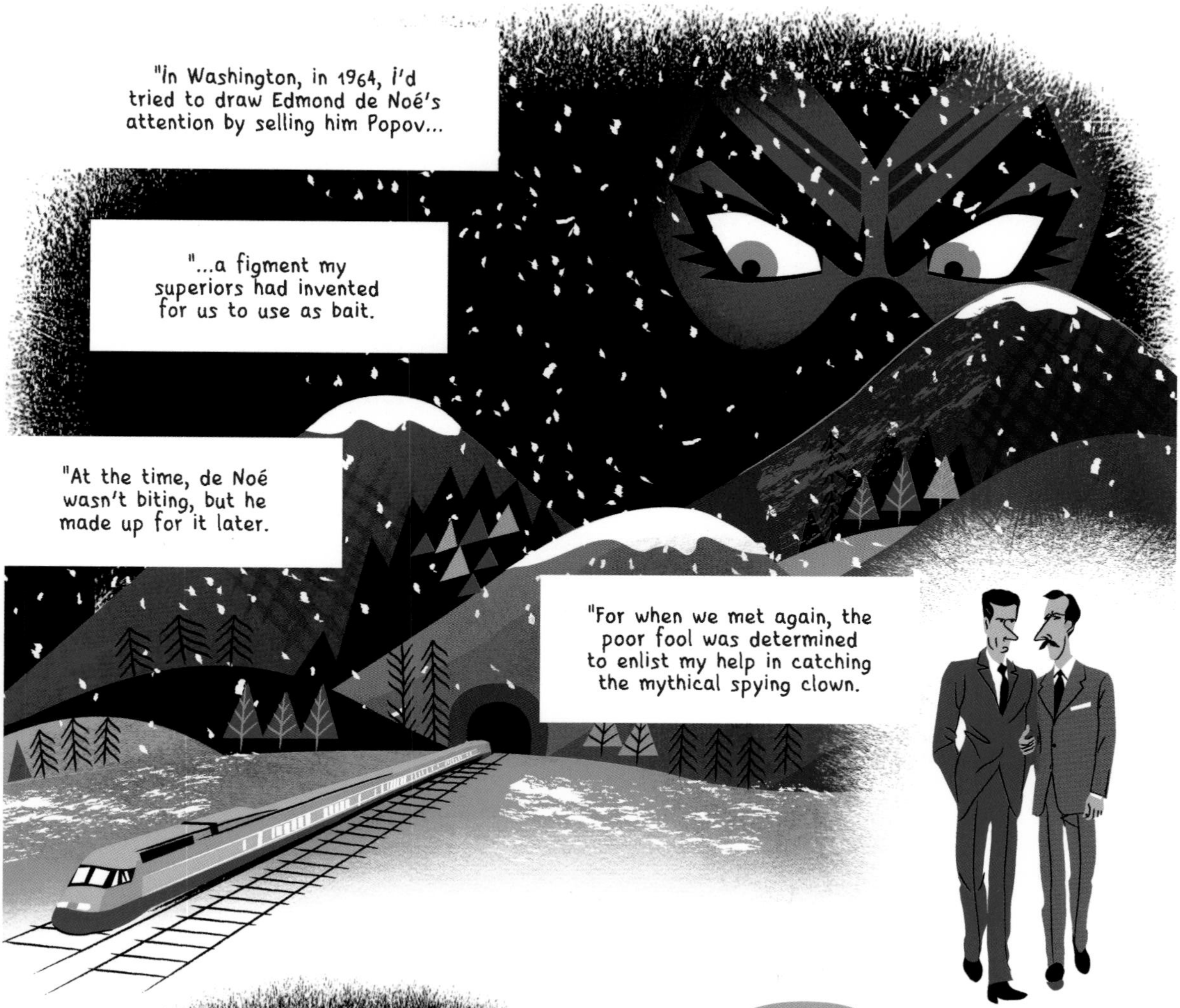
"In Washington, in 1964, I'd tried to draw Edmond de Noé's attention by selling him Popov...
"...a figment my superiors had invented for us to use as bait.
"At the time, de Noé wasn't biting, but he made up for it later.
"For when we met again, the poor fool was determined to enlist my help in catching the mythical spying clown.

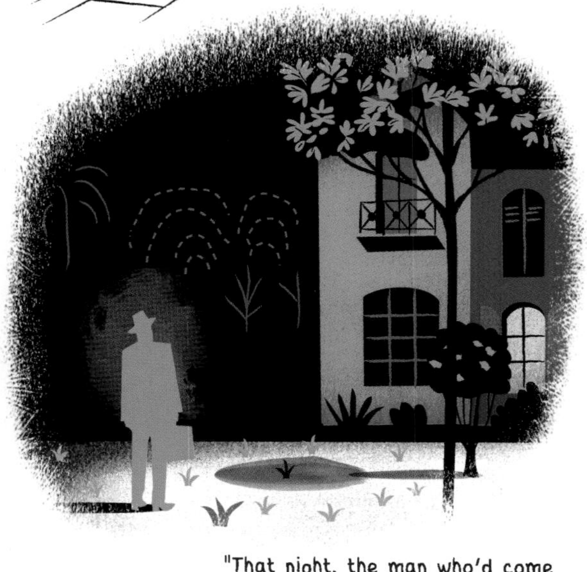
"That night, the man who'd come to extract me left empty-handed.

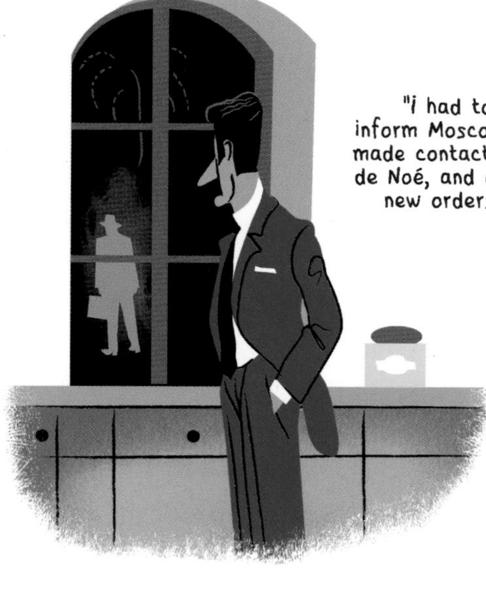
"I had to inform Moscow I'd made contact with de Noé, and await new orders."

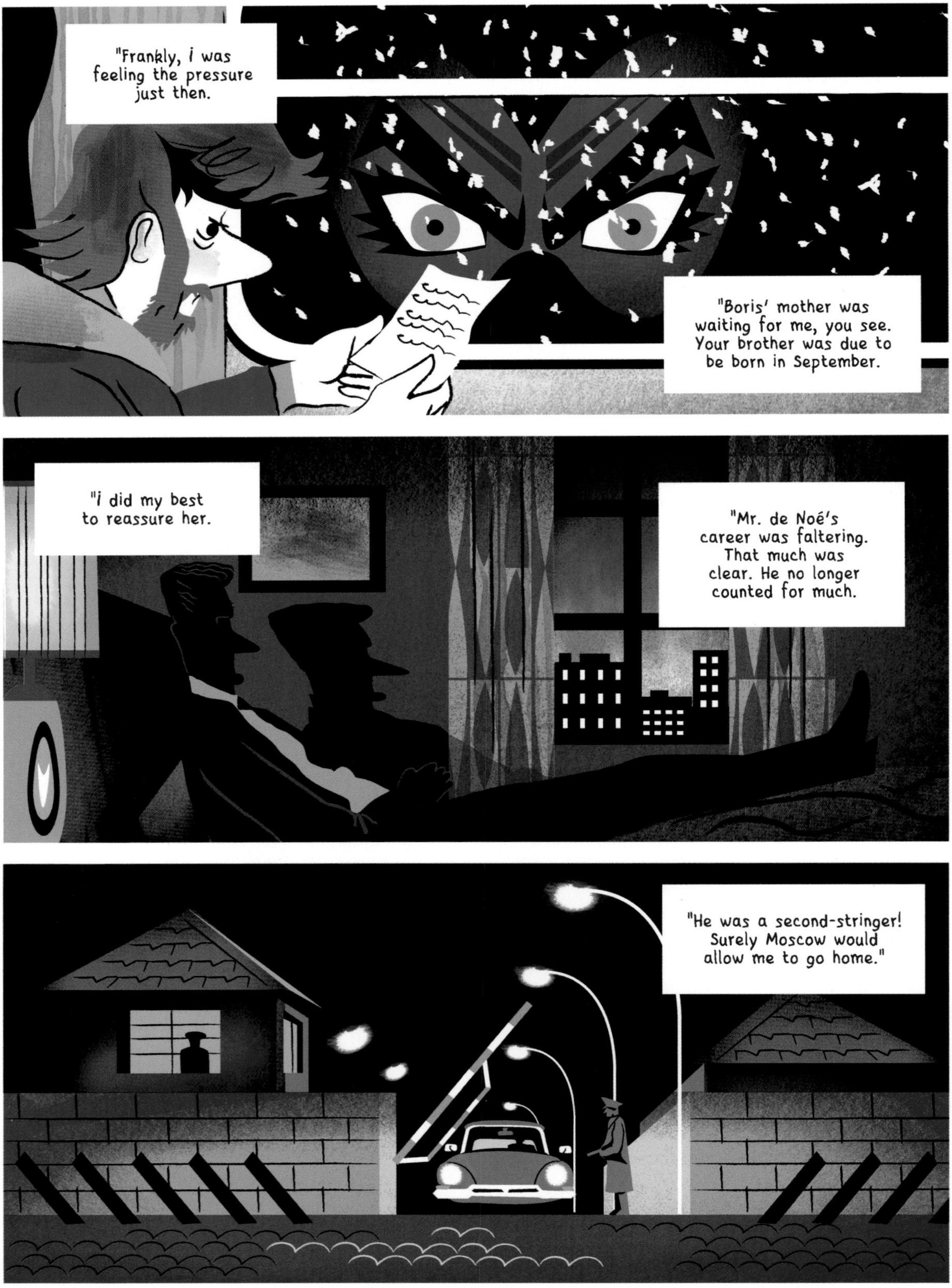
"Frankly, i was feeling the pressure just then.
"Boris' mother was waiting for me, you see. Your brother was due to be born in September.
"i did my best to reassure her.
"Mr. de Noé's career was faltering. That much was clear. He no longer counted for much.
"He was a second-stringer! Surely Moscow would allow me to go home."

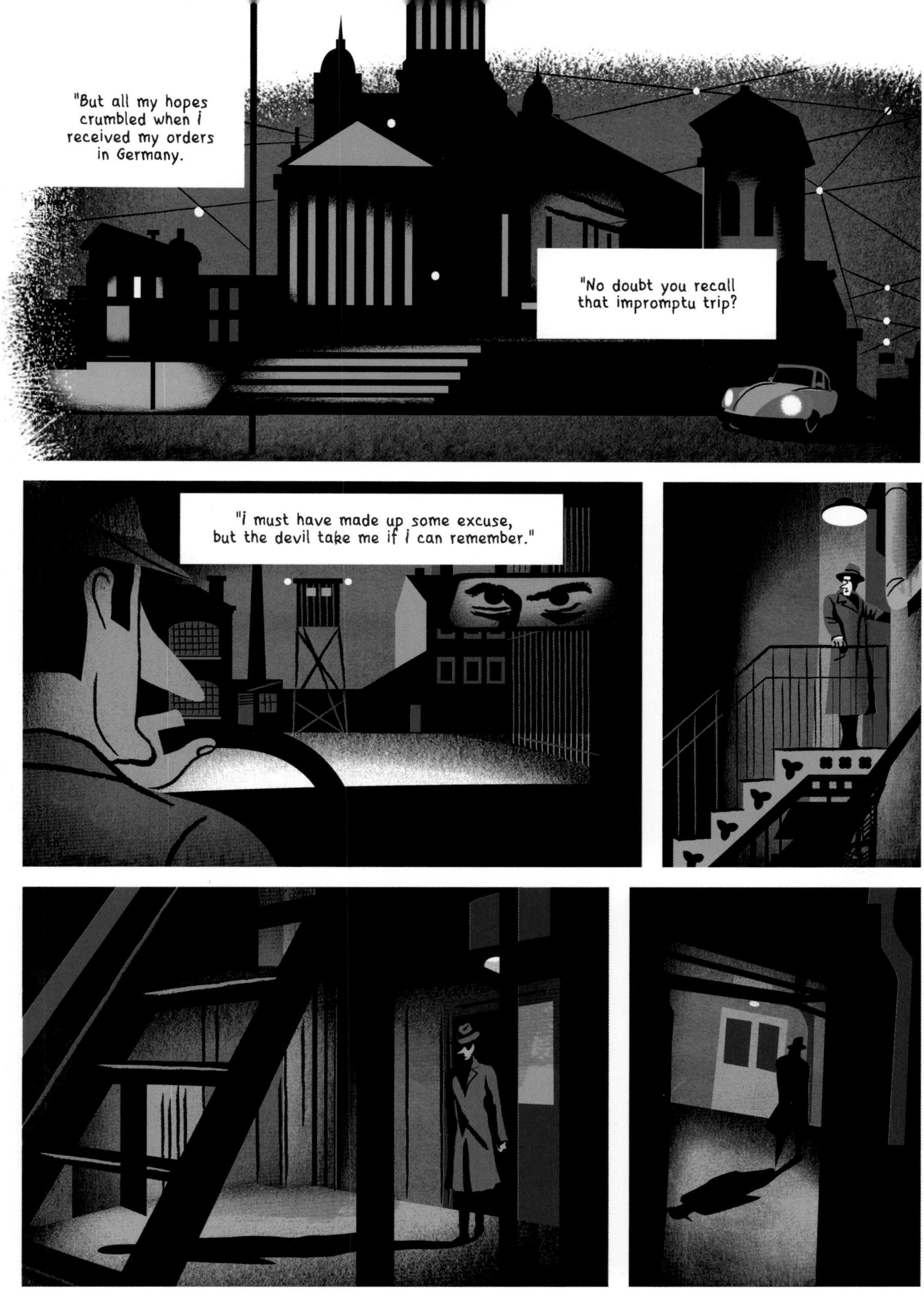
"But all my hopes crumbled when I received my orders in Germany.
"No doubt you recall that impromptu trip?
"I must have made up some excuse, but the devil take me if I can remember."

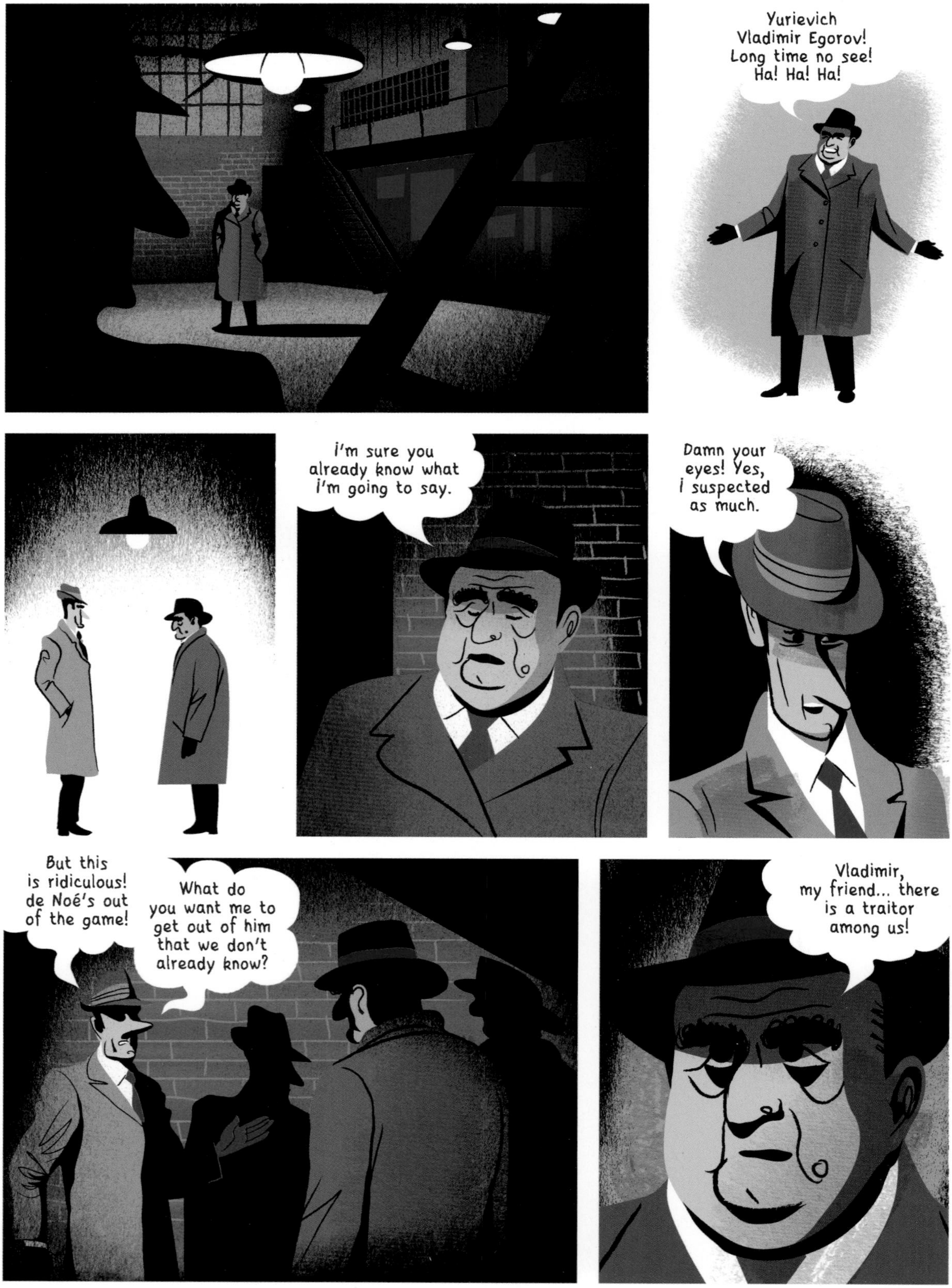
Yurievich Vladimir Egorov! Long time no see! Ha! Ha! Ha!
I'm sure you already know what I'm going to say.
Damn your eyes! Yes, I suspected as much.
But this is ridiculous! de Noé's out of the game!
What do you want me to get out of him that we don't already know?
Vladimir, my friend... there is a traitor among us!

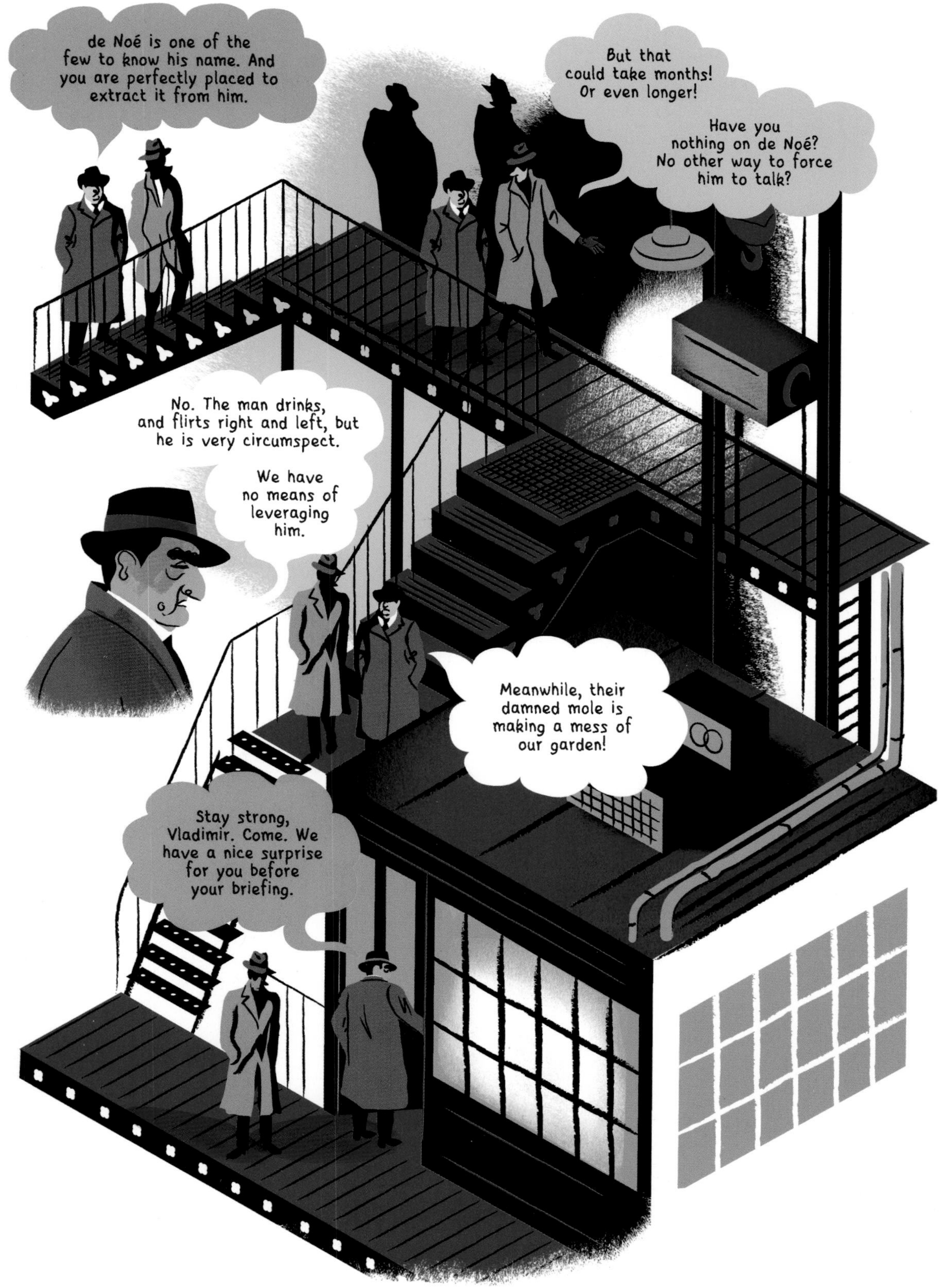
de Noé is one of the few to know his name. And you are perfectly placed to extract it from him.
But that could take months! Or even longer!
Have you nothing on de Noé? No other way to force him to talk?
No. The man drinks, and flirts right and left, but he is very circumspect.
We have no means of leveraging him.
Meanwhile, their damned mole is making a mess of our garden!
Stay strong, Vladimir. Come. We have a nice surprise for you before your briefing.

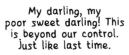

My darling, my poor sweet darling! This is beyond our control. Just like last time.

i'll do everything i can to wrap this up as soon as possible. i promise!

Vlad! Please be careful!

Your wife's words are worth their weight in gold, Yurievich. Bring us the name of the mole. That is all we ask.

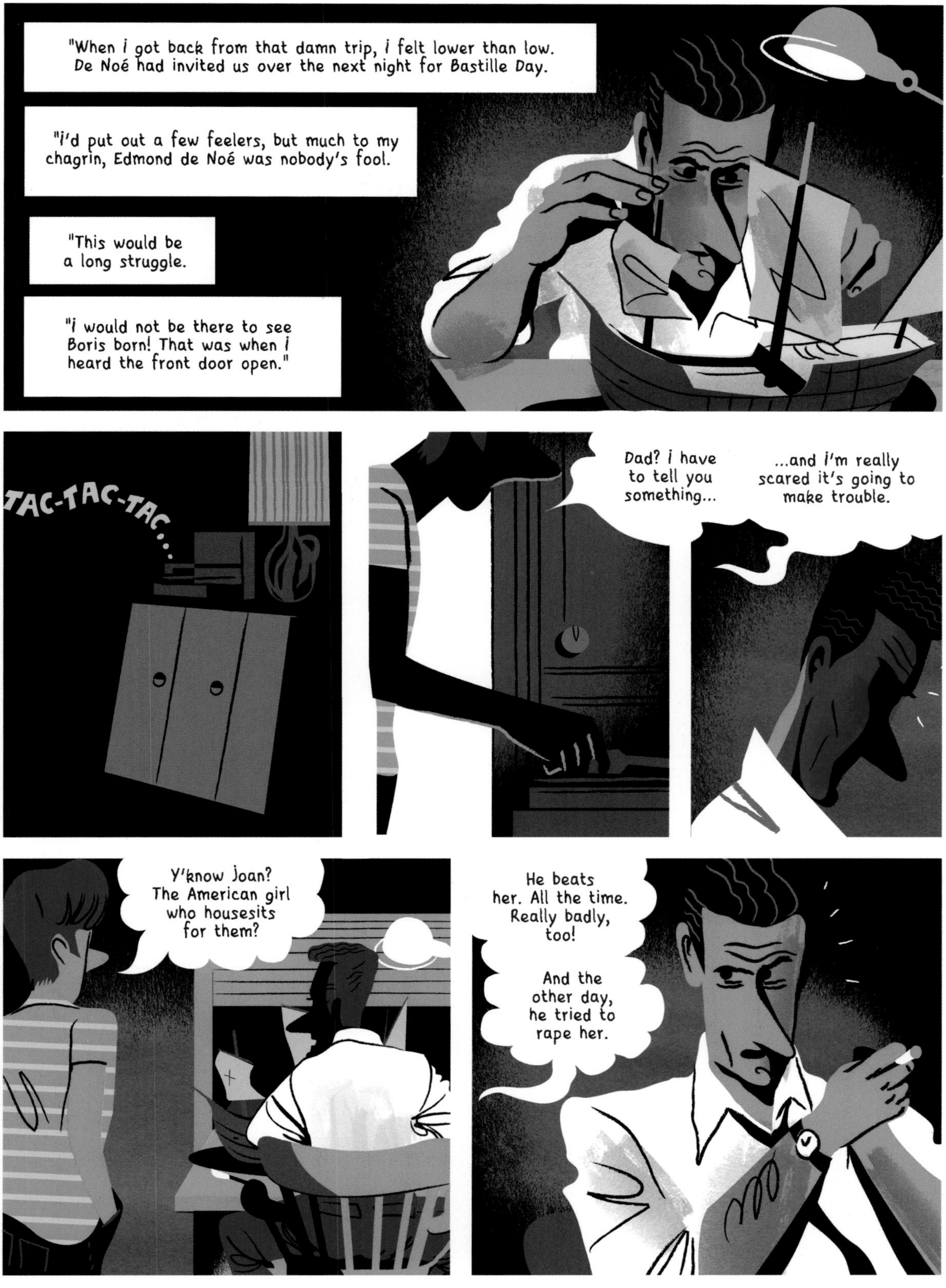
"When I got back from that damn trip, I felt lower than low. De Noé had invited us over the next night for Bastille Day.
"I'd put out a few feelers, but much to my chagrin, Edmond de Noé was nobody's fool.
"This would be a long struggle.
"I would not be there to see Boris born! That was when I heard the front door open."
TAC-TAC-TAC...
Dad? I have to tell you something...
...and I'm really scared it's going to make trouble.
Y'know Joan? The American girl who housesits for them?
He beats her. All the time. Really badly, too!
And the other day, he tried to rape her.

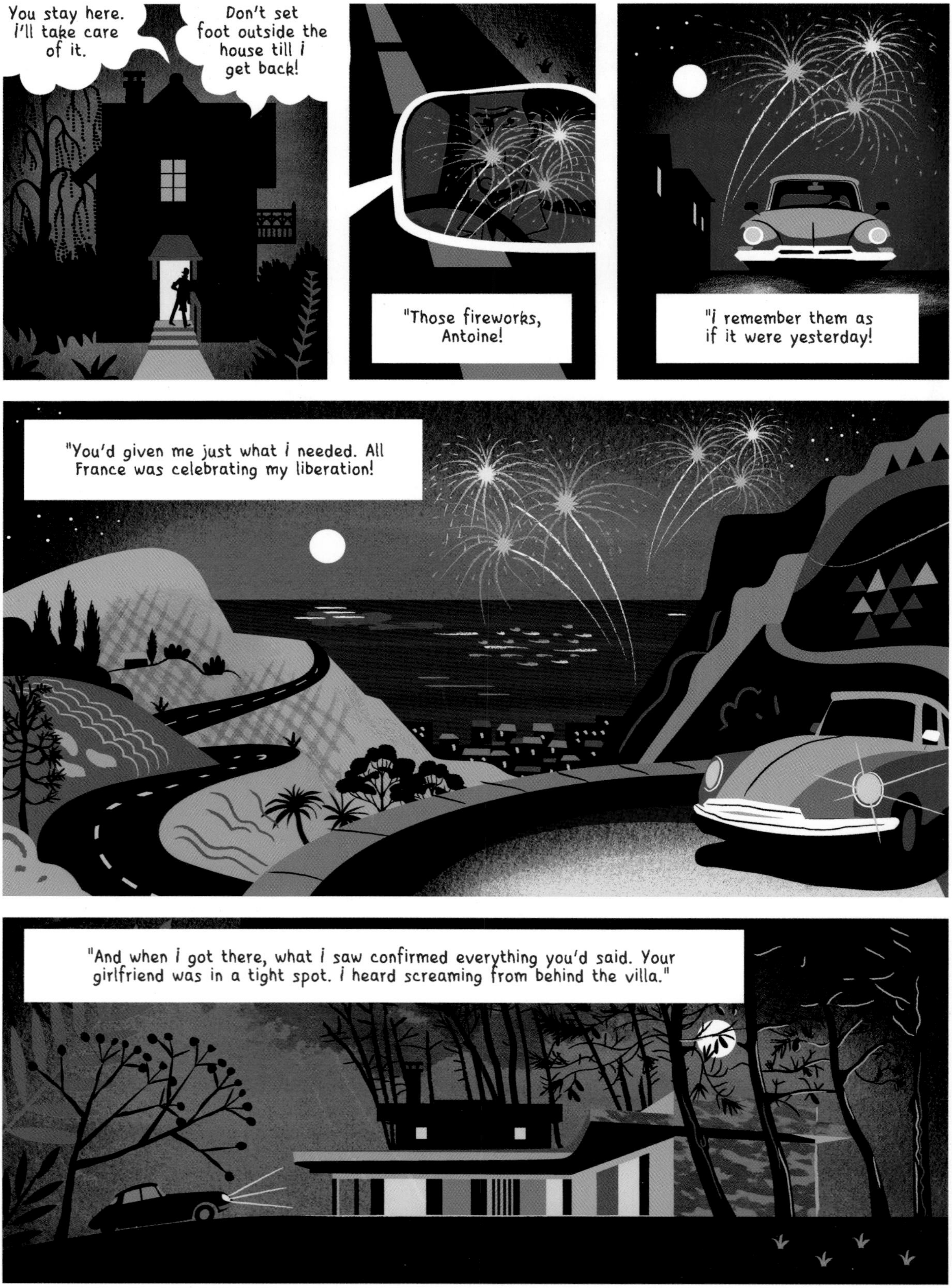
You stay here. I'll take care of it.
Don't set foot outside the house till I get back!
"Those fireworks, Antoine!
"I remember them as if it were yesterday!
"You'd given me just what I needed. All France was celebrating my liberation!
"And when I got there, what I saw confirmed everything you'd said. Your girlfriend was in a tight spot. I heard screaming from behind the villa."

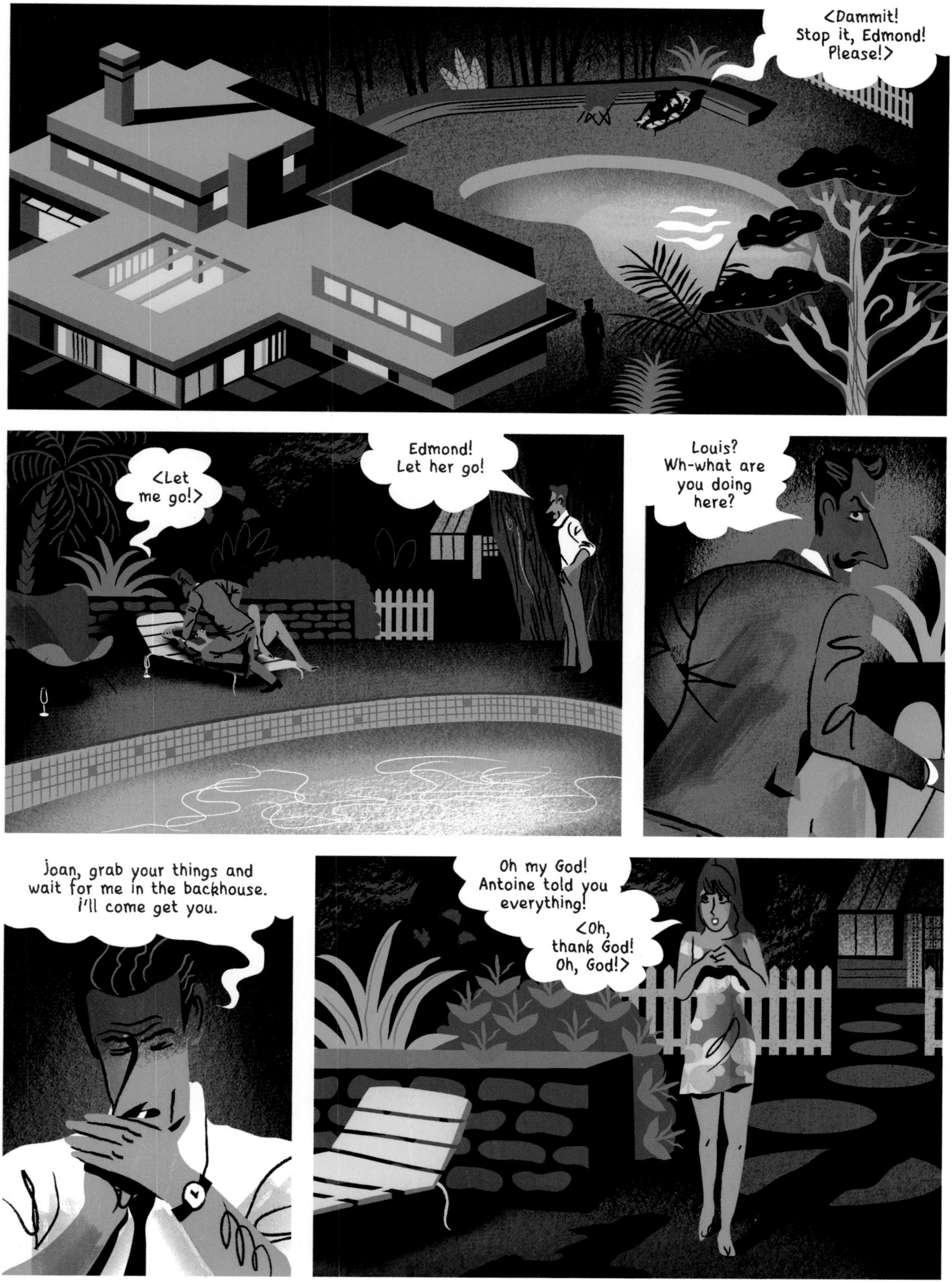
<Dammit! Stop it, Edmond! Please!>
<Let me go!>
Edmond! Let her go!
Louis? Wh-what are you doing here?
Joan, grab your things and wait for me in the backhouse. I'll come get you.
Oh my God! Antoine told you everything!
<Oh, thank God! Oh, God!>

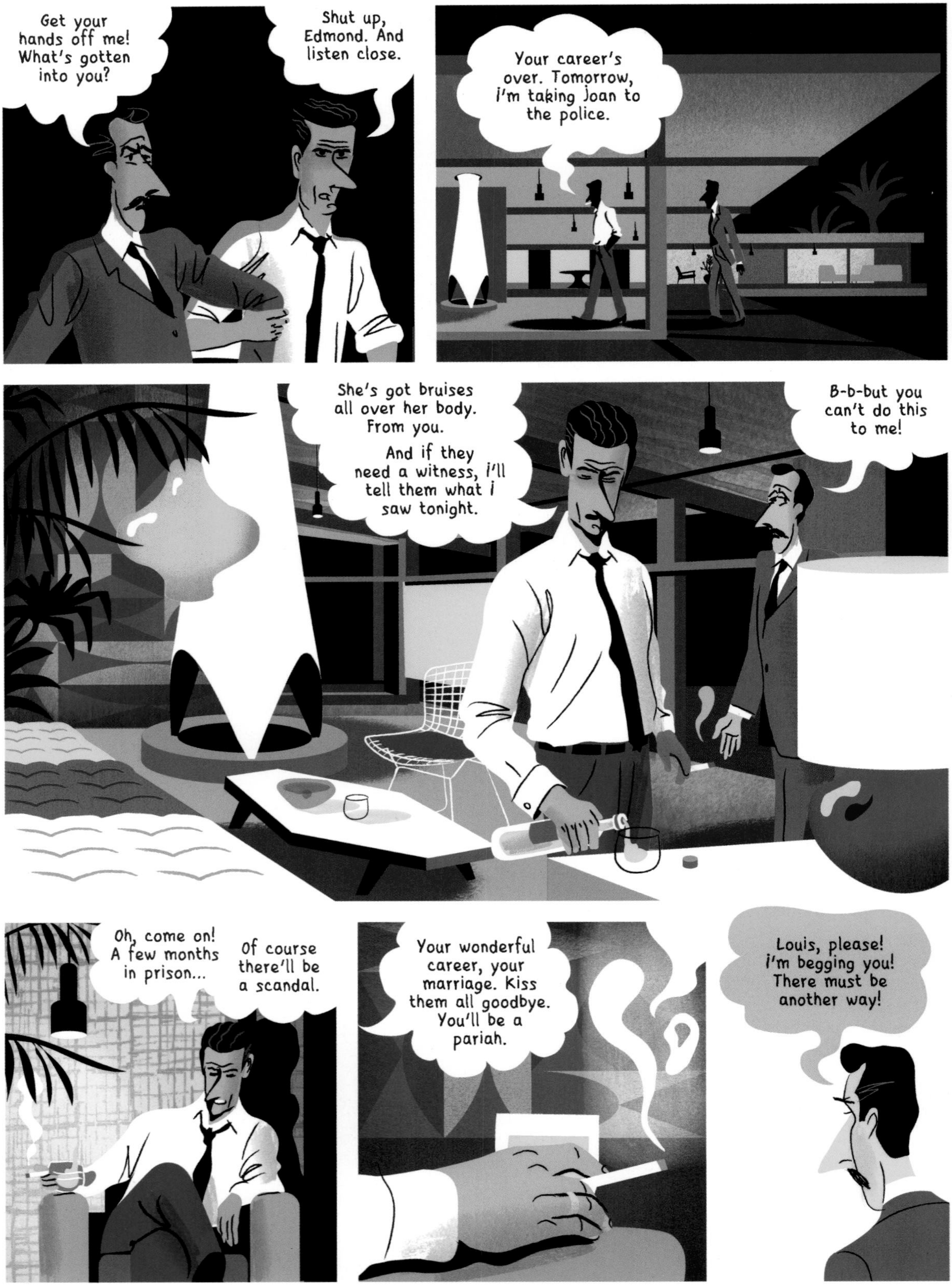
Get your hands off me! What's gotten into you?
Shut up, Edmond. And listen close.
Your career's over. Tomorrow, I'm taking Joan to the police.
She's got bruises all over her body. From you.
And if they need a witness, I'll tell them what I saw tonight.
B-b-but you can't do this to me!
Oh, come on! A few months in prison...
Of course there'll be a scandal.
Your wonderful career, your marriage. Kiss them all goodbye. You'll be a pariah.
Louis, please! I'm begging you! There must be another way!

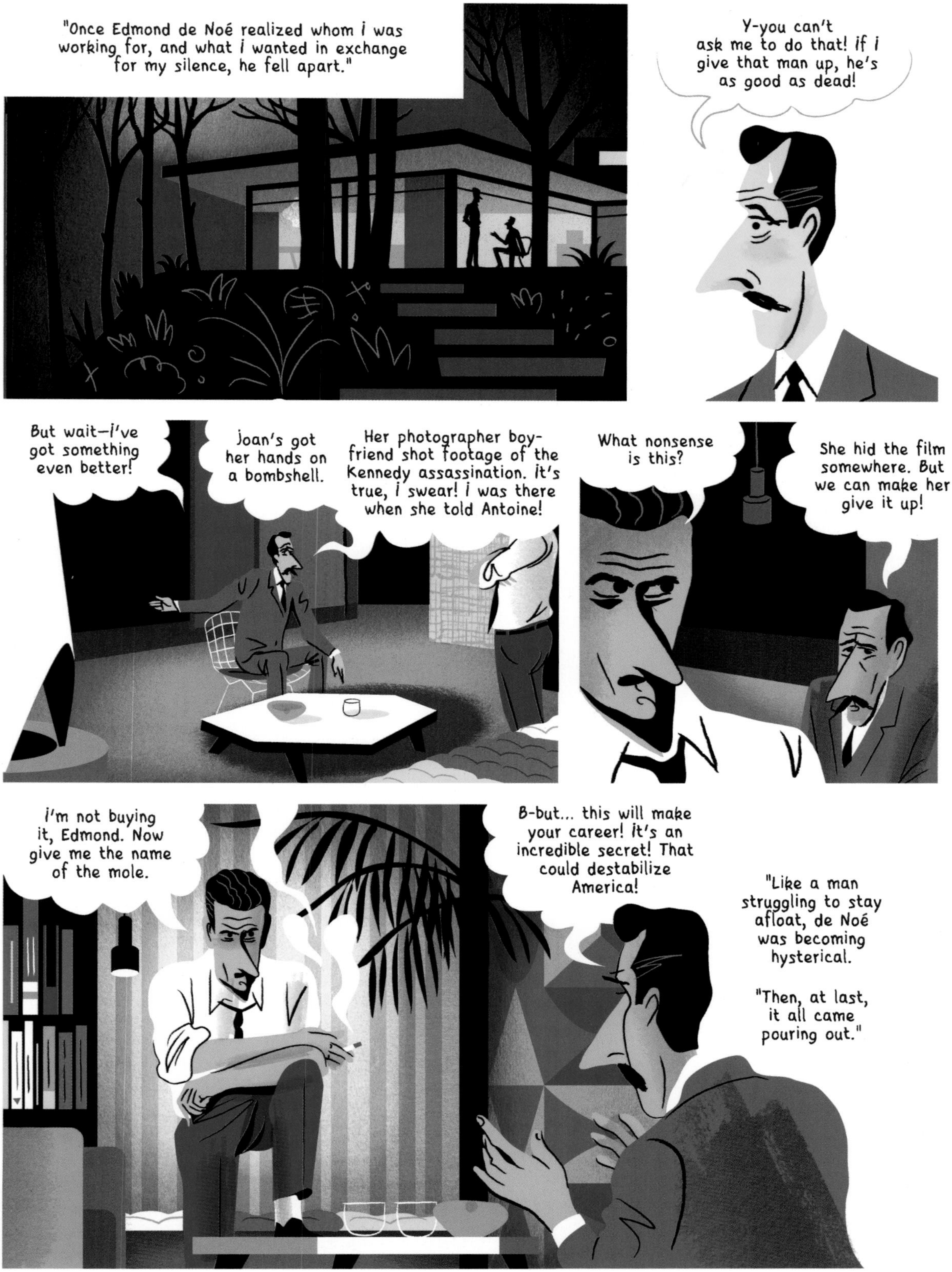
"Once Edmond de Noé realized whom I was working for, and what I wanted in exchange for my silence, he fell apart."
Y-you can't ask me to do that! If I give that man up, he's as good as dead!
But wait—I've got something even better!
Joan's got her hands on a bombshell.
Her photographer boyfriend shot footage of the Kennedy assassination. It's true, I swear! I was there when she told Antoine!
What nonsense is this?
She hid the film somewhere. But we can make her give it up!
I'm not buying it, Edmond. Now give me the name of the mole.
B-but... this will make your career! It's an incredible secret! That could destabilize America!
"Like a man struggling to stay afloat, de Noé was becoming hysterical.
"Then, at last, it all came pouring out."

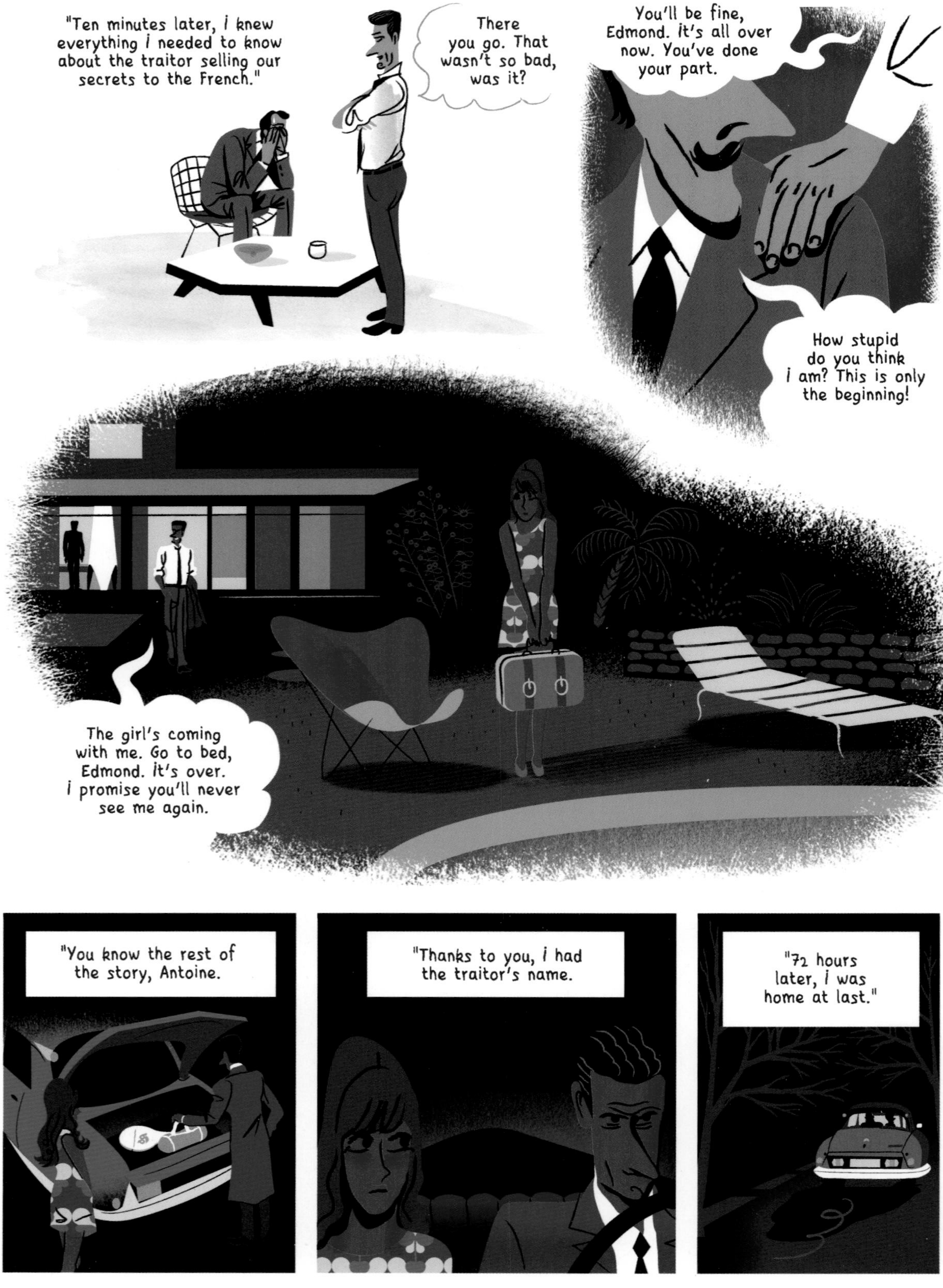
"Ten minutes later, I knew everything I needed to know about the traitor selling our secrets to the French."
There you go. That wasn't so bad, was it?
You'll be fine, Edmond. It's all over now. You've done your part.
How stupid do you think I am? This is only the beginning!
The girl's coming with me. Go to bed, Edmond. It's over. I promise you'll never see me again.
"You know the rest of the story, Antoine.
"Thanks to you, I had the traitor's name.
"72 hours later, I was home at last."

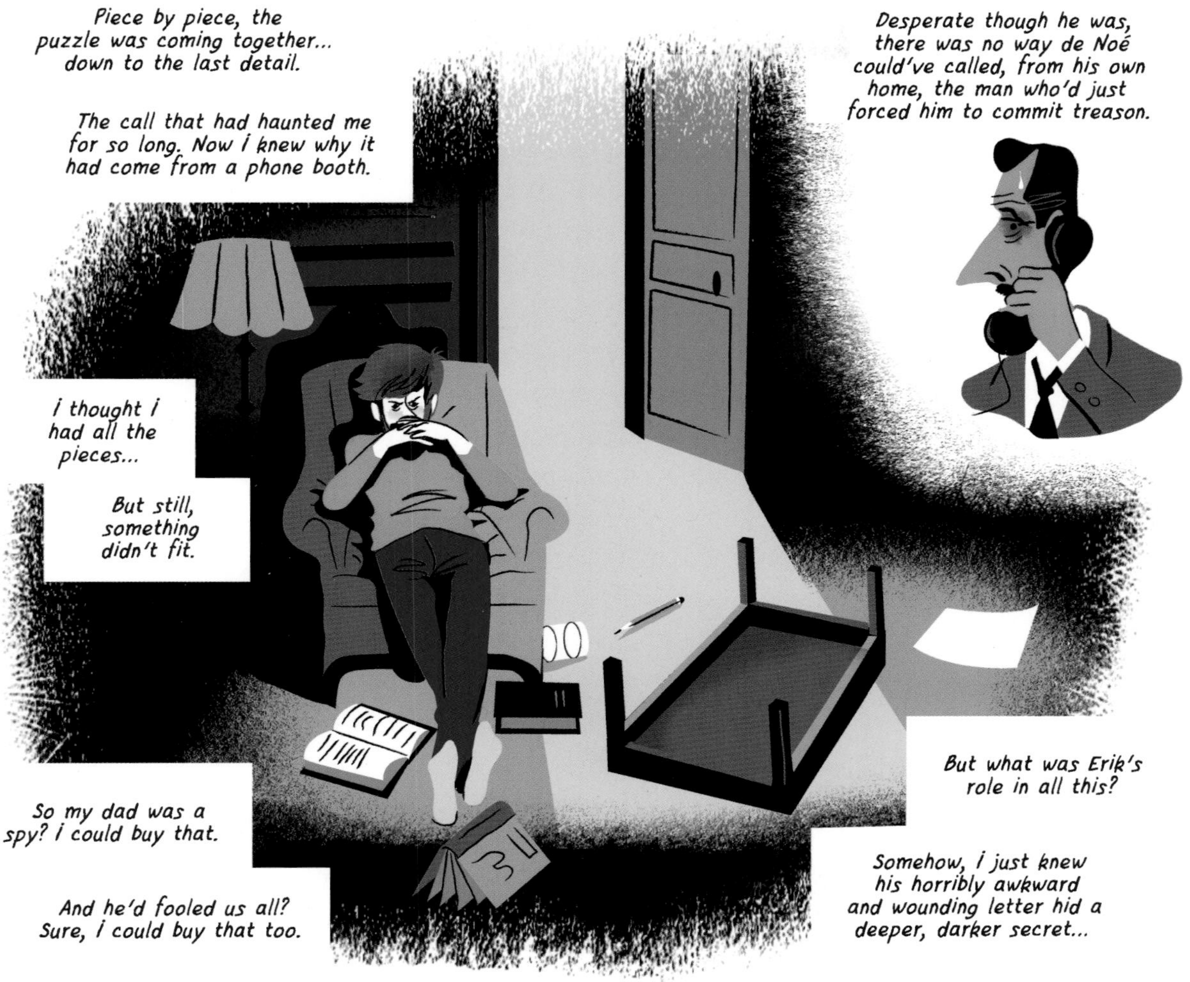

Piece by piece, the puzzle was coming together... down to the last detail.
The call that had haunted me for so long. Now I knew why it had come from a phone booth.
Desperate though he was, there was no way de Noé could've called, from his own home, the man who'd just forced him to commit treason.
I thought I had all the pieces...
But still, something didn't fit.
So my dad was a spy? I could buy that.
And he'd fooled us all? Sure, I could buy that too.
But what was Erik's role in all this?
Somehow, I just knew his horribly awkward and wounding letter hid a deeper, darker secret...

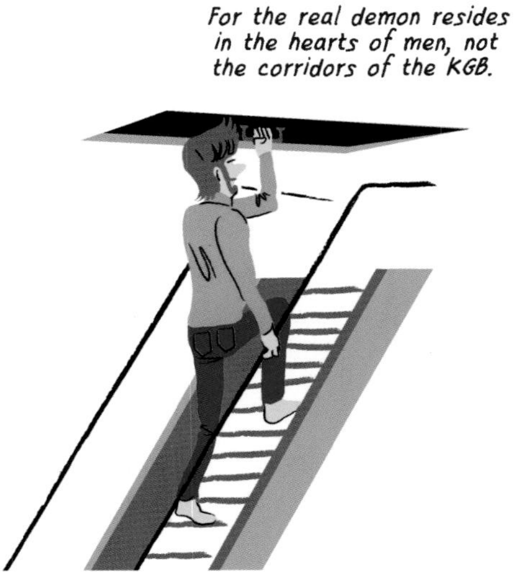

For the real demon resides in the hearts of men, not the corridors of the KGB.

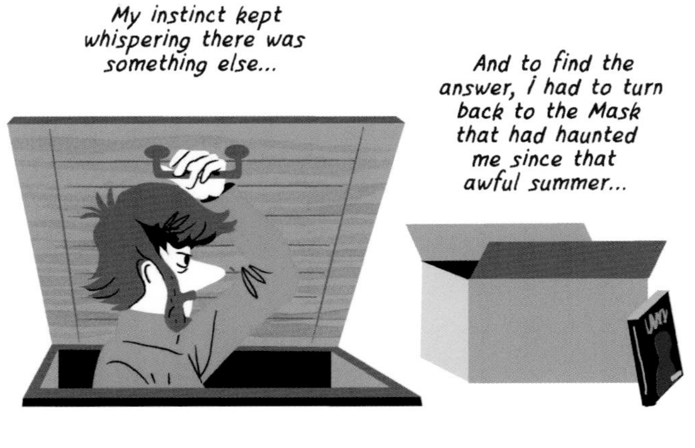

My instinct kept whispering there was something else...
And to find the answer, I had to turn back to the Mask that had haunted me since that awful summer...

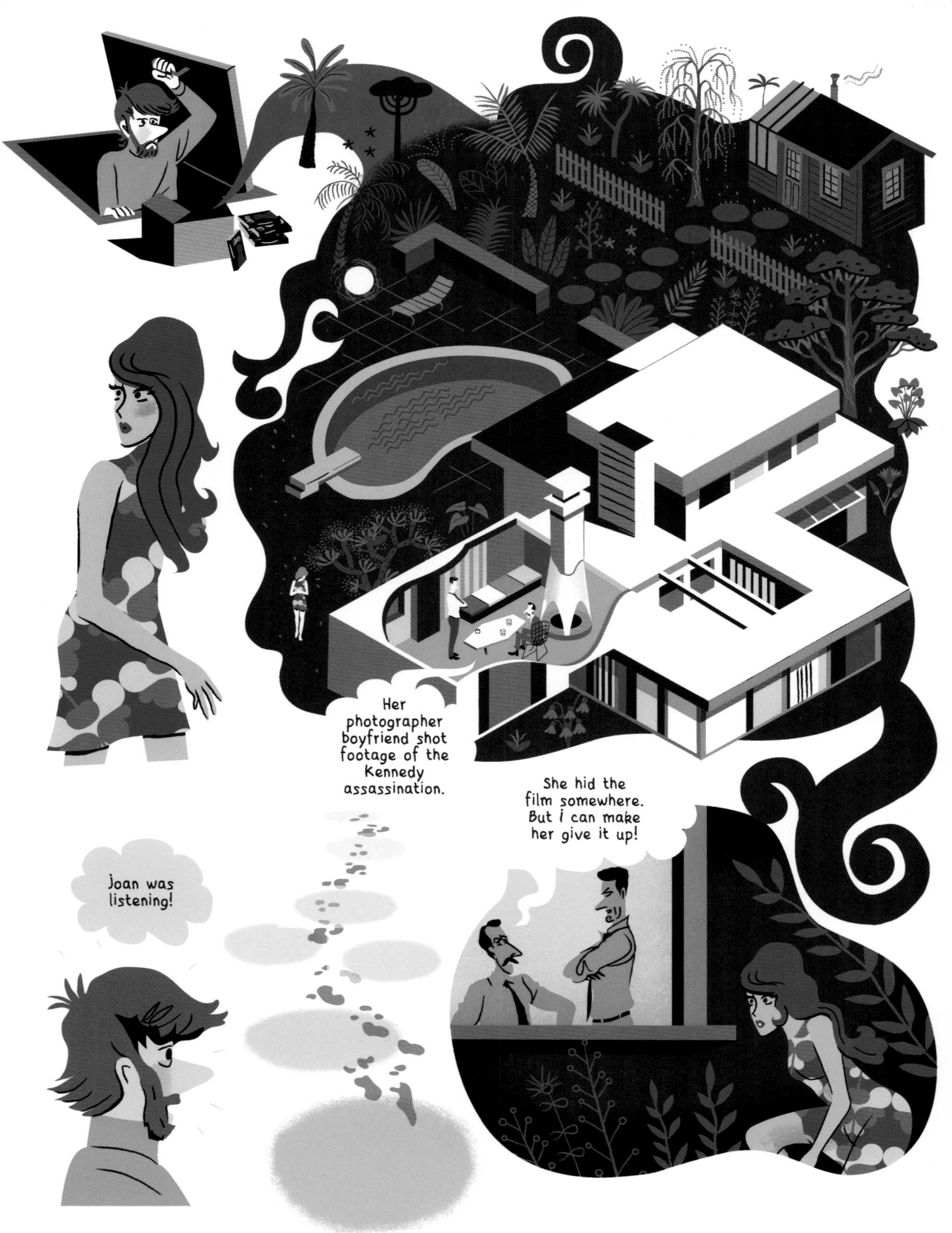
Her photographer boyfriend shot footage of the Kennedy assassination.
She hid the film somewhere. But I can make her give it up!
Joan was listening!

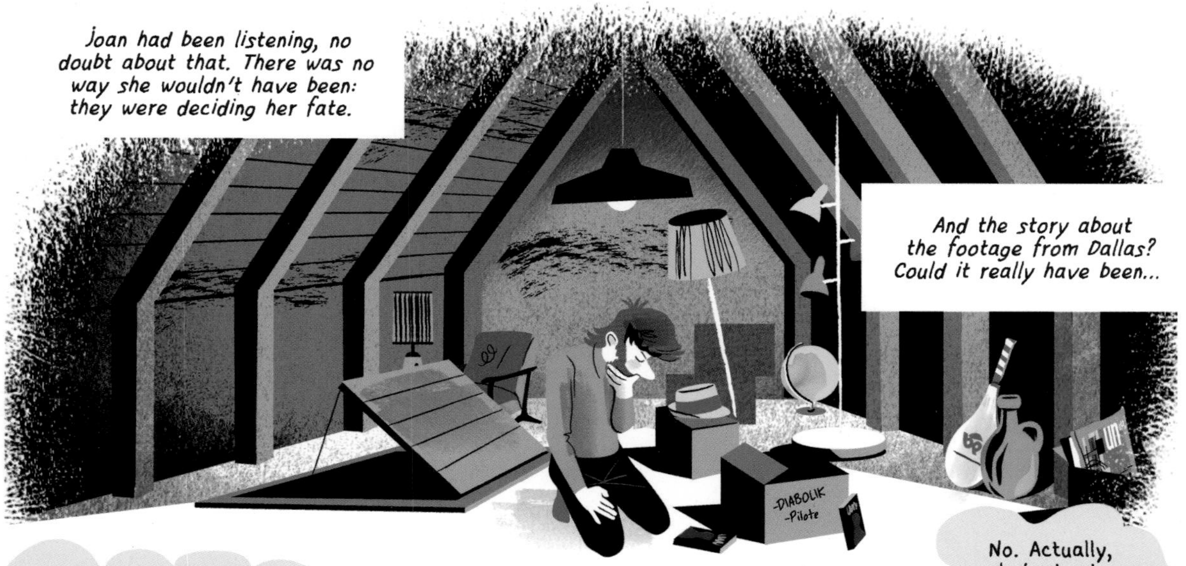
Joan had been listening, no doubt about that. There was no way she wouldn't have been: they were deciding her fate.
And the story about the footage from Dallas? Could it really have been...
-DIABOLIK
-Pilote

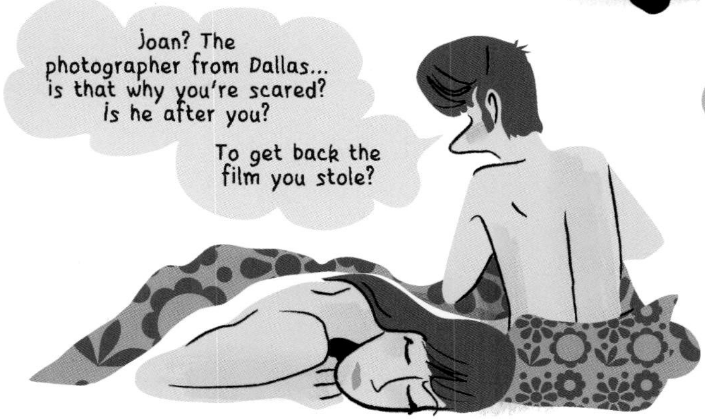
Joan? The photographer from Dallas... is that why you're scared? Is he after you?
To get back the film you stole?

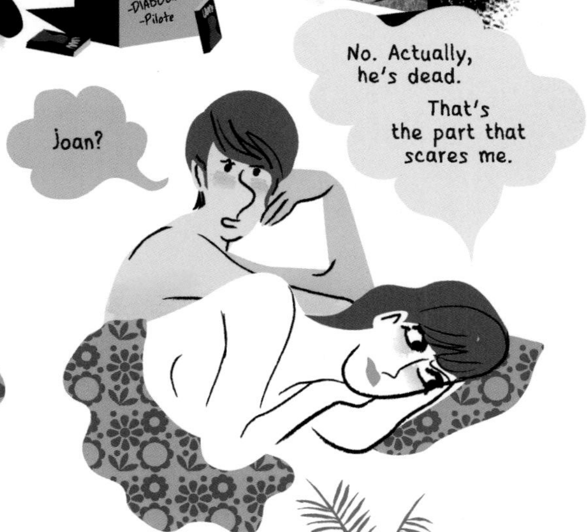
Joan?
No. Actually, he's dead.
That's the part that scares me.

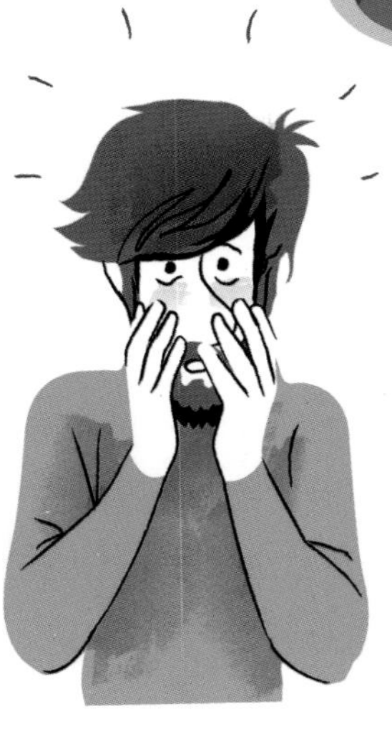

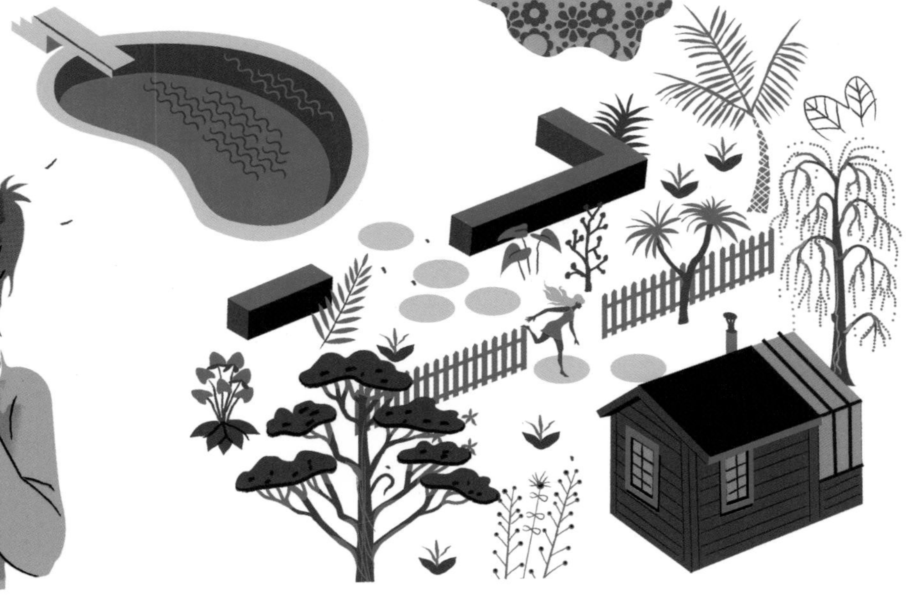

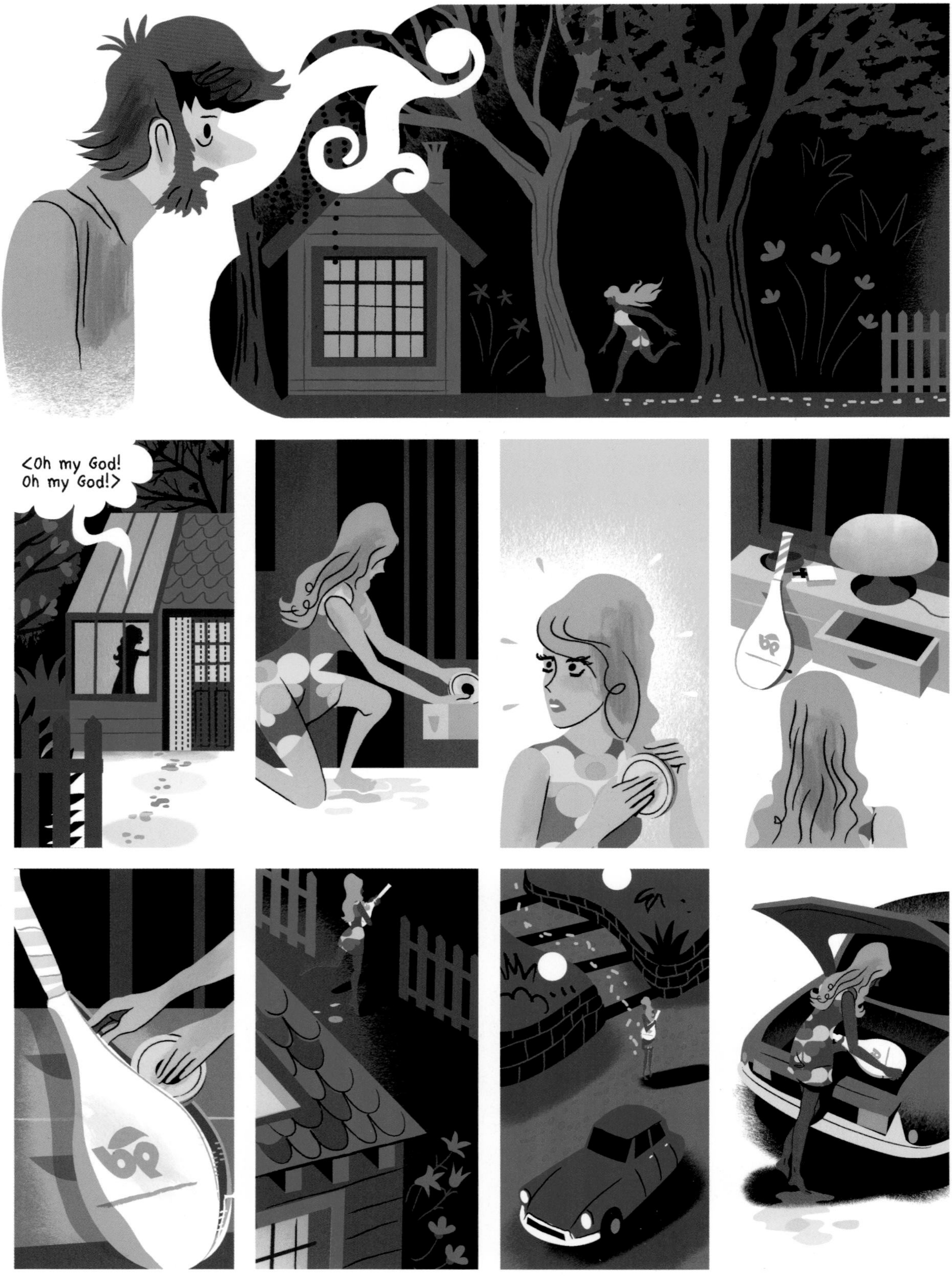
<Oh my God! Oh my God!>

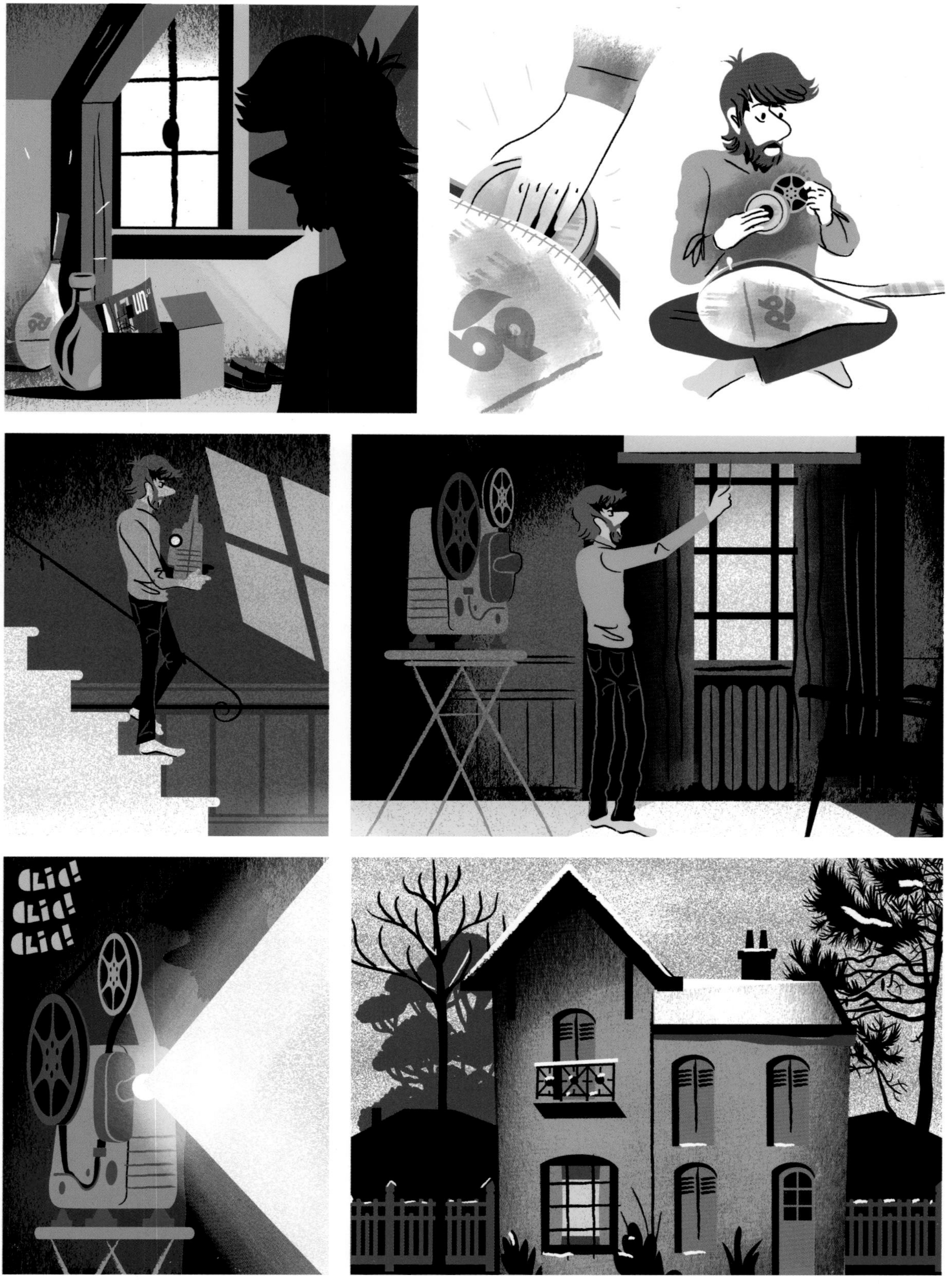
Clic!
Clic!
Clic!

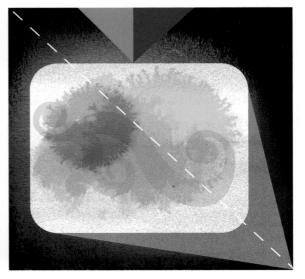

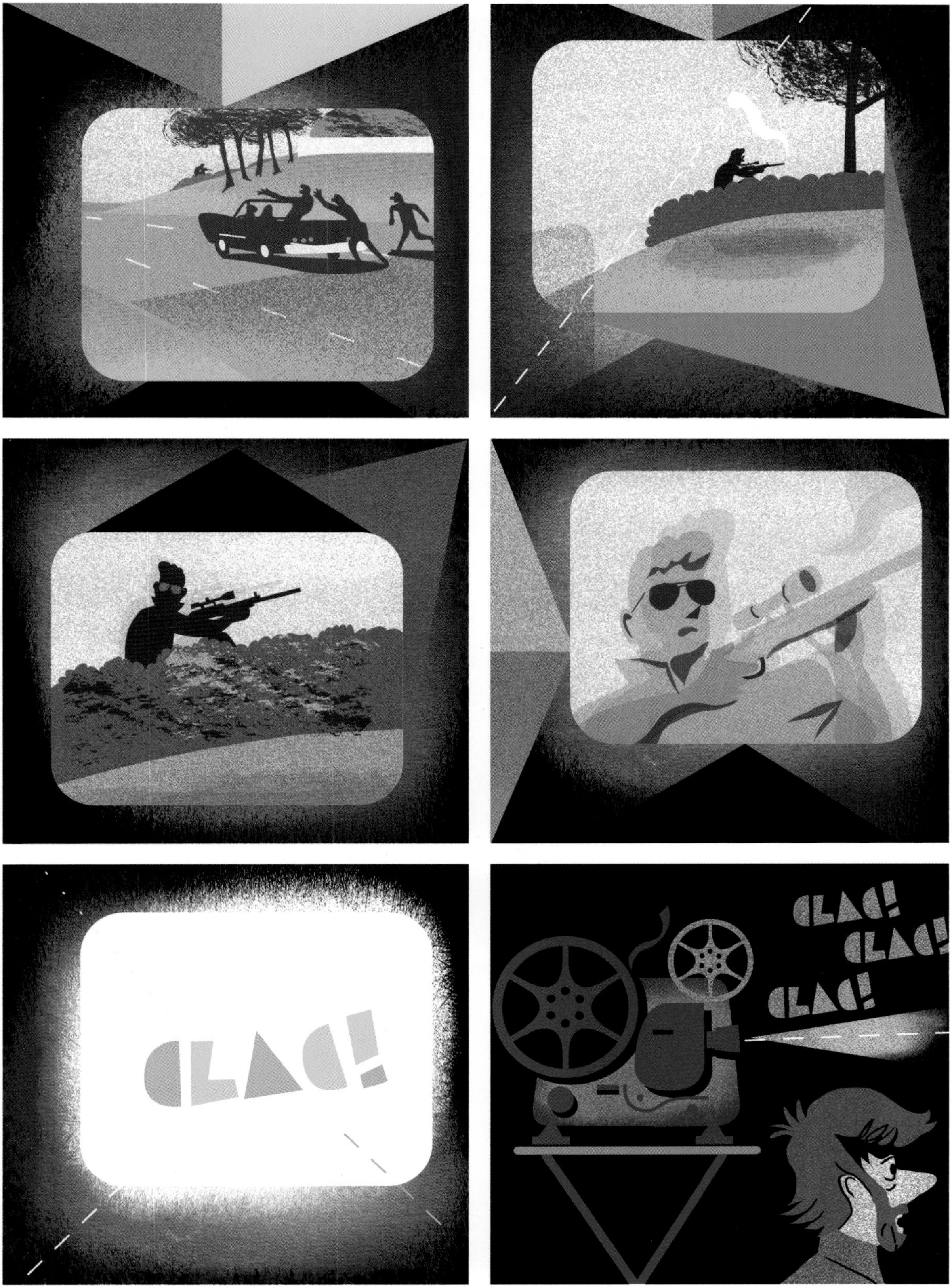
CLAC!
CLAC!
CLAC!
CLAC!

So this was what Joanie had been so scared of...

The source of all her fear and torment.

A few seconds of a blue movie shot in Dallas the day President Kennedy died.

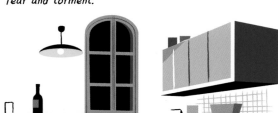

The truth about the conspiracy of the century... coiled up like a viper in its plastic canister...

Just waiting for a projector's beam to dart out, hissing, from between Joanie's thighs.

To each their nightmares, to each their demons. She'd left me her own....

...and now she was free.

Wherever she was today, I hoped she could feel the final shackles falling away...

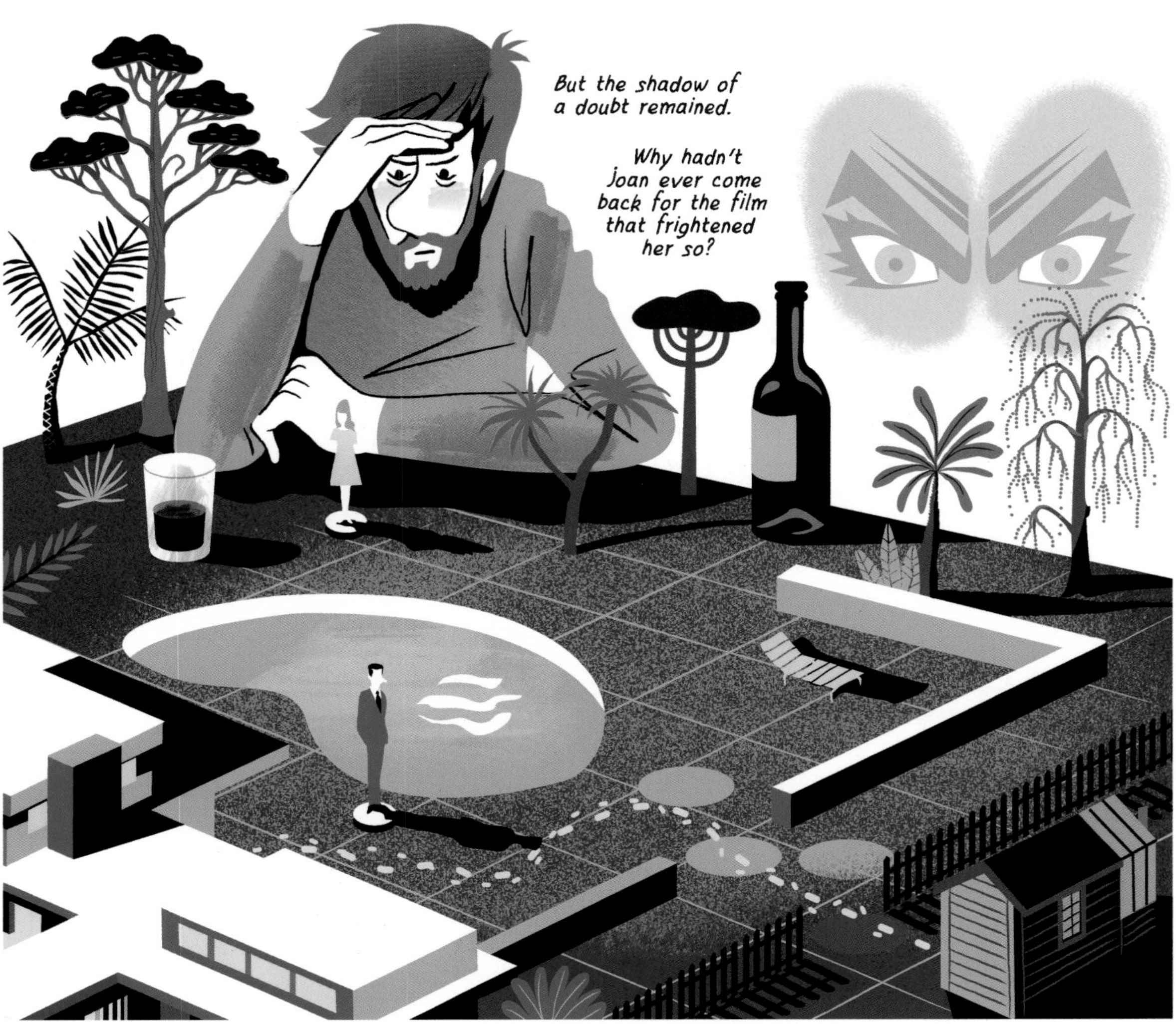
But the shadow of a doubt remained.
Why hadn't Joan ever come back for the film that frightened her so?
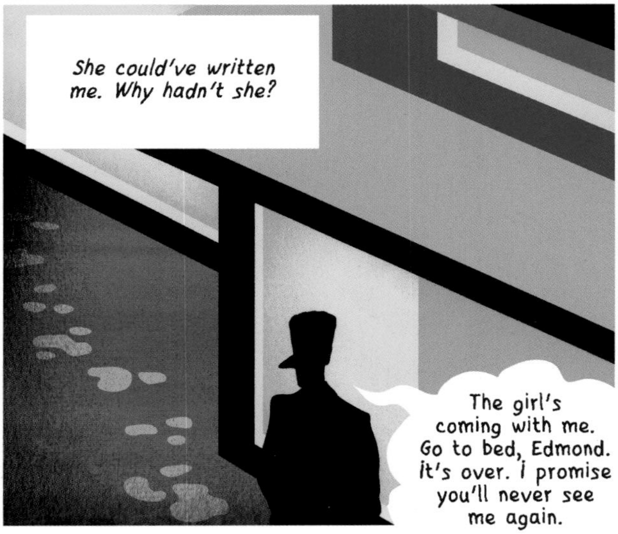
She could've written me. Why hadn't she?
The girl's coming with me. Go to bed, Edmond. It's over. I promise you'll never see me again.
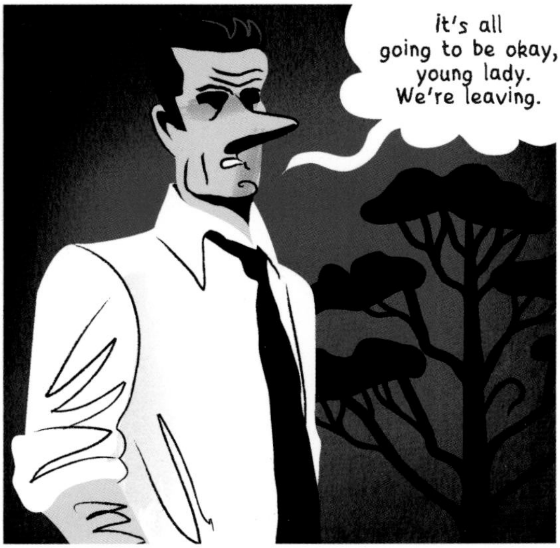
It's all going to be okay, young lady. We're leaving.

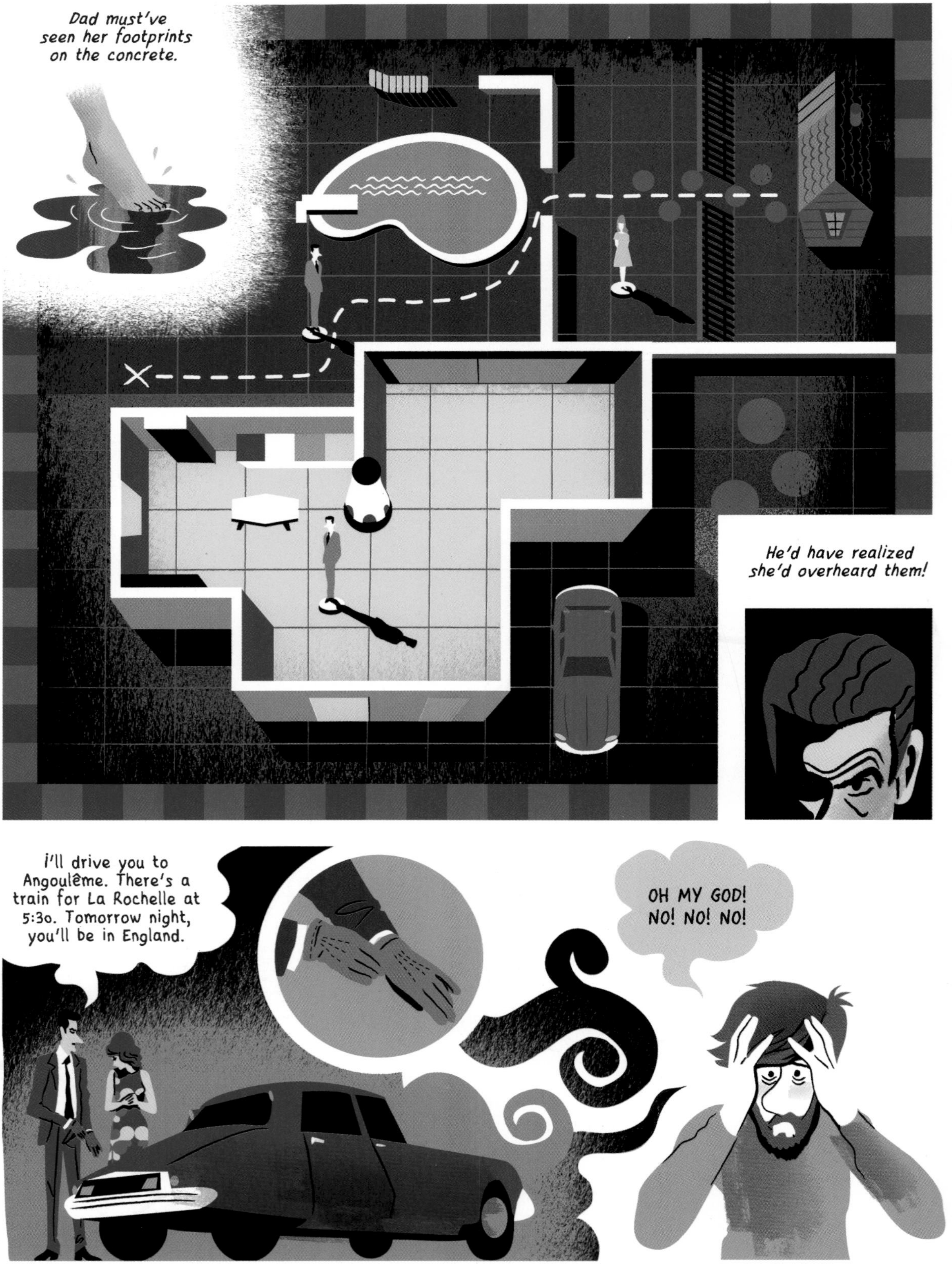
Dad must've seen her footprints on the concrete.
He'd have realized she'd overheard them!
I'll drive you to Angoulême. There's a train for La Rochelle at 5:30. Tomorrow night, you'll be in England.
OH MY GOD! NO! NO! NO!

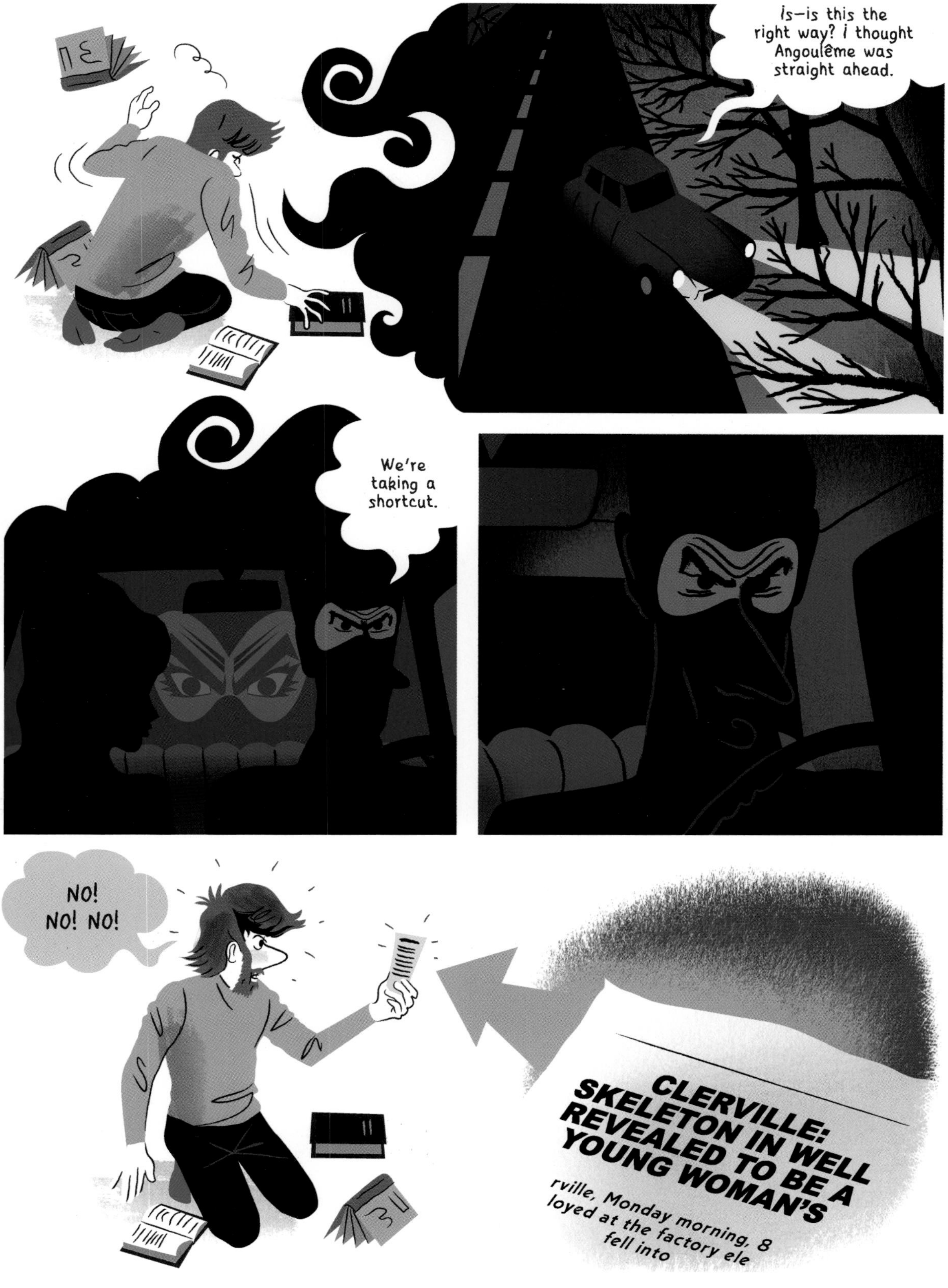
is—is this the right way? I thought Angoulême was straight ahead.
We're taking a shortcut.
NO! NO! NO!
CLERVILLE: SKELETON IN WELL REVEALED TO BE A YOUNG WOMAN'S
rville, Monday morning, 8
loyed at the factory ele
fell into

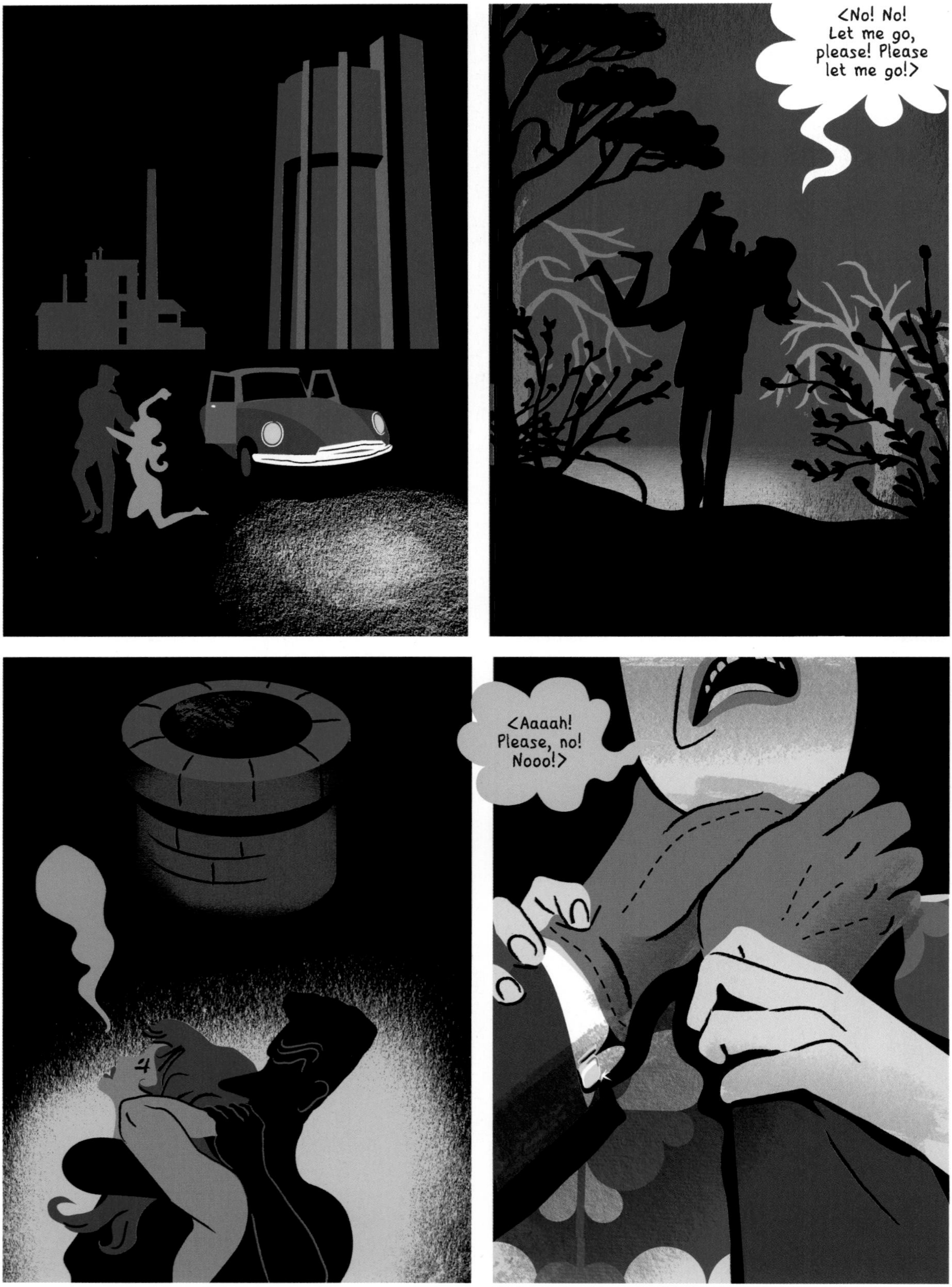
<No! No! Let me go, please! Please let me go!>
<Aaaah! Please, no! Nooo!>

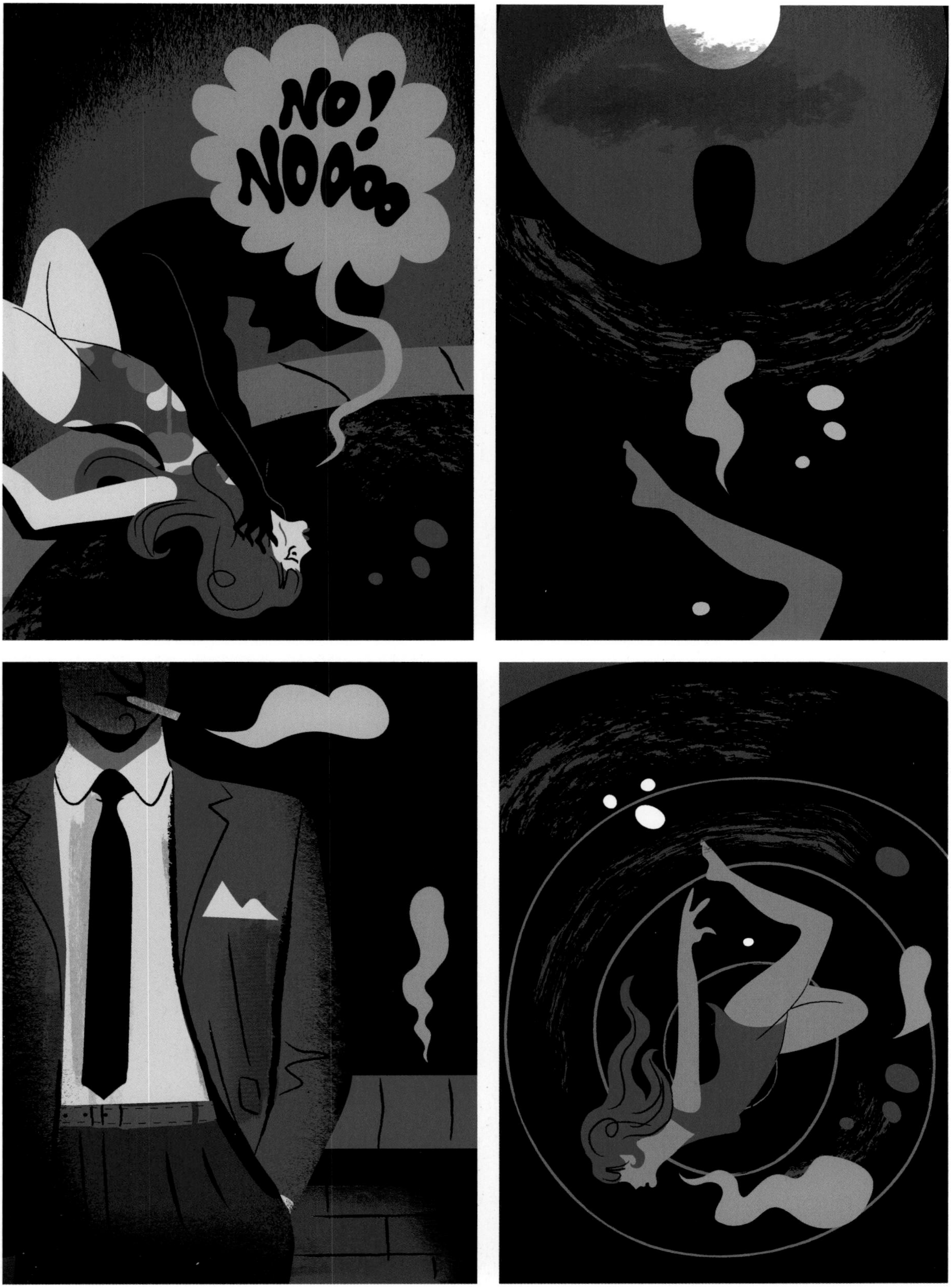
NO! NOOOO

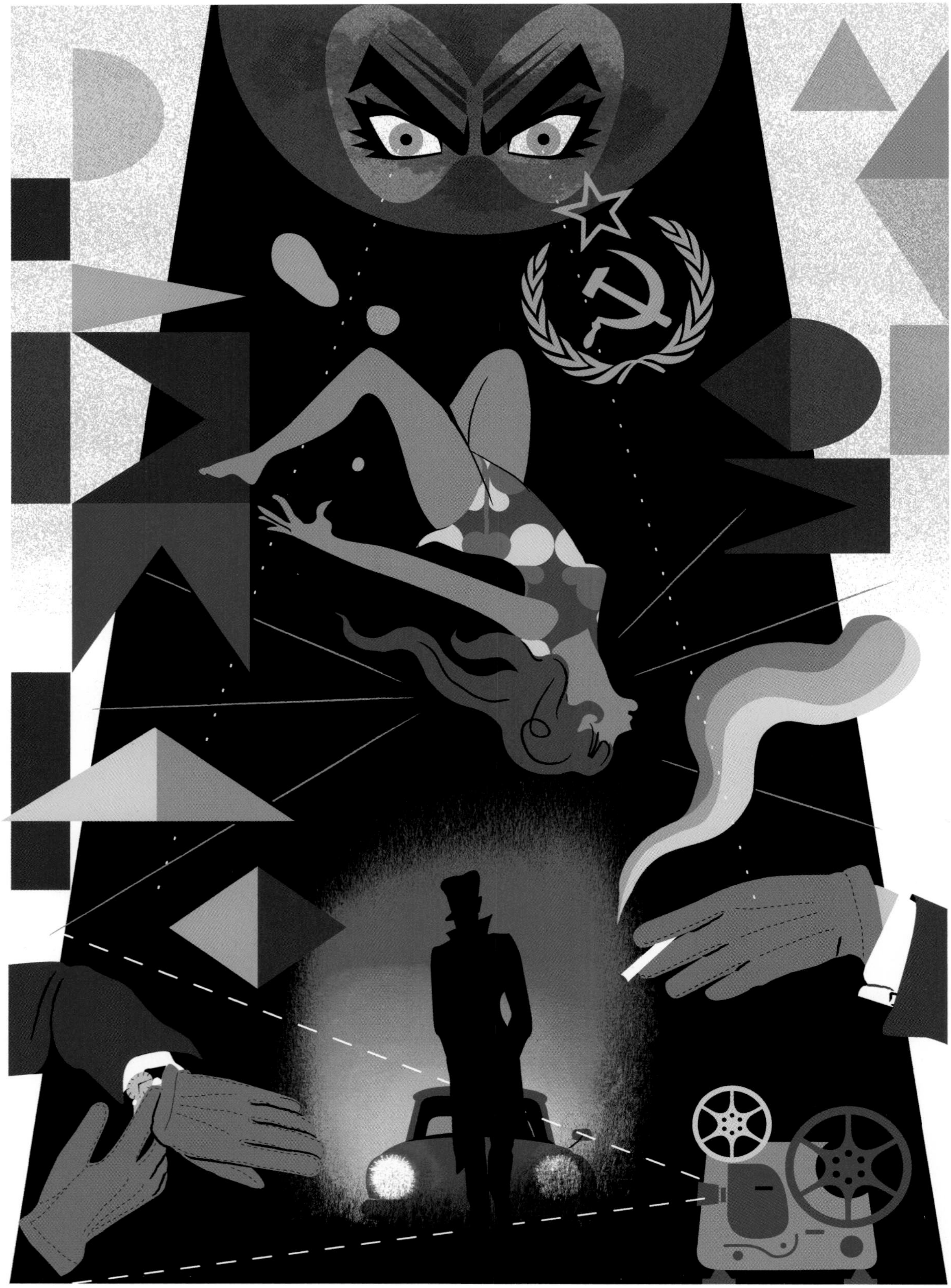

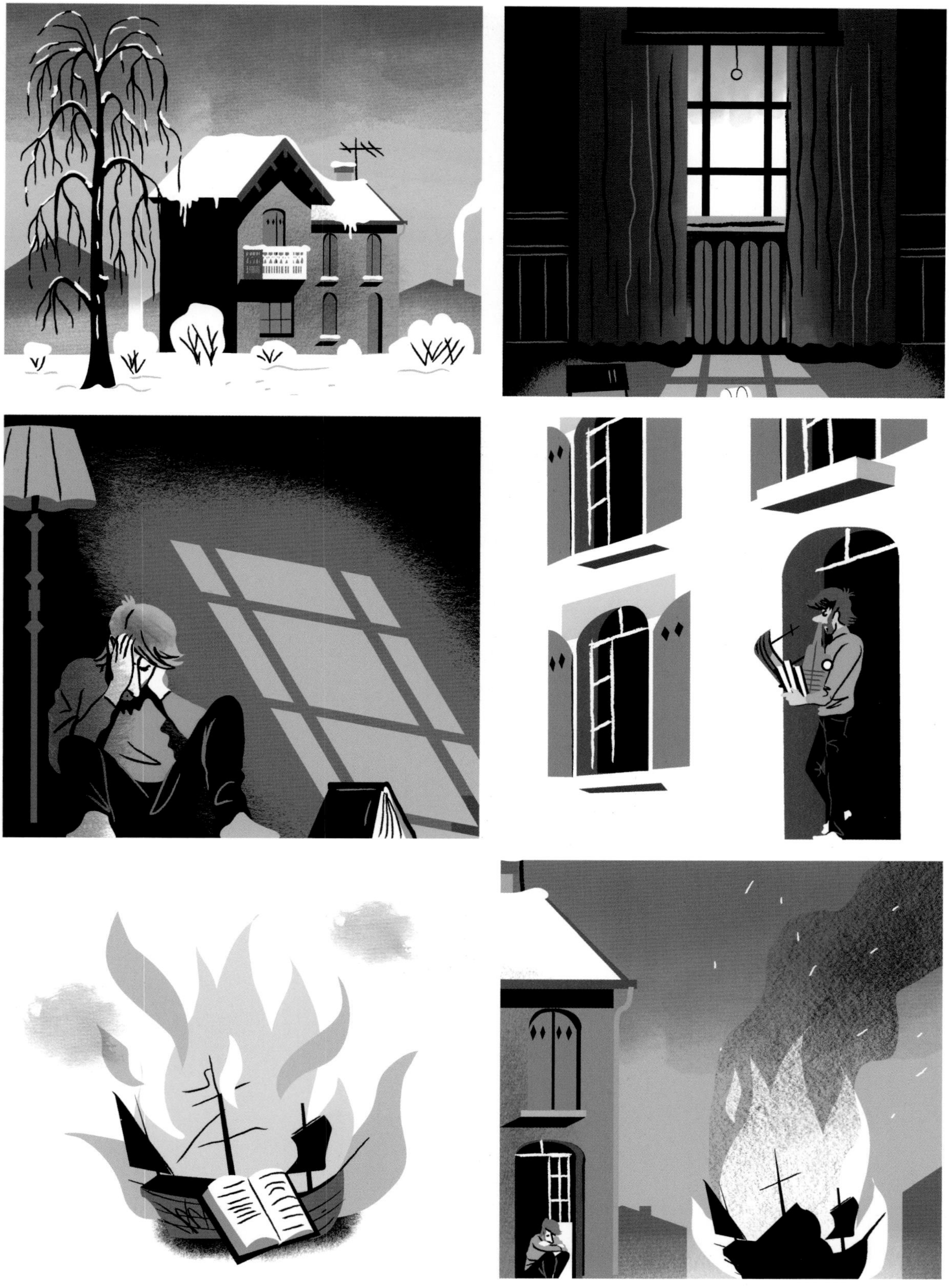

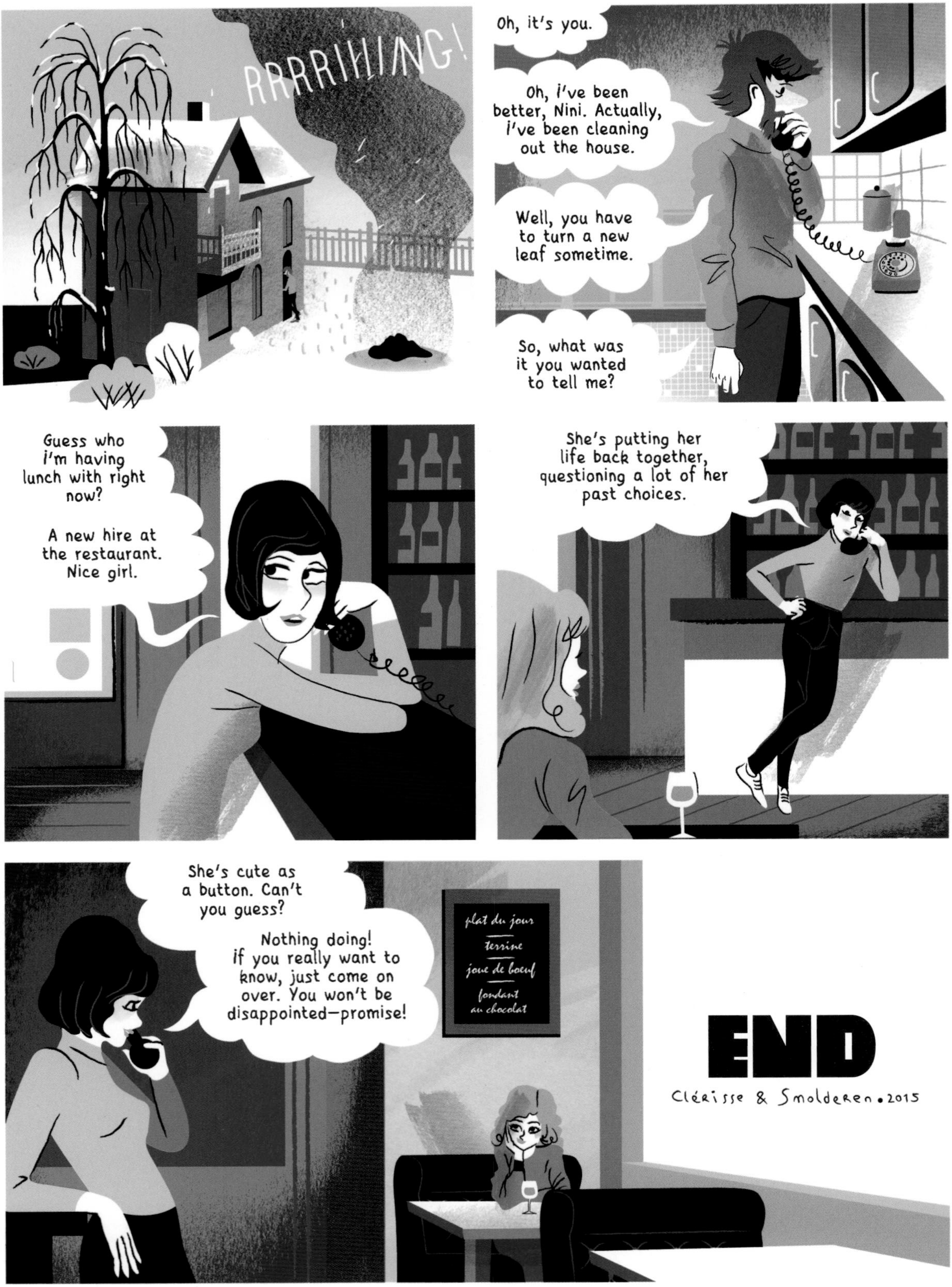
RRRRIHIING!
Oh, it's you.
Oh, i've been better, Nini. Actually, i've been cleaning out the house.
Well, you have to turn a new leaf sometime.
So, what was it you wanted to tell me?
Guess who i'm having lunch with right now?
A new hire at the restaurant. Nice girl.
She's putting her life back together, questioning a lot of her past choices.
She's cute as a button. Can't you guess?
Nothing doing! if you really want to know, just come on over. You won't be disappointed—promise!
plat du jour
terrine
joue de boeuf
fondant au chocolat
END
Clérisse & Smolderen.2015

Born Under the Sign of the Newsstand

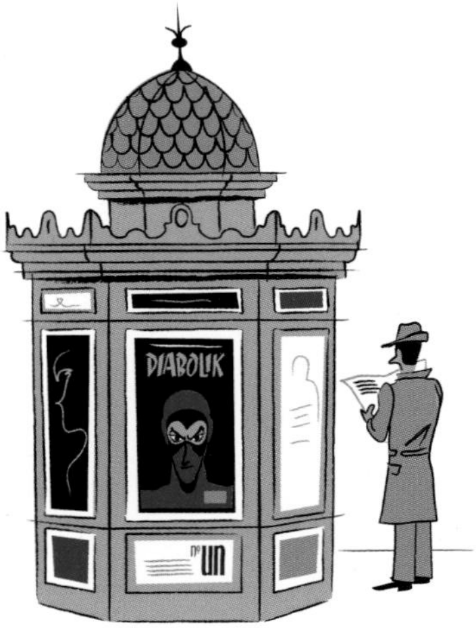
DIABOLIK

THIERRY SMOLDEREN with
ALEXANDRE CLERISSE

« Whatever are they doing in our cloisters, beneath the eyes of reading monks—these ridiculous monstrosities whose misshapen beauty and beauteous misshapenness awe and astonish? »

Bernard of Clairvaux (known as St. Bernard), Letter to Abbot William of Saint-Thierry 1135[1]

The nefarious, shadowy presence hovering over *Diabolical Summer* stands among those unusual figures that have haunted the fringes of Western culture for thousands of years. In St. Bernard's time, gargoyles, chimeras, and demons dwelled in the margins of illuminated manuscripts and the dark corners of cathedrals; in the 20th century, they have taken refuge in newsstands and movie theatre marquees.

In the late '60s, I'd dash off every morning to see what new monster or masked man was now emblazoned on the clapboard newsstand that presided over the small suburban train station near my house. I was fifteen, and at the time, my tastes ran more toward heroes from the early part of the century (Arsène Lupin, Fantômas, Tigris) up to the '30s (Mandrake the Magician, The Phantom). Insatiable, I'd raid my friends' attics in search of lurid pulp magazines from the '20s and old issues of *Hop-là!* and *Robinson*. But from those attics it was only a hop, skip, and a jump to the station newsstand: the same glowing crime and fantasy-inspired vein had been giving off radiation since the century began. And a new king of crime and terror now reigned supreme over the small, marginal world of illustrated magazines. His name was Diabolik, and in those days, his glinting, pitiless gaze stared daggers out from above all his competitors.
Created in 1962 by sisters Angela and Luciana Giussani, this masked man was obviously an avatar—the latest in an occult lineage that I had no trouble tracing back to its early roots. Given his Italian origins, there was an instant connection with Hugo Pratt's first hero Asso di Picche, published in the '40s and clearly inspired by the adventures of *The Phantom* (in the handsome pre-war monthly *Aventures et Mystère*—I had every issue). Created by Lee Falk and Ray Moore, *The Phantom* was among the American comics from the '30s that had met with great success abroad (much more so

PUBLICATION DE SERIE NOIRE DESSINEE
DIABOLIK
MENSUEL - N. 42 | 2 F
BELGIQUE 20 FB - ALGERIE 2,30 DA
SUISSE 2 FS - MAROC 2,30 DH - CANADA 50 CTS

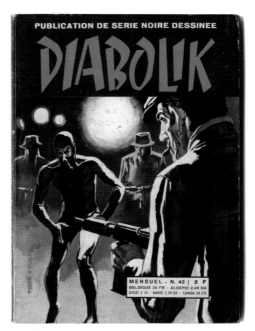

Diabolik, created by Angela and Luciana Giussani in 1962. French edition of the adventures of the infamous criminal (Gemini, 1969).

(1) Quoted by Michael Camille in *Images dans les marges: Aux limites de l'art médiéval* (Gallimard, 1997). Originally published in English as *Image on the Edge: The Margins of Medieval Art* (Reaktion Books, 1992).

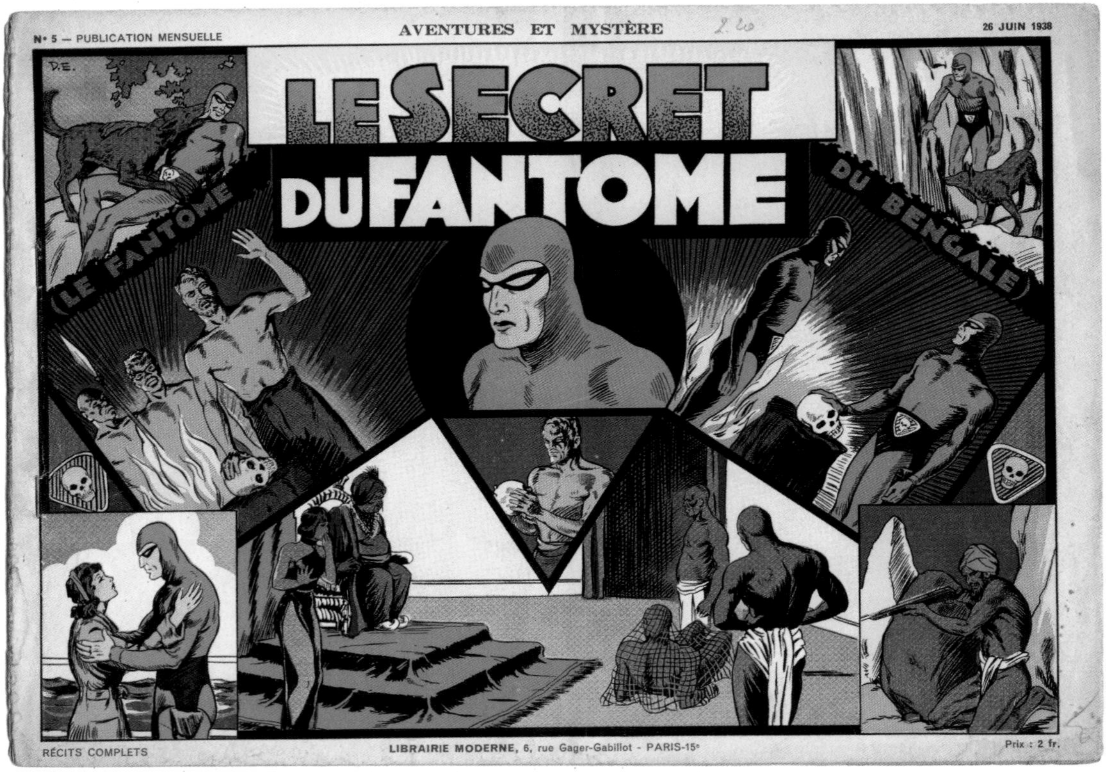
N° 5 — PUBLICATION MENSUELLE
AVENTURES ET MYSTÈRE
26 JUIN 1938
LE SECRET
DU FANTOME
(LE FANTOME
DU BENGALE)
RÉCITS COMPLETS
LIBRAIRIE MODERNE, 6, rue Gager-Gabillot - PARIS-15e
Prix : 2 fr.

The Phantom, known in French as *Le Fantôme du Bengale* (The Phantom of Bengal), created in 1936 by Lee Falk and Ray Moore. Cover of Issue 5 from the handsome monthly *Aventures et Mystère* (*Adventures and Mystery*, 1938). From the author's personal collection.

than back home in America). The serial translated well: there weren't many references to the idiosyncrasies of American society and lifestyle. The Phantom's eyeless, iconic mask traveled easily from one continent to another. In this incarnation, the crimefighter's costume and features even leapt nimbly from one generation to the next, as if providing an early model of transference, the curious phenomenon that concerns us here.

I will not make the fashionable mistake of treating such figures that populate the margins as orphan products: there are, behind each and every one of these avatars, human creators of flesh and bone. In creating *Diabolik*, the Giussani sisters clearly gave form to their dreams and desires (not to mention their intimate fantasies). But nevertheless, there is something crepuscular about these margins that bring down one's defenses and inhibitions, an aspect the Surrealists certainly remarked on in *Fantômas*, by Pierre Souvestre and Marcel Allain. Perhaps we should speak instead of a liminal ecology, which partakes of fairgrounds and their intoxications, a pact made in the earliest days of capitalism between the chaos of the carnivalesque and the trade in private urges. In this ecology of attraction and fascination, the bizarre and the horrific come to seem two fixed constants, and the source of *Diabolik*'s power lay in reconnecting with this dark side.

The truth is that these fictional masks never stop slipping into the *danse macabre* of current events. Today, the 9/11 attacks and decapitations posted on the Internet do-si-do with Hollywood's *Avengers*; yesterday, Diabolik haunted the wings of the Kennedy assassination and the urban legends surrounding it; yesteryear, Fantômas, Nosferatu, and Dr. Caligari led a farandole around the Great War. And were we to trace the genealogy of these masks,

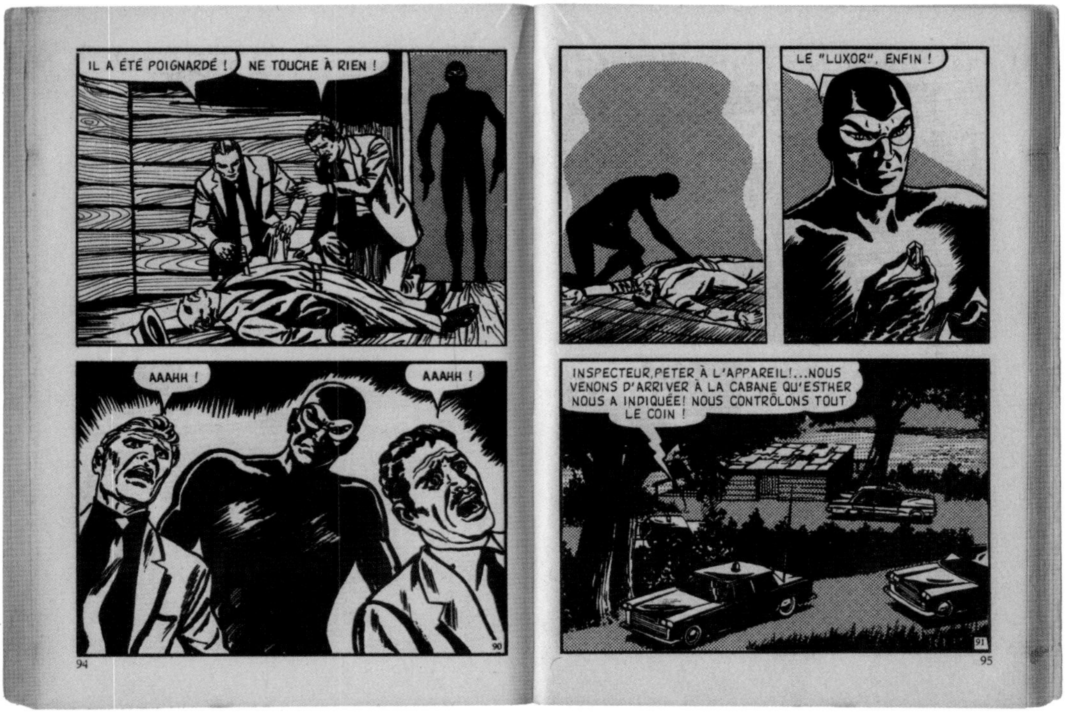
IL A ÉTÉ POIGNARDÉ !
NE TOUCHE À RIEN !
AAAHH !
AAAHH !
90
94
LE "LUXOR", ENFIN !
INSPECTEUR,PETER À L'APPAREIL!...NOUS VENONS D'ARRIVER À LA CABANE QU'ESTHER NOUS A INDIQUÉE! NOUS CONTRÔLONS TOUT LE COIN !
91
95

From *Diabolik* (Gemini, 1969).

which offer an intimate and portable interface capable of connecting us personally with the global forces of current events, we would end up back at the very first of them, in which all the usual features can already be found: Harlequin Faustus, Harlequin the Criminal, the superhero of English pantomime, who electrified the London stage in the early 18th century.

Descended from Renaissance Italy's *commedia dell' arte*, the Harlequin of London was a master of metamorphoses, a magician able to transform himself into a dog or a piece of furniture (thanks to special effects that presaged 19th century magic shows).
In his first triumphant appearance (in 1722), the progenitor of all masked heroes took on the role of Faustus. After making a deal with the devil (or stealing Gutenberg's secret—it's not very clear), he went to Paris and sold perfectly identical copies of Bibles that seemed to have been written by a demon's hand.

Shortly thereafter, Harlequin slipped into the role of Jack Sheppard, the greatest English criminal of the 18th century. This highwayman, who prefigures Arsène Lupin, Fantômas, and Diabolik, is the first modern escape artist. When his execution was played out on a London stage in 1724, Harlequin Sheppard's body broke apart into a thousand brightly colored pieces, only to re-assemble themselves miraculously once outside the noose—an astounding escape every bit the equal, we must

Actor John Rich
in the role of
Harlequin Faustus
(circa 1723).

admit, of Fantômas scandalously dodging the guillotine.

So it is that masks travel through time and space, cavorting from actor to actor, character to character. They act as an interface between our most intimate desires (and fears) and the macabre sideshow that is reality.

No doubt I had all this vaguely in mind when an image came to me, the one that gave rise to *Diabolical Summer*. A very simple image, really: *a man—a magnate, maybe—glancing at his rearview mirror and glimpsing, at the wheel of the car behind him, the figure of Diabolik, the Giussani sisters' anti-hero. The outlandish vision fades almost immediately from the man's mind, but a few days later, it happens again.*

And he cannot, for the life of him, figure out why.

Admittedly, not much to go on, but then something in Mario Bava's incredible pop masterpiece *Danger: Diabolik!* (1968), rewatched for research, did much to reinforce it. In one scene, the title character is speeding along in his Jaguar E-Type (white, in the movie). He's not wearing a mask, but for a split second, an oblong of sunlight reflected from his rearview mirror stripes his eyes with a virtual one. The entire script for this comic developed from this play of light.

But of course, what motivated Alexandre Clérisse and I the most was the arsenal of prisms and graphic lenses we could apply to refracting this story. We'd just finished *Atomic Empire*, and the idea of going back again, this time to dive into the swingin' '60s, was irresistible.